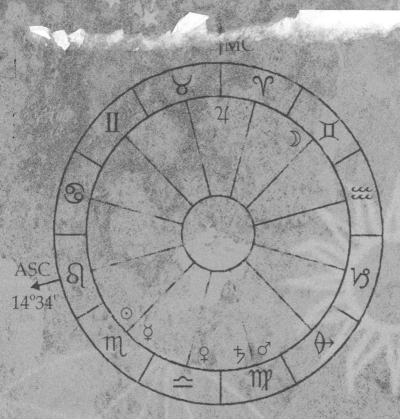

ASC

14°34'

St Bartholomew's Day

24th August 1572

3.00 a.m.

Paris, France

48°N52' 02°E20'

☽ △ ♂

♃ ☌ m.e.

♂ ☌ ♄

☽ ☍ ☿

THE
NOSTRADAMUS
PROPHECY

THE
NOSTRADAMUS
PROPHECY

THERESA BRESLIN

DOUBLEDAY

THE NOSTRADAMUS PROPHECY
A DOUBLEDAY BOOK 978 0 385 61308 8
TRADE PAPERBACK 978 0 385 61309 5

Published in Great Britain by Doubleday,
a division of Random House Children's Book
A Random House Group Company

This edition published 2008

1 3 5 7 9 10 8 6 4 2

Astrology charts in the endpapers based on charts calculated using Solar Fire Software

Map illustrated by Jo Buchan

The Random House Group Limited supports the Forest Stewardship Council (FSC),
the leading international forest certification organization. All our titles that are
printed on Greenpeace-approved FSC-certified paper carry the FSC logo. Our paper
procurement policy can be found at www.rbooks.co.uk/environment.

Mixed Sources
Product group from well-managed
forests and other controlled sources
www.fsc.org Cert no. TT-COC-2139
© 1996 Forest Stewardship Council
FSC

Set in Adobe Garamond by
Falcon Oast Graphic Art Ltd.

RANDOM HOUSE CHILDREN'S BOOKS
61–63 Uxbridge Road, London W5 5SA

www.kidsatrandomhouse.co.uk
www.rbooks.co.uk

Addresses for companies within The Random House Group Limited can be found at:
www.randomhouse.co.uk/offices.htm

THE RANDOM HOUSE GROUP Limited Reg. No. 954009

A CIP catalogue record for this book is available from the British Library.

Printed in the UK by
CPI Mackays, Chatham ME5 8TD

This book is for Sue Cook
– editor *extraordinaire*

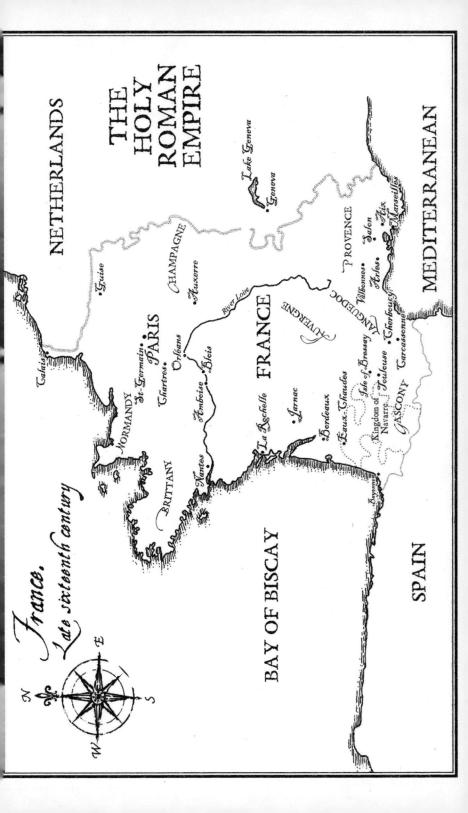

PART ONE
THE PROPHECY

The south of France,
Spring 1566

Chapter One

'**M**urder!
Murder and foul betrayal!'
The old man with the long white beard trembled as he spoke.

'Listen to me, I beg you! Blood runs red in the streets of Paris!'

In the great hall of Cherboucy Palace nobles and courtiers pressed forward to hear. The soothsayer reached into the folds of his cloak and drew out a crumpled parchment. He held it aloft and declaimed in a loud voice,

'With fire and heartless hangings
The treachery of royal line holds sway.
Deeds done by stealth will come to light and all but one
   consumed
Safe from the sword, saved only by the word.

'O most vile iniquity!'
His finger stabbed at the paper and his voice rose in a wail.

'A hundred dead!

'No! More! Two hundred!'

White flecks of spume gathered at the corners of his mouth.

'Yet more! And more still! Three! Four! Five hundred! Five times five!' He moaned and pulled his hair. 'The bell is pealing. Paris screams in agony.

'Babies torn from their mother's breast. Put to the sword, battered and clubbed to death. No one is safe. People try to escape. Look!' The old man's eyes started from his head. 'See them flee! In vain they run. Their bodies pile in the streets, their corpses choke the river. The king's life is forfeit! Murder most foul!'

From her seat on the raised dais, Catherine de' Medici, Queen Regent of France, leaned forward listening intently. But her son, the young King Charles, only laughed. 'Paris is a city most favourable to me. I hold my court in the royal residences there without fear.'

The soothsayer raised both hands above his head. 'Death is in this very place! Here! Tonight!' he cried out. 'I feel its presence near me!' He looked up in terror at the ceiling rafters. 'Hark to the beating of wings! Even as I speak, the Angel of Death hovers above our heads!'

A murmur ran through the assembly. All craned their necks upwards. Some gasped, others sniggered behind their hands.

'Sire, you should pay heed to Nostradamus,' Catherine de' Medici hissed at her son. 'He is no ordinary prophet.'

'Enough of this.' King Charles held up his hand for

silence. 'We thank you for your time, soothsayer. Now, you are dismissed.'

It was plain to see that the queen was vexed, for she frowned and bit her lip. But she did not protest, only took out her purse and gave a servant some money to hand to the old man.

Nostradamus regarded the coins contemptuously and then dropped them at his feet. 'I came here to give you warning,' he replied with dignity, 'not for you to give me gold.'

'Minstrel,' King Charles called to my father, 'play me a tune.' He clapped his hands. 'A merry tune. And ask your daughters if they would dance a little.'

My father beckoned to my sister and me.

'Chantelle, Mélisande.' He put his hands on our heads. 'I think the king needs a distraction. A madrigal followed by a lively roundel, would you agree?'

My father plucked the strings of his lute and began to sing in a tranquil voice. My sister Chantelle and I shook our finger cymbals in time to the music and waited for the right moment to run into the middle of the floor.

Nostradamus, the soothsayer, stared at the king. 'You do not listen today,' his voice boomed out. 'I tell you, one day you *will* listen. But it will be too late!'

And, leaving the gold coins where they lay, Nostradamus turned and strode out of the room. He brushed against my sister as he passed. A shudder seized his body. He stopped and looked back. Huge dark eyes under hooded lids.

'Dance well tonight,' he said. 'For you will not ever dance before this king again.'

Chapter Two

We *did* dance well that night, my sister Chantelle and I.

Many of the courtiers stopped their chatter to watch us, for we had newly returned from England where we'd learned the Morelia, the latest dance popular at the court of the English queen, Elizabeth. I took the part of the man, and as we performed the steps, and dipped and swayed, some of the lords and ladies joined us on the floor to copy our movements.

Our money basket soon filled up. My father was the most talented troubadour in Europe and in demand at all the royal courts. King Charles applauded vigorously when we'd finished, but we did not manage to lift the mood of the queen regent. Catherine de' Medici barely glanced in our direction. She requested permission from her son to withdraw, summoned her ladies to her side and retired for the night.

We were allowed to keep the gold left by the soothsayer.

Although Chantelle was older than me and the better dancer, when we counted it later she divided it equally between us. My sister was the kindest that anyone could hope to have. She had reason to want all of the coin for she was secretly engaged and hoped to be married soon, yet she insisted that I take half share.

Before going off to spend some of our earnings on drink and card playing, our father had taken us to our chamber and made sure we were safe inside with the door barred. Even in royal castles under the king's rule some men, with drink or without it, take advantage of unprotected women.

As Chantelle and I sat down to embroider another section of her bridal gown, I made up a new song and we sang it to each other. My voice was heavy, too low in tone to be considered sweet, and I was not so graceful in the dance. But my fingers were nimble on the man-dolin and I loved to compose music and verse. So I picked out a tune and we sang a song of chivalry, of noble deeds and unrequited love. And then we went to bed, Chantelle lulling me to sleep describing the flowers that would adorn our hair on her wedding day.

Of Nostradamus and his dire prophecy we did not think at all.

Towards midnight there was a tap on the outside shutter. Chantelle slid from her bed and walked barefoot to the window. I heard a male voice. It was her betrothed, Armand Vescault on the terrace outside. She knelt up on the window seat and they began a whispered conversation.

I pretended not to hear. I had no anxiety about Armand being there with her, unchaperoned. He would not harm or dishonour her.

It was another man, in the wickedness of his heart, who chose to do that.

Chapter Three

The next day Nostradamus was called to the presence of the queen regent.

He remained in her apartments all day while she conferred with him. Catherine de' Medici was much given to mysticism and astrology and worried that there was some truth in the prophecy that foretold harm to the king. Nostradamus had travelled especially from his home in Salon to meet up with the court near Carcassonne to deliver his message. The queen regent took him very seriously. She thought that the warning could be a sign sent from on high to protect her son.

'It's all nonsense,' said Chantelle.

We were sitting in the palace gardens tuning our instruments when our father found us to tell us this news. In my lap was my beautiful Italian mandolin whose strings, when plucked, made a sound like falling water.

'You know that we have met others like Nostradamus before on our travels,' Chantelle went on. 'There are dozens of these soothsayers wandering Europe making prophecies of doom at every opportunity.'

'Nostradamus was very specific,' I said. 'He spoke of the Angel of Death. He said he felt its presence.'

'But there were so many people in the great hall last night,' Chantelle protested, 'that one of them is sure to die within a twelvemonth. It will happen anyway, but when it does it will seem as though the soothsayer is proved correct.'

'You should not dismiss portents so readily,' said my father. 'The death of the king's own father was foretold. He was warned not to take to the field in single combat. On the day he died Queen Catherine herself cautioned her husband against jousting. He thought he was in no danger as the tournament was a mock one, using wooden weapons. But his opponent's lance broke as it struck his helmet. A long splinter entered his brain through his eye. Nine days later he died in agony.'

'Armand agrees with me,' said Chantelle. 'He says that his own liege lord's wife is ill near to death, and not expected to live beyond the end of this week. Armand says that when she dies in a few days then all will believe that Nostradamus saw a vision of the Angel of Death.'

'Does he indeed?' My father raised an eyebrow. 'And since I saw this same Armand ride out on an errand with his master early this morning before you rose, it would appear that you must have had this conversation with him after you retired last night, when I left you under a solemn promise not to leave your chamber.'

Chantelle's face flushed bright pink.

'Sir—' she began.

'Chantelle did not leave our chamber,' I said at once, anxious to defend my sister. 'Armand came to the window and they only spoke through the opening for a short while together.'

'You were awake!' Chantelle turned to me.

'I hope that your conversation was such that it was fitting for the ears of your younger sister,' my father said to Chantelle. 'She is still a child.'

'I'm not a child!' I protested.

'You are not quite a woman yet, Mélisande,' my father said. He came and embraced us both. 'And I'm glad of that, for I would lose you to some gallant as I am about to lose your sister.'

He hugged us and stroked our heads. Then he regarded Chantelle severely. 'I am not pleased with you,' he told her. 'A girl's reputation is a most precious asset. It is something that you should guard at all times. With more care than you do your speech,' he added.

'I am sorry, Father,' my sister said contritely.

My father sighed. 'I see that I must make an arrangement for you to be married now. I will speak about this matter to Armand's master, the Count de Ferignay, this week.'

'Thank you, Papa!' Chantelle cried out in joy. 'Thank you!'

'I'll wait until after tomorrow's hunt. Hopefully it will be successful and the king and his companions will return in good humour.'

The smooth running of the French royal court

depended very much on the king's temper. At fifteen, just two years older than me, King Charles was famed for his petulance and fits of rage. It was said that his mother had smothered, not mothered, him and his outbursts of anger were his way of releasing his tension. Yet, since we had joined the court on its present tour of southern France, it seemed to us Catherine de' Medici's main concern was the welfare of her son. I suppose that Chantelle and I, missing our own mother who had died when we were small, saw the queen's acts as a manifestation of love.

'I'll sew the lace on my wedding dress tonight,' Chantelle whispered to me, 'and in my night prayers I'll ask for the huntsmen's aim to be true.'

Since early boyhood King Charles had loved hunting and this part of the south of France, where the palace of Cherboucy was situated, had many large woods full of deer and boar. The weather was set to be fair and even now the squires and the grooms and the armourers were preparing horses and weapons for tomorrow's chase. The dogs were being exercised in the yard below the gardens when suddenly they let loose a frenzied yapping and high-pitched howls of alarm.

My father rose from his seat to see what was amiss. Looking from the garden wall, he exclaimed, 'It's a leopard! The king will be delighted. He has always wanted to hunt with one of the big cats.' Then I saw my father's face become troubled. 'Yet the bearer of this gift will not be welcomed by everyone here.'

Chantelle and I joined him at the balustrade. An elegant leopard stood in the courtyard. Its pelt was the colour of mellowed ale, studded all over with ink-black spots. Its ears lay flat upon its head as it turned its neck this way and that, gazing around. The hunting dogs were now frantic with fear, straining against their leads. It took all the strength of the kennel lads to prevent them from bolting. The person handling the leopard was himself not much more than a boy, yet he only loosely gripped the chain attached to the animal's collar.

Behind the boy, on horseback, was an older man wearing a black hat adorned with neither feather nor plume. His clothes too were of plain black, except for white ruffs at his throat and sleeve edge.

'His name is Gaspard Coligny,' my father told us in a quiet voice, 'admiral in the State Council, one of the most pre-eminent Frenchmen to embrace the new reformed Protestant faith. And a courageous man,' he added, 'to venture here unguarded, where the men of the Catholic house of Guise surround the king so closely.'

Suddenly there was the sound of laughter from one of the upper windows. King Charles had appeared and was highly amused at the dogs' state of terror.

On seeing the king, Admiral Gaspard Coligny removed his hat and called out to him, 'If it pleases your gracious majesty, your blood cousin, Prince Henri of Navarre, has sent you something to aid you in the hunt.'

'The leopard?' the king almost shrieked. 'This leopard is accustomed to hunt with men?'

'It is, sire. The leopard, Paladin, and the boy, Melchior, who trains the beast, are both offered to you for tomorrow's royal hunt with the good wishes of

Prince Henri and his mother, the Queen of Navarre.'

In his excitement the king leaned so far out on the windowsill that he nearly toppled over. He called on the leopard-handler.

'Melchior!'

The boy raised his head and tossed back wild tousled hair. His face had the dark complexion of the southerners, firm brows, and underneath these his eyes were as tawny as those of the great cat chained to his wrist.

'Bring the animal closer to me!' the king commanded.

Melchior led the leopard into the centre of the courtyard. They were now directly beneath us and, although he spoke in a low voice, I could clearly hear the boy talking to this magnificent animal. His tongue was not northern French. He used the language of the south. The Languedoc had been my mother's country, where I had spent my girlhood before setting out on journeys with my father and sister, and I understood his words.

'Ignore these foolish beings, o Paladin, proud warrior,' Melchior said softly. 'Noble prince, swift son of mighty hunters, thy spirit is like the wind, free and unfettered. Thou art more royal than the churls who try to make thee submit to their will.'

Head held erect, the leopard stood quietly by his side.

'Look.' Chantelle tugged my sleeve. 'There is Armand.'

I felt her tremble as Armand Vescault rode in under the entrance archway with his master, the Count de Ferignay.

'My dogs!' the Count de Ferignay cried out. 'They will be terrorized and useless for tomorrow's hunt!' He leaped from his horse and ran forward. 'You fool! Get that animal out of here!' And he raised his whip, intending to strike the boy across the back of the head.

Behind its muzzle the leopard opened its mouth in a snarl, showing huge, sharp teeth in pink gums.

'Hold your hand, Ferignay!' King Charles shouted from his window. 'I ordered the leopard to be brought near that I might view it.'

'Your majesty' – the Count de Ferignay composed himself – 'I was unaware of your presence.' He glared venomously at the boy and then strode on into the palace.

A vague mood of disquiet came over me as I watched him depart. Once she was wedded to Armand, my sister Chantelle would enter the household of this man.

I thought to myself that I did not care much for the Count de Ferignay.

Chapter Four

As he led his master's horse away, Armand contrived to come close to the wall of the garden where we stood. He glanced up to my sister. Such a look of adoration was on his face as made me catch my breath.

My sister plucked one of the wild flowers, the pink-petalled *artema*, that grew among the stones on the wall. She let the bloom fall from her hand. Armand caught it, kissed it and tucked it inside his tunic. If my father noticed he said nothing. I knew that his own life story was a romance – he had often told us of how he'd wooed my mother with little hope, being only a minstrel, but in the end had won her love.

We passed the rest of the day in the palace gardens with the intention of rehearsing our repertoire of songs. But the murmured words of the leopard-keeper to his animal had insinuated themselves into my head. They now moved in my mind like fish in a deep pond, making their own eddies and currents, occasionally flicking a tail to disturb the calm surface. Eventually I conceded their presence and, taking my mandolin, I began to pluck at the strings to seek out the tune that best accommodated the spirit of the lyrics.

My father smiled as he watched me. 'Another new song, Mélisande?'

I nodded, but I did not tell him the source of my inspiration. That, I decided, would be my secret.

The business of the court went on about us. The purpose of this royal tour of France was to show the young king to his people in all parts of his kingdom. His mother, the queen regent, was hoping that such an overwhelming display of splendour and power would enhance the monarchy and quell the warring Catholics and Protestants. The king was enjoying his new status, meeting with local magistrates, hearing grievances and dispensing justice. Lords of the regions presented themselves as ambassadors of goodwill and pledged him fealty.

However, messengers also arrived bearing unwelcome tidings: the previous week in a monastery not five leagues away sixty monks had their throats cut while hearing Mass. In retaliation a group of Huguenot families meeting to pray in a barn had the roof set alight over their heads. All were slaughtered as they tried to run to freedom. This last atrocity was thought to be the work of members of the powerful Guise family. Of royal blood and influential enough to attempt to take the throne of France, the Guise were also rigidly Catholic and had objected vehemently to the terms of the recent royal Edict of Amboise giving freedoms to those of the Protestant faith, in particular the Huguenots. Their actions in attacking Protestant church gatherings and putting to death well-known Huguenots on any pretext was interpreted as deliberately flouting the king's rule. The Huguenots, now growing in number and strength, retaliated with their own killings and assassinations.

Although the king himself seemed less ruffled by these threats, his mother, the queen regent, constantly strove to keep both factions in check. Firmly believing it was by divine purpose that her family was chosen to rule France, she actively sought out mystic signs to show her the way forward.

Nostradamus stayed all day in the apartments of Catherine de' Medici and in the evening she summoned her son and insisted that he attend while they discussed matters of state. The Count de Ferignay was one of the lords of the chamber and Armand told us later what had happened.

Nostradamus had shown the king's mother, Queen Catherine, his book known as *The Prophecies*, which he had published years earlier. It contained a quatrain where he had correctly predicted that Charles's elder brother, Francis, married to Mary, Queen of Scots, would die before reaching his eighteenth birthday. There was documented evidence that the four lines had been written prior to the event. The printer who had made the book testified to the truth of this. By evening everyone in the Cherboucy Palace had it by word of mouth.

The first son of the widow, of an unexpected illness
Will leave the monarchy without any children
But with two Isles in strife,
And before the age of eighteen will die.

So now here was proof of the soothsayer's accuracy in foretelling the future. King Charles's elder brother's death had been accurately predicted. He had come back from hunting one day complaining of a pain behind his ear. A strange tumour had been found to be growing there and he had died just before his seventeenth birthday. He was his mother's first son, she was a widow, and his death had caused a deal of strife. Even I, who did not pay much heed to prophecies, felt an unaccustomed thrill as this was told to me. Perhaps the king *should* be concerned about this new prophecy of Nostradamus?

'*No one is safe!*
'*Murder most foul!*
'*The king's life is forfeit!*'

When he had concluded his audience with his mother, the king returned to his own apartments in high bad temper.

'She does not wish me to take part in the hunt to-morrow,' he was heard to complain loudly. 'I agreed to this royal procession, dragging the whole court halfway round France to encourage support from minor nobles. And to what end? None that I can see, apart from putting our own anointed personage in danger from religious factions who would murder each other on the slightest whim. We are away from Paris, from our châteaux on the Loire, from civilization. But I say, I *will* hunt tomorrow.' Charles threw a chair across the room and tore the curtains from his royal bed and trampled them on the floor.

In a fit of pique, King Charles went to have dinner in the rooms of the scandalous Duchess Marie-Christine. His musicians were summoned to entertain them, so my sister and I dressed with care and went with our father to play as they ate.

The leopard was there. Unmoving as a statue, it sat on its haunches, long tail curled around its feet. The boy, Melchior, stood beside it, staring straight ahead, his gaze fixed.

I saw his lips move as he stroked the animal's head, but this time he was too far away for me to hear his speech.

Suddenly the words I'd heard him crooning to his leopard earlier in the day rearranged themselves inside my head. The notes of the tune slid into their proper place. I lifted the mandolin and as I played I sang,

> *'Proud prince of royal blood art thou,*
> *Paladin, so nobly named,*
> *Prisoner of others, yet*
> *Thy spirit, like the wind, untamed.*
>
> *'Swift son of a mighty hunting race*
> *Conquest falls to thee,*
> *Silent shadow, fleet among the chase*
> *Chained now, yet thou shall be free.'*

Melchior did not turn his head but the posture of his body altered.

I glanced up, and our eyes met.

Between us there was a flash of recognition.

More than the words. More than the music. I saw something naked in his soul.

Then a veil dropped over his eyes and his face became impassive.

I bent my own head.

'I like that song.' King Charles lolled back in his chair. He had drunk too much wine. 'I fancy the words are about me. I am a prince chained to do the bidding of others. My mother bade me pay the soothsayer one hundred gold coins. She believes utterly in his prophecies. But can anyone truly see into the future?'

'Of course they can, my lord.' The duchess, dressed in a gown that exposed most of her breasts, leaned forward provocatively. 'I too have the gift of foresight. I prophesy that I will put this grape into my mouth.' She reached into the fruit bowl and plucked out a fat green grape. 'See?' She held it up and popped it between her lips. Then she rolled it on her tongue and said in a throbbing voice, 'Now, I prophesy that the King of France will eat this grape!' She opened her mouth again to smile at the king and everyone could see that she held the fruit firmly between her teeth.

King Charles's face flushed and he leaned across and put his lips clumsily to hers. She pretended to be compliant, but at the last moment she drew away. He moved closer. She rose up from her chair and made to run off. He chased after her and caught her easily. She laughed deep in her throat. Then King Charles put his mouth over hers. She sank against his chest, and with him supporting her they collapsed together on a couch.

'Time to go, my sweets,' my father said to us with a sigh.

I wonder now if this display of lovemaking saddened him, as it reminded him of the loss of our mother. Or did he wish to protect us from the immoral ways of the court? It was not that my father did not have his faults – a lot of our money was lost to his gambling and he drank more than he should, but for all that he held against loose morals in love. He wasn't particularly religious, being frequently absent from church, yet he would urge us always to say our night prayers and greet each new day with a song of praise to the Creator. Once upon a mountain he stood and spread his hands wide and laughed out loud in joy, saying, 'Can anything be more wonderful? No palace or prince is equal to this.' On another occasion he lifted a ladybird onto his finger and bade Chantelle and me watch as the insect opened its wings and flew away. 'Look at how unique is the construction of this creature who can fly untrammelled by any care that we humans must suffer.'

But this was a time in France when a person's individual freedom was held in the control of others. My father's non-attendance at formal worship could engender comment and his mode of life be viewed with suspicion.

'Just when it was becoming interesting,' grumbled my sister as we prepared ourselves for bed. 'How am I supposed to learn the ways of love if I'm never to be allowed to watch how others conduct themselves when courting?'

'It was not true love that was on display tonight.' I was quoting my father. 'The Duchess Marie-Christine is married. Her husband is away in Paris and she is seducing King Charles for her own ends.'

'I will be ill-prepared for my marriage,' Chantelle

continued to complain as she helped me unlace my gown. 'I don't know any of the tricks a woman needs to know in order to beguile a man.'

'I saw you drop the wild flower to Armand in the garden this morning,' I told her as I put on my night shift. 'You were as bold as any cunning courtesan.'

Chantelle giggled as she pulled her own night shift over her head. 'Did you see how he kissed it and placed it in his tunic next to his heart?'

'*Oh, Armand! I love you so much. I will die if I cannot lie with you soon,*' I gasped, making loud kissing noises to tease my sister.

She replied by pulling my hair and we wrestled together, laughing. Then we jumped into our cot beds and settled down to sleep, whispering to each other in the dark.

'Tomorrow will be a glorious day, Mélisande,' said Chantelle. 'When the hunt is over our father will present me to the Count de Ferignay and ask that Armand and I may be married. Imagine! I might be wed within the next few weeks.'

Distantly the noise of the palace drifted into the room. Messengers came and went, their horses' hooves clattering on the cobbles. We heard the rough voice of the captain of the guard checking the night watch as he made his rounds each hour.

And as I listened to these sounds and my sister's chatting I too looked forward to the morrow. Not because of the wedding arrangement to be made but because we would accompany the hunt. Earlier, when my father had begged leave for us to retire, the king had said that he would definitely hunt the next day, and that we could ride behind him for at least part of the chase.

I lay in my cot that night and thought of the others who would be there.

I thought of the leopard. And I thought of Melchior.

Chapter Five

Mist was rising from the meadows on either side of the river as the royal hunt assembled the following morning.

'It's too early to be abroad.' Chantelle shivered and drew her cloak closer round her shoulders as we stepped outside.

Beside her I too shivered, but more from excitement than from cold. I gave my sister a quick hug. I knew she hated to rise early and did not care to take part in the hunt. She was only doing it because I had begged her to accompany me, for without her presence I would not have been allowed to go.

Before the main gates of Cherboucy Palace the king's chief huntsman, the Grand Veneur, was assembling the hunters. Nobles and courtiers, men and women on horseback and on foot, horses, dog handlers and weapon carriers took their places according to his instructions.

About a field away a number of peasants from the locality stood watching. Most had a sack or game bag over their shoulder. All forest land belonged to the king, although sometimes parts of it were gifted or leased to the aristocracy or senior clergy. No common man had a right to kill any forest animal or bird, but today they might follow in our train and take the leavings not gathered by the royal servants. Anything they found was deemed the king's largesse and the food or furs used to sustain them through the winter.

I heard Chantelle sigh as she caught sight of Armand Vescault.

Immediately I felt better at having coaxed her from her warm bed. She smiled a happy smile and we mounted the horses that a groom had readied for us to ride. Chantelle sat tall in the saddle in the hope that Armand would see her. She'd said that he would contrive to be close to her at some point during the day. In the frenzy of the hunt all things were possible. But then maybe not, for now our father approached to ride with us. He was careful of our honour and had managed Chantelle and Armand's courtship with prudence and care. It was over a year since they had met and fallen in love at the royal court in Paris, but Papa would not agree to my sister's marriage or even allow Armand to speak to his own liege lord at that time. He'd insisted that Chantelle wait a while and took us away to England so that they could test their feelings for each other. But now we were back in France and it was plain that their love had not dimmed.

The sous-lieutenant had a note of the order of the courtiers who would be grouped around the king. This was a matter of strict protocol according to rank and favour. We were ushered through the squires and the huntsmen, the various aides and weapon-carriers and a score or more of mounted and unmounted valets to our allotted place. King Charles's mother, the queen regent, had chosen not to attend the hunt. Out of concern for her son she had, however, sent her own surgeon and an apothecary laden down with boxes containing instruments and medicines. When the king arrived he barely acknowledged their presence and they were assigned to the rear, with only the peasants trailing behind them. King Charles could not have made his irritation at their presence more plain.

The king's groom had just led his majesty's horse to the centre of the line when a restless shifting rippled among the ranks of the assembled nobles. There was an angry murmur of voices. Then one, louder than the rest said, 'How dare these Protestants approach the king without Queen Catherine's permission!'

'It's the Huguenot leader, Admiral Gaspard Coligny,' my father told us. 'He must mean to join the hunt today.' Then he too gasped. 'And he has brought young Prince Henri of Navarre with him!'

I shook my reins to move my horse so that I might better see this prince, a cousin of the king, and distant heir to the French throne. Navarre was a small kingdom on the western border of France and its ruler, Queen Jeanne, had converted her country to be Huguenot. Their prince, Henri, was younger than King Charles, but with a more healthy, open look about his face. Admiral Gaspard Coligny was leading the way, guiding his horse to follow the master of the king's kennels, who was bringing the king's deerhounds that they might be loosed to begin the hunt. Prince Henri sat straight in his saddle. Coligny's hair was streaked with grey and his face showed the scars of sword fights fought and won. In their dark clothes the Huguenots exuded an air of gravitas. Both were daring indeed to come among the Catholic lords, who were known to be violently jealous of their places next to the person of the king.

I was not the only rider who tried to move forward. Ahead of me a handsome young man dug his heels into the flanks of his horse, intent on intercepting Admiral Coligny's progress. This noble I knew by sight and reputation. At just fifteen years old the wilful and head-strong Duke of Guise had inherited his title when his father was treacherously assassinated by some Protestants. He blamed Gaspard Coligny and had declared himself sworn enemy of all Huguenots. Instantly, the duke's uncle, the Cardinal of Lorraine, who was positioned alongside him, leaned over and pulled on his rein.

'Not now!' The command was low and urgent. 'Not now! This is not the place. Our time *will* come, I promise you. Then we will strike these heretics down so that they will never rise again.'

The Duke of Guise scowled but held his horse in check and we watched as Admiral Coligny presented Prince Henri to the king.

'I wish to thank you for bringing me Paladin, the leopard!' the King said, holding out his hands towards Gaspard Coligny.

The Huguenot leader took the proffered hand, bent his

head and kissed the fingers of his king. 'It is an honour to serve your majesty,' he said.

'And you, beloved Henri, prince of the blood royal, such a generous act I will never forget!' King Charles stretched across his saddle and embraced his cousin. Both young men, direct descendants of the saintly King Louis of France, seemed genuinely glad to see each other. 'You must ride one on either side of me today,' the king declared.

There were murmurs of annoyance and discontent from the lords, who had to shift from their privileged positions to make room for the two Huguenots.

Then the dogs began to yip and the horses to whicker and neigh in alarm and I knew immediately that Melchior and his leopard had arrived. Most of the other riders reined in, but the king pushed his horse on and I urged my own mount into the space created so that I had a better view. Melchior and Paladin were by the outside gate. The leopard was not muzzled.

'Now, sir.' The king waved his hand to his cousin. 'Introduce me to this most exquisite beast.'

Prince Henri dismounted and with a firm step went up to Melchior and Paladin and placed himself before them. The leopard stretched out its neck. Now its face was almost on a level with Prince Henri. Its eyes stared and it opened its mouth wide and licked its chops. But Henri stood his ground. Melchior spoke once and the leopard sat back on its haunches.

'King Charles' – Prince Henri bowed low – 'be pleased to make the acquaintance of Paladin, the leopard.'

The king laughed and clapped his hands. When he

called on the rest of his court to applaud the bravery of the Huguenot prince, the scowl on the face of the Duke of Guise deepened.

In the midst of this Chantelle whispered to me,

'Armand is here.'

Chantelle's betrothed had managed to come as near to her as he dared. But it was Count de Ferignay who caught my attention. He edged his horse closer to the Duke of Guise and I saw them, with lowered glances, exchange some words.

The king held up his hand. The long shuffling line of people and animals quietened. The king let fall his hand. The clarion call of the hunting horn echoed from the palace walls to meadow and valley beyond.

The hunt was up!

Chapter Six

To the thunder of horses' hooves, the barking of dogs, and the whoops and shouts of those taking part we streamed away from the palace of Cherboucy.

Melchior and Paladin ran ahead, and from the outset the pace was swift. Those taking part in the hunt wore special hunting clothes. The men's leather jerkins were split at the back for ease of movement while most of the women had adopted the queen's mode: when she hunted, she wore long pantaloons under her dress so that she could preserve her modesty, for she had the habit of hitching up her skirts to allow her to hook one leg around the pommel of her saddle. Ladies wishing to keep to the forefront of the hunt now adopted this method of sitting on their horses as it helped us to ride as far and almost as fast as many of the men.

The king and Prince Henri cantered beside Melchior and the leopard. The king's outfit of Florentine purple slashed with crimson silk contrasted with the plain black and white of his cousin's Huguenot clothes. Beside the muted garb of Admiral Gaspard Coligny and Prince Henri's attendants the rest of the company dazzled colour. Fine silverwork decorated the horse trappings and the tunics of the vassals and squires showed the coats of arms of their masters. Members of the House of Guise, to show their royal lineage, wore tunics decorated with the lily of France.

We reached the outskirts of the forest and drew rein. Horses and riders and huntsmen on foot milled around while the dogs ran up and down, tracking here and there, trying to pick up a trail.

Melchior stood some way off and unhitched the chain from the collar round the leopard's neck. He gave it to one of the servants to carry. Then he removed his shirt. The women beside me glanced at each other. One ran her tongue around the edge of her lips and the other giggled. The skin on Melchior's chest was a lighter hue than his face, a creamy bronze that gleamed like gold dust. He laid his hand on Paladin's head and then turned to face the forest. As he did so a little gasp went round the company and I felt my own pulse quicken.

Intricate whorls, like a circular maze, covered Melchior's back. Painted in hues of violet, green, yellow and indigo, the lines spiralled and twisted across each shoulder and down his spine to the waistband of his breeches.

'Pagan symbols,' one of the huntsmen growled to another.

I stared at the pattern. It was of another age, another belief. From the depths of antiquity, closer to Nature than the rituals of the religions of our time, they reminded me of deep carvings I'd seen on standing stones in the south of England, in Carnac in western France, and somewhere else that I could not quite recall. They were not the same, yet they had a fleeting familiarity, like a tune absorbed in childhood which haunts your memory when falling asleep.

The dogs began to sound and the cry went up.

'The staghounds have the scent!'

'So soon!' Charles cried in delight. 'Why, on previous days I have wasted hours thrashing around in dense bush before starting an animal.' He shouted to Admiral Gaspard Coligny, 'You have brought me luck today!'

The Huguenot leader beamed with pleasure. Then, as the king was absorbed elsewhere, he sent a triumphant glance in the direction of the Duke of Guise.

The king glanced around. 'Where is Melchior? Where is the leopard?'

Melchior was already there. He had wound his shirt around his waist and tied it like a scarf. Now he bent to speak in the leopard's ear.

Boy and beast sprang forward, and we were off!

Melchior and Paladin ran with easy strides. Muscles rippling beneath their skin, they loped together after the staghounds, and we followed.

Many of the court ladies were not there for the sport of hunting animals, but rather to parade a new costume or hat. Their true intention was to ensnare another gallant for their amusement. Therefore some of the men found it more diverting to slow their pace to accommodate these women and thus pursue their own quarry. We soon left them behind. I had travelled on horses through the woods and hills of England, Spain and France, and I could keep my saddle with the best of them.

Before long we glimpsed the stag. Again Charles cried out in a high-pitched voice, hysterical with joy. 'Magnificent! With full antlers! A true king of the forest! Worthy of a king of France!'

The animal plunged away into dense wood and now we were relying on the dogs. The huntsmen listened intently to their baying, then hacked through bushes and guided us. For a while we struggled on, until Paladin and Melchior veered down a different path. King Charles hesitated. Prince Henri pointed to where the leopard had gone, and he and King Charles galloped off in that direction. Those closest to him, including myself, went too. A short way behind us, the remainder of the hunt crashed off through the trees in the wake of the hounds.

Our small group burst into an empty clearing and scrabbled to a stop. Melchior was standing beneath a massive tree. His great cat lay along one of the wide spread branches.

The Duke of Guise cried out, 'The leopard has lost its way!'

'It has not,' said Melchior.

King Charles reined in and trotted his sweating horse over to Melchior. 'Why then does it not pursue the stag?'

'It is not a cheetah or a panther.' The boy spoke quietly, but with authority. 'The leopard hunts in its own distinct way.'

'It's not hunting,' the Count de Ferignay remarked loudly, to much amusement. 'It's hiding!'

'Hush!' The king waved for quiet.

He had seen the leopard's ears prick up.

'Move back!' Melchior spoke in such a way that all, even the king, obeyed him, melting into the surrounding cover.

A huge stag came bounding from the trees. It reared and stopped, sniffing the air.

'Ahhhh!' Charles looked as though he might swoon in ecstasy. Bright spots of red coloured his cheeks.

'If you want the leopard to make the kill,' Melchior told him, 'you must hold the dogs.'

The king glanced at Prince Henri, who nodded. Charles jumped from his horse and gave orders. Men went to call the dogs and try to prevent them running in. Now the other huntsmen who had caught up came creeping from the bushes. The weapon-carriers distributed the spears, and crossbows primed to fire. One man carrying a long knife the length of a man's arm presented it to King Charles. Two others, similarly armed, stood on either side to protect the king lest the stag should charge him.

'Stay!' the king commanded. 'I want to see the leopard make the kill.'

And suddenly I felt sorry for the creature. The stag pawed the ground, drool hanging from its mouth. I know that it is necessary that animals should die that we might live. It is part of their cycle. As we in turn must quit this earth at the end of our allotted time else there would be no room for our descendants. But seeing this noble beast at bay made my heart quake.

Barking furiously, some hounds who'd escaped being restrained pelted into the clearing and flung themselves at their prey. The stag lowered its antlers, gored and gathered them, and threw them into the air. The tortured animals hurtled to the ground, blood pouring from their ripped bodies.

The king cried out. It was a cry of joy. The dogs' screeches of pain served to inflame his senses.

With supple agility Paladin launched himself into the next tree and climbed up to a higher branch.

'The leopard is a coward!' The Count de Ferignay spoke out loudly. 'See how it backs away. Let me finish off the stag before we lose it.'

Without taking his eyes from Paladin, Melchior spoke again to the king. 'I tell you, sire, in the wild it is from a tree that this cat makes its kill. The leopard will not fail you.'

'Do you hear, Ferignay?' The king's voice shook with excitement. 'The boy assures me that, in their own habitat, this is how these beasts capture their prey.'

Ferignay directed a look of fury at Melchior.

Again the leopard moved lithely, choosing its best position as the stag tossed its antlers in anger at being menaced by the encircling hunters.

But now surely the hunted animal must try to break for freedom?

The moment came. The stag chose to fight. It straightened its forelegs and thrust forward its massive head.

'I thought the leopard would make the kill.' King

Charles put his fist to his mouth to stifle a moan of disappointment.

The stag prepared to charge.

And then the leopard pounced.

In one lithe movement Paladin leaped from the tree onto the back of the stag. Claws extended, it dug them deep into its victim and with powerful fangs bit into its neck. The stag struggled, trying to throw off its attacker. Snarling in fury, the leopard clung on. But the stag was strong and flexed its shoulder muscles again. Paladin slipped to one side. The king howled in despair. The stag twisted round, attempting a final move to dislodge the leopard.

A fatal mistake.

Turning this way exposed its front. With incredible speed the leopard loosed its hold on the back of its prey, opened its jaws once more and fastened its teeth deep into the stag's throat. Blood spurted out from the throat of the mortally wounded beast.

The king gave a squeal of ecstasy.

'You were wrong, Ferignay!' he called out. 'The leopard is a fighter!'

The stag shook its head. It battered the leopard against the ground but Paladin would not let go. And now the stag was on its knees, blood pouring from the gaping wound. Its eyes rolled in its head and we heard its death rattle.

'Use your knife,' I heard Prince Henri urge King Charles. 'One strike to the heart. Be merciful and hasten its end.'

But the king ignored him. 'Loose the dogs!' Charles

shouted. 'Loose the dogs! They must have some fresh blood to taste!'

I turned my head away as the dogs ran in.

To Melchior it was the order of nature, one animal taking the other as natural prey. To the king it was his right to decide how to dispense death.

To the Count de Ferignay it was the opportunity to settle a score.

The leopard was busy with its kill. Prince Henri and Gaspard Coligny had moved to one side. The king, fascinated by the blood pumping from the stricken animal, went close to kneel down and gaze spellbound at the death throes of the stag. Melchior stood, waiting and watching over Paladin.

The Count de Ferignay made a signal to the man on horseback beside him. This man swiftly handed him a whip he had coiled at his belt.

The count raised his arm and, directing his aim at Melchior, he flicked the whip. The length of leather unfurled with a crack and the lead tip at the end chipped a gouge from the skin on Melchior's back. The boy grunted and, spinning round, he caught the end of the whip. He yanked it hard and Ferignay had to brace himself in his stirrups or he would have been unseated.

I heard myself cry out, 'No!' and my heart stalled. To unseat a noble and send him crashing to the ground would be a step too far. Even the protection of the king might not save Melchior from the consequences of that insult.

Melchior looked at Ferignay with disdain. He dropped his hand and released his end of the whip.

The Count de Ferignay drew in the long leather lash and rolled it in his hands. There was a satisfied look upon his face that had nothing to do with the successful killing of the stag. My uneasy feeling about this man solidified into one of dislike.

I realized that with the Count de Ferignay a grudge would be held until revenged.

Chapter Seven

This feeling of unease was with me as I returned to the palace.

I dismounted from my horse and as the groom led it away I decided to go by the servants' stairs to reach the accommodation I shared with Chantelle. I was walking along the upper corridor when I saw the prophet Nostradamus standing by a window, leaning on a silver walking stick. With his long robe and tall figure he was very distinctive. It was not surprising that I should recognize him. What surprised me was that he recognized me.

'Mélisande,' he said.

He had the accent of his home town in Provence, and in pronouncing my name he gave an emphasis to the 's' and the latter syllables which gave it an air of mystery I had never appreciated.

'Something has distressed you,' he said, looking at me acutely. 'Yet it is not you, rather for your sister Chantelle that I—'

'Sir,' I interrupted him. 'They say that you can see into the future. What do you see there for me?'

He looked into my eyes. I felt he probed my very soul. 'In addition to my three sons, I have been blessed with three daughters of my own.' He spoke slowly. 'Diane, the youngest, is no more than a baby. I also have one a little older, and another who is a little younger than you. So . . .' He hesitated. 'I see what any young girl might hope for. You will grow into your womanhood. Men will pay you compliments.'

I shook my head. I was not interested in men saying sweet things to me. I had watched this kind of wooing many times, at the courts of England and in France. Such liars, men were. They would say anything in order to win over a pretty girl. Too lazy or untalented to do it themselves, often they came to my father and paid him to compose a line or two of verse, or make up a song that they might pass off as their own. They then used these to woo their fancy. Even if I believed such compliments signified true love, it was unlikely that I would receive many. My face was too plain, my body too angular, with none of the plump curves that men liked so much.

Nostradamus smiled at me. 'I see that my words do not please you. What would you have me say?'

I recalled my sister's words. '*Things can be made to fit round any prophecy.*' Master Nostradamus had told me what he thought a young girl would want to happen to her. 'Do you say that which you think people want to hear?' I demanded.

'The young maid has a keen tongue.'

I thought he was angry at my boldness, but he pondered on my words.

'Yes,' he replied. 'There are occasions when I do in fact do that. I have to eat and pay for bread for my wife and children.'

'Then you are not a truth teller.'

'I am not a charlatan,' he replied. 'Life is hard and comforts are few, especially for those who have no income, or connection to a noble household. I take a lot of care when making up my almanacs. I spend many, many hours composing them to be ready for the year ahead. They give practical advice and simple effective remedies for a variety of ills, and also indicate the best times to sow and reap.'

'But predictions of the weather and the tides and the harvest are practical things and can be done by any person versed in country lore.'

He had been studying me as I spoke. Suddenly he raised up his head and shoulders and towered over me. I wilted under the intensity of his gaze. 'I will tell you what I see. But beware, you have asked for the truth. It may be hard to bear.'

I stepped back. Now I was unsure that I wanted to listen to what he had to say. But I could not stop him.

'Grievous harm surrounds you, Mélisande. The minstrel is unable to defend his daughters. You will be called upon to be very brave. Your father will have great need of you. And another, also, will require your intercession. Yet . . .' He paused. 'I do not know if you are equal to the task.'

At this, Nostradamus walked away from me, and I was

left wondering. When he'd first spoken to me he had mentioned Chantelle's name. If his concern was for my sister, then why did he say my *father* would need my help?

I shook my head to clear my thoughts. In any case I didn't have time to worry about these things for I had to hurry to our chamber to change my clothes. It had been arranged that in the early evening Chantelle and I were to be presented to the Count de Ferignay.

The evening sun had set and the pitch torches in their sconces lit the courtyards when my father came to escort us to the apartments of Armand's lord and master.

When he saw Chantelle arrayed in her best dress and with her hair braided, my father's eyes filled with tears.

'You are so like your mother,' he said. He took from his purse a string of seed pearls and fastened them around my sister's neck.

Chantelle began to cry and flung her arms round my father, who embraced her. Then we all hugged one another. My father and I both held onto Chantelle. We knew that if a marriage was agreed tonight, there would be no long engagement. The wedding might take place very soon. The days when we would have free access to my sister were coming to an end.

'Dry your eyes, my beautiful girls,' Papa commanded us. 'And let us go and inform the Count de Ferignay how fortunate his family is that it may be joined to mine.'

Chapter Eight

'Your lordship, may I present my daughters to you?'

My sister and I waited at the entrance to the apartments of the Count de Ferignay, as my father walked forward to introduce us formally to Armand Vescault's liege lord.

Chantelle's eyes searched the small salon before us and alighted on the one she sought. From his place at the window Armand fluttered his fingers in greeting. In these circumstances my sister did not dare acknowledge his salute, but a little smile came to her lips. I was more concerned with the count and the man standing closest to him. This was the man I had seen earlier at the hunt who had handed the count his whip with which to punish Melchior. By his rough features and size, and the dagger prominently displayed in his belt, I guessed him to be the count's personal bodyguard.

'Pay heed, Jauffré' – the Count de Ferignay turned to speak to this man – 'there are some things I wish you to deal with over the next few days.' Ferignay then numbered a series of unimportant tasks.

Anger prickled under my skin as I saw that the count was deliberately making my father wait while he ostentatiously dealt with minor matters, in order to emphasize his own superior position. But if my father was put out by such a display of bad manners he did not show it in any way.

When he had come to the end of his list of instructions, the count stood up and surveyed my father haughtily. He too had changed from his hunting clothes and was now richly dressed in a long tunic of maroon velvet. I noticed that the cut of the cloth was skilfully done to cover his thick neck and heavy belly. His face displayed the ravages of years of overindulgence. A greedy man, I thought. Greedy. Proud. And from what I had witnessed today, cruel.

Ferignay indicated for my father to step closer. 'Now then,' he drawled, 'Monsieur the Minstrel.'

My father said nothing, only inclined his head. Then he raised his eyes and looked at the Count de Ferignay.

'Of course you are not any common jongleur,' the count went on, 'but the famous troubadour that the high-born Lady Beatrice de Bressay married some years ago in defiance of her parents, who cast her out because of it.'

My father spoke quietly. 'My wife was reconciled with her parents before she died, my lord.'

'Is that so?' A note of interest crept into the count's voice. 'And now that they are both dead with no other heir, then you must own the manor house and the lands of the Isle of Bressay?'

My father nodded again, and, young that I was, I knew him well enough that I could tell by the tilt of his head and the set of his shoulders that the count would not deflect him from his purpose.

'Good income from farming and fishing, so I'm told.' Ferignay seemed keen for more information.

'The people who work the land and fish the waters round the Isle of Bressay live to enjoy a just reward for their labours.' My father's reply was enigmatic, but Chantelle and I understood his meaning. We knew that our father was no feudal overlord who forbade his tenants hunting rights, and he did not inflict ruinous taxes.

'So why would a man choose to be a wandering minstrel when he can live the life of a lord either at home or at court?' Ferignay regarded my father with genuine curiosity.

'When my wife died a few years ago the place held only sadness for me,' my father answered. 'I felt that my solitary mourning was upsetting my daughters so I sought employment in the royal courts of England and France, that we might make music together. Besides which I do not truly own the Isle of Bressay. It is kept in trust for my daughters. Half will go to Chantelle and half to Mélisande. They will inherit when they reach their majority or when they are wed, whichever comes first.'

'A woman inherit in her own right!' exclaimed Ferignay. 'The law does not permit this.'

'In our part of France we are faithful to the old ways of the Occitan,' said my father.

'You rebellious southerners,' said Ferignay in a mocking

46

voice. 'Yet . . . I can see that there could be advantages in such an arrangement.'

'As my lord has so wisely observed' – my father quickly took the opportunity to further his case – 'it means that, should my daughter Chantelle be wedded to your kinsman, Armand Vescault, then she brings with her half of the Isle of Bressay.'

Ferignay considered this. He looked towards Armand, who walked quickly from the window and went down on one knee before him.

'I would beg my lord to give his consent,' Armand said humbly. 'My service to you would in no way be impaired and to be married to this lady would make me very happy.'

'Ah, a love match.' Ferignay's eyes glinted.

I was watching him closely, and it seemed to me that for the merest second an emotion I hardly recognized burned in their depths. Was it malice?

'Armand Vescault is not without substance.' Ferignay addressed my father again. 'As you have said, he is kin to me, though distantly, by a long-dead cousin, and I am attached to the house of Guise, and therefore to the blood royal.'

The Count de Ferignay obviously wanted to impress upon my father that it would be a high honour for Chantelle to be allowed into his family. My father murmured a suitably neutral response, for it was common knowledge that the fortunes of the house of Guise were in flux. Some years ago it had been a daughter of the house of Guise, Mary, Queen of Scots, who had wed the eldest son of Queen Catherine de' Medici while he was a boy. With this marriage the Guise family had hoped to rule France. But the boy prince had died, Mary had been sent back to Scotland, and Queen Catherine's next son, Charles, was now King of France. This downturn of fortunes had left the Guise family frustrated in their ambitions.

'My colours are royal blue with the lily of France incorporated,' the Count de Ferignay continued. 'You will have noted that when we rode in the hunt today.'

Only that my father had given my sister and me both strict instructions to remain silent unless spoken to, or I would have asked the Count de Ferignay if he had not observed that it was us that the king had chosen to ride just behind him at the start of the chase.

'And our shields are gilded to indicate the ties to the royal house of France.'

'I am aware of this, my lord,' my father said diplomatically. 'My daughters and I know the colours of the royal houses, for we have travelled abroad. In fact I took Chantelle away for the last few months to test her love for Armand and ensure that theirs would be a true and lasting marriage. We have only just returned from England.'

'Then you have seen their queen, Elizabeth. Is she as vain as they say?'

My father hesitated and then said, 'She would defy being described as pretty in the conventional sense, yet she has a noble bearing.'

'More noble than our king?' the count asked slyly.

But my father had too much experience of court life to be snared in such a trap.

'As you yourself have said, my lord, the nobility of France has the blood royal.'

'And you aspire to have your daughter be a part of it?'

I glanced at Chantelle. She was twisting her fingers and held her face down – as I should be doing. My father flashed me a look of reprimand and I dipped my head, but I soon raised it again. With the formalities out of the way some negotiation had begun and I found this too interesting to miss.

'I desire my daughter's happiness,' said my father.

'I repeat: Armand is no ordinary squire that you wish your daughter to marry,' the Count de Ferignay replied.

'In addition to her dowry my daughter is graceful and an accomplished musician.'

'The queen regent, Catherine de' Medici, and the royal ladies favour needlework.'

'My daughter can embroider skilfully. The clothes she wears are decorated by her own hand. And' – my father pressed his advantage – 'I am given to believe that the queen rates musical talent highly. Chantelle is a sweet songstress and plays many instruments.'

'Let us see her then.' The count waved his hand imperiously.

My father beckoned to us to come forward.

The Count de Ferignay's eyes flicked over me – and paused as our eyes met. I did not drop my gaze from his. He arched an eyebrow at my impudence and travelled on to Chantelle.

And there he lingered. She did not see his avid look for she bent her head demurely when my father spoke her name. But I watched the count react to her presence.

Chantelle was unaware of her effect upon men. Hers was a natural beauty that was all the more gracious for being unaffected by artifice. Her face and form were very lovely. Where I was flat-chested, her bosom swelled beneath her bodice. My hips were bony like a boy's while hers were rounded. Her face was small and heart-shaped, mine was angular with high cheekbones and flat planes. My hair was often tangled, hers shone smooth like wet silk.

'Most becoming,' the Count de Ferignay purred. '*Most* becoming.' He took her hand and raised it to his lips.

My father and Chantelle smiled. They seemed untroubled at this scrutiny of my sister. I had a curdling in my mind, a scent of danger – there was an aura about this man that I did not like. Ferignay held my sister's hand a fraction longer than was seemly. His kiss lingered upon her fingers.

'Do we have your permission, sir, my lord?' It was Armand who spoke.

'What?' Ferignay looked at him and then at my father. 'Oh, yes, yes, permission is granted. I will allow this.'

A calculating smile curved on his lips as he watched Armand and Chantelle embrace.

'One thing,' he called to us before we left his apartments. 'I wish to be kept informed as to your plans. Do not forget this. I most specifically want to know in advance the date you set for your wedding.'

Chapter Nine

When we got back to our room Chantelle took me by both my hands and swung me round and round.

'I am to be wed!' she cried. 'I am to be wed to Armand!'

There were tears on her cheeks and on mine too for she was so wondrously joyful. At last she tired of spinning in a circle and she let me go and fell upon her bed.

'I am so happy, Mélisande. You have no idea how happy I am. I am so very lucky to have found a man that I love and who loves me in return.'

I was glad on her behalf for I wasn't so ignorant as not to know that the majority of marriages were political arrangements. From high estate to the humblest, girls were used in alliances to broker power between men. It did sometimes happen that a couple could fall in love, but it was a thing of chance and often occurred after the wedding had taken place.

Chantelle lay there exhausted with the emotion of the day and soon she fell into a light doze. There was plenty of time before dinner, when we might be called to entertain, so I decided to take advantage of my sister being asleep to be very bold and undertake an errand of my own.

The palace of Cherboucy was built around several court-yards with the service staircases set in the corners. These spiralled down, connecting at their lowest level to the kitchens, and via long subterranean tunnels to the stable block. Taking a small dish from the medical box that we carried with us on our journeys, I opened our chamber door very quietly and slipped into the passageway.

On the upper levels the corridors were quiet. Most of the nobles were resting after the hunt, or using the time to have their hair dressed and to choose what outfit they would wear that evening. A huge dinner was planned to celebrate the king returning safely and to quieten any alarm caused by the ominous forecasts of Nostradamus.

Below ground level things were very different. Every inch of space was heaving with people. Porters were carry-ing sacks of onions and chestnuts and plates of fat truffles and mushrooms. The slaughtered animals from the hunt had been brought inside and butchers were busy jointing and quartering the carcasses. Cooks squabbled with them over the best cuts, while every grade of kitchen servant ran with dishes and all manner of kitchen utensils. In the mêlée the least of these, the scullions, were cuffed and kicked for any reason.

As I paused to check my bearings, one of them, a child of no more than six or seven, came past me staggering under the weight of a pail of brock. He tripped, and the contents spilled out. He sat down among the mulch of leavings and began to sob. Quickly, before anyone saw, I scooped most of it back inside his bucket and handed it to him. He took it from me gratefully and continued in the direction of the kennels. I went past the open fires with the long spits roasting haunches of venison, hare and other game killed this morning.

I found my way partly by instinct, and partly helped by my memory of yesterday when I'd watched the boy, Melchior, lead his leopard away after presenting it to King Charles. The king had commanded that a special place must be set aside to house the animal and the master of the king's horse had been summoned to attend to this. I'd stood with my father and Chantelle by the wall in the palace garden and seen him indicate where Melchior was to go.

Beyond the grain bins I came to the place I sought. Here was a wide passage sloping up to the main courtyard outside for carts and wagons to deliver to the storerooms on this level. To one side a half-sized timber door had been erected to fence off a section of the cellar.

I raised myself on tiptoes and looked over the top of the door. A window set high up in the wall allowed enough light to show me the scene before me.

In one corner was a large wheeled platform upon which stood a cage made of metal bars. Curled inside, on layers of straw, lay Paladin, the leopard. Outside the cage there was a small mattress unrolled on the floor. Upon it, half naked, sleeping, was the boy, Melchior.

The door scraped as I opened it to go inside.

Immediately the leopard stood up and regarded me, unblinking. I stepped inside and looked down at the boy. In repose his face was quite beautiful. Long lashes rested against his cheeks. His breath trembled the downy hairs on his upper lip. I kept very still and made no threatening movement, but the leopard was unhappy. Tail swishing, it began to pace the floor of the cage. I knew better than to touch its master. I knelt and put the dish I carried beside his bed. As I rose to leave, without opening his eyes, Melchior spoke quietly.

'What is your business here?'

I was so startled my voice squeaked, mouse-like, in reply.

'I brought a salve.'

He sat up then. His eyes, like the leopard's, were unflinching.

I returned his gaze with one equal to his own.

He looked from my face to the dish on the floor.

'What does it contain?'

'Arnica, an ointment made from yellow flowers, with borage added. It would help to heal the wound. The one you sustained in the hunt today.'

He reached behind his shoulder to try to touch the place where Ferignay's whip had gouged a chunk from his flesh.

'Yes,' he said. He picked up the dish and gave me it. Then he presented his back to me. 'Will you do this? I am unable to stretch so far.'

I removed the lid and put my fingers in the ointment. Then I applied it to the raw flesh. My fingers touched his warm brown skin.

The leopard made a small noise in its throat.

'Be easy, Paladin,' said Melchior. 'She is a friend.' He murmured some more phrases that I couldn't comprehend.

'What are you saying to the leopard?'

He twisted round to face me. 'I thought you knew my language. The other evening you sang my words very well.'

I blushed. 'I did not mean to eavesdrop. I was in the castle garden and heard you speak, and the music came into my head.' I hesitated. 'It's difficult to explain. When that happens I cannot ignore it.'

'I understand.'

He said this so very clearly and with such assurance it made me believe that he did actually understand.

He turned away from me again and I looked at the pattern on the skin of his back, the scrolls and symbols of the ancients. I searched the rings and ellipses and it seemed to me that among them there was a tribute to the prey. The stag. Honour paid to the animal hunted that we might eat to live. And the hunter too. The leopard. These circles were its spots, the shapes made by the finger of God when he breathed life into the beast.

Melchior didn't say anything but the silence between us was not uncomfortable. I felt that he was waiting.

But why? For me to speak?

Or to act?

I reached out. With the tip of my index finger I traced the outline of the superior pattern. And as I did so it began to reveal itself to me. It was a symbol to be read on more than one level, using more than one sense.

Like my music.

Ah! That was why Melchior *did* understand.

Under my touch the shapes shimmered in my mind. The swirling loops leading me in, to the core of the labyrinth; marking a pattern, as the stars do in the skies above our heads, holding their course since the world's beginning.

'It is life,' I whispered.

He reached back and put his hand over mine and drew my own hand flat, deeper into the complex rhythm of the lines, into the vortex.

I closed my eyes.

Under my touch I felt his life-blood thrum.

And suddenly my own breath was unsteady.

I blinked my eyes wide.

He turned to me. His eyes were shut.

His face was so close. Sweetness flooded my senses. Around us Time hung motionless, awaiting our signal to continue.

The leopard shifted position and laid its head upon its paws.

Melchior moved his own head at the sound. He opened his eyes and I sat up straight.

With shaking hands I replaced the lid and held out the dish of healing salve. 'Here,' I said, 'take it in payment for the lyrics of my song. It is a good remedy,' I added. 'You must be careful against infection. There are rats in the tunnels and they carry disease.'

Melchior laughed softly. 'Where my leopard is, there are never rats close by.'

I laughed too.

He took the dish from my hands, made a small formal bow of his head and said, 'I thank you. This is perhaps the one act of kindness that I have received since I entered the employ of your king. I fear he will not be as civil a master as the Prince of Navarre.'

'How did that come about?' I asked curiously. 'That you and Paladin serve Prince Henri?'

'I had the leopard as a cub when I was only a young boy. My father found it where we lived in the great forest of the Pyrenees, lying beside its mother, who was dead. He brought it home and it grew with me and we taught each other to hunt. The fame of it spread and men came to buy the leopard but my father would not sell it. So they killed my father, but they kept me alive as they knew they needed me to control the animal. We hunt well together, Paladin and I. The man named Gaspard Coligny heard of our skills. He brought a large sum of money to the men who held me and thus they sold me and Paladin to him. And now Gaspard Coligny has used us as chattels to win the good graces of your king.'

'I am sorry about your father's death and that you are held against your will.'

Melchior smiled. 'We will wait,' he said, 'Paladin and I. One day we will be in the mountains again. When our moment comes, then we will be free.'

The sound of the dinner bell pealed through the palace.

I started up. 'I must go. My presence will be required to entertain.'

Melchior got to his feet and held open the half-door that I might pass through. I was conscious of his eyes watching me as I ran along the tunnel towards the kitchen and the spiral staircase leading to my own chamber.

Chapter Ten

When I returned to our room my father was there with my sister.

'Where have you been?' he asked me sharply.

'I – I went to the kitchens,' I answered him.

'Ah, Mélisande, you always were a hungry child,' he said. 'But you know it's not a wise thing for a young maiden to wander the corridors of any palace by herself.'

'Yes, sir,' I said, and bent my head, conscious of my lie of omission in not revealing that it wasn't in quest of food that I had gone down to the cellars.

'The king is a little fevered,' my father began.

'The prophecy!' I cried out. 'It's coming true!'

My father held up his hand. 'Mélisande!' he said severely. 'Curb your tongue!'

My face flushed and again I hung my head.

'To continue,' said my father. 'His majesty, King Charles, is suffering a weakness after the exertions of the hunt and will dine in his own bedchamber this evening with a few guests. We are to go there and play soft music discreetly in the background at his pleasure.' He turned to Chantelle. 'Beautiful as you are in that dress, my dear, I would ask that you both wear' – he cleared his throat – 'less revealing clothes for this evening's entertainment.'

As he left us to prepare, it occurred to me then that perhaps my father had not missed seeing the looks that Armand's master, the Count de Ferignay, had earlier bestowed upon my sister.

It is a great honour to be commanded to play in the private bedroom of any monarch and Chantelle and I dressed with care. My sister had more regret than I at not being allowed to wear her most becoming dress. Usually I gave scant thought to such things, but Chantelle impressed upon me the importance of the occasion. She made me pay attention to arranging the skirts of my sage-coloured dress and smoothing the trim of gold lace at my neck. My hair was a more unruly challenge for her, but she succeeded in securing it in a snood of pale green gauze latticed with thread of gold.

'You have a fine high forehead, Mélisande,' Chantelle commented as she was doing this. 'It's a very fashionable attribute. You should show it off to best advantage. When your hair is clasped back like this one can see your eyes and how blue they are, so like in colour to our mother's.'

I liked it when Chantelle said things like this to me. Our mother had died when I was six or seven, and as the years passed I was beginning to forget her more. It wasn't a thing I wished to do. It was just that as our life changed and we travelled I seemed to drift further away from her. I think our father realized this. It was one of the reasons he'd wanted to join the French court at this time. As soon as he'd heard that a royal tour was planned to encompass the whole kingdom he talked to us of his idea of travelling with the royal party. He knew their itinerary included the Languedoc and that after Carcassonne they would come near to our mother's land of the Isle of Bressay. When this happened my father intended that we should take time to make a detour to visit there. Chantelle and I would be able to reacquaint ourselves with our birth home, and he would catch up with the business of the estate.

Carrying our song sheets and musical instruments, the three of us waited in the outer rooms of the king's apartments for our summons to enter his chambers. People went constantly to and from these rooms: lackeys bearing messages, servants of the king's household and of other lords and ladies, equerries on state business. All were screened and dealt with by the king's personal attendants. Although many nobles asked to speak to the king or at least be allowed a glimpse of his majesty, none were permitted to do so. The Cardinal of Lorraine, uncle of the Duke of Guise, arrived and made a similar request. He looked dumbfounded when he was refused admittance by the king's chamberlain.

'Stand aside!' he ordered the quaking man. 'I have heard that the king is sick and I have come to bestow upon him a blessing of Holy Mother Church.'

'No one is to enter, sir,' the chamberlain stammered. 'It is his majesty's express orders. No one.'

'You would deny the king, his most Catholic majesty,

the comfort of his religion at a time when he is unwell?' roared the cardinal.

'Your eminence, I have a list here of persons who are to be admitted and your name is not upon it.'

'Let me see that document!' The cardinal snatched the paper from the chamberlain's fingers. He had scarcely brought it near his face to scan it, when there was a rustle of taffeta and the paper was, in turn, taken from his hands. 'How dare you presume to—?' The cardinal whirled round and faltered. He was facing the queen regent, Catherine de' Medici. 'Your majesty,' he began.

In one seamless movement Catherine de' Medici returned the paper to the king's chamberlain. 'You may now destroy this list,' she ordered him. Then she grasped the cardinal firmly by the hand and kissed his ring. 'It pleases us greatly that you are so concerned for the welfare of our son, the king. Be assured that you are the first person I personally would call upon if I thought King Charles needed spiritual solace at this time.' The queen lowered her voice in a confidential tone. 'Let me go in now and speak with his majesty,' she said. 'Allow me to inform him of your good wishes and desire to comfort him. I'm sure he will be gratified to know that you, above others, have rushed to his side to attend to him. I will beg him to make an exception in your case and that you be permitted inside.'

At that moment the king's chief surgeon, Ambroise Paré, came from the king's rooms. He spoke out loudly. 'The king has asked me to make an announcement. His majesty is suffering from fatigue, nothing more. By the grace of God he will be recovered, and strong enough to attend worship at Mass in the chapel tomorrow.'

The courtiers turned to one another and the news spread rapidly through the rooms. The Cardinal of Lorraine went to speak with his nephew, the Duke of Guise, who had just entered the chambers in the company of the Count de Ferignay. Their frowns made me think that this information had not so much cheered them as cast them down.

Catherine de' Medici beckoned to my father and we went forward. 'Permit these musicians to enter after me,' she told the chamberlain. As he conducted us inside she drew him to one side and added, 'But on no account admit anyone else. That includes all members of the house of Guise, and in particular the Cardinal of Lorraine.'

As we followed the queen regent into the king's private rooms my father whispered to Chantelle and me, 'Do not speak unless spoken to. Do not listen to the royals' talk. Do not make any comment or display an opinion, by movement of your body or expression on your face – no matter what conversation you might hear this night.'

Chapter Eleven

It was as well our father gave us his warning about self-control, for the king was not alone as his surgeon had indicated.

The first person I saw when I entered the room was Melchior.

My heart tightened in my chest. Melchior stood with his leopard, Paladin, at the end of a long table that had been set up in the king's bedroom to accommodate his dinner guests. Although I came into the room to one side of them and out of their sight, upon my entry, both leopard and boy turned their heads to look at me. Neither acknowledged my presence, but I saw a subtle change in their stance. I kept my face composed and walked with Chantelle and my father to our appointed place by the window.

King Charles was very tired. He sat, half supported by cushions, on an enormous chair at the head of the table. Three of the places were occupied by the king's two younger brothers and his twelve-year-old sister, Princess Margot. The king's brothers were, like him, spindly and thin-chested, but Margot, with her bright complexion and shiny dark curls, displayed vibrant good health. In the remaining seats sat the prophet Nostradamus and, closer to the king, the Huguenots, Henri, Prince of Navarre, and Admiral Gaspard Coligny. No wonder the queen had given orders to the door keeper to refuse entry to any member of the Guise family!

Queen Catherine embraced her son and took her place by his right hand. 'The royal surgeon, Ambroise Paré, made the announcement as to your health,' she told him. 'It gladdens me that you are not seriously incommoded.'

'How was the news received?' King Charles asked his mother. 'Were my people happy that I am not ill?'

'They become concerned when they do not see you, my son,' Catherine de' Medici answered obliquely, 'although some are always eager to pursue their own ends. That arrogant Cardinal of Lorraine, uncle of the Duke of Guise, tried to bluster his way through, but I defeated him in his intentions.'

'One day we will need to deal with the insubordinate house of Guise at the point of a sword,' the king said angrily.

'It may be that the day will come when you do have to deal with them, but it is not this day,' his mother replied soothingly.

'Ah, the minstrel.' The king noticed us. 'His music always eases my mind.'

King Charles waved for us to begin playing and for the food to be served. The royal family and guests chatted as they ate, much as any other family might do. I was surprised at the warmth and familiarity that was accorded the young Prince Henri of Navarre. By following their conversation, although my father had forbidden me to, I learned that Prince Henri had lived some of his boyhood with Catherine de' Medici's children. His mother, Jeanne d'Albret, Queen of Navarre, had then adopted the new reformed religion. Thus there had been a parting, with some suspicion on both sides. Prince Henri's country of Navarre lay north-west of Languedoc, situated on the border between France and Spain. More and more French Huguenots, aware of a sympathetic reception, sought refuge in that area. They were not only congregating in Navarre itself, but also filling up towns in the west of France, like La Rochelle and Jarnac. This was displeasing to the queen regent, Catherine de' Medici, and she said as much:

'We do not wish parts of the kingdom of France to become a protectorate of Navarre,' she stated.

Admiral Gaspard Coligny replied on behalf of Prince Henri, who was sharing a joke with Princess Margot at this point.

'Queen Jeanne d'Albret of Navarre has no wish to encroach upon French territory, your highness. She seeks the way of reconciliation.'

'From your position on the State Council of France you will be aware that the French crown does too, most strenuously,' Catherine de' Medici replied tartly. 'His majesty has already conceded many liberties to the Huguenots in their religious practices. Do remember that in France, unlike some other countries in Europe, a citizen may, under law, hold to either religion. In his wisdom and goodness the king has steered his country on this hazardous course to achieve harmony among both sides.'

It was clear that King Charles had done none of these things. They were all machinations of his mother, as queen regent. The king was not even interested enough to keep up with the political discussion at his own table. During the meal King Charles chatted to his siblings and from time to time played with Paladin. He ordered that the leopard be brought to him and its muzzle removed that he might feed it morsels of meat from his plate. If Melchior objected to his animal being pampered in this way, he gave no sign. And even though throughout the evening he also made no further obvious glance in my direction, I knew that he listened to my music.

We made music and sang for an hour or more. Then King Charles gave us leave to rest, and to eat from the remains of the royal meal now lying in dishes on the sideboard. I desperately wanted to speak to Chantelle, to ask my sister her opinion on the things we'd heard. But I did not, for my father, once again, gave us both warning looks. Talking less made me concentrate my mind and I slowly came to see that my father's countenance was more than one of a parent attempting to instil good manners in a child – the expression on my father's face was one of apprehension. But what could he be frightened of? We were in the king's good graces and would do nothing to offend him. I sat on a stool and rested and listened to the sounds of the palace, inside and outside the room, and felt again the quickening within me that presaged a song forming in my mind. I tried to analyse this sensation as it occurred. Did the words and the notes spring like a stream from the earth? What tributaries in the mind feed into the soul whence the muse is nourished? Words were tumbling in my head. I looked at the leopard and the amber of Paladin's eyes reflected green grass. What story could this animal tell of the dark Pyrenees where it was once suckled by its mother? There was grass there, and stones, and a pattern . . .

'Do you know the source of your inspiration?'

These words spoken in the room, so similar to the ones inside my head, brought me abruptly back to the present.

The question had been asked of Nostradamus by the king.

'The Lord God is the source of all inspiration, sire,' the prophet replied.

In some relief Catherine de' Medici broke off from the intricacies of her sparring with Gaspard Coligny. 'Ah, yes, Master Nostradamus. Would you be good enough to make some predictions for my family this evening?'

'Your son the king will recover from this present weakness,' Nostradamus said confidently. 'He will live for years to come.' The prophet paused. Then he added, 'The reign of King Charles will be marked out in history.'

'There!' Catherine de' Medici exclaimed in delight. 'There, you see, my beloved Charles. The prophet says that your reign will be one of note. You will be famous for evermore!'

I wondered why no one asked the question: in what manner would King Charles's reign be thus marked?

King Charles inclined his head to Nostradamus. 'Your doom and gloom of yesterday is gone then?'

His young sister Margot giggled. As she did so, Nostradamus started and looked at her. Then he turned to the king and said stubbornly, 'That which I saw, I saw.'

'And what else do you see?' Catherine de' Medici pressed for more information. 'Will my other sons reign too?'

Nostradamus nodded, but he seemed distracted. 'You spoke of a way to bridge differences . . .'

'Yes?' Catherine de' Medici asked eagerly. 'Have you any observation to make on that subject? Any indication of a way forward?'

Gaspard Coligny moved his chair in annoyance. Clearly he thought it frivolous to be asking this question of a soothsayer. And I, recalling what Melchior had told me, saw why. At his own expense Coligny had engineered this meeting of the two young men. He'd heard that King Charles desired a leopard, had sought one out, and procured it for Prince Henri of Navarre. Then he'd arranged for it to be brought to the palace of Cherboucy, knowing the heavily armed ultra-Catholic men of Guise were attending court. At great personal risk he'd escorted Prince Henri and joined the hunt, anticipating that King Charles in gratitude would grant them a private audience. He wanted to ingratiate himself and gain favour for the Huguenot cause. Now the vague predictions of a soothsayer threatened to overshadow a serious discussion.

'Surely the way forward is to—' Coligny broke off as Nostradamus rose to his feet.

The prophet's eyes had become fixed.

'*Five times three.*'

He said this flatly, without emotion, as he stared into the distance.

'Five and three,' Catherine de' Medici repeated. 'Three is a magical number.'

All in the room looked at Nostradamus. But not I. Instead I followed his gaze and saw where his sight was fixed. Above the sideboard hung a long mirror. In it I could see his image.

And my own.

'*A great King of France is in this room.*'

The prophet intoned the words.

Before my eyes the surface of the mirror rippled and was still. I blinked. It was tiredness, nothing more. I had risen very early this morning and had kept up with the hunt all day. And when others rested in the afternoon I'd taken the salve to Melchior. I was tired. That was all.

I closed my eyes.

'*A great King of France is in this room.*'

The words echoed in my head. Had Nostradamus spoken again? I opened my eyes. The surface of the mirror was calm. I saw my own eyes, the pupils huge and dark. My gaze moved to the frame, embossed silver with a complex spiralled design.

'*A great King of France is in this room.*' Nostradamus raised his hands above his head; his moonstone ring shone dully on his finger.

'*Two persons joined in holy bond,*
Two realms,
One—'

He stopped.

'One what?' Catherine de' Medici asked him.

'There is one here whose purpose is yet to be determined.' Nostradamus gazed around him. His eyes were as milk-white as the moonstone ring he wore on his forefinger. 'I cannot see clearly.' Drained of energy, the old man sank into his chair.

'We were talking of a way to bridge differences,' Catherine de' Medici pursued him. 'That means between Catholic and Protestant. '"Two realms joined . . ."' She mulled over his words. 'I know!' She rose to her feet. 'Two realms. Two persons! *I* can see it, even if you do not!'

Nostradamus lifted his hand feebly. 'You do not have the gift,' he said.

'Elizabeth of England!' Catherine de' Medici cried. 'My son will marry the Queen of England.'

My father played an incorrect note on his lute. He quickly picked up the tune again and kept his eyes concentrated on the strings.

'Send for Throckmorton, the English ambassador!' Catherine ordered. 'Tell him to bring a picture of his sovereign, Queen Elizabeth!'

This was momentous. Protestant England and Catholic France united! Was this what Nostradamus had meant when he'd uttered those words?

The prophet looked confused. He began to shake.

Without heeding any protocol I went to the sideboard and brought him a glass of water. He took it from me. As his fingers touched mine his hand twitched as though stung. He stared at me. 'Mélisande,' he whispered.

'The Queen of England?' King Charles questioned his mother. 'Is she not much older than I?'

'Your majesty,' Nostradamus began to protest.

Catherine de' Medici waved him into silence.

'It is clear. It makes perfect sense. Our two kingdoms will become one. Then we will be stronger and able to resist the might of Spain, which seeks to surround us with its conquests in the Netherlands. A marriage of France and England will heal the wounds of division that rend us apart. We will unite and so will these two religions, and followers of both will find favour.'

The door opened and the very bewildered English ambassador, Throckmorton, was admitted, bearing a miniature of his queen.

In haste Queen Catherine took it from him. 'Look!' She thrust the likeness under the nose of her son. 'Do you think this woman would make a suitable consort for you?' Then, recalling our presence in the room, she called out to my father. 'Minstrel! You have recently come from the land of England. Do you deem her queen worthy enough to be a match for my son?'

We had met Elizabeth of England. Her grandeur and majesty were awesome. She would gobble up this stripling boy as a lizard does a stick insect.

My father looked up. 'The Queen of England has great majesty,' he said in an even voice. 'Indeed . . . Yes.'

'She seems a handsome enough woman,' Charles said reluctantly. 'If you so wish it, my beloved mother.'

Throckmorton had the stunned look of a man whose house ceiling has fallen in upon his head. Whether by dint of the wine he had consumed that evening, or by the fact that the proposal was so unexpected and, to his mind, preposterous, he could not take it seriously. And perhaps in the genuine belief that this was one of the japes that Catherine de' Medici was wont to play on people to amuse herself, he reacted in a most natural but catastrophic manner.

The English ambassador laughed.

Chapter Twelve

B y the time ambassador Thockmorton realized his
mistake, there was no way he could retrieve the
situation.

'O gracious Queen,' he improvised. 'I have suffered a
headache these last three days, and my thoughts lack
clarity.'

'You are dismissed, sir,' Catherine de' Medici told him
icily.

Throckmorton, now fully aware of the gaffe he'd made,
sought to make amends. 'Your majesty' – he directed his
entreaty towards King Charles – 'forgive me, I thought
only, only . . . ahem, my own queen is of an age, and you
are . . .' He stopped as he saw the pit opening before him.
He could not now rescue the situation without denigrating
one or other of the parties involved. He began to cough. 'I
fear I have eaten something, a piece of bread, perhaps . . . It
has lodged in my throat.' Throckmorton covered his mouth.
'If I may retire to my own lodging and speak with you again
tomorrow.' The hapless man backed from the room.

'It is he who sticks in *my* throat!' Catherine de' Medici was incandescent with rage. 'And I will spit him out!' She strode up and down the king's bedroom, striking her fist into the palm of her hand. 'How dare he mock me! How dare he try to thwart my good intentions!'

'It is of no importance.' The king tried to console his mother. 'We can easily make another match for me.'

'Don't you see he has offended your person? Has offended all of us?' Catherine de' Medici ceased her pacing and gave Charles and the rest of her children a fierce and condescending stare. 'Do none of you appreciate the significance of statecraft? Can you not foresee the ends we strive for?' When she received no reply she moaned in despair and tore the veil from her head. 'Why is it that everyone misinterprets what I try to do?'

Her children sat upright in their chairs. I saw that all of them, especially the Princess Margot, were very scared of their mother. The girl's face was stricken and had become palest white. She sat without moving, more cowed than a servant in the presence of a cruel master

'I will have revenge on that odious toad and his heretical queen,' Catherine de' Medici declared.

Gaspard Coligny coughed.

But the queen regent did not hear him or chose to ignore him, such was her passion. Coligny must have felt it wiser not to point out that if Elizabeth of England was a heretic, then so too was he, and also the young Prince of Navarre who sat at the king's table.

Catherine de' Medici took her seat and resumed eating. Although she had already consumed much food she now ate more, and quickly; stuffing all kinds of sweetmeats into her mouth simultaneously. This seemed to calm her and she tried to restart the conversation, but everyone at the table was subdued and disinclined to join in.

Very soon Nostradamus begged to be excused, saying he needed to rest to enable him to make further prognostications for the queen. Leaning heavily on his silver walking stick, he went out by the way we had entered. However, when Gaspard Coligny and the Prince of Navarre stood to depart the queen insisted that they left as they had arrived, secretly.

King Charles, who by this time had drunk many glasses of wine, made a protest about this. 'Am I not king in my own kingdom,' he demanded shrilly, 'that my invited guests are unable to come and go when and how I say?'

'It would be unwise, my lord' – his mother's manner changed dramatically as she sought to coax her son to do as she thought best – 'and you are not an unwise king. It would be foolish to openly antagonize the house of Guise too much. Remember they have a large force of men-at-arms and command the loyalty of the citizens of Paris and much of Catholic France.'

'Sire, I have no mind to run the gauntlet of the men of your outer bedchamber,' Prince Henri quipped. 'And in any case I rather like secret passages. Don't you recall' – he turned to the Princess Margot – 'how we played in one as children at the château of Blois?'

Margot nodded happily, the colour at last coming to her face. Impulsively she ran forward to embrace her cousin and laid her head on his shoulder.

Henri laughed and teasingly tugged at her hair. I saw that he had referred to this childhood memory to relieve the strain and I also saw that, unlike Catherine de' Medici, the Prince of Navarre was a natural diplomat.

King Charles fussed and complained but in the end did as his mother wished.

A curtain by the king's bed was pulled aside to reveal a hidden door. It led indirectly to an outer courtyard where horses waited for Prince Henri and Gaspard Coligny. In this way it was hoped that the Guise family would not be alerted to their presence in the palace and the fact that they'd had a private audience with the king.

King Charles embraced his cousin and bade him farewell, saying, 'Good Prince, my cousin, I wish that we could dispense with the differences that keep us apart.'

But they were different in more than religion, I thought. Although younger than Charles, Prince Henri had thick curly hair and already the beginnings of a beard. The king's hair was sparse and lank. Taller than his cousin, he was thinner and appeared stooped beside the stockier figure of Henri. Their clothes too contrasted wildly. Prince Henri's formal dining clothes were plain grey while Charles wore yellow silk slashed at arm and leg to show froths of lace. A diamond sparkled in one ear and more jewels shone from his finger rings and from around his neck. But rather than displaying majesty he appeared foppish beside the solid build of the younger man.

'I would hope to spend more time together,' Prince Henri agreed. 'I enjoyed our hunt with my leopard today.'

At the mention of the hunt King Charles became more

animated. 'It was a glorious kill.' He looked to where Paladin and Melchior stood by the table, both impassive. 'I would so much love to hunt again with such a peerless beast.'

Prince Henri glanced at Coligny, who gave an almost imperceptible nod of his head. I wondered later if what followed had been rehearsed in advance.

'My dearest cousin,' said Prince Henri. 'Why not keep the leopard whilst you are in the south of France?'

'A splendid idea!' Gaspard Coligny interposed smoothly. 'The leopard and the boy would serve you well on your hunting days, sire, as you make your royal progress. Then at some future date, when you are travelling north towards Paris, we might arrange for the leopard to be returned.'

Tears of joy spilled down King Charles's cheeks. 'So we will meet and hunt together again!' He hugged his cousin in gratitude.

When Prince Henri and Coligny had finally gone, the king declared his intention of retiring to his bed. He dismissed us and made to call for his valets.

'I will stay a while longer,' his mother told him. 'We must speak further.' Her eyes glittered as she seated herself once more at the table.

With relief my father, my sister and myself quitted the king's bedchamber. I do not know exactly what was in my father's mind for I did not ever have the opportunity to ask him, but I knew that for myself I was heartily glad to leave that place of intrigue and deceit.

Chapter Thirteen

B y noon the following day the whole court was aware
that the Huguenot Prince of Navarre and Admiral
Gaspard Coligny, the unofficial leader of the French
Protestants, had dined privately with King Charles the
previous evening.

'Everyone knows,' I told Chantelle, as we practised our
repertoire in the garden with my father the next afternoon.
'It is the main topic of conversation, from kitchen cellar to
bedroom ceiling.'

'I wish you would not speak like that, Mélisande,' my
father tutted. 'Such expressions make you sound like a
gossiping washerwoman.'

'I'm sorry, Papa,' I said. 'But how can it be that everyone has heard that which the queen regent desired to be
kept secret?'

'You have much to learn about the ways of court life,'
my father replied. 'The king cannot piss in his chamber
pot without the world knowing its contents two minutes
later.'

'Armand says every noble has a network of spies,' said Chantelle.

'And even the spies have spies,' my father laughed. He stood up and looked out to the north-west. 'In that direction, beyond Toulouse, lies the Isle of Bressay. When you are married, Chantelle, and secure with Armand, I will take Mélisande away so that she may have some respite from this polluting atmosphere.'

There was a sound of rapid horse's hooves followed by yelling from the courtyard at the main gate. My father went over to the wall and looked down. 'Yet another messenger bearing ill tidings, I'll warrant,' he said gloomily.

Suddenly we heard the loud tones of the Cardinal of Lorraine. 'Outrage!' he shouted. 'In God's Holy Name! This is sacrilege!'

There was the clatter of more horses and then women wailing and sobbing. Chantelle and I hurried to see what had caused the commotion. Escorted by some peasants and farm workers, a group of nuns had arrived. Their habits were bloodied and torn. Their wimples had been pulled from their heads and their poor shaved skulls exposed to show bruises and cuts. They huddled together, crying in the most pathetic manner, bursting into even louder sobs as several carts trundled behind them into the courtyard, bearing the dead bodies of the remainder of their community.

'Holy Mother!' Chantelle blessed herself.

Men and women came running from the palace. The Cardinal of Lorraine hurried towards the nuns and blessed them, giving comfort to each in turn. Then he gathered up his robes and clambered into the first cart. Ignoring the pools of blood, he began to bestow the Last Sacrament of the dead on the bodies that lay there.

A few minutes later, the Duke of Guise came cantering from the direction of the stable yards at the head of a column of soldiers. They were fully armed and paused only to confer with the cardinal before galloping headlong out of the main gate.

My father furrowed his brow and murmured to himself, 'It will go ill with any Huguenot who crosses their path this day.'

It was evening when the soldiers returned. We were playing quietly behind the king's chair during dinner in the main hall when the door crashed open. The duke's soldiers dragged in two men and flung them into the middle of the room, where they fell upon their knees.

'We have captured two murdering heretics,' the Duke of Guise declared, 'and brought them here for the judgement of the king.'

King Charles half rose from his seat. 'This is an impertinence,' he said. 'I am at dinner. I will convene a judgement tomorrow. Or . . . or when it suits me . . .' He tailed off.

His mother plucked at his sleeve. He tried to shake her hand away but she persisted. 'At least pretend to listen to them.' She mouthed the advice to her son.

The king was feeble in his body and not fit to stand unsupported. He settled back in his chair. 'I will hear what you have to say,' he said, and signalled for us to stop playing.

The Duke of Guise listed the men's offences.

'These men are Huguenots,' he said. 'Today is Sunday. We espied them at worship with some others in a barn in a field. Huguenots are not permitted to worship on the Sabbath day. Also, they are only allowed to come together for prayer within their own homes and they were in a public place. This place is in close proximity to the Convent of the Child of Hope, where the good sisters were butchered and violated.'

'The barn where we worship is on my own property more than twenty miles away from the Convent of the Child of Hope.' From his position on his knees one of the prisoners spoke out. 'I donate grain to the sisters there. I would no more harm them than I would my own wife and children. My own wife and children,' he added, his voice breaking, 'that your soldiers murdered without mercy.'

'Twenty holy nuns have been slaughtered!' The Duke of Guise raised his voice. 'This man has blood on his sleeve.'

'That is where you wounded me with your sword, sir. It is my own blood that you see. Can you bring the nuns here and ask them if we were the men who assaulted them?'

The Duke of Guise went forward and struck the prisoner across the face. 'How dare you make demands, you filthy cur! Do you think we would bring holy women, women whom you have violated, into your presence? Your very request is shameful and indicates your guilt.'

At this point the other prisoner, a lad of about fifteen years, spoke up. 'We are innocent,' he said. 'But may I remind you: "Vengeance is mine sayeth the Lord"?'

'We do not seek vengeance.' The Cardinal of Lorraine now stood beside his nephew. 'The Catholics of France seek justice. The king's justice.'

The king gave his judgement the next day. The two prisoners were to be burned at the stake.

All courtiers and foreign dignitaries were compelled to attend. Throckmorton, the English ambassador, was made to occupy a seat close to the queen regent. Catherine de' Medici had dressed as if for a great occasion of state, with a necklace of heavy jewels and a full-length cloak of white ermine furs draped about her person. Her widow's dress of black taffeta was relieved with a wide collar of stiffened white lace which rose up behind her headdress to frame her face, giving her a most majestic appearance. The executioner from Carcassonne had been summoned. This man's reputation was one of extreme cruelty, and he displayed it that day in the courtyard of the palace of Cherboucy. He did not strangle the men mercifully before their burning, but disembowelled them where they stood tied to the stake before setting the torch to the bonfire. Their groans and screams could be heard above the noisy chatter of the crowds. My father made Chantelle and me stand well back among the people who jostled for a good view of the executions.

'I do not think anyone believes these men to be guilty of attacking nuns,' I whispered to my father. 'Why then does the king condemn them to death?'

'Most likely the king's mother, Catherine de' Medici,

will have advised him to do this to appease the Catholic faction who believe her to be in collusion with Protestants,' my father whispered. 'Perhaps it is also to show Throckmorton, the English ambassador who offended her, what she is capable of. It may even be because her son's frail health will deny him his hunting over the next few days and she thinks he needs some other diversion to occupy his mind.'

I recalled how King Charles had revelled in seeing the leopard rip the throat from the living stag.

'Who knows?' my father went on. 'Certainly we must hasten Chantelle's marriage. Allied to Ferignay she will have protection and after the ceremony is over you and I will leave for the Isle of Bressay.'

Why did we need to leave? What had we to fear? We had done nothing wrong.

Chapter Fourteen

There was widespread reaction to this act of savagery.

The King of Spain, who supported the Catholic cause, applauded France for dealing swiftly and decisively with heretics. An angry but formally polite letter arrived from Queen Jeanne of Navarre, enquiring, if it was the case that Huguenots enjoyed the full protection of the laws of France, why had the prisoners been denied a trial?

To these royal missives Catherine de' Medici was supposed to have replied, 'Both Catholic and Protestant try my patience every day.'

Claiming ill health, King Charles withdrew to his rooms. It was believed that this was a pretext to avoid receiving the flood of messages either supporting or condemning his actions. But these political manoeuvrings did not deter our plans for Chantelle's marriage.

'Papa has permitted that I may walk with Armand to celebrate our official betrothal,' Chantelle told me one afternoon, 'but I must not go alone. You are to accompany me as chaperone.'

We clung to each other and giggled. Me! A chaperone!

I pretended to take my duties very seriously. 'You must cover your head with a veil,' I instructed her. 'And look at your dress! It is quite immodest. Who do you think you are? The Duchess Marie-Christine?'

Chantelle pulled her neckline higher to conceal the v of her cleavage.

'That's better,' I informed her primly. I held out my arm. 'Now we may go forth and meet your suitor.'

Armand was standing under one of the arches of the courtyard. He rushed forward when he saw us approach.

'There is a place I wish to take you, Chantelle.' He made a small bow to me. 'If it is permitted by your sister chaperone?'

I nodded my head, thoroughly enjoying this new-found power.

Armand led us through the main courtyard past the stable blocks. By the open door of a horse stall stood an elderly man. It was the prophet Nostradamus. He was waiting while his horse was being strapped with saddle-bags. They were stuffed with books and papers, but nothing much in the way of rich clothes or jewellery. For a man who commanded the respect of Catherine de' Medici, the Queen Regent of France, he travelled very plainly.

'Mélisande,' he said.

I stopped. Armand and Chantelle walked on as if they had not heard. I glanced after them. My duty was to be beside them. I should not loiter, yet . . .

I looked at the prophet.

'I wondered,' he said, 'if you would mind telling me how old you are?'

'I am in my thirteenth year, sir,' I replied.

'And the date and month of your birth?'

'The fifteenth day of January.'

'Could that be it?' He murmured these words so low I hardly heard them. Then he went on, speaking more loudly, 'Five times three is fifteen, and January marks the beginning of the year, month number one.'

'Yes,' I said, for I could not disagree with his statement, but I felt awkward standing there so I asked him, 'You are leaving?'

'The king and the queen regent have graciously given me leave to return to my home in Salon,' he told me.

Now I was anxious to quit his presence. Standing in the bright spring sunlight, his predictions and the unease that they had caused me seemed remote. Besides which, Chantelle and Armand were now almost out of sight and I did not know where Armand was leading us.

'I will return to my home in Salon,' he repeated. 'Salon, which is in Provence.'

'I wish you a safe journey, sir,' I said, and ran to catch up with my sister and her betrothed.

They had gone into a smaller, less-used cobbled square. We crossed to the furthest tower and entered by a wooden door. Up and up the spiral stair we followed Armand until finally, on the top floor, he opened the door with a flourish.

'I approached the master of the king's household and he has allowed us these rooms as our own apartments.'

'It seems so selfish to think of our wedding when the king is sick,' said Chantelle.

'His doctors have diagnosed marsh fever, nothing more,' Armand told us. 'Although my lord Ferignay says the Medici lineage has polluted the royal blood of France. He blames the queen regent for the constant bad health of the king and his younger brothers.'

No one remarked on the fact that King Charles's sister, the Princess Margot, enjoyed good health. It seemed to me that Catherine de' Medici was blamed for the ill luck that beset the family but received no credit for any good. But that afternoon the health of the King of France was of little concern to us. We were so taken up with exploring the two rooms that would become Armand and Chantelle's first home. The inner chamber was very small, but sufficient, as Armand pointed out, to hold a bed.

'I have ordered a wool mattress and I'll have a carpenter make a bed platform over the next few days.'

Chantelle dipped her head and blushed. I walked to the window and glanced down. It was dizzyingly high. Below was the stableyard where the tiny figures of the farriers and the grooms walked around tending to the horses.

'I will be the maiden in the tower,' said Chantelle dreamily, coming to look out of the window.

'And I will be your prince,' murmured Armand, his mouth in her hair.

I withdrew quietly to the outer room and left them alone. This was not the correct behaviour for a chaperone but they would be married shortly and I knew that Armand was utterly trustworthy.

The window of this room was much larger. From here I could see the double-walled city of Carcassonne with its towers and crenellated battlements. Between it and us the countryside of the Languedoc spread out, forest, field and river. To my mind my sister *was* a princess, and it was fitting that she should be wedded here in this land of our mother, one of an independent people who shared a noble history. I would write them a ballad, I decided, as a wedding gift. It would tell of the romance of Armand and Chantelle and would be in the form of the *tenson*, which is sung by two people, each taking an alternate verse.

I imagined them here, sitting by the window, Chantelle strumming her lute and singing in her beautiful melodious voice, and he gazing at her, his eyes and heart full of love. The words presented themselves and they were bound in with the view before me, part of nature and its bounty, wine and herbs, and the song of the birds like the song of my sister's name.

Armand would speak first, and my sister would reply.

'O lady in your bower,
what do you see
from thy tower
as you gaze longingly?'

'I see a fine chevalier
leaving the city rampart
to come riding here
and make claim upon my heart.'

Almost of their own accord my fingers tapped on the windowsill. I wanted to write immediately, while the song was fresh in my mind. I stirred myself, impatient to be away. I needed an instrument, something to trap the tune before I lost it in my head. Crossing the room, I rapped on the door and opened it and they were standing there by the window entwined in each other's arms.

Armand leaped away.

I laughed to see this handsome chevalier so put out by the appearance of a young girl.

Chantelle's face was suffused with love.

When I think of my sister now, this is the image that I try to bring to my mind – not the other starker memory I have. That day is the one I want to remember, when she was safe and happy in the arms of her lover.

Chapter Fifteen

For the next week or so, while Papa formalized the marriage contract and arranged the ceremony, Chantelle and I busied ourselves furnishing her love nest.

I purchased some lengths of muslin and together we sewed curtains for the windows of her tower rooms. She was gifted a table and two chairs by the Count de Ferignay; Armand's friends bought them a small stove. My father gave an oak chest and paid for rush matting to be laid and all was ready on the morning of Chantelle's wedding day.

Chantelle wanted to come from her tower to be married. Although we had begged him to allow us both to spend the eve of her wedding there, my father in his strictness refused. It meant that Chantelle and I had to rise very early on her wedding day and transport her dress and all our other accoutrements from our room in the main part of the palace. With our travelling cloaks wrapped round on top of our night shifts, we giggled together as we hurried back and forth across the courtyards. On one of these journeys I broke away and ran to the garden to pick some of the *artema* flowers that grew there. This was Chantelle's love token and I meant to weave them into her hair ribbons.

My new friend, the little kitchen scullion, brought us a shovelful of hot coals for the stove, where we heated some water. We removed our night shifts, shivering in the coolness. Then we washed each other before getting ready. Chantelle slipped her wedding gown over her head and I plaited the hair on her crown into many small braids, tying these with white ribbons and interlacing them with the pink wild flowers. We arranged the mass of her shining dark hair across her shoulders, where it curled in tendrils on the delicate embroidery of her dress.

'You look so beautiful it makes my heart ache,' I told her.

Chantelle went into the bedchamber and strewed the remainder of the flowers on her marriage bed. Then she opened up the window. The muslin cloth wafted in the breeze that blew in from the plains. Chantelle hugged me tightly.

'We will not be separated,' she vowed. 'You will come and visit me often as I travel with the court. I will have Armand, my husband, command my father to allow it.'

We both laughed at this – how she might outrank my father in her new role as the wife of a vassal to a high lord. She promised that as soon as she was pregnant she would come to the Isle of Bressay and spend her confinement with me. We held hands together and wandered back into the outer room.

The Count de Ferignay stood there. His bodyguard, Jauffré, was by the outer door.

'Why, sir,' Chantelle said in surprise, 'the arrangement is that my father is going to escort me to my marriage. Besides which, you are an hour too early for the ceremony.'

'I did not come here to escort you to your wedding, girl. I came to claim my right – *Droit de Seigneur*.'

'What?' Chantelle had turned pale.

'I would have had you last night except your tiresome father always ensures that your room door is well bolted.'

'I do not understand.' Chantelle looked desperately towards the door, where Jauffré stood with a leer upon his face.

'I think you do,' the count replied. 'Your sister here might be more uncultured but you have enough experience of the world to know that it is the right of a lord to claim his vassal's wife on the eve of the wedding.'

'Sir, you are saying this to tease me.' Chantelle's voice now sounded very scared.

'No, I am not. Although I think you mean to excite my passion by your pretence of innocence.'

'I do not!' Chantelle cried out. And it was this cry that roused me to action as I realized this man meant to harm my sister in the most shameful way.

'I will go and fetch my father,' I said. I ran towards the door, but Jauffré came into the room and grabbed me roughly by my wrists.

'Be sensible,' Count de Ferignay told my sister. 'That way you will come to no harm.'

'I will not submit to you!' Chantelle told him.

'You will,' said the count.

'She will not!' Armand Vescault elbowed Jauffré aside and entered the room.

'Armand!' Chantelle cried out and made to go to him.

The Count de Ferignay seized her by the arm, tearing her dress as he did so. He shoved her violently into the corner of the room and pulled his sword from its scabbard. Armand was unarmed yet he did not hesitate. He ran in front of Chantelle to protect her.

'You must not do this,' he said to Ferignay. 'There are plenty of ladies at court who would consider it an honour to please you. Leave me and my bride alone, I beg you.'

'Get out of my way!' snarled the count. 'I will not be ordered about by a vassal of the lowest kind.'

Jauffré had moved forward to protect his master and I saw my chance to slip away to get help. I ran again for the door. But he was too quick for me and caught me, dragging me by my hair.

I shrieked and so did Chantelle. Armand launched himself at Ferignay and, being faster and stronger, managed to wrest the sword from the older man before he could raise it to strike. Armand flung the sword down and grappled with the count.

Jauffré threw me into a chair with such force that both it and I tumbled backwards and I lay on the floor, half stunned.

'You must leave off!' Armand was shouting. 'The minstrel is favoured by the king. He will not allow this desecration of his daughter!'

'Kill him!' Ferignay shouted at Jauffré. 'Kill him. *Now!*'

And Jauffré took his dagger from his belt and plunged it hilt-deep in Armand's back.

Armand staggered forward, clutching the count around his waist. But he had no strength in him and the count pushed him away quite easily.

There was blood. A lot of blood, spreading down the back of Armand's white shirt. He fell on his face and still the blood came. It was on Armand's face, coming from his mouth.

'You have killed him,' Chantelle wailed, and she ran and knelt and lifted up Armand's head and tried to hold him to her. A great pool of her lover's blood seeped into Chantelle's white wedding dress, staining it crimson.

'That was my wish,' the count stated. He smoothed his clothes and addressed Chantelle. 'And now I will fulfil my first intention.'

'Armand is dead.' Chantelle lifted her head and gazed at me. 'Armand is dead. Mélisande, what am I to do?'

'I have told you what you must do.' The count removed his scabbard and laid it down upon the table. He was shaken, but seemed more determined now to continue his wicked purpose.

Chantelle stared at him. She seemed to come to herself. She looked to Armand again and at the count.

'Yes,' she said. 'I see what I must do. If you would grant me a moment with my sister?'

I did not understand what Chantelle was saying. My head ached so much I could not stand.

Chantelle came to me. She bent and kissed my face. 'Adieu, dearest Mélisande,' she whispered. She trailed her fingers across my cheek. 'Farewell, sweet sister.'

95

I raised my head and watched Chantelle walk calmly into the bedchamber. She could not mean to give herself to this fiend. I knew my sister better than anyone alive. We talked and shared secrets. She was both my sister and good friend, and when our mother had gone, she'd been like a kind mother to me. Her heart was true. Although not as rash and foolhardy as me, she had her own quiet courage. What was she thinking of? There was no weapon in that room with which she could defend herself. No table or chairs. There was nothing there; only the bed and the window.

The window.

'Chantelle!' I screamed. '*Chantelle!*'

Chapter Sixteen

I crawled on my knees into the bedchamber.

The room was empty. The muslin curtain billowed at the open window. I stumbled over and looked down. Far below me the body of my sister lay broken on the cobblestones. She can't have screamed as she fell for there was no one there beside her. But there *was* someone screaming. I realized it was me. I put my fist in my mouth and bit down on my knuckles with my teeth.

A footstep in the room.

I whirled round. The Count de Ferignay was behind me. For the briefest moment I believed he was going to tip me out of the window, but then he swivelled abruptly and left. I heard him call to his bodyguard.

'Bring the body of that young fool and get out of here before that hellcat rouses the whole palace.'

I turned to the window and swayed against the casement. Now people were gathering round and looking upwards. I began to rock myself backwards and forwards. 'Chantelle, Chantelle,' I moaned. Then I saw what I too must do. I grasped each side of the window frame, and began to climb through. I would have flung myself after her, except someone caught at me. I fought hard. I bit and scratched and kicked the man who'd stopped me, the one I thought was her murderer, only to find that it was my father who had captured me in his arms.

'Mélisande.' He held me fast until I quietened down. 'A scullion boy came battering at my door and told me to come here as fast as I could. What has happened? Where is Chantelle?'

I did not answer him; only fell to weeping and pointing at the window. A look of horror came on his face. He set me to one side and peered out. He turned back, his face ashen. He shook and trembled and could not speak. 'What happened?' he whispered. 'There was an accident?'

'No accident,' I stuttered. 'No accident. Chantelle is dead by the hand of the Count de Ferignay. He came here to claim his right over her body as Armand's Seigneur. Armand died trying to defend her and was stabbed to death on Ferignay's command by his henchman. And when this happened Chantelle cast herself from the window. Murder!' I screeched and I beat my fists against my father's chest. 'Murder!'

My father put his arm around my shoulder and led me out of the room. We went down the spiral staircase, the same one Chantelle and I had so happily tripped up only an hour before. We came out into the courtyard and I saw the little scullion's terrified face among the crowd. The people parted to let us through.

The king's own doctor, Ambroise Paré, was by the body of my sister.

'She is dead, I'm afraid,' he told my father. 'Take comfort that it would have been a swift death. Her neck was broken in the fall.'

'I thank you, sir,' my father replied dully. He reached in his purse to find a coin, for it was customary to pay the doctor who attends at a death.

Monsieur Paré put his hand over my father's. 'There is no charge, minstrel. Keep your money for your daughter's funeral costs. For fear of Plague she needs to be buried without delay.'

We did not even have the satisfaction of knowing that Chantelle and Armand would lie close to each other in their graves. No trace could be found of Armand's body. The Count de Ferignay stated that Armand Vescault had disappeared on the morning of his wedding day. He said that his vassal had told him that he had changed his mind about marrying such a lowly lady. He'd seen Armand ride out of the palace. He suggested that Chantelle, unable to bear the humiliation, had committed suicide by casting herself from the tower window.

We did not hear any of this until our return from the place where we had buried Chantelle.

'We will go to the king and demand justice,' I said to my father. He was rushing around our room in the palace, stuffing music sheets into a satchel and clothes into saddle-bags.

'We must leave before another day goes by,' he said.

'Leave?' I said. I looked around the chamber Chantelle and I had shared and had left so happily that morning. Our sewing basket lay open, spilling the bright threads we'd used to embroider Chantelle's wedding dress. The quill sat on the portable writing block. There was the music score where I'd begun to write a wedding song for Chantelle and Armand as my gift to them. 'We cannot leave until the Count de Ferignay is brought to trial for the murders of Chantelle and Armand.'

'Without witnesses, there will be no trial.'

'There will be those that will testify.'

'Against Ferignay? I do not believe so.'

'I am a witness to what happened.'

'Mélisande,' my father said firmly. 'We are leaving this place within the hour.'

'Papa!' I cried, incensed at what I saw as my father's weakness. 'Papa! Did you not love Chantelle?'

He wept then. 'I adored her. As I do you. And it is for love of you that I know we must take this course of action.'

'What has your love for me got to do with us leaving?'

'Mélisande' – he spoke desperately – 'the complexities of court life are too devious for you to appreciate.'

I stamped my foot. 'I am not a child. I am a woman and if you persist in running away I will go and plead with the king myself.'

'No! You must not do that!'

'I will!' I shouted in hysterics. 'I will! I will! I will!'

And then my father did something he had never done in all the years of my life. He struck me.

100

I fell back with both hands to my face where he had slapped it.

'Don't you see that you are now the one in danger?'

I shook my head, unable to reply.

My father fastened the straps of the saddlebags. 'I will go to the keeper of the king's purse and ask for the money that is due me. I'll be lucky if I get even half of it. But that will do, as long as I have enough to enable us to get to the Isle of Bressay. While I am away doing this you must barricade the door, Mélisande, and admit no one. Change your dress to prepare for a journey. You may bring your travelling cloak and mandolin, that is all. I'll find my horse in the stable and put these saddlebags on it. Then I will come here for you and we will quietly leave this palace at dusk.' He lifted the satchel and saddlebags and was gone from the room.

I sat down on the edge of my cot. I was too numb now to cry any more. My father was betraying my sister and Armand, and there was nothing I could do about it. I must obey him. I took up my mandolin and put it in its chamois leather carrying bag. Then I looked around for my travelling cloak. I recalled that it was in the tower room. In order to be ready to leave with my father on his return I would have to go and fetch it now.

I took my mandolin and went to the door. There I hesitated. Turning, I lifted the long scissors from our sewing basket and tucked them into the waistband of my dress. Then I opened the door of the room and cautiously went out.

The palace was quiet as the courtiers were now

assembling for dinner in the main hall. I made my way through the courtyards and into the turret room. My cloak lay beside the chair. I snatched it up and stuffed it into the top of the bag that held my mandolin. I swung this across my back, and hurried down the turret stairs, unhappy to be even one moment in those rooms.

I came into the main part of the palace and stepped into the first corridor.

My way was barred. A man stood before me.

It was the Count de Ferignay.

Chapter Seventeen

'Let me pass,' I said.

My anger with this man was such that I had no fear of him at this point.

'We must speak together, you and I.' He glanced up and down the corridor then grabbed my arm and manhandled me into a nearby alcove. He surveyed me up and down. 'With the older one gone, I suppose you will have to do.'

'I don't know what you mean,' I said. 'Allow me to go.'

He had hold of my arm and now he shook me quite roughly. 'You have no figure. Your face is plain. You are much more forward and opinionated than a girl should be, but my whip will soon beat that out of you.' He laughed. 'I might even enjoy taming you.'

'What do you want with me?' I struggled to understand what this man was after. 'I know you desired my sister. When we were presented to you, I saw how you looked at her.'

'It would have been a bonus to have her, but a man as deep in debt as I am cannot afford to be choosy.'

'You want *me*?' I stared at him.

'You don't think I want you for your person, you stupid girl?' he said. 'It is your estate that makes you desirable. It was to obtain the land that I gave permission for my vassal to marry your sister. Armand Vescault was so naive that I would have sequestered it from him quite easily once they were wed. Unfortunately my appetite overcame my good sense in that instance. She was a particular beauty, your sister, unlike the painted harlots of this court who jade my palate.'

Anger flooded through me as I heard him speak of Chantelle in this way. I wrenched my arm from his grasp. But he moved quite easily across the width of the alcove and blocked me in.

'Here is the situation,' he said. 'Now that your sister is gone, all of the estate will fall to you when you marry. The Isle of Bressay has very rich pickings for a lord who can manage it more shrewdly than your father does. He seems unaware that tenants are supposed to work the land for their master, not for themselves. I had my agents look into it when your father first mentioned it as the dowry for your sister. You and I will be wedded. I will have your land, which will help me repay my debts and give me an income beside.'

I could not believe his effrontery but began to realize that he was very serious and that I was in great danger here. If I called for help, who would rescue me? I could hear no footsteps in the corridor. The courtiers would be assembled at dinner. Even if they heard me scream, none of the servants would dare interfere in the business of a nobleman, especially one with a connection to the House of Guise.

'Your wife is alive,' I said. Perhaps if I stalled for time, my father would return to our room, find me gone and come looking for me.

'Only just,' Ferignay replied. 'She lingers, but Monsieur Paré has said that she will not last more than a day or two. You and I can be married within a week.'

'I will *not* marry you,' I said.

'I will leave you no option.' He lunged at me.

But I had remembered the long scissors tucked in my waistband and had them in my hand. My gown ripped as he tore at me but I had the point of the blades at his throat.

'There is a vein there,' I gasped. 'If I plunge these in, you will bleed to death before you can cry out for help.'

'You will not do it,' he said, but his tone was uncertain.

'I will,' I said. And in that second I would have done it, for vengeance for my sister if no other reason.

He must have heard the purpose in my voice for he said in a placating manner, 'Listen to me. You are being foolish. If you kill me they will find the body and you will be hanged, and your father too most likely, for they will certainly believe he had a hand in it.'

He must have felt me waver. He went on more confidently, 'We can make a deal on this, you and I. Marry me and I will leave you alone. I have women friends enough and you may have your own male companions, as long as you're discreet. Both you and your father will be safe with a mighty lord to protect you. Otherwise you become a murderer. You will both be fugitive and hunted down. Think on it.'

I began to reflect on what Ferignay had said. If I married him, I and my father would have a barrier between us and the world. For he was right: if I killed him, we would never escape the palace. And I remembered the punishment the Guise had arranged for the two Huguenot farmers, who had been innocent of anything other than worshipping God in their own way.

'You may even play your silly music,' Ferignay added, 'if that's what takes your fancy. As may that shiftless, worthless thing that is your father.'

The spell shattered. Whatever else my father was, self-effacing, fond of drink and gambling maybe, he was neither shiftless nor worthless. His soul was filled with love of life, and music. As mine was.

'No,' I said. 'I will never marry you.'

But I had relaxed my grip and the fiend took immediate advantage. His fingers snaked around the hand that held the scissors. And he gripped me by the wrist.

'You will do as I say, madam. Maybe if you promise to behave I will not whip you every day – only every second day.'

With my free hand I clawed out at him. My nails scratched his face. I opened a long ragged tear running from eye to chin.

'You cat!' he yelped, clutching both hands to his wound. 'You minx! I will have you, and beat you every day for the rest of your life!'

I eluded his grasp and ran. And as I ran I thought what

I might do. The court was at dinner. I would go to the main hall. To where the royals sat at table. I would go to the king, our king, who had taken sacred oaths before the altar of God to care for his people, and I would ask for justice. King Charles, who looked favourably on my father, would listen to me.

I had forgotten that the king was ill.

The person presiding over dinner that night, and dispensing justice for his majesty, was the queen regent, Catherine de' Medici.

Chapter Eighteen

'*Justice!*' I screamed, as I ran into the main hall and flung myself on my knees in front of the high table. 'I ask for justice in the king's name!'

'Who is this child?'

Catherine de' Medici stopped in the act of raising her spoon to her lips.

The courtier who stood behind the queen's chair leaned forward and said in a low voice, 'It is the minstrel's younger daughter. The older girl died this morning by casting herself from a tower in the palace due to a broken marriage promise.'

'Ah, yes.' The queen looked at me not unsympathetically. 'My ladies-in-waiting have talked of nothing else today. How men do deceive us. A most unfortunate death.'

'It was not an unfortunate death,' I said through my tears for I had begun to cry at the mention of Chantelle. 'My sister's death and that of her lover were caused by the Count de Ferignay.'

Upon my saying this, the Duke of Guise and the

Cardinal of Lorraine, who were seated not far from the queen regent, exchanged looks. The duke called his servant and spoke to him and the man hurried off.

'Are you saying that your sister did not cast herself down from the tower in order to kill herself?' Catherine de' Medici asked me.

'She did, your majesty, but it was the Count de Ferignay who compelled her to do this.' My voice shook, but having got this far I was determined to continue. 'She killed herself because her lover, Armand Vescault, was murdered before her eyes by the Count de Ferignay.'

Catherine de' Medici regarded me sternly. 'That is a grievous charge.'

'I know this. Yet still I make it.'

'Mélisande!' There was a stir among the groups of people at the side of the hall. It was my father. He tried to reach me but was prevented by some men in the livery of the house of Guise who had come into the hall and now stood about in clusters.

Queen Catherine glanced around. 'Where is the Count de Ferignay? Let him stand forward.'

'Am I being accused of stabbing my own bondsman, Armand Vescault?' Feigning astonishment, the Count de Ferignay walked to the centre of the room. 'This girl has been rendered hysterical by the shock of the death of her sister. Armand was my cousin's child whom I'd taken into my personal service. He was a young man, orphaned and without fortune, and I treated him as my own son.'

'You did not strike the blow personally but you shouted

to your bodyguard to kill him as he tried to defend his bride, my sister, from your unworthy attentions,' I said.

'This is nonsense,' replied the count. 'Armand Vescault left the palace this morning. I saw him go.'

'How came you then, count de Ferignay,' asked Catherine de' Medici, 'by that scratch to your face?'

'Ah.' The count put his hand to where there was a weal of red where I had scratched him.

And now we have him, I thought in triumph, for it was obvious what kind of action had caused that wound. I blessed the queen regent for her sharp eyes and mind.

'I am ashamed to say, your majesty.' The count bowed his head.

'I do insist,' the queen replied.

'I had an assignation with a lady of the court. This lady has a singular way of expressing her passion for me.'

Such a liar this man was! Had he thought of this in the short time that had elapsed since I'd injured him or did falsehoods come readily from his lying tongue?

There was a titter among the onlookers. 'The Duchess Marie-Christine is wont to mark her conquests in this way,' some wag quipped.

'You had this tryst while your wife lies dying?' Catherine de' Medici observed dryly.

'In such circumstances a man needs comfort,' replied the Count de Ferignay.

'Perhaps it is your wife who should have comfort from you in her last hours,' the queen said acidly.

'I am deservedly rebuked, your majesty.' The count bowed his head.

'His story is not true.' I raised my voice. 'The count lies. His face is marked because—'

The Count de Ferignay interrupted me in a bolder and more confident tone of voice. 'Yes, there are lies being told here, your majesty. And we must wonder why. Before he ran off Armand confided in me. He told me that he was becoming disinclined to marry this girl's sister. Since they joined our court he had been party to some of the conversations within this family. He was becoming suspicious as to the true intent of these musicians in the presence of our king. It is known that they have recently come from the court of Elizabeth of England, where they entertained that false queen who has sworn enmity with France. And now they have insinuated themselves into the good graces of his majesty, gaining close access to his person. Who knows what harm they intend?'

'Bring me the minstrel!' Catherine de' Medici called out.

My father walked forward. My spirits faltered as I saw that he was escorted by two of the Guise men-at-arms. What had I led him to in my reckless foolishness?

'Explain yourself,' the queen commanded.

'Your majesty,' said my father. 'I first came to your court in Paris, where my elder daughter Chantelle fell in love with Armand Vescault, and he with her. I took my daughter away, so that she might consider whether she wished to marry this man. I reasoned that it would be a test if their love was true. I did not want her to marry and later regret it, she being so young.'

The queen said nothing. Perhaps Catherine de' Medici

would not be in sympathy with this novel idea of a woman having a choice in whom she married. Her own marriage to the previous King of France had been arranged for her at a very early age.

'We were invited to the court of Queen Elizabeth of England to play at the occasion of the baptism of the son of the Earl of Henley,' my father continued.

'This baptism,' interrupted the Cardinal of Lorraine, 'would it have been a true sacrament of the Church or some false ceremony of a spurious reformed faith?'

Now Ferignay's side had scored a hit. For, although the queen regent was sympathetic to the Protestants, she was under public pressure from the house of Guise to maintain only the Catholic faith as the one religion of France.

My father, never confident in speech, allowed himself to be distracted and hesitated in his explanation.

'Your eminence, I do not know. My daughters and I did not attend the service. It was afterwards at the celebrations that we were required to play music.'

'Ah yes, let us examine the circumstances of the performance of your music,' said the Duke of Guise. 'You played to the king in his private rooms the other night, and now he is taken ill. Were you near the food that was served to his majesty that evening?'

Catherine de' Medici was at once alert. 'You and your daughters were permitted at the sideboard dishes,' she said. 'I recall you being there. And' – she paused – 'you made comment on the greatness of the majesty of Elizabeth of England, did you not?'

Now I began to see why my father had tried to warn me

of the snares of court life. He could not publicly state that he had only been agreeing with the queen when she said that Elizabeth of England might be a worthy match for her son. If he did then he would betray something that she obviously would not want the Guise faction to know.

I saw the queen's eyes once more range around the hall. There were more Guise men-at-arms present than any others. She spoke directly to the Duke of Guise. 'You think there is some plot here?'

'I think this warrants careful investigation,' the Duke of Guise replied. He gave Ferignay a look, but it was one of annoyance. His own conspiring had been thrown out of order by this matter, yet he must defend his kinsman.

'Your majesty,' I said. 'I came to ask you to look into my sister's death, and Armand's murder.'

'These people are wandering minstrels.' The Count de Ferignay spoke out again. 'They had not been given royal permission to depart, yet when I went to their rooms to express my grief at their loss they were packed to leave. You may wish to know that the minstrel has a home in the Isle of Bressay which lies near the border of Navarre.'

'Is this true?' the queen asked my father.

'Yes, but—' he began.

She raised her hand. 'I will delay our evening meal no longer. Tomorrow we must remove the king and the court to a more suitable place to tend him in his illness and that he may deal with the affairs of state. Your case will be heard then. In the meantime I think it best to have you and your daughter kept close guarded. But' – she looked coolly at the Duke of Guise – 'by my own soldiers. Have your men stand down.

And the Count de Ferignay must remain with the court until this matter is resolved.'

My father had contrived to come near to me where I stood in disbelief. The murderer was allowed his liberty while we were to be close guarded! We could be assassinated in any number of ways, or kept and forgotten about for twenty years or more, or even executed without trial, as the Huguenots had been.

My father stretched out his hand and, under the pretext of stroking my hair, whispered, 'If you can seize an opportunity as they change guards, then run, Mélisande, and save yourself.'

And for once I obeyed him without arguing. There was ill feeling between the two sets of soldiers who nudged and prodded each other as we were ushered towards the main exit. People had gathered there, pressing forward to see the father and the sister of the girl who had killed herself for love. In among them I saw the face of the scullion boy. He made a sign to me with his hand and shouted, 'A rat! I see a rat! A huge one. On the table, there!'

The people at whose table he pointed jumped up, over-turning their stools. My father pushed through the soldiers surrounding us and ran one way, pretending to escape. I ducked behind the soldier nearest me and raced in the other direction and out of a side door. Ahead of me was a staircase ascending, and beside it an outside door. It was closed. I ran and pulled it open. But strong arms captured me, one wrapped round my upper body, pinioning my arms.

And then a hand over my mouth.

Chapter Nineteen

A voice in my ear.

Quietly.

'It is I, Melchior.'

He pulled me in against the wall and up the stairs.

'If we go up we are caught inside the palace,' I said.

He put his fingers to his lips. 'Trust me,' he said.

And I did.

He pointed upwards and I followed him as fast and as silently as I could. We heard men rushing outside through the door below. On and on we climbed until we were at the top and there was, as I had suspected, no outlet.

'We are trapped,' I said.

'Not so.' Melchior shook his head. 'In here.'

At floor level there was a long slim aperture. He got down and squeezed himself inside. He stretched out his hand. 'Come.'

It was more difficult for me, hampered as I was with the bag containing my mandolin and travelling cloak, but I would not leave it, could not leave it behind, for it would show the way we had gone. And already there was a noise of many feet upon the stairs. I knelt down and rolled into the roof space beside Melchior.

'Follow,' he said. And began to crawl away from me.

In the blinding darkness I went after him. Then we came to a place where it opened out. There was more room and more light too. We reached the point where the flooring stopped. I looked out and a wave of vertigo engulfed me. We were in the ceiling above the great hall.

Melchior pointed. 'We must cross to the other side,' he said.

'How?'

He indicated the roof beams that were here exposed and extended from one side of the hall to the other.

I shook my head and backed away.

'Give me your hand.'

His voice was neither pleading nor commanding. He held out his own. I looked down. I felt my head sway and my whole body was drawn towards the edge.

'Look at me!' His voice more insistent this time. I looked into his eyes. They were calm yet within their depths I saw determination. 'You can do this,' he said. 'You *can* do this.'

I put my hand in his.

He walked out onto the beam. Perfectly balanced, like a cat.

'Place your feet with care,' he said.

I glanced down to see where to position my foot.

The yawning depth of the floor rushed up to greet me.

'Thou must not look down!' His voice was compelling. 'Feel your way as you go.'

But I could not help but look.

In the hall below us the soldiers threw over benches and chairs as they searched for me. If any one of them raised their eyes I was doomed.

We were both doomed.

I was suddenly aware of what an enormous risk Melchior was taking in helping me. The Count de Ferignay bore him a grudge. He believed the boy had terrorized his dogs and humiliated him before the king. Ferignay would be glad of any excuse to have Melchior punished.

We had reached the centre part of the hall. Here there was an intersection of the ceiling rafters. We could pause and take rest. I clung on and breathed. The huge chandelier hung below us. The lights of the hundred candles flared as it moved slowly in the disturbance created by the search. The cross spars of the sconce supports cast their shadow over the room.

'We must go down there.' Melchior indicated the sloping roof joist.

I stared at him. The beam fell at an angle. I would be unable to walk upon it.

'It is necessary. There will be some space where it connects under the roof edge and we can get through to the other side of the palace.'

Swing myself over and slide down the beam, hampered by my dress and carrying the mandolin? It was impossible.

'It is the way to freedom. You will do this.' Melchior nodded encouragement. And then he did something unexpected. He grinned at me.

117

I was taken by surprise. The normal solemn appearance of his face changed. His teeth showed dazzling white and his eyes lit up with humour. I could not help myself and smiled at him in return.

And I thought I understood at least one of the reasons Melchior was helping me. In my escape he would have the satisfaction of outsmarting those who hunted us, the ones who thought they controlled his life. He and his leopard were prisoners, but part of him would flee with me.

And despite being in imminent danger, at some level my mind thought: There should be a song for this – how the hunted outwits the hunter.

'I will go first.'

Melchior swung himself over easily and lay astride the beam, much as the leopard had done along the tree in the forest. Then he reached out an arm to help me do the same.

We slid down between the stones and the underside of the roof. I was small enough to get between the solid bulwark of the palace wall and the overhang. Melchior was supple, his body as lithe as the big cat who was his companion. Within minutes we were outside on the roof tiles. There he grasped my hand and we manoeuvred our way to the chimneys. He hoisted me up and joined me above a kitchen service chimney.

'Down here,' he said.

I looked inside. There were no footholds.

'There is a way to do this, if you brace yourself against the sides of the wall. I will go first and show you.'

It also occurred to me that should I lose my footing he would break my fall.

'We will hear them searching for you as we pass by each floor.'

He looked up at me and smiled, his teeth flashing white in the gloom. My heart lifted. And I believed that I might live.

We did hear the guards and Ferignay's men, who were soon joined by others as they hunted for me. In lieu of any other diversion it became their evening's sport. And as I listened to them, I shook with apprehension at what my father's fate would be. But I knew that he would want me to escape and I tried not to think what might happen if the soldiers found me. I did not know if I would be brave enough to choose my sister's way of release.

I faltered then as I thought of her, my Chantelle. Tears flooded my eyes.

'What's amiss?' Melchior's whisper was far below me. 'There is no time to delay,' he said. 'We must reach our destination before the soldiers.'

Where were we going? I had not thought to ask him.

The palace of Cherboucy was not so big that I would be able to hide safely for long. We were almost at the kitchen. Having prepared the food, the kitchen staff were eating their own meal, scullions and cooks' boys squatting where they could, scrabbling with the house dogs and cats for the scraps and leftovers. We came from the chimney in the corner. To be covered in soot with torn clothes was not so out of place here. I went where Melchior led me, padding on soft feet.

I knew now where we were headed.

To the lair of the leopard.

'The Count de Ferignay is an insidious and vicious man,'

I said as Melchior opened the door of his cellar room. 'He will search everywhere for me, including here.'

'There is a place where you might hide where he will not look.'

'Where?' I asked him.

He answered my question with one of his own. 'How brave are you?'

And stretching out his hand, Melchior opened up the leopard's cage.

I took a step back.

The leopard got to its feet and padded towards us. I stepped behind Melchior.

'Never do that,' he said. 'Never show a wild beast that you are afraid.'

Melchior moved so that we were again side by side. Then he put his arm around my shoulder. 'It is not widely known, but a leopard does not view man as his prey. Little children, yes, a leopard will eat them.' Melchior appraised me. 'But you are not a child, Mélisande, are you?'

I shook my head.

'So. I want you to come into the cage with me.'

I hesitated. My heart was thudding.

'This then is your choice,' said Melchior. 'Enter the cage. Or remain outside and be captured when Ferignay's men search underground.' He tilted his head. 'Listen. They are already in the kitchens.'

We could hear the sounds of yelling, dishes breaking, and pots and pans being thrown against walls.

Melchior looked at me. He walked into the leopard's cage.

And I followed him.

Chapter Twenty

The leopard's ears pricked up.

'Be steadfast,' Melchior said in a quiet voice.

He knelt down and breathed into the animal's face. Then he undid the muzzle and cast it aside. The leopard opened its jaws to yawn and I saw its teeth and the full length of its throat. I felt again the sickness of terror. It turned its head to look at me.

'If Paladin remains muzzled then the soldiers might be tempted to enter the cage and look amongst the straw.' Melchior pointed to the heap of straw in the corner. 'The straw in which you are going to hide. Now!' He urged me as the sound of marching men came nearer. I knelt down and crawled in among the straw.

I heard Melchior refasten the cage. Then came the noise of the half-door being kicked open.

'What a stench!' one of the soldiers said. 'It's the boy and the leopard. Though which is which is hard to say.'

His companions guffawed as they threw Melchior's pallet bed up in the air and knocked over his food dishes.

Paladin growled and a soldier banged his pikestaff against the rails of his cage. 'Quieten down,' he ordered. 'You're not above the king's law even though you be a beast.'

'But the king loves the leopard, don't you know,' said another soldier nervously. 'So don't be annoying it. If the animal won't hunt next time then we'll get the blame.'

'We're supposed to search everywhere,' said the captain. 'So who's going into the cage?'

My heart quailed for, if they did, there was nowhere to run.

I heard Melchior's voice utter a command. The next instant a fearsome roar came from Paladin's throat.

'I'm not going in there,' said the first soldier.

'Ha! Ha! Only joking,' said the captain.

Their feet echoed away but I waited, unmoving, until Melchior came into the cage and re-muzzled Paladin.

We sat down then and tried to think of a way that I could leave the palace.

'The court is moving tomorrow,' said Melchior. 'Already servants are being sent on ahead to prepare the next castle. It may be that you could go out with a group of them. Let me go and see what is happening at the exit gates.'

It was over an hour before Melchior returned, carrying an assortment of clothes.

'The lower servants are assembling in the courtyards,' he told me. 'They are being scrutinized as they climb into the carts that are taking them to the next castle. I found out that after the king leaves tomorrow some soldiers will wait behind and search every room in the palace until they find you.'

'Then I must hide as best I can,' I answered him. 'Perhaps in one of the chimneys. I am slighter than most men. I can go where they cannot.'

Melchior shook his head. 'They will have hunting dogs. Remember the Count de Ferignay has his own pack of hounds. And you will have left enough clothes behind for them to take your scent.'

I looked into the leopard's cage. 'I cannot travel out lying among the straw,' I said. 'In daylight there is a greater chance of me being seen.'

'This is true,' said Melchior. 'But it may be possible for you to get away now' – he held up the bundle of clothes he carried – 'disguised as a servant.'

'But you said they are studying each person as they climb into the carts,' I protested. 'They will see instantly who I am.'

'They are looking for a girl,' Melchior replied. 'You will not be a girl.'

That night Melchior cut my hair. He made it so that it flopped over my face and down my neck. When he had done he admired his handiwork.

'Already you are unrecognizable.' He grinned at me and handed me my boy's clothes.

As I began to unfasten my dress Melchior courteously went and busied himself by going back into the leopard's cage to conceal the bag containing my mandolin and travelling cloak under the straw. I dressed myself in the breeches, tunic, cap and sandals that he had stolen for me.

'I am ready,' I said.

He turned and tilted his head to one side. He walked all around me, then he bent and dug his fingers into the earth of the floor. Straightening up, he took my chin firmly in one hand and, using the forefinger of the other, he began to streak my face with dirt. When he had completed this to his satisfaction he said, 'Now you must do the same with your own hands and the parts of your legs that show between your breeches and sandals.'

As he said this his face was very close to mine. I could see deep into the tawny eyes. Their depths flickered with a strange wildness.

'Yes,' I said. My voice was hoarse.

He had not released his grip on my chin. And I did not move to free myself.

His gaze went slowly over my face, forehead, nose, cheeks, mouth.

He brought his own mouth close to mine.

'Mélisande.' He breathed my name.

With extreme tension in my stomach and a pounding in my head I walked behind Melchior into the kitchen court-yard. We had delayed my departure until the darkest watches of the night when we reckoned the soldiers would be less vigilant. Under the arches of an outside corridor we waited for a suitable moment. When a squabbling group of cooks' boys and scullions came trailing past us Melchior gave me a small push.

'Go now,' he whispered. 'And do not look back at me.'

I did as he said, but just before we parted I reached

behind me with my hand and for the briefest second his fingertips touched mine.

Then he murmured something else. It chimed so exactly with the words in my head that I was never sure if Melchior had spoken, or it was merely my own thoughts I heard.

I slipped out and joined the other servant boys. With shaking legs I shuffled forward in the line. The kitchen master in charge of this batch yawned as he held his lamp and looked at each of us in turn. He frowned as he caught sight of me.

'You're not one of mine,' he said.

My tongue and throat were so dry I could not reply.

He brought the light closer.

'Are you with the Spanish cook, Alvaro?'

I nodded.

He made an expression of annoyance as he added a stroke to his tally sheet. 'Leave this cart at the first stop and go off and find your own,' he ordered me.

I nodded my head.

Clambering onto the cart, the boys jostled and slapped each other in the type of rough play that I was totally un-accustomed to. At first I shrank away from them but then I realized that I might be left behind and I grabbed the arm of the one nearest me and levered myself up. Copying their ways, I shoved myself rudely in among them and managed to find a place to squat in the depths of the cart.

At the gate the guard shone his lantern into the cart. But he was not interested in examining us. He only checked that the number of persons on board matched the number on the sheet presented by the person leading the carthorses. His enquiry as to whether there was any girl amongst us was met with whistles and crude remarks. He waved us on and as dawn light flooded the sky we trundled out of the gate of Cherboucy Palace.

Later, as the sun came up, I could see rolling along behind us the leopard's cage on its wheeled platform.

We'd arranged that as soon as there was a stop Melchior would come and give me my bag and I would slip away. The court was moving north-west to Toulouse. That was also the road to the Isle of Bressay.

The Isle of Bressay. My home. The place where my father had intended we should go.

But that was not the direction I was going to take. I'd had all night to think on my situation. By morning I had made my decision. When my chance came to leave I would head a different way. I knew where I needed to go and to whom I needed to speak. I would seek out the person who might be able to tell me more about my sister's death, and who might aid me in clearing our family name and rescuing my father. The one whose word Queen Catherine de' Medici would believe.

PART TWO
THE HOUSE OF
NOSTRADAMUS

Chapter Twenty-one

It was spring market day when I arrived at the town of Salon in Provence.

With so many people on the road I was able to mingle easily with the folk going there to sell their goods. I joined up with some farmers and their wives and servants, who were herding livestock and carrying produce in baskets and handcarts. There was a holiday atmosphere with this group, and their banter, combined with the cackling of the geese and bleating of the goats, made the last mile or so a very pleasant walk. Although I'd been sleeping in barns and under hedgerows since parting company with Melchior some weeks ago, I'd taken care with my appearance, shaking out my clothes each morning and washing my face and hands. Troubadours and jongleurs were not unusual on market days and I guessed that one more wandering musician would attract no special attention from the town guards.

Why is it that certain places, like people, make an instant impression on you? My father used to say that he could tell the character of the citizens by the smell of a city as he rode through the gates. Chantelle always looked into people's faces. She claimed it was in their eyes that she saw a person's true worth. With me it was sound. My ear was sensitive to all things, both natural and man-made. My mood was always affected by my surroundings. The royal court had made me uncomfortable. Both the queen regent, Catherine de' Medici, and King Charles were surrounded by self-seeking courtiers, their words slithering with deceit. I was most content in the countryside, where birds and animals reign supreme. Yet I loved the clamour of cities: the rowdy bawling of the street sellers, the quips of the messenger boys, the laughter of women. Therefore I should have been happier as I approached the walls of this bustling town.

But I was not.

The crowd had become denser and in the press of people were some rough-looking individuals: armed mercenaries, women with painted faces, men in the garb of beggars who began to limp when within sight of the soldiers guarding the gates. Their language was bad, even in the presence of children, and I considered turning away. Once inside the city I would have to fend for myself without the protection of the farmers. Only my hope of justice for Chantelle and freeing my imprisoned father made me continue and I allowed myself to be carried on with the rest up to the outer gate.

Above it, on the rampart, a man stood, surveying the people as they passed below. He was older than me, more than three times my age, I reckoned, with a lightly tanned face and hair the colour of sun-bleached wheat. His cloak was thrown back to show a black surcoat richly embroidered in red and he had taken up a stance there, where his keen glance could inspect faces in the crowd. By his side was the sergeant at arms, who was hurrying to and fro at this man's bidding. I looked about and saw what was happening. The man – he must be some noble or lord – would point to a person he considered unsuitable and the sergeant would run to command his soldiers to seize the unfortunate, who would be taken off protesting loudly.

'It's the Lord Thierry.' The farmer ambling along beside me had noticed my interest in what was happening. 'Salon falls under his fiefdom and he's very strict about who goes in and out of his towns.'

As the nobleman's gaze roved over the crowd my heart began to beat more quickly. I did not know this Lord Thierry but that was not to say he had not seen me at Cherboucy. His rigorous weeding out of potential trouble-makers might be something he did every market day. But supposing the Count de Ferignay had sent letters all around for law-makers to be on the lookout for me? In that case, I reasoned, they should be seeking a girl. Dressed as I was, with my travelling cloak around me and my cap set low across my brow, this man had no cause to pick me out.

I began to hum a tune to calm myself. A young minstrel carrying a mandolin should not seem out of place here. I was almost at the gate. It would be foolish to turn back now, would only serve to attract attention to myself. I was almost beneath him when his glance fell upon me.

Our eyes met.

I should have looked down. But I felt compelled to return his imperious look with one of my own. Later I regretted my brashness; heard my father's voice:

'Mélisande, you are too forward. Your look is impertinent. Be careful, such manners will bring misfortune to your door.'

Pushed forward by those behind me, I went under the arch and through to the other side. There. It was over. I was safely inside the town, unchallenged.

I glanced back.

The Lord Thierry had walked to the city side of the rampart and was watching me. I gulped, and this time I did look away at once. There was a market stall in the vicinity. I sauntered over, trying not to appear in too much of a rush. I was sure the nobleman's eyes were on me yet. I selected a ripe apple and promised the young girl tending the stall that I'd make her the heroine of my next ballad if she gave it to me for free. She blushed and dipped her head, then giggled and nodded and told me her name. I hoped the noble lord on the rampart was seeing a carefree youth engaging in some innocent flirting. I recalled one of the remarks that I'd heard men at court say to ladies and exchanged another word with the apple seller. Then I bit into the fruit and bade her farewell. How I longed to turn round to see if Lord Thierry still held me in his sight, but I forced myself to stroll on, slowly, slowly, past a shop front displaying wool and yarn, then down a narrow street and into a little square.

I waited. There was no sign of pursuit. He had not ordered his sergeant to send soldiers after me. I exited the square. Now that I was away from the main passageways I felt safer. But I had no idea where I was. There was no one about to ask directions – most likely everyone was at the market in the town centre. I walked on. The streets I was in were meaner, the houses more shabby. I was by the canal in an area which even I in my youthful innocence knew was unsafe. I decided to turn back, go towards the town centre and ask someone the way. I'd just begun to do this when in front of me two young men lurched out of a tavern. The nearest one tottered. His companion clutched at him, tripped, and both of them fell against me.

'Ho! Who have we here?' The larger one pushed his wine-flushed face into mine.

I stepped past them, but as I did so, the large man reached out and grabbed my shoulder. To protect my mandolin I swivelled it quickly to the front of my body.

'A merry minstrel,' said the other man, in a mocking voice. He had a more closed and cunning look to him.

'I am that, sir.' My years at court had taught me that, as far as possible, it was best to placate those who had drunk much.

'Play us a tune,' said the large man.

'Perhaps another time. I have an appointment elsewhere.' I laughed and tried to ease myself away from them.

He scowled at my reply. 'Do you know who I am?'

I shook my head, trying to keep a distance from them both. I was not so sure that my disguise would be effective if they came close enough to examine me further and touch me again. And if they learned I was a girl and unprotected, they might take more cruel advantage of me than some roistering badinage.

The large man loomed above me. 'I am the Duke of Marcy and I *command* you to play a tune,' he slurred. Now his face was flushed, not just with drink, but with temper at being thwarted.

'Very well, good sir.' I made a low bow. 'I will certainly do as you wish.'

I took the mandolin from its chamois leather bag and played a song, a plain but popular melody that they might catch the rhythm and join in. The cunning one started to stamp his feet and snap his fingers.

'I like that,' he cried out.

Sensing his mood, I moved on then to an older ballad, a more vigorous tune. He began to dance, capering about in the middle of the street. I smiled and tapped my own feet to encourage him. If I could get them both occupied dancing then I might manage to escape.

Some people from the tavern had come to the door and were clapping and shouting.

The music began to have an effect on the larger one, the Duke of Marcy. 'Let's dance!' he shouted. 'Let us all dance!'

I needed to choose my moment. I'd already marked out a nearby alley where I might go. 'This is thirsty work,' I called to the nearest person.

'A drink!' he responded. 'A drink for the minstrel boy!'

The Duke of Marcy's companion looked at him slyly.

'A drink for us all!' he said. He skipped over and slapped the duke on his back.

'Yes. Yes. A drink for all here!' the duke agreed without quibble. 'Tell the tavern master I will pay.'

'By squandering the money your father gives you.' A cold voice cut into the merriment.

My hands stilled on the mandolin. I turned. Behind me was a man in a black and red surcoat. It was the nobleman from the ramparts.

My heart twanged and vibrated like a plucked string.

'It's Lord Thierry.' A murmur went through the on-lookers.

Lord Thierry looked at me appraisingly. 'You have more skill than most itinerant musicians.'

His glance was piercing. It took in my sandals, my clothes, and then the mandolin. As his gaze returned to my face I pulled the collar of my cloak higher. My throat was constricted in fear. I shrugged and tipped my finger to my forehead to acknowledge his compliment.

'I will not be told what to do by an upstart lordling,' the Duke of Marcy proclaimed. 'Innkeeper!' he bellowed. 'Bring me a jug of wine.'

'This gathering should disperse,' Lord Thierry said in a firm voice. 'There has already been too much wine taken.'

'*I* will decide when this dancing is finished and how much I will drink,' the duke said angrily.

'It is my duty to keep the peace in this town,' Lord Thierry retorted. 'And keep it I will.'

'And allow us no fun or pleasure with your dour Huguenot ways,' snarled the duke.

A hiss went round the company in the street. Lord Thierry frowned in irritation. 'This has nothing to do with religion. It is to do with protecting property and safeguarding citizens.'

'Sire' – the Duke of Marcy's wily friend caught at his arm – 'we can find other sport elsewhere.'

'Leave off, Bertrand.' The duke shrugged his friend away.

The owner of the wine shop appeared with a fresh jug of wine. The Duke of Marcy snatched it from him and drank straight from the jug.

The Lord Thierry spoke to the innkeeper. 'You sell these young men more drink than is good for them. You know it is not allowed under the city rules.'

'It's market day, my lord.' The innkeeper spread his hands. 'I mean no ill.'

'You mean to make a tidy profit.' Lord Thierry lifted a flagon that someone had set down upon a windowsill. He took some wine into his mouth then he spat it onto the street. 'This has been watered once yet is twice the price, I'll warrant.'

The innkeeper looked nervously at his customers, who had overheard this exchange, and he hurried into his shop. The men outside began to tell each other about how they had been cheated. Now anyone could see that trouble was not far away. I prepared to go, and bent to pick up the leather bag that held my mandolin.

But the Lord Thierry, seeing my movement, glanced at me and said, 'I would speak with you more.'

I left the bag where it was and inclined my head. He must not think I'd anything to hide.

'You are a talented minstrel. I would like you to come to my castle at Valbonnes. I could give you employment there—'

He was interrupted by the crashing sound of breaking crockery. The innkeeper came from his shop, his face bleeding. From inside came the sound of a bench being overturned and a woman began to scream.

The face of the Duke of Marcy contorted in fury. He fumbled his sword from his scabbard. 'You have ruined my afternoon. I will call you to account for it.'

Lord Thierry drew his own sword, and at the same time took a whistle that hung from his neck and blew upon it. The people in the street scattered and I went with them.

I jumped into a doorway at the sound of boots on cobblestones. Hopefully it was the sergeant-at-arms and some of the guards. I slid along against the wall of the alley and, once clear, I ran and ran until I was out of breath. Now I must find the house I sought and get shelter as soon as I could.

On the corner opposite was an old woman street pedlar. I asked her the way. She immediately knew where and whom I was looking for.

'Why would you go there?' She regarded me speculatively.

'A remedy,' I replied, with the first reason I could think of. 'I have an ailment.'

'Look' – she indicated her tray of goods – 'I have remedies of my own, very powerful potions. I've lavender to aid sleep, chamomile to soothe, rosemary, parsley.'

'I have no money,' I answered her.

'These are the best of cures and worth more than gold, but I would let you have some for a small coin.'

I knew these herbs – the scent of them perfumed the air of the Languedoc and Provence, brightening the bushes and fields and mountain meadows where they grew. 'I know they are good for all manner of ills. I am not unwell like that.' I hesitated. Better to give her another reason for going there. 'I need some advice on a private matter.'

'No, no.' She shook her head. 'You don't need to go there, young man.' She tried to take my hand. 'Let me look at your palm.' As she did this she glanced up and down the street to ensure we were unobserved. Officially, fortune-telling was banned by the Church. 'I can foretell the future as good as any.'

'No,' I said. 'I *must* speak with him.' I had only two coins left in my purse and in desperation I gave her them both.

'The place you seek is in the middle of the town,' she told me, 'within sight of the Château Emperi, where the Lord Thierry takes residence when he visits Salon.'

She led me through the winding alleys and lanes until we came out close to the mound where the château towered above us.

'There.' She pointed. 'That is the house.'

I'd imagined it would be very grand but, although taller than the houses round about, it was very plain to look at.

'He's often seen up there on his roof terrace. By night, especially when the moon is full. And the noises one hears . . .'

'What kind of noises?'

'I don't know, creaking and moaning, souls in torment.' She made the sign of the cross on her forehead and across her breast. 'Be careful,' she warned me.

But I was not very afraid. I had seen death. Witnessed foul murder. My sister's broken body smashed on the cobblestones of the courtyard of the palace. And I needed to know more.

So I went forward to the door of the house of the prophet, Nostradamus.

Chapter Twenty-two

I lifted the heavy knocker and let it fall.

Inside I could hear a child howling. A woman opened the door. She had the worn look of a woman who cared for many children. Her face was lined, her apron crumpled, and she held a little one in her arms.

'I've come to see the prophet Nostradamus—' I began.

'My husband is too tired to see anyone else today,' she said and shut the door in my face.

I knocked again but although I could hear those inside moving about, no one came to the door.

I looked up at the building. There was a light burning in the room at the top. If I cried out, would he hear my voice? I glanced around me. The pedlar woman had gone away and the street was deserted, but for how long? I already knew that this was a well-patrolled town. I could not risk making a disturbance else the guards would come to investigate. There was a lane at the side of the house. I went down it and came out at the back. The top half of the kitchen door was open and I could hear the child squalling louder than ever. The woman was holding this girl child and walking up and down trying to get her to cease crying. She glowered when she saw me.

'Be off with you. You've no right to come round here and annoy me.'

'Please,' I begged her. 'I need to speak to Nostradamus, if only for a moment.'

'That's what everyone says. "Only for a moment."' She placed the child on her hip and turned to face me. 'But it's never that amount of time. People always want more, and then more. They need to know this thing. They need to know another thing. And they take and take and take from him, until he is drained. And they become angry if he doesn't tell them that which they wish to hear.'

'I don't want him to prophesy anything,' I said.

'Then what do you want?'

'He made a prophecy. I did not realize at the time that it was about my sister, and it came true—' I broke off. I thought I might break down if I spoke about the fate that had befallen Chantelle.

'So you've come to complain?'

'No, not that. I only want to understand.'

'There is no understanding of it. That's what people do not appreciate. Even *he* does not understand the half of it,' the woman said wearily. She began to close the door.

And I, with the memory of Chantelle in my head, and exhausted with my various escapes, and in fear of being left to wander the streets at night in a strange town on my own, and frightened that I would meet Lord Thierry again, or some other band of rough young men, did what any girl might do in the circumstances. I burst into tears.

'Come now,' the woman said, 'you mustn't cry. I don't like to see anyone cry, especially a boy. It isn't seemly.'

'My sister,' I sobbed. 'My sister died. I cannot bear the grief of it.'

'Yes, yes, it's very sad to lose a sister. But these are hard times we live in. Only last year the Plague took away six hundred souls from this parish. Six hundred! And many of those were children, brothers and sisters.'

'It wasn't an illness. It wasn't anything like that. Her death should not have happened. She was so young and beautiful and a good person.'

'Nevertheless' – the woman spoke more briskly – 'a young man of your years should not be crying. How old are you anyway?'

'Not very old,' I sobbed. I'd forgotten to deepen my voice. But now I did not care.

'There's something amiss here,' I heard her say as I did not ease off my crying. 'What is wrong?'

'My sister . . .' I said. I wanted to tell her what had happened but I could not say the words.

'You are but a child yourself, aren't you?'

I nodded, swallowing tears and snot.

'I'll give you some hot milk but that's all, mind. Then you must go away. My lord Nostradamus is unwell today. He's an old man, and becoming weaker and more seized by frights and fits. It's not fair for him to be tormented with so many visitors.' She took my arm. 'Come this way. There is a place here where people are allowed to sit and wait for him to speak to them.'

She led me to a shed set against the wall of the garden. It contained a long bench and I went inside, rested my mandolin on the floor, and sat down. 'I'll summon my eldest girl to nurse my baby and I'll return in a little while.'

After about ten minutes the good wife came back bearing a cup of warm milk.

'Drink,' she said. She held the cup for me and when I'd finished she said, 'Now listen. When Master Nostradamus is well again he is in the habit of seeing common folk on the first Monday of each month. He does not charge for these consultations. As you may imagine, a long line forms from the previous day, so you must be here very early in the morning or the evening before.'

'Do not send me away,' I whispered. 'I have nowhere to go.'

'Go home to your mother.'

'My mother is dead. She died when I was very young.'

'Your father then. Where is he?'

I could not tell her that my father was imprisoned on the orders of the king himself, and that I was on the run from a powerful lord who had vowed to hunt me down.

I shook my head. 'I have none.'

'There is a lodging house at the canal bridge. I see you have a mandolin there. You may sing for your supper. There is money flowing on market day. You will do well enough to pay for bed and board.'

I saw that it was useless to plead further. I stood up.

A shadow filled the room.

The woman turned round. 'Husband,' she cried, 'you are too unwell to be out of bed.'

Master Nostradamus tottered on his feet and put an arm on the door lintel to steady himself.

His wife ran to support him.

'Bring the girl into the house,' Nostradamus said.

'My husband, you are confused. There's no girl here. Just an urchin boy.'

For answer, Nostradamus pointed at me. 'This is Mélisande, the minstrel's daughter. I have been expecting her.'

His wife stared at me and back at her husband.

'Let her enter the house,' said Nostradamus. 'It has been so decreed.'

Chapter Twenty-three

Nostradamus's wife's name was Anne Ponsarde and although she was unhappy and suspicious at this turn of events, she didn't argue with her husband. 'Follow me,' she told me brusquely as she helped Nostradamus into the house.

I wiped my face with my hands and bent to gather up my mandolin. It was only then I realized that earlier, in my haste to escape the street brawl, I'd neglected to pick up the leather bag that protected my mandolin against the elements. I could feel tears beginning again behind my eyes. My father had paid a good sum of money for the mandolin with its bag as a gift to me for my twelfth birthday. I'd considered it a token of my maturing to womanhood and had vowed never to be parted from it. Now I had lost the bag which was of the finest chamois leather.

'Don't dawdle,' the seer's wife scolded me. 'It's almost supper time and I must encourage my husband to eat something. He has only taken water all day.'

We entered the house via the kitchen and, as we did so, I saw a way to be of help to her. 'I could switch some eggs together and make a hot drink with herbs that Master Nostradamus might manage to swallow.'

She stared at me over her shoulder with a look of mistrust. Somewhere else in the house the child mewled but another voice was now trying to pacify it. 'My eldest daughter is busy with the little one, else I would ask her—' Mistress Anne broke off, and then I saw where her hesitation lay. In her eyes, I, as a young man, would have no household or kitchen skills. I pulled off my cap and smoothed my ruffled hair. I softened my voice as I spoke and said to her, 'My sister taught me how to make basic herbal dishes.'

'Very well,' she conceded. 'When it's ready, bring it to the first floor. Knock on the double door at the front of the house and wait.'

'No,' Nostradamus interrupted. 'The top floor, Anne. Ask Mélisande to bring the food to my study on the top floor.'

His wife groaned in exasperation. 'You should come to our bedroom and rest, husband,' she said. 'You are not well enough to work.'

'I must,' he whispered. 'If you could see what I do see then you would know that I cannot rest.'

There were three storeys in the house of Nostradamus. Holding the cup of warm eggnog that I had prepared, I climbed the stone spiral staircase to the top level.

The stairs giving access to this top floor were steeper

and the staircase coiled more tightly. I came out upon an open landing where an arch led through to a suite of rooms. As I approached the entrance to the first room I could hear the murmured conversation of Nostradamus and his wife. He was protesting at her attentions, saying that he was feeling much better. She was scolding him, but not in an angry way, more like a mother chiding a favourite son.

Holding the drink carefully in my hand, I stepped inside the open doorway.

And stopped, utterly transfixed.

It was now heavy dusk outside but the room was bright. The reason for this was a wonderment of blazing candles. There must have been a hundred or more set about through these apartments and all were of expensive beeswax. There were hanging lamps, several tall floor-standing candelabra and a host of candlesticks. Many, many more individual flames shone from candles and lamps placed on tables, windowsills and shelves. On this floor where Nostradamus worked, the rooms led from one to the other and the doors between them were kept open. The walls were covered with inscribed scrolls, ancient texts and tapestries, but also with mirrors of every size and shape, and pieces of coloured glass placed on the ceiling, on shelves, and in corners. The whole effect was as if I had entered a moving, shifting, shimmering world where reflection upon reflection was caught up, mirrored, and sent spinning.

I swivelled slowly, mouth agape.

'In here.' I heard Anne Ponsarde's voice call me from an inner room.

I took a pace forward. At the same instant a lanky figure with tousled hair moved ahead of me. A figure carrying a cup clutched to its chest. I turned my head, and it did too.

I stopped.

It stopped.

'Oh,' I breathed. It was myself, seen from a side view. I regarded my image as if I were a stranger. Did I really look like that? So unkempt and bent over? I straightened up and walked more quickly as Mistress Anne called me again.

Master Nostradamus was propped up on a couch in one corner of the smaller room and Anne was tucking a blanket at his feet. I went towards them, and a dozen or so images of myself walked with me.

His wife held out her hand. 'Give me the cup,' she said, and she took it and held it close for him to drink.

Nostradamus's face was grey and grooved but his great hooded eyes had lost none of their lustre. 'Come nearer, Mélisande,' he instructed me.

I went closer. He looked at me for a long moment. Then he raised the cup to his lips and drank the thick yellow liquid. 'It's good,' he said. 'You have more than one talent.'

His wife Anne smiled in relief that he had taken some sustenance. She was about to hand me the empty dish to take away when he prevented her.

'Do you know why you have come to this house?' he addressed me.

'I came about my sister,' I said.

'Your sister?'

'My sister, Chantelle.'

'What does your sister require of me?'

I stared at him. Why did he ask me that? Did he not know that Chantelle was dead?

His wife drew in her breath. 'This person's sister' – she hesitated – 'Mélisande's sister has recently died.'

'And I believe that you foretold her death,' I added. 'Don't you remember? In the great hall at Cherboucy, in the presence of the king?'

'Ah, yes.' He passed his hands over his eyes. 'Ah, yes. The older girl, who was about to dance. I recall it now. The shadow of death was upon her.'

'You *did* see something!' I cried out. 'I must know what it was, and why Chantelle had to die. That is why I am here.'

He shook his head. 'No, Mélisande. That is not why you are here.'

I thought then that he must sense when all of the truth was not being told, and that he had an inkling of the circumstances of Chantelle's death. Therefore I gave him my whole sad story. And I could not tell it without shedding tears, and even his wife, who had earlier shown me not much sympathy, put her hand to her mouth when I related what had happened to my sister, Chantelle.

'My father is taken by the king to stand trial for these false accusations by the Count de Ferignay,' I finished. 'I know that you have influence with the queen regent, Catherine de' Medici, and I hoped that you could help me in some way. These, Master Nostradamus, are the reasons I am here.'

Nostradamus shook his head. 'No,' he said and his voice

had become remarkably stronger. 'No, Mélisande, that is not why you are here.'

He lay back upon his pillows and closed his eyes.

I was at a loss. There was no other cause for me to seek him out other than to save my father and have justice for my sister.

'You may *think* that is why you have come here,' Nostradamus continued with his eyes closed, and speaking as if more to himself than anyone else in the room. 'But it is not so. It is for another reason altogether that you have been sent to me.'

It was now dark outside.

Inside, the candles burned with warm light but I felt a chill in my bones.

'What lodgings have you obtained here in Salon?' Nostradamus came out of his half-sleeping state.

'None,' I replied.

'Do you have anywhere to go?'

'I know no one in this town.'

'Anne,' he said to his wife. 'We must find room to shelter Mélisande.

His wife clicked her tongue. She was not best pleased. I wondered how many other waifs she had been compelled to give shelter by her husband's charity.

He seemed to become drowsy so we left him to sleep and tiptoed out of the room. Downstairs Anne showed me a large cupboard in the hall. It contained some matting and old cushions.

'This will have to do you,' she said.

'I am grateful for it.' I was so exhausted that I could have lain down to sleep on the stone floor of the kitchen.

The squalling infant, whom we had not heard for a space of time, resumed its lamenting with a whining, sickly cry.

I pointed to my mandolin. 'If you would allow me,' I said, 'I know a berceuse that might soothe your child.' It was a cradle song that I'd heard in Normandy, a very simple three-chord tune.

'You may try, if you wish.' Mistress Anne shrugged, and led me to the family room on the first floor where the child lay in its crib, flushed, and rubbing one side of its head. She left me as I began to strum my mandolin.

> *'Little child, hush*
> *Little child, shush*
> *Little child, don't cry*
> *I will tell thee why*
> *Papa's coming home*
> *He's been gone so long*
> *He will want to see*
> *His child upon his knee*
> *Not crying*
> *But smiling, laughing.*
>
> *'Little child, hush*
> *Little child, shush*
> *Little child, don't cry*
> *I will tell thee why*
> *Mama's making cakes*
> *To soothe away thy aches*

She will want to see
Her child upon her knee
Not crying
But smiling, laughing.'

I kept my foot on the cradle rocker and repeated the song until the child's eyes drooped and closed in sleep. Then I tiptoed from the room, went downstairs and found my own place of rest. I'd hardly settled myself when the door of the cupboard opened and Mistress Anne thrust a blanket at me and went away.

I was left in the dark and although it was cold, even with the blanket, I slept, for I felt safer than I had felt for the last few weeks.

The house was quiet. I whispered my night prayers into the silence and asked God to allow Chantelle and Armand to find each other in Heaven, and hold my father in His hand until I could reach him and rescue him.

I began a slow slide into sleep. Within this house I felt secure. No one would attack me here, so in that respect I was untroubled. Only one thought shifted in my head to disturb my dreams – the mysterious words of Nostradamus.

'*No, Mélisande. That is not why you are here. It is for another reason altogether that you have been sent to me.'*

Chapter Twenty-four

'*Sweet sister.*'

I opened my eyes.

Chantelle stood at the door of my room. She was wearing her bridal gown. The room was filled with the smell of the fresh flowers that adorned her hair and her cheeks were blushed pink like the morning sky.

'Sweet sister.' She spoke again, and her melodious voice quivered in my head.

'Chantelle!' I gasped. I raised my head and gazed and gazed at my sister in an ecstasy of pleasure and relief.

'Mélisande,' Chantelle whispered. She seemed to want to take a step into the room but something prevented her from doing so.

I saw that her wedding dress was neither stained nor torn. The bodice was clean and the tiny pearls sewn along the neckline were intact. Nothing was ripped, there were no blood spatters violating the clean cloth, no scratches or bruises on her face to defile her loveliness. All my wild thoughts and the violent happenings of the last weeks had been nothing but a bad dream. Some dreadful nightmare visited upon me by an unnamed fever.

I knelt up in bed. There was a light glowing behind and around her – I was unsure of the source.

'Where is Armand?' I asked.

'He is here.'

'I cannot see him.'

She laughed in her throat. 'He is with me, I assure you.'

I stretched out my arms to her.

'You cannot touch me, Mélisande,' Chantelle said gently.

I began to cry.

'Hush, sister dear. Don't fret. You have a life of your own to live now.'

'I don't want to. I want to be with you. So that we can be happy again together.'

'I am as happy as I can be. And you,' she said, 'you, Mélisande, have been given your own time to live, a path to follow, and a special destiny to fulfil.'

But I was barely listening to her. I wanted so much to hug her and have her stroke my hair like she did when I was very small and she was as much a mother as a sister to me.

I *would* touch her.

I blundered up from my makeshift mattress, reached out with my hands and flung myself at her. With a hard thump my body connected with the solid door of the cupboard and the figure I saw was my own, reflected in a long glass mirror pinned to the inside. It was myself, just myself, and the horrible realization came to me that I had been asleep and was now wakened. What I had just experienced was a pleasant wish-dream of my sister. The true and awful fact was that Chantelle was dead and I would never see her again as she was in this world. I began to cry in earnest and I knelt down and beat my fists upon the floor. But I soon stopped, for I thought I must cease my wild weeping or the ailing child would wake and begin to bawl, and Mistress Anne would come and tell me to quit her house.

I sat back upon my heels and it struck me then that one thing had not altered between my sleeping and waking, and that was the lovely scent of meadow flowers in the room. I looked down. Beside my knee was a crushed flower, the *artema*. It was from those I'd gathered to place in Chantelle's hair on the morning of her wedding day. I lifted it into my palm. It must have attached itself to my clothing over the days when I had taken shelter where I could as I walked the road to Salon and then fallen out as I prepared for bed last night.

Where else could it have come from?

I knew I would not get any more sleep, so I placed the flower inside the hollow bowl of my mandolin. It was very early so I made sure that I was quiet as I unbarred the back door and went outside to the privy. As I washed my face and combed my hair with my fingers the words of my sister Chantelle echoed in my head:

'. . . *a path to follow, and a special destiny to fulfil.*'

But I knew the particular path that I must take. I had already determined what it was. My special destiny was to find my father and save him from imprisonment or worse.

Chapter Twenty-five

O n my return from the privy I noticed that there was a well in the garden. I filled a few buckets, carried the water to the house and poured it into a pot that hung over the hearth. I raked the ashes and found enough embers to light some kindling and then I placed a log or two in the grate from the woodpile stacked outside the door. Thus the pot on the fire was simmering by the time the house began to stir and Mistress Anne arrived in the kitchen.

She glanced at the hearth and nodded in approval. 'I see that you are not an idle child and I am glad of that, although I have a kitchen maid who comes in each morning to help out.'

'Would you like me to make another eggnog for Master Nostradamus?' I asked her.

'He is sleeping,' she said wearily. 'He was awake most of the night. I could hear him moving about in his rooms above my head. It will do him good to rest for a while. And anyway, we two have business that must be attended to.'

As I looked at her in puzzlement she went on, 'We need to decide what to tell people about the circumstances of how you came into this household. The rival factions of Protestant and Catholic in Salon are always seeking to cause discord. There are informers everywhere who run with any snippet of news to Lord Thierry, or to the bishop and his friend the Duke of Marcy. So let us concoct a good plain story of your background before any servant or visitor arrives here and you become the subject of gossip or speculation.'

'I may already be the subject of speculation,' I said. I told her of the brawl outside the tavern the previous afternoon, of how I had slipped away and been conducted to the house of Nostradamus by an old pedlar woman.

'I think I know that woman,' Mistress Anne replied. 'She goes about the streets and is harmless enough in her own way, but she is very poor with no children to support her. If she hears that the Lord Thierry has an interest in a minstrel boy, then, in the hope of a small reward, she'll certainly inform the captain of the town watch that she guided such a boy to my house.' Mistress Anne surveyed me critically. 'We must think of how to deal with you.'

'Deal with me?' I said. 'In what way?'

'Tush, child. Look at you. You are quite bedraggled and you still have the appearance of a boy.'

'It is as a girl that I am being sought by the king and the Count de Ferignay,' I reasoned, 'so it would be best if I remain as a boy.'

'Not here,' said Mistress Anne, speaking slowly as she was thinking aloud. 'No. You have been involved in an incident in the town where Lord Thierry was present. He is a very astute man and if he admired you as a musician and wanted you to go to his castle at Valbonnes to play for him as you said, then he will try to find you. Know this: he is the type of person who once he starts to investigate something or someone does not leave off until he's satisfied.'

I recalled the keen look of the man in the black and red surcoat as he stood on the ramparts and also later as he had gazed at me while sorting out the rabble in the street outside the tavern.

'I think it would be best if this wandering minstrel ceased to exist,' Mistress Anne went on, 'and you became a girl once more. That means we can devise a more ordinary and natural reason for your presence in my home. I have a twin sister and there are many cousins in our family. I think you will be Lisette, who has come from the country-side to learn skills in the apothecary shop that we run from one of the rooms at the front of the house. Yes' – she nodded her head – 'that will do. I'll find you a dress and a suitable scarf that you may cover your head and conceal your short hair until it grows longer.'

I saw the wisdom in her words and knew that it would be sensible to put on a dress and become a girl again. But the realization was tinged with regret. I had become somewhat used to being a boy, enjoying the exhilaration of swaggering along a street with no escort or chaperone, the freedom to make a joke or pass a remark as I pleased, the ability to come and go on my own whim.

'One thing.' Mistress Anne held out her hand. 'You must give me your mandolin.'

This I resisted. 'No, I cannot.'

'You must.' She said this more kindly. 'Mélisande, it is the one consistent part in any description of you, both as the minstrel's daughter sought by the Count de Ferignay, and as the unnamed boy who arrived in this town and ran away from the law maker, Lord Thierry, when he had done no wrong.' She held out her hand again.

I went then to the cupboard where I had passed the night and I brought her my mandolin. As Mistress Anne took it from me she said, 'When it is dark and everyone is in bed you may play it. But during the day it must be out of sight.'

She pulled the kitchen table near to the shelves that ran along one wall. She put a chair on the table and, climbing up, placed the mandolin on the highest shelf, pushing it back so that it could not be seen by anyone standing in the kitchen.

'There,' she said. 'You are taller than me so by dint of doing what I've just done you may retrieve it at any time, but I beg you not to be foolish. We do not want any official investigation brought here. It is hard enough to keep clear of trouble without another load being added.'

'What kind of trouble?' I asked, as we moved the table back to the centre of the room. I was curious to know this. I'd thought that this must be one of the safest houses in France. With the protection of the highest in the land what kind of retribution could Mistress Anne fear?

'Catherine de' Medici has always valued Master

Nostradamus and she favours us,' Mistress Anne explained. 'But the royal court does not hold so much sway here in the south of France, and even though the queen may believe that certain people have been given a gift to foretell the future, there are those who do not view it so kindly. Many see it as the work of another, darker, force. It would not take very much for us to be denounced to the courts of the Inquisition.'

The Inquisition!

I had once seen an example of the doings of the courts of the Inquisition. Papa, Chantelle and myself had just entered a town across the Spanish border where there was to be a fiesta in a few days' time and we hoped to make some money playing to the crowds in the streets. On approaching the main square we'd had to stand aside to allow a long file of people to pass. On the outside of the line were figures clothed in black robes, their faces and heads covered in tall hoods with sockets cut for eyes. They carried torches of burning pitch and were escorting two men and a woman who had crosses tied to their backs. The woman's nose had been cut off and she was staring out from bloodshot eyes with a demented look. The crowds surged all round the procession, calling out horrible words and spitting at these unfortunates. In answer the woman gave out a loud braying laugh like a donkey. My mouth hung open in stupefied fear at the noise issuing from her throat. It was only later that I was told that they had probably also cut out her tongue. One of the men was singing. His voice was not tuneful but it had tremendous power as it carried across the square. The other man trudged along as if he would crumple to the ground at any moment.

'I'll warrant no Simon of Cyrene will go forward and carry any of their crosses for them,' my father said harshly.

In the crowd someone nudged him roughly. 'Why don't you go then if you're so smart and quick to criticize? Eh? Eh?'

A few more people turned to stare at us. One of the men leered at Chantelle. 'Now that's a pretty one you've got there.' He spoke to my father. 'How much for her?'

My father grasped both our hands and began to withdraw.

'Just for the hour,' the man called after us. 'Then I'll let you have her back for your own pleasure.'

Over their rude words and vulgar suggestions I could hear the tortured woman screeching, the bellowing of the singer, the chanting of the hooded men, and the ratcheting sound of wooden clappers. Being young and curious to know what was happening, I tried to twist round to see, but Chantelle covered my eyes with her hands and my father gathered us to him and we went quickly from that town.

Everyone knew that the Inquisitors had far-reaching powers, and travelled around the country holding courts to torture and condemn those accused of heresy. I remembered how the pedlar woman had glanced around the street yesterday before offering to read my palm and foretell the future. A man like Nostradamus would have to be extra careful not to attract the attention of those who might condemn him.

'And, indeed' – Mistress Anne looked out of the kitchen

window in alarm – 'here comes one who loves gossip more than she does work.'

A stout woman, whom I guessed was the morning maidservant, was bustling up the path.

'Quickly now.' Mistress Anne took me by the arm into the hallway of the house and pushed me ahead of her upstairs to her own bedroom. 'We must get you some clothes and rehearse your story before Berthe has a chance to see you.'

Chapter Twenty-six

'**Y**ou are very thin.'
Mistress Anne tutted as I undressed, taking off my sandals and breeches and tunic.

'It is the way I am made,' I said quickly. In truth I had lost weight, for I'd not had a good meal for a week or more. I'd never worried much about food before. My father always ensured that Chantelle and I were provided for. In recent years he'd secured employment with royal courts, both in England and in France, where there was food aplenty. During the last weeks it had been a new experience for me to know dull hunger, which depresses your body and spirit.

As if she sensed my thoughts Mistress Anne said, 'The life we lead here is not like that of the grand palaces you may have been used to. We have six growing children to support and although Catherine de' Medici awarded Master Nostradamus a royal pension, there is not enough money for me to pay you as a proper servant.'

'I don't expect payment,' I said. 'I will help you as best

I can and will be grateful for any food that is left when the family have finished their meals.'

'Tush, child.' She clicked her tongue against her teeth. 'You will eat with the rest of us. Now let's see what's to be done with you. Those clothes!' She wrinkled her nose as she gathered them up. 'They look as though you have slept in haystacks!'

I didn't like to tell Mistress Anne that I had in fact been sleeping among hay for the last few nights. 'My cloak is still serviceable,' I said.

'But too distinctive.' Mistress Anne fingered the russet wool and the collar with its gold embroidery. 'Did you sit with your sister and prick out this pattern together?'

I bowed my head as a warm memory came to me. I felt again Chantelle's skilful hands guiding my fingers, teaching me how to make the template in fine paper, and showing me how to transfer my own design to the material.

'I know what it's like to have a sister very close to the heart,' said Mistress Anne. 'I have a twin, and in our girl-hood we shared secrets and whispered together as we sat together sewing in the heat of the afternoon.'

A fat tear oozed from one of my eyes and slid down my face.

'Your sister's suffering is over,' Mistress Anne said firmly. 'Take comfort from that.'

I was tempted then to tell Mistress Anne of my dream last night, of how Chantelle had come to me and told me she was happy. But something stopped me. A sense of oppression. The very walls of this house seemed to ache with dreams and things unsaid.

Mistress Anne spread the cloak wide and wrapped my cap and sandals and breeches and tunic inside. Then she raised the lid of a chest that stood at the foot of her bed and buried the bundle among the rest of the goods inside.

'Now here is your story. Mind what I say so that we both tell the same tale. You are Lisette de Ponsarde. There, I have given you my own family name. And you have just travelled to Salon from a country farm near Montvieulle.'

'I have been in that area,' I said. 'We passed through it before arriving at the court at Cherboucy.'

'Very well, any description you can give as to the land and features of that countryside will add credence to your identity. My cousin Guillem has a small farm there where he lives with his wife and large family. He keeps livestock and hens and sells eggs. They have no riches but neither do they starve. As you have been growing up my cousin noted that you showed a bit of intelligence. I will say that he wrote to me and asked if I would train you to help in the apothecary shop and be a house-help to me in return for your bed and board.'

As she was speaking Mistress Anne had taken a basket of clothes from a cupboard in her room and was sorting through it. First she pulled out a scarf of pale blue and then a pair of wooden clogs. The clogs were very worn and too large for me, but they looked as though they might fit if I stuffed straw in the toes. Next she brought out a long dark blue dress with a row of pin tucks at the bodice.

'Whose dress was this?' I asked her.

'It was mine. Before I bore my husband his six children

165

I had a waist that a man could encircle with his hands.' She sighed. 'Alas, no more.'

I placed the dress over my shoulders and let it fall. The end of the skirt swung free, some inches from the floor.

'You can unpick the hem later, and if need be sew a strip of ribbon along the bottom.' She took the pale blue scarf and wound it around my head. 'What enormous eyes you have, Mélisande,' she declared. 'Excuse me, I must remember to call you Lisette.' She gave me a smile. It was the first welcoming one that she had bestowed upon me since we'd met. 'Don't look so scared. If you tell no one else your true life history and keep yourself to yourself, you should be safe enough now.'

I looked beyond her head at the mirror behind the door. Once again I did not know myself. I was no longer the gawky minstrel lad, nor was I the bold but innocent Mélisande of the royal courts. Now I was Lisette, pale of face and plain of dress. And, if Mistress Anne was believed, a girl of humble origin to whom no one would pay much attention. But I fancied that the face of Lisette that looked back at me was shadowed with sorrow and this would be obvious to any observer.

Mistress Anne took my hand. 'Let us go and introduce you to Berthe, the kitchen maid. I need to give her orders for the day or she'll sit with her feet in the fireplace and do nothing.' She paused before going out of the room and lowered her voice to a whisper. 'I say again to you. Be very careful when Berthe is in the house. Her ears are longer than those of the wild hare, and her eyes miss nothing.'

Chapter Twenty-seven

B erthe, the maid, scrambled up from her stool as we entered the kitchen.

She had been sitting close to the grate with her aprons hitched up and the calves of her legs were blotched crimson by the heat from the fire. Quickly she placed her hand on the kettle and swung it off the flames.

'I have the water here boiling ready, mistress,' she said.

I saw then that she was a crafty servant, this Berthe. But her attempt to make it look as though she had been attending to her duties did not fool her employer.

'I have been downstairs already, Berthe,' Mistress Anne retorted crisply. 'It was Mél' – in her annoyance she almost said my name – 'my cousin's child, Lisette, who drew the water from the well and set it to boil.'

Berthe flicked a look of resentment at me and thus we began badly, for I saw that in some way she blamed me for this scolding.

'Well, yes,' she said, 'I knew that someone different had been working here since yesterday.'

Mistress Anne pursed her lips. 'How so?' she asked.

'The table has been moved.' Berthe grinned slyly. 'I can see the marks on the floor where the legs once stood.'

I glanced up to where my mandolin was hidden.

Mistress Anne saw me and gave her head a little shake.

Berthe was watching us both. Had she seen me glance at the top shelf?

With her next words Mistress Anne swatted Berthe as she might do a bluebottle.

'I'm amazed that you draw attention to your poor house-keeping skills in this way!' she exclaimed. 'The kitchen floor should be in such a state after you have mopped each evening that it should not be possible to tell if the table has been moved. In future see to it that you shift the table and the chairs and stools so that you do not merely clean around the furniture but also below and beneath it.'

'Yes, mistress.' Berthe bent her head under this on-slaught.

'My cousin's daughter, Lisette, has come in from her father's farm at Montvieulle to stay with me awhile. He wants her to learn to assist in our apothecary, but she will come and go as she pleases here and you will treat her as a daughter of the house.'

'Yes, mistress,' Berthe repeated. She raised her head enough so that her eyes could assess my clothes and face.

'Begin by cooking the soaked oatmeal.' Mistress Anne pointed to a covered dish which stood on the sideboard. 'Afterwards mix up some flour. I want a pie made for—'

She was interrupted by her older daughter coming into

the room carrying the sick child, who had obviously just woken up and was moaning and fretting and tossing its little head from side to side. Upon seeing its mother the child shrieked, 'Mama! Mama!' and began to yell loudly.

'There, there.' Mistress Anne took a big outdoor shawl from a hook on the kitchen door, coddled the toddler in it and tried to comfort her. 'Get dressed and prepare for your lessons,' she directed her older girl. 'Berthe will make some breakfast for us and will bring it to us when it's ready. 'Lisette' – she turned to me – 'go into the apothecary shop and introduce yourself to Giorgio, who is Master Nostradamus's trusted apothecary. Even though it is early Giorgio will be there. Do not be put off by his manner. He is a learned man with many skills. Explain the situation to him and ask if he has anything that will ease my baby's distress.' The child moaned again, shook her head and screamed and clawed at her mother's face. 'Tell him she howls as if possessed.'

At these words Berthe crossed herself, and when Mistress Anne had gone from the room with her children she muttered, 'Possessed they may be. I'd say it's a judgement of God for those who meddle in what they shouldn't.' She stared at me inquisitively. 'What do you say, farm girl?'

I didn't give her any reply, but went out of the door into the hallway. Going past the cupboard where I had spent the previous night I went to the front of the house. Beside me was the staircase leading to the upper rooms, in front of me was the main outside door, and on my left, another door with a key in the lock. I turned the key and pushed it open and found myself in a long narrow room with windows and its own outside door, which gave onto the street on the other side of the house.

The room was both a shop and a workplace. Before me ran a counter where customers might wait to purchase their goods. Behind this, on either side of the doorway in which I stood, were numerous rows of shelves with dozens of jars and bottles, and below these, banks of drawers of various sizes. All were labelled and numbered in fine script. At one end, partly concealed behind a screen, was a stove, several sinks, a table and some workbenches. Over one of these a man stooped. He was spooning powder into a small wooden box, but stopped and looked up as I opened the door.

'A new face,' he said. 'Enter. Enter. Tell me your business.' He beckoned with his hand to bid me go near to him.

As I approached he did not straighten up and I saw that he could not. His body was bent yet he was not a true hunchback. As I hesitated, he came towards me with a shambling gait as if his bones did not quite connect to each other.

'And who are you, miss, who has forgotten her manners and stares at poor Giorgio in such a rude way?'

My face reddened and I gabbled, 'I am – I am Lisette. I am kin to Mistress Anne, the daughter of her cousin who lives at Montvieulle, and I've come to live here for a while.'

'What! Yet another refugee for this already over-burdened family to take care of?'

'No, no,' I said hurriedly. 'I will earn my keep. I can

work as hard as anyone else. I've been told that I am to assist you. And in particular this morning Mistress Anne has sent me to see if you have a remedy to ease her youngest child, who is in pain.'

'Well, then' – Giorgio was now close to me and being shorter than I was obliged to look up into my face – 'let's find out if you are to be of any use to me in this apothecary shop. What kind of pain is the child suffering?'

'I – I don't know what you mean,' I stammered.

He limped back to his place and took up the spoon to continue what he had been doing when I'd come into the room.

'Think about the question I have asked and then answer me.'

'You want me to describe the pain the child is suffering?'

He nodded. Despite being engaged in his work I saw that he was attentive to me.

I recalled how loudly the child had screamed. 'It was a sore pain.'

'Ah!' Giorgio said in a false tone of wonder. 'A *sore* pain. That makes it all so much more clear.'

'Don't mock me,' I said, rising to his taunt. 'I have no expert knowledge to describe the child's condition. And it seems to me that rather than using this situation to teach me a lesson in humility, it would be better if you explained to me the information you seek. We are wasting time when a child is suffering.'

'Oh, well uttered!' He tilted his head to one side. 'Although, a somewhat tart reply for a mere country girl.' He shook his spoon free of any remaining loose powder and used it to gesticulate at the shelves. 'There are a dozen remedies here that will ease pain. Some of which could stupefy the child unto death, even. To be of best help I need to try to determine what is *causing* the pain. So this is what I would like to know.' He held up his fingers one by one as he itemized his list. 'The location of the pain. The severity of said pain. Is it constant or intermittent? Be it an ache or a stabbing pain? Is the child vomiting? Are the bowels loose? Is there an accompanying fever, or is the child producing normal sweat?' He paused and gave me a piercing look. 'Now, speak, and let us judge how observant you are, Miss Lisette.'

I rhymed off my answers in the order he had asked the questions and held up my fingers in rotation to mimic him. 'The pain appears to be in the child's head. It is very severe. It comes and goes, but when it comes it causes the child to rub the side of its head and howl. To my knowledge the child has not vomited or soiled itself. There is a fever, yes.'

'Good. Very good.' As I was speaking Giorgio had pulled out a wooden ladder and was kicking it before him along the row of shelves.

He did this in a practised but awkward manner, but I felt I already knew enough about his character not to offer assistance.

'Is there any other, even minor piece of information that you can add to help my diagnosis? The slightest thing, which might at first seem unimportant, may assist.'

I shook my head.

'Did she sleep at all last night?'

'Only after a long time. I play—' My tongue tripped over the word 'played', and I felt a stab of fear. I had nearly given away the fact that I was a musician! I hurriedly changed my sentence. 'I placated her with a lullaby.' Giorgio did not appear to notice anything odd but I thought to make a joke to distract him so I added, 'She did sleep then, poor mite. But I fear it was more to do with her exhaustion from crying than my good singing.'

Giorgio placed his ladder against a shelf. He hauled himself up a step or two and, opening a large bottle, took out what appeared to be a piece of tree bark. 'Did Mistress Anne offer a suggestion as to what might be wrong?'

'No,' I replied, and then, hoping to show him that I could match wits with him, I added, 'But the kitchen maid, Berthe, did. She declared it to be a judgement of God.'

'Myself,' Giorgio said as he clambered down the ladder, 'I declare it to be earache. And with this' – he held up the piece of tree bark – 'we may effect to give the child some relief.' He peered up into my face with a calculating look. 'Now, Miss Lisette. Whose judgement will you abide by? That of God or that of Giorgio?'

I stepped away from him. It was a question worthy of any Inquisitor.

He laughed at my confusion. 'Would we be thwarting God's will by making a preparation with willow bark to help this child?' He addressed the remark to me from over his shoulder as he shuffled back to his workbench.

'It cannot be God's will that a child suffers,' I said as I followed him to see what he was doing. I had met doctors and apothecaries aplenty in the courts of England and France but mostly they preferred to keep their recipes secret.

Giorgio handed me the tree bark and a small metal food grater. 'Take some thin shavings from the inner side,' he instructed me, then he continued our discussion by saying, 'There are those who would argue that when God sends an affliction then man must bow his head and suffer, as Job did in the Bible story.'

'God made the plants for us to harvest,' I replied. Grasping the grater, I applied myself to obtaining the finest bark shavings possible.

Giorgio broke off a piece of honeycomb and added it with the shavings to a small pannikin of water simmering on his stove.

'And the same God endowed you with the intelligence to devise this concoction,' I added.

'And did he also grant you the intellect, Miss Lisette, to remember the ingredients, the amounts, and the method to prepare a similar concoction if so requested?' Giorgio folded his arms and waited.

I recited his recipe to him and was rewarded with what I detected to be a small gleam of approval in his eyes. But he did not gratify me with any kind remark. I was to learn that Giorgio was very spare with compliments. When the mixture had boiled for some minutes he strained it into a cup and added a dollop of amber liquid which smelled to me like mead. This he gave to me, saying, 'Take this to Mistress Anne and say that the child must swallow all of it.' He reached under the counter and took the stopper from a large jar that was kept there out of sight. 'Here is a sugar stick for the child to suck, that it might be easier to get her to take the medicine.'

I took the items from him and went to do as he asked. I was conscious that he was watching me, so in order not to spill any drop I set the cup on the counter while I pulled open the door leading to the house.

Berthe, the kitchen maid, fell against me. She must have been leaning close to the door on the other side.

'Mistress Anne said to bring in some breakfast for you both,' Berthe said, walking past me quickly carrying two bowls of porridge.

Had she been loitering to listen? And if so, how long had she been there? Had she heard Giorgio and me having the type of conversation that some might consider blasphemous?

I found Mistress Anne in the upstairs family room rocking the grizzling child upon her knee. 'Ah' – she glanced up in relief as I entered the room and reached out her hand for the medicine – 'I knew that Giorgio would not fail me.'

I helped her coax her little girl to drink the medicine.

'Did Giorgio make you welcome in the pharmacy?' Mistress Anne asked me as she gave me the empty cup to take away.

'He is a singular man,' I answered her.

Mistress Anne smiled. 'Yes,' she said, 'that is true. He has his own distinct way of coping with life. But if you pay him good attention you will learn a great deal.'

Chapter Twenty-eight

A
nd in the time that followed I did learn a great deal from Giorgio.

From the very beginning he did not treat me as the type of assistant who was there to sweep and dust and clean the various utensils. He sought to train me as a true apprentice. On my return to the shop that morning with the empty cup he instructed me to put on an apron and prepare a large batch of the liquid he called *Salix verum*.

'Inflammation in the inner ear frequently takes more than one treatment to dispel,' he said as he supervised me boiling up more of the infusion. 'Therefore we must have some phials ready in case the child has another attack. And do not be surprised if, when we open for business today, some of our customers bring children with similar symptoms. In my experience the same sickness spreads within a community. That is something you should note, Miss Lisette. Speaking of which,' he added, 'I expect you can read a bit. But can you write?'

I nodded.

'Very good. I will give you a blank book and you may make such notes as you see fit. I warn you, there is much to learn and I do not wish to keep repeating myself.' Giorgio went to one of his store cupboards and took out a leather-bound notebook, which had a pencil attached to it with a fine cord. 'There, take that and keep it handy by you.'

I put the book in the pocket of my apron and made notes in it all the time I worked in the apothecary shop. When we closed up in the evening I would open it and read and re-read it to memorize the new recipes and ingredients I had learned. There was never any free time to do this during the day. Every morning, even in the worst of weather, there was usually a customer waiting outside to be let in. And when we closed for siesta Giorgio often used these hours for us to mix and prepare more medicines. Most of the herbs we used came from Nostradamus's own extensive physic garden. Some of these I was familiar with, as Chantelle had instructed me in their effects: comfrey as a poultice to treat bruises, mint and marjoram for colds and sore throats, rosemary and anise to aid digestion. Others were entirely new to me, and came from seeds and plants obtained from the Orient and the New World. I learned their medicinal properties, how to accurately weigh amounts, and chop and grind these with pestle and mortar.

The first few weeks I was there, Master Nostradamus was too weak to rise from the day couch in his study and his wife forbade anyone apart from her to come into his presence. I fretted with impatience and worry. I wanted to speak to the prophet as soon as possible to beg him to petition the king

177

and queen regent on my behalf and to question him as to
what he meant by saying that I had been directed to his
house for another reason altogether. Mistress Anne attended
to him faithfully. I ran up and down the four flights of stairs
keeping the lights replenished and carrying food and drink,
medicines and poultices. Mostly I stayed in the outer rooms
and heard only the murmur of her voice as she entreated
him to eat. But one time she did call to me for help to prevent him rising up from his sick bed.

Evening was approaching and I was lighting the candles
and lamps when suddenly his voice sounded out like rocks
crashing down a mountainside:

'See the world as it turns! The lands to the west! Fire and
fury will rain down from Heaven's door!'

Did he mean the New World? Those countries recently
discovered to the distant west, beyond the great ocean, and
already claimed as their own by the kings and queens of
Europe?

'By a tree man first came to life and by a tree will he
perish!'

Was this the tree in the Garden of Eden?

'Are you there, girl?' It was Mistress Anne's voice I heard
now. 'I need some assistance if you are.'

I ran into the inner room. This was the sanctum where
the prophet pored over his mystical texts and where he
kept his aids to divination. On either side of the window
shelves bowed under the weight of books and manuscripts,
some crumbling with age. The other walls were covered in
charts depicting human and celestial bodies. It was
rumoured that he had dissected cadavers in his quest for

knowledge. I shuddered as I saw the tall posters of two skeletons showing the human bones stripped of their flesh. One was that of a man, the eyeless sockets of his skull staring out at me. Beside it was the woman, long hair trailing low across her body to preserve her modesty. On the ceiling, in a great wheel, were depicted the signs of the zodiac, and above and below them were many numbers and symbols, known and unknown. Along the top level of the walls the planets were numbered and named: Mars, Venus, Jupiter and the rest. As I stared at them it was as if their influence reached out to me. There were drawings in Nostradamus's own hand showing the movement of the planets, tracing their course in the skies above us. And here was his wide desk with its astrolabe and a half-completed horoscope, his quill pen discarded, the ink crusted on its tip. His silver walking cane stood propped beside his day bed.

Nostradamus had flung off his blankets and was pushing his wife aside as she wrestled with him to make him lie down. His face had sunk in, his skin was grey. He appeared too feeble to resist her, yet his eyes started from his sockets as he saw me and he tried again to rise up.

'Who is this? Who is she who comes with the torch of hope burning when the Angel of Death is close on her heels?'

I realized then that I still held a lit taper in my hand.

'Hush, hush,' Mistress Anne calmed him as I'd heard her do her youngest child. 'You are having a nightmare due to fever.'

'Am I fevered?' Her husband grasped her hand and put it to his brow. 'Tell me true. Am I fevered?'

She bit her lip. 'Not so much, no.'

'Then 'tis not a nightmare, but a vision I see. Woe and lamentation in our land.' He managed to sit upright and cried out in a terrifying voice, 'Pity the children for they will be butchered! The innocent are blamed. Blood runs red in the streets of Paris!' He pointed a long bony finger at me. 'The women cry for succour and you, Mélisande, can do nothing to help them.'

I stood there, unable to move. This was the same prophecy that he had uttered in the, palace of Cherboucy at the time he had foretold the death of Chantelle. He fell back on his pillows, exhausted, and Mistress Anne indicated for me to leave them alone.

I came down into the shop and went about my business very quietly. Giorgio gave me a curious look but made no comment. I knew him well enough to gauge that he was sensitive to a person's mood or nuances in atmosphere. It was one of his skills in the diagnosis of an illness. He could not fail to notice now that I was disturbed, so I pre-empted any enquiry by saying, 'Master Nostradamus seems troubled in his mind today.'

Giorgio gave me a sidelong glance. 'It would seem that your mind is also troubled.'

'He proclaimed a great disaster to come.'

'Master Nostradamus is wont to use a fanciful turn of phrase.'

'He warned of death and destruction upon the land.'

'There has been death and destruction on Earth since ancient times,' Giorgio pointed out. 'It is the way of things.'

'He said that the blood of the innocent would be shed.'

'The blood of the innocent is always spilled more profusely than that of the wicked. By very dint of them being wicked, the wicked contrive to avoid justice.'

I saw that he was trying to lift my mood yet I was not amused. My sister Chantelle had also pointed out that certain things happen, whether prophesied or not.

But Chantelle was now dead.

'You know one can induce visions in one's brain,' said Giorgio. 'If you stare at the moon long enough then you will see a shape there that will talk to you.'

'Don't you believe in the predictions of Master Nostradamus?' I asked in surprise. I had always assumed that being his closest assistant Giorgio would believe in the prophecies.

He shrugged.

'What *do* you believe in?' I asked him

'I hold faith in the efficacy of medicine. I believe that for every illness Nature has, if not a cure, then a way of helping. Sometimes only to ease our passage through this world.'

'Or out of it,' I replied.

'For a homely farm girl you possess a formidable wit.'

I lowered my gaze. Giorgio shuffled nearer.

I made to move away, but he blocked me. Why could I not keep my tongue quiet in my head? Mistress Anne had warned me about Berthe but had not said anything about Giorgio. Either she thought he would be less interested or she trusted him more. If she gave him the keys to the pharmacy then she must have some faith in him.

181

'There is something I have noticed about you, Miss Lisette, as I watch you help me in my work.' Giorgio reached out, took my hands in his own and turned them, palms up. 'These are not calloused and rough with farm work. They look as though they belong to a lady at court.'

I was quiet for a moment. Then I laughed. 'My father spoiled me,' I answered lightly, 'for he deemed me intelligent. That is what he always desired for me. To catch the attention of a royal knight and become a noble lady.'

Giorgio tipped my chin up with his fingers. I lowered my eyelids but not before we had exchanged a brief glance. 'Don't play a bucolic lass with me,' he said. 'Those eyes blaze out intelligence and impudence. You have a manner that belies your station.'

'And so have you, sir,' I countered. 'You must have had some more important position elsewhere before you became an assistant in a pharmacy.'

He winced and I saw that I had made a hit. I pushed forward my advantage. 'What were you before you came to Salon?'

'I was a court physician.'

My heart tripped, but I knew that I must ask the next question else it would appear odd. 'Which court?'

'The most wondrous court in all of Europe,' he replied.

The French court claimed their court to hold this honour but then so did Elizabeth of England.

'England? France?'

'Not royal.' He shook his head. 'I said the most *wondrous* court of Europe, not the richest or the most grand and ostentatious. This court patronized and encouraged the natural talent of men of genius and produced the most sought after artistry in the world. It was the one held by the Medici of Florence.'

'That of the family of the queen regent, Catherine de' Medici?'

'The very one.' He bowed low. 'Doctor Giorgio was one of the most respected doctors there.'

'So you knew Catherine de' Medici before she was married to the King of France?'

'I did. I knew her as a child. I'm not much older than she.'

Yet he looked more aged, and walked hunched, dragging his legs like an old man.

He guessed my thoughts and said sadly, 'Ah yes, I'm not as robust as I once was. This is courtesy of Signor *Strappado*.'

He saw my puzzlement and went on to explain. 'The *strappado* is an instrument of torture much favoured by the Florentines. The victim is tied with rope around the wrists and the rope flung over a high beam. The rope is then raised and the body let fall just short of the ground. This is done many times until one's bones jolt out from their sockets. I was lucky. My punishment ceased ere every bone had been loosened from its joints.'

'What wrong did you do?'

'None. One of their noblemen took a fever and became very ill, retching green bile. Fortunately for me he recovered but they suspected I had attempted to poison him.'

'And had you?'

'No. Had I done so I would have despatched him properly and left no trace.'

'That is not a skill to boast of,' I laughed.

'I know as much about poison as any Medici, and the Medici are very skilled poisoners indeed. This duke had been poisoned but it was a clumsy effort, more like the work of the Borgia family who once ruled the Papal States. They used a white powder, mendoril, mixed with soup or the sauce of any dish. It is odourless and tasteless, but the victim begins to have fits of vomiting and diarrhoea so it's obvious that poison has been administered. The Medici and those who work for them know more sophisticated methods . . .'

'Such as?' This was not quite the thing a young girl should be interested in but my curiosity was piqued.

'There is a particular mixture of substances that is easily absorbed by the skin. It can be blended into a beauty cream, or an ointment to remove blemishes. And once administered there is no cure. Even inducing vomiting or administering a purge will not rid it from the body. You become as one of the walking dead.'

'And there is nothing to show that any poison has been given?'

'Oh, if you have a keen eye, you might determine a faint mottling of the neck, the skin on the back of the hand yellowing, a smell like that of cherries. But it doesn't matter what symptoms you espy, there is no antidote. The Medici poison is very swift and efficient.'

A fragment of court gossip came into my head and I repeated it aloud: 'They say that when the queen came to

France from Italy she brought her own poisoner with her.'

Giorgio's head snapped up. He sent a look of alarm towards the door leading to the house.

'Perfumer!' He spoke sharply. 'Perfumer,' he repeated the word. Yes,' he said distinctly. 'I heard that the queen regent brought her own *perfumer* with her from Italy.'

I followed his glance to the door and remembered the presence of Berthe in the house, who could be listening. 'Yes,' I hastened to agree with Giorgio. 'I heard that too. The queen is very interested in perfumes.'

With my heart beating fast I began to tidy the shelves. Giorgio limped slowly to the house door, opened it and looked into the hallway and up the stairs. I'd seen that Giorgio always treated Berthe with caution. Every morning the kitchen maid brought us both a bowl of porridge laced with honey and a jug of milk. He was always very polite to her, bowing as he accepted the porridge. I don't believe she considered him in any way a suitor, but you could see that she was flattered by his manner, the little compliments he paid her. I recalled someone questioning an unlikely alliance at court between a cruel and powerful older woman and a young man who had taken up with her.

'That's what love can do,' another courtier had replied.

'Or fear,' my father had observed.

If Giorgio's body and spirit had been broken by the *strappado* then he would fear torture all the more for having once suffered it and escaped. A picture of the woman and the two men on their way to be burned at the stake in Spain came to my mind.

Giorgio closed the door and returned to the shop.

'There are those who set more store by the prophecies of Master Nostradamus than by his medicines and cures,' he continued. 'Myself, I wish he could shake off his visions. It debilitates him and attracts too much unworthy attention. People add their own interpretations to his proclamations and invent stories of strange happenings within this very house.' Giorgio pointed out of the window. 'See, over there is a mill. The paddles go round and the machinery creaks and groans as any mill does. But now it is widely put about that these noises emanate from the spirits that the magician Nostradamus summons to speak with him.'

This was exactly what the pedlar woman had said to me when she'd guided me here! She'd told of weird noises coming from the house and claimed it was souls in torment.

'But he does make true prophecies,' I said. 'Did he not prophesy the death of the queen's husband and her first-born son?'

'Some do say so,' Giorgio replied in a neutral tone.

I nearly blurted out then that Nostradamus had accurately foretold the death of my sister. But I stopped myself. It was not that I thought that Berthe might be listening, but more out of deference to the wishes of Mistress Anne, who had said that no one must know of my true life history.

Chapter Twenty-nine

Despite Giorgio's medicines and Mistress Anne's attentions it was the first week of June before Master Nostradamus was fit enough to rise from his bed.

I quickly learned how much work the house required. It was a task in itself just to keep the candles and lamps burning but it was the one I loved most, especially tending those on the upper floor. Just before the shop reopened for the evening hours I would go upstairs to trim the wicks and replenish the oil, lighting each lamp and candle in turn. While doing this I took time to look at the books and ornaments and astrological aids in Nostradamus's outer rooms.

I touched the fossils and strange stones that he had collected on his travels. I saw the ragged outline of the coasts of the New World on the huge globe that stood near the fireplace. This was where, in the vision I had heard Nostradamus declare, fire and death would rain down from the sky. What peoples lived there? Did they have prophets and seers of their own who would warn them of the coming catastrophe? On the walls of these rooms hung many charts of numbers set in grids and circles. I could not understand these, and they did not attract me as much as the ones showing the positions of the planets and the stars. I kept returning to them, to wonder at their mystery and majesty, and to consider our place within their pattern.

It was here also that he kept copies of his published works, *The Prophecies*. These revelations, each one made in four lines of free verse, known as quatrains, were the source of speculation and fascination to the world and to me. Why did my heart beat faster when I looked upon these pages and read the words? Imbued with a terrible force, they opened a fissure in my mind. I struggled to understand his visions, spilling raw from his fevered mind. Was he writing what he saw, what he heard, or merely what he imagined?

Downstairs in the shop Giorgio and I worked mainly alone. Prior to my arrival Mistress Anne and the older children had helped out. But of the six children of Mistress Anne and Master Nostradamus, only four were at home at this time. The oldest boy had recently left to travel abroad with an uncle and one of the girls had gone to live with an aunt for a while. Of the rest, the two young boys were schooled daily outside the house, while the remaining girl had a tutor who came to teach her at home each day. In addition to tending to her husband, Mistress Anne's time was taken up with her smallest child, Diane, the little girl who was still sickly and constantly sought her attention.

Nostradamus's presence was missed in the shop for, as Giorgio told me, he was in the habit of consulting there two or three mornings a week. During opening hours part of the space behind the screens was used for this and Giorgio now did the diagnoses there every morning. Sometimes our customers would be members of the aristocracy who had journeyed especially to Salon to meet the famous Nostradamus. Their servants would push their way to the front and demand that Master Nostradamus attend personally to their particular lord or lady. They gave Giorgio scant attention when he informed them that Nostradamus was unavailable but that he, Giorgio, was a qualified doctor and could offer a consultation at a lesser fee. I had a certain sympathy for these frustrated persons who went away crestfallen, for more than anything I wanted my own private meeting with the prophet.

Yet Giorgio was patient, even with the most humble petitioners who presented themselves. He often gave consultations without charge to the common people, to compensate for the cancellation of Nostradamus's free sessions held on the first Monday of each month. Some came looking for a cure for nonexistent illnesses. It seemed to me that Giorgio often spent more time than was necessary with such customers, when it was clear they only wanted to unload their troubles. For these patients Giorgio recommended a variety of water tinctures. He would invent a long and complicated history of success for the particular remedy he prescribed; of how this potion had cured the youngest son of a Spanish princess, who herself was eighth in line of succession to the throne, or how that infusion had healed the favourite wife of the second Sultan of Arabia. In some patients' minds the more convoluted the story, the more potent the medicine became.

I queried this with Giorgio, saying, 'These infusions you give out are no more than liquorice boiled in water.'

'They will do no harm,' he informed me. 'And sometimes believing you will get better is more than half the cure.'

But to balance these cases, the desperate and the hopeless also arrived in the apothecary shop, and on occasion caused us both to be depressed for the remainder of the day. To look into someone's face and tell them there was no cure for their terminal illness is a melancholy task. Once a woman arrived carrying a dead baby. She laid her piteous bundle on the counter and begged us to have Nostradamus put his hands on her daughter, thinking that he could restore her child to life.

'You must go to a priest,' Giorgio told her. Even he, who must have seen many deathly sights, was disconcerted. 'Only God Almighty has the power of life. Doctors can stave off death, and Master Nostradamus is an expert in this, but he is not a worker of miracles.'

As word spread that the prophet was unwell, business fell away and the shop became quieter. Giorgio made a remark about this when doing the accounts at the end of one week.

'Everyone thinks that we make a fortune here. But the ingredients we use are expensive. There must always be some prepared ahead of time, so we are obliged to outlay money, even though our income drops.'

The biggest expenditure was on rosewater, which was

delivered in huge jars made up to Nostradamus's own recipe. The rose grower who did this was contracted to him alone, and used thousands of rose blossoms in the preparation.

'It seems a waste of so many roses,' I commented. 'Why spend so much on this, a product used to beautify the body, while others die for want of proper medicine?'

'Master Nostradamus is a good doctor, and a wise man,' Giorgio replied. 'Rosewater is also used to make the pills that curtail the Plague. His own first wife and their two children were struck down with Plague and he could not save them. Thus he has dedicated himself to finding a cure for this affliction. Also, the money paid by the rich for their beauty treatments subsidizes the medicine for the less fortunate.'

It was the less fortunate who Giorgio contrived to help the most. He always had a sugar stick for the ragged children of his poorer customers, and would sometimes entertain them with simple conjuring tricks when the shop was less busy. He had a repertoire of these. By dint of twisting his fingers and holding them up to the light he could make shadow shapes of animals cavort on the window blinds; he showed them unbreakable eggs and many card tricks, and once even perplexed me by having a coin slide across the counter to him as he beckoned to it. After the children had gone he revealed the secret – a piece of magnetite chipped from a block of lodestone that he had concealed in his hand and which had attracted the metal in the coin to move towards it.

Meanwhile Mistress Anne moved my bed from the

cupboard to a curtained alcove in the family room upstairs and I was allowed to use the candle stumps to read by after supper each night. This was when I most missed my mandolin. My fingers ached to pluck the strings and send music cascading through the air. I had to content myself with playing songs in my mind and bend my head to study my notebook.

Then, near noon one day, Mistress Anne arrived in the shop to say that her husband had woken up and asked for some chicken to eat. She had given Berthe a day off to visit her mother and wished me to go to the shops in the main square, where there was a poultry seller and I might get a joint of chicken for two pennies. I put the money in my apron pocket and went to do as she asked. As I left, Giorgio pulled down the window blinds and locked the street door.

'I will go out too,' he said. 'I heard a pedlar has come to town carrying Secren seeds from Marrakesh. It's a rare commodity and I want to obtain some before the other pharmacists buy them all up.'

Giorgio regularly went off for an hour or more when the shop was shut to track down obscure ingredients. It was a sign of how much he was trusted that he was allowed to take such money as he wished from the cashbox to do this.

The poultry seller's shop was easy to find. Like the rest of the traders in Salon, as soon as the month of June began, they set up their tables outside with awnings on top to give shade. I pointed out a fresh piece of chicken and, as the shopkeeper wrapped it up, I placed my two pennies on the table top.

He glanced at my face, and then at the money.

'Two pennies!' he exclaimed. 'I think not! Such a fine piece of chicken is worth far more than that!'

I was taken aback. Mistress Anne had only given me two pennies. Then I recalled I had a penny or two in my apron pocket, for occasionally a grateful client would return and give us a coin as gratuity for our services. I rooted around in my apron pocket and took all the money I had – three more pennies.

'Is that all you have?' the shopkeeper asked in a belligerent voice.

My face went red and I nodded.

'You are robbing me,' he declared, 'but I suppose I will have to take it.'

Five pennies was more than double what Mistress Anne had given me. But I had never in my life bargained for food in the market, so I did not really know the best price. And Master Nostradamus had asked especially for chicken and I did not want to disappoint him. Yet I hesitated.

The man glanced beyond my shoulder. 'Quickly now,' he said. 'Else I'll raise the price again.'

I looked to see what had caught the shopkeeper's attention. A tall figure was making his way down the street from the direction of the Château Emperi. It was the Lord Thierry. He had with him his sergeant at arms who was carrying a solid long box.

Some murmurs of discontent sounded around the stallholders.

'What is our noble Lord Thierry poking his nose into today?'

'Look! His sergeant carries the box of the official weights. He must mean to check our scales are accurate.'

'He's always bothering someone about something, that one. Why can't he leave honest traders in peace to go about their business?'

I was about to say that if they were honest traders then they should not fear an inspection of their scales and weights, but now I was experiencing my own flutter of disquiet. Weeks had passed since the spring market and my encounter with this man. My hair had grown a little and I had altered Mistress Anne's dress so that it looked more fitted to me but I did not want to be near him and come under his scrutiny.

'Come on, girl!' the poultry man said in an anxious voice. 'Are you buying this chicken piece or not?'

If he was hastening to do the deal, then so was I, albeit for a different reason. I gathered my money and made to give it over, when a hand reached out and over mine.

'Stop!'

I whirled round. Giorgio stood beside me. 'Put your money in your apron,' he told me. Then he addressed the shopkeeper. 'That is an absurd sum of money to pay for a piece of chicken, as well you know. Shame on you, to take advantage of a young girl.'

'I did not, I did not,' the man protested. 'We were bargaining, that's all.'

'Then let me bargain on her behalf,' said Giorgio tersely. 'I will give you one penny, and one penny only for that chicken piece. And if you do not hand it over immediately I will raise my voice so that the Lord Thierry may hear. We'll let him be the judge if you have given this innocent girl a fair price, shall we?'

The man thrust the chicken at me. 'Here take it for nothing and go away from here.'

I took the chicken and picked up my pennies. When I turned to thank Giorgio he had disappeared among the passers-by. What would he think of me now? It was clear to any observer that I was no country girl as I did not know the price to pay for ordinary farm produce. With the life I'd led in my youth I might have been able to spy a bargain in a ribbon or a piece of cloth, but I had no idea when it came to purchasing livestock or kitchen goods.

But now Lord Thierry and his sergeant were approaching the row of stalls where I stood. I slipped into a doorway. He passed near to me and, without thinking, I leaned out to watch him. Even from the back he was a handsome man with an air of superiority. His golden hair shone out among the dark southerners. He glanced over his shoulder and I hurriedly drew back.

I returned to the house. As I was unwrapping the chicken piece Mistress Anne came into the kitchen. 'I will prepare this meal for my husband myself,' she said. 'Come upstairs with me now. Master Nostradamus was asking as to your whereabouts. He said that on your return he would speak with you.'

Chapter Thirty

Nostradamus sat in a high-backed chair in the inner room of his apartments.

His face was still gaunt but there was more colour in his cheeks and his eyes within their hooded eyelids were less fevered than before. On a small table at his side were his astrolabe and the uncompleted horoscope he had been working on when he had first been taken ill.

'I hear that you have been very industrious during the last weeks,' he said as I approached him. 'Mistress Anne tells me that you have been working hard in the pharmacy, and have been taking special care of my rooms, trimming the candles and replenishing the lamps each morning and evening. I want to thank you, Mélisande.'

'Lisette.' His wife glanced towards the door and placed her finger on her lips. 'You must remember to call this girl Lisette and also the story we have decided upon. We know that Berthe loves to gossip about everything that happens in this house.'

'But Berthe is not allowed to come onto this top floor,' Nostradamus pointed out.

'My dear, she hovers on the stairs and listens outside doors.'

Nostradamus smiled at me. 'My wife is very protective of my person. She thinks all the time that there are those who seek to destroy me even though I intend harm to no one.'

'My sister was innocent and good,' I replied. 'It did not prevent her life being taken from her.'

'Ah, I recall, that was the reason you said led you to my door. Your sister. She was . . . ?'

'Chantelle,' I said. 'I think you foretold her death.'

'Yes.' He passed his hand across his brow. The movement required effort on his part and I saw how very tired he was. 'Chantelle. She was petite while you are tall. Her face more rounded and—' He broke off.

'And what?'

'Nothing. It is hard for me to recall the exact details of some occasions. It depends on many factors. And now . . . the visions are coming more often and they are more confusing than ever. I see things in my sleep and then in my waking moments, and I can no longer distinguish between them. They seize my mind and I have no control.'

'That night,' I persisted. 'In the palace of Cherboucy. What did you see?'

'Cherboucy . . . Cherboucy. That was before Easter, was it not?'

I nodded.

'My prophecy was about the king.' He paused. 'The

true King of France.' His face tensed. 'More and more the visions I have are about the rulers of France' – he hesitated – 'and about the rulers of the world. This world, the old . . . and the other. There are ones who seize power, and ones who have it thrust upon them. I see that those who rule walk with death. Always. It stalks them in the street, in their palaces, in the carriages they ride. Those who would be rulers, beware!'

'My sister,' I said, to try to bring his mind to what I wished to know.

'Husband' – his wife leaned over him – 'perhaps you might want to talk more another day when you are recovered in your health.'

'No!' he said, and his voice had new strength. 'There is not much time left and this girl must have her answers.' He took his wife's hand. 'Leave us alone. Please,' he added, as she wavered. 'It is for your own safety, and that of our children.'

She did not hesitate then, but went away out of the apartments and descended the stairs.

Nostradamus indicated for me to sit beside him. 'I felt the presence of death in the palace of Cherboucy,' he began, 'the shade of everlasting night creeping across the hall. It fell upon those of the house of Guise. It fell upon the seed of the Medici. It fell upon the throne itself.

'That night, the night of which we speak, the shadow was very distinct. I saw, spread out across the great hall, the wings of the Angel of Death.'

And quite suddenly, sitting there on a stool by his feet, I saw what Nostradamus saw.

He stopped speaking as I gasped and covered my mouth with my hand. Now I was with Melchior again on the beam. I could smell the acrid smoke, see the flames of the torches, the upturned benches on the floor of the hall.

'Do not look down,' Melchior commanded me, his voice once again in my ear. 'Thou must not look down.'

Melchior's hand clasped my hand. His arm along mine, giving me support.

But I *had* looked down.

The great hall below me. We were high up among the roof beams, positioned above the enormous central chandelier.

A hundred candles or more burned in their sockets. I saw again the pattern they made as they cast their light. The two outspread wings of a huge angel.

Nostradamus's hand gripped mine. 'You see it too?' he cried. 'Don't you? You see it too!'

I nodded. 'Yes,' I said, 'but—'

'And at the outer edge,' Nostradamus continued, 'on the very tip of the angel's wing, that was where your sister was standing on the day I made my prophecy to the king.'

It was true. We had been standing behind the pillar and Chantelle had taken a step back as the prophet had passed. By doing that she had placed herself where the shadow fell.

'As I left the hall,' said Nostradamus, 'I brushed past her and a chill entered my soul.' He passed his hand across his face. 'I felt that her shade was disconnecting from her body. That her soul was preparing to leave.' He slumped in his chair, exhausted.

There were many things I wanted to know now. How could he prophesy a specific thing from his feelings and from his perceptions? This would need discussion and I saw that he required rest. But there was one thing more than any other that I wished to know.

'My sister Chantelle was in love,' I said. 'She loved Armand Vescault with a passion, and he loved her too.'

'I believe you,' Nostradamus said.

'So they are together now?' I asked him. 'Please tell me that they are together.'

'I cannot tell you that which I do not know.'

'They *must* be together.' I was becoming distraught.

'If it pleases you to so believe,' he said.

'I do believe it.'

'Then believe it.'

'Why couldn't you prevent her death?' I asked him.

'There is very little that I can prevent,' Nostradamus replied. 'It may be that things are set in their course and I only have the gift to see what will be, what must be. And yet, even if these happenings could be altered, how could that be effected? You might give a warning. But people do not listen. They choose not to. They would have to change their lives, and' – he paused – 'the lives of others.' He looked at me then, most intensely. 'It takes an exceptional person to change the course of an event.'

His eyes held my own fast in his gaze. It was as though he was searching for something in my soul. An answer? But he had not asked a question. Perhaps he himself did not know the question to ask.

'An exceptional person,' he repeated. He closed his eyes.

The room filled up with silence. The sputtering wick of the candle became louder.

A voice, unlike his even though it came from his mouth, said clearly, 'And if such a person does exist, then that person must choose to be the one. They cannot be forced or coerced. For sometimes in order to save a life, a person must sacrifice their own.'

'I would have given up my life to save my sister!' I cried.

Nostradamus replied, 'It was not arranged thus. Perhaps you have been spared for a greater deed.' He seemed to muse on this and fell into a kind of reverie. After a few minutes he spoke without opening his eyes. 'It would be best if you left me now for a space of time, for I must think on—'

He did not complete the sentence.

Mistress Anne came hurrying up the stairs in a state of agitation. 'The Lord Thierry is at the door,' she said. 'I told him you were not fully recovered from your illness but he insists on seeing you!'

Chapter Thirty-one

I jumped to my feet in fright.

'What ails you, child?' Nostradamus asked me.

'I have encountered this man before and I don't want to meet him again.'

'At court? Are you sure? The Lord Thierry spends no time there. He loathes the royal household with all its falseness and decadence. And he's not long returned from travelling for many years in the east. You must be mistaken.'

'No, not at court,' Mistress Anne explained quickly to her husband. 'The first day Mélisande came here, on spring market day, Lord Thierry rescued her from a bunch of drunken men.'

I nodded. 'He bade me wait for he wished to make me minstrel in his own castle, but I ran off.'

'You were dressed as a boy then,' said Nostradamus. 'He'll not know you now.'

The words Nostradamus spoke made sense, yet I was uneasy. I remembered the way Lord Thierry had examined

my clothes, how he had shown up the innkeeper to be selling watered wine. As Mistress Anne had said, this was a
man who was more astute than others.

'You cannot go now,' said Mistress Anne. 'I left my
daughter to take his cloak and gloves and then guide him
here. I am only a minute or so in front of them. If you
went away now you would meet him on the stairs and that
would mean passing close to him. Stand in the corner and,
as soon as I can, I'll send you out on some errand.'

She was right. Already we heard the firm tread of boots
on the staircase. I took my place in a corner of the room as
the Lord Thierry appeared in the doorway.

Mistress Anne went to meet him. 'Forgive my husband
not rising to greet you, my lord,' she said. 'He has been in
ill health these past weeks.'

'Such formality is of small consequence.' Lord Thierry
nodded to Nostradamus. 'I am pleased finally to make
your acquaintance.'

I heard him say this and thought how stark the contrast
was between him and the Count de Ferignay, who had
insisted on servility from others he considered his inferiors,
and made my father wait until he chose to speak to
him.

'How may I serve you, my lord?' asked Nostradamus.

'You know who I am?'

'Your name is well respected in this town.'

Lord Thierry snorted. 'By some. By others, well reviled.'

From my place in the corner I had a chance to study this
man more clearly. He was perhaps not as old as I'd first
judged. His face was sun-browned and wrinkled about the

eyes, not so much with age but rather as one used to spending time out of doors.

'As is my own,' said Nostradamus.

'A fair comment,' agreed Lord Thierry.

'Have you come to consult with me?'

Lord Thierry shook his head. 'I have no need of divinations.'

'You do not believe in such matters?'

'On the contrary,' Lord Thierry said seriously as his eyes ranged over the room, taking note of the multitude of books and charts. 'I would not scoff at any prophecy made with good intent. I have journeyed through many lands and seen sights that if I told of them here my listeners would think me mad or bewitched. No, it is not that I would not give credence to your foresight. It's only that I prefer to remain in ignorance of my fate.'

'Then how can I help you?' Nostradamus asked him.

'Ah.' His eyes rested on me where I stood, head meekly bent, then moved on. 'I thought you might have a text here that I am interested in, *De viribus quantitatis* by Luca Pacioli.'

'Lisette' – Nostradamus indicated to me – 'you will find that book somewhere on the third shelf to the right of the window.'

I searched through the titles until I found the book. Then I carried it across the room and, keeping my gaze on my own hands, I gave Lord Thierry the book.

'A servant girl who can read?' he said with interest in his voice.

'She is a relative of my wife,' Nostradamus explained.

'More of an assistant to me and Giorgio in the apothecary shop than a house servant. You may borrow that volume if you so wish,' he added.

'I am honoured that you trust me with your precious manuscripts. I assure you that I will return it safely.'

'Is that all?'

Lord Thierry held the book loosely in his hand. 'There is another matter,' he said. 'I am looking for a minstrel boy.'

There was a space of a heartbeat. Nostradamus repeated the words slowly. 'A minstrel boy?'

'My lord, I'm sure if you go around the town on market day there will be any number of troubadours for hire.' Mistress Anne offered the information with a smile.

'This is a particular one,' said Lord Thierry. 'On spring market day I interrupted a street brawl where he was an innocent onlooker. I bade him stay until I had dealt with the miscreants, but when I turned to look for him he was gone. Later he was seen knocking on your door.'

So the old pedlar woman who had given me directions and led me to this street had given up her information just as Mistress Anne had predicted she would.

'Many people knock on our door, to beg or ask for consultations with my husband,' Mistress Anne replied. 'But I don't recall a boy coming here on that day.'

'I took ill just prior to Easter and my family had to attend to me.' Nostradamus looked to his wife for support.

'Yes,' his wife agreed with him. 'Palm Sunday was the day that both my husband and our youngest child were struck down with fever. They were both sick for weeks afterwards.'

'Is this boy wanted for a crime?' asked Nostradamus.

'Not as far as I know.' Lord Thierry kept looking at Mistress Anne, as he replied. 'Although it's strange that he should run from his rescuer, especially as I offered him employment and he did have the appearance of needing money and food.'

'You are certain that you don't seek to punish him for some wrongdoing?' Nostradamus persisted.

'I do not.'

'Then why not find another minstrel? The summer market will take place soon and there's bound to be one just like him.'

'Not quite like him, I do not think.'

'How so?'

'He played a most exquisite mandolin. Even the bag he carried it in is of superior quality. I have it here.' And from a pouch that hung from the belt at his waist Lord Thierry pulled out my chamois leather bag.

I was glad that for once I had sufficient self-control not to make any sound or strain forward to see.

Nostradamus took the bag into his hands and his wife came to admire it. 'As you say, it is fine leather,' he said.

Lord Thierry nodded. 'This person cares for their musical instrument and is also someone who, I think, loves music dearly.'

'Indeed?' Mistress Anne feigned an interest.

'Indeed,' said Lord Thierry. 'His first song was a well-known folk tune, but then he played a ballad which was composed at the same time as the Song of Roland. It is a text that few have even heard of, and even less would have the ability to play. And he played it well. At some time in his life he must have had a singular teacher.'

Lord Thierry had been fooled by my disguise and thought me a boy, but in his assessment of the music he had guessed correctly. I'd had a singularly most talented teacher: my father. I felt tears beginning behind my eyes.

'If the bag is expensive your minstrel would have no need to knock on my door,' Mistress Anne pointed out.

Lord Thierry made a grimace.

'I wonder, sir,' said Nostradamus, 'if you have more need of this minstrel than he does you.'

'You are a shrewd man,' Lord Thierry replied. He folded the chamois leather bag and replaced it in his pouch. 'I love music. I find it lifts my spirits when I am fretful or melancholic. This lad played merry tunes and has at least one unique song in his repertoire. And that is a rare thing. I know this, for I have heard many songs from all the lands I've travelled.'

'I hope you find what you are looking for,' said Nostradamus. 'But I can tell you plainly that no young man came knocking at our door.'

'Master Nostradamus, I have not been to visit you before this,' said Lord Thierry, 'for I have been occupied with setting my domain to rights since I returned from my wanderings. But in this short acquaintance I would have warranted that you would tell the truth.'

'It is the truth that I speak,' said Nostradamus firmly.

'It is the truth that you speak.' Lord Thierry repeated the words of Nostradamus. He paused. 'And yet . . .' His voice tailed off.

No one made any comment so he began to speak again.

'A person who has no reason to lie says they saw the minstrel boy knock on this door.' He turned quickly and stared at me. 'Perhaps your cousin's child saw or heard of this boy.'

'Lisette,' said Mistress Anne. 'Lisette!' she said again. I looked up then. 'The Lord Thierry is asking if you know anything of a minstrel boy.'

'I do not,' I said. My voice trembled as I spoke but I reassured myself that this would be the natural reaction of any country girl in the presence of a noble lord.

'Very good,' said Mistress Anne. 'Now I do believe I hear the child crying, and her older sister has been nursing her all day. Would you be good enough to go and help?'

'Certainly, Aunt Anne,' I said and bent my head and made to leave the room.

To do this I had to cross the floor near to where Lord Thierry stood. As I passed him he stretched out and touched my arm. A current went between us as if he had fingered a nerve. It startled him as much as it did me.

'Sir?' I faltered.

'I saw you in the main square this morning, yes?'

'Lisette often runs errands for the household,' Mistress Anne said quickly.

'So you go out and about, Lisette?'

I nodded, keeping my eyes on the floor.

'If, when you were on these errands . . .' He paused. 'If this minstrel boy appeared, I would be grateful if you would send word to me.'

'Sir.' I nodded.

'You may tell him that I am looking for him.'

'Yes, sir.'

I kept my head well down. I would not risk our eyes meeting again.

'You may tell this boy,' he said courteously, 'that I wish him no harm. I'm very fond of music and he played very well. He had a distinctive gift.'

He waited, but I said nothing.

'If he came into my employ he would not be ill treated,' Lord Thierry went on. 'If there was anything he was afraid of, something he had done, a theft perhaps, then let him know that I am the law in these parts and I would not pursue some petty thief.' Once again Lord Thierry stopped. But again I said nothing.

'You will tell him that if you see him?'

'I do not know the person of whom you speak,' I replied unsteadily.

'No, of course not.' A curious tone had come into his voice and I was very aware of how close he was to me and the smell of him, the smell of the sweat of a man, and of the fact that his hands, which I could see with my lowered gaze, had fine tapered fingers. I bunched my own fingers into fists and hoped that he would not notice, as Giorgio had done, that I did not have sun-reddened skin.

'You may go now,' he said at last.

'Thank you, sir.' I forced myself not to run from the room.

I had been in these apartments often enough now to know where the mirrors were situated. I knew how each one was placed and what images they captured. I could not help but glance into the large oval one that stood by the door leading to the staircase. It threw out my reflection. But it also gave me a view into the room I had just left.

Lord Thierry was watching me.

Why? Had I aroused some suspicion in him? Was it simply that this man watched everyone? Or was it something else? Had he been compelled to study my retreating form just as I felt compelled to look back at him?

Like the lodestone that Giorgio had shown me; the stone called magnetite that has the property to attract iron. These elements cannot help this happening. It is in their very nature. The stone cannot be prevented from attracting the iron.

And the iron cannot resist.

Chapter Thirty-two

I fled to the safety of the apothecary shop.

If Giorgio saw that my face was flushed he made no comment. He gave me a tray of pills he'd been making as a treatment for stomach worm and asked me to package and label them. I stood at the counter and did this task while he went on compacting his powders in the moulds to make up another tray. We worked together until we heard the front door of the house bang closed and the sound of a horse trotting away.

'So our illustrious visitor, the noble Lord Thierry, has left,' Giorgio said, glancing towards the door that led through to the house.

'How did you know who had come to call?' I asked him. 'The shop windows only look out onto the lane at this side of the house.'

'Ah, now . . .' He hesitated. 'You have me there, Miss Lisette.' He tilted his head to one side. 'She who cannot assess the price of a chicken joint, yet whose quick mind asks right away how it is Giorgio knew who had entered the house to consult with Master Nostradamus. Come here and I will show you,' he said before I could think of any reply to this.

He shuffled to the door between the shop and the house and pointed at it. 'What do you see?' he demanded.

I looked at the door with its panels of ornate carvings of flowers and leaves. 'I see the keyhole,' I said, 'but you cannot peer through there for the key is always kept in the lock.'

'Look more closely at the right-hand panel,' he instructed me.

I went nearer the door.

'Run your hands over there about eye height.'

I did as he bade me and soon discovered among the carvings the tiny rounded peephole he'd wanted me to find. I put my eye to the opening and saw clearly through to the other side. It gave me a view of the front door entrance, the staircase, and part of the hall going towards the kitchen.

A person watching here would have knowledge of who came and went and also an insight into a lot of the family business, and I said as much to Giorgio.

'Remember a peephole works both ways,' he replied.

'Of course!' I exclaimed. 'Berthe!'

Spying from the house side of the door, the kitchen maid would be able to watch everything that transpired in the shop. She would know who came seeking help and for what ailment. In this way she could garner a lot of information about the people of the town. It did not occur to me at the time that the spyhole was too high for Berthe to reach. And if Berthe had constructed it, she would have no need to lean against the door to listen, as was her custom, to find out what was happening inside the shop.

'Why did you feel the need to look though it?' I asked Giorgio.

'As I returned from buying the Secren seeds I saw Lord Thierry in the next street. When the door knocker sounded I looked to ascertain if he had decided to honour us with a visit. Given the type of business we run here and him being the inquisitive overlord that he is, it is advisable to know what he is about.'

'But this shop is a very helpful one,' I said. 'We sell goods that cure ills and ease pain.'

'We also sell those.' Giorgio pointed to a quantity of printed books arranged on a shelf behind the counter.

'The almanacs?' I went over and opened one. I riffled through the pages. 'There are hundreds of these sold throughout Europe. People buy them for guidance in all sorts of things.'

'The almanacs prepared by Master Nostradamus have more information than the ones for sale elsewhere. You may take one to read and you will find that what I say is true.'

I put one into my apron pocket to look at later.

'Don't you like Lord Thierry?' I asked.

Giorgio responded with a question of his own: 'Did he get news of his minstrel boy?'

I started. How did Giorgio know that Lord Thierry sought a minstrel boy?

Seeing my look of surprise, Giorgio laid his finger

alongside his nose. 'The Lord Thierry may keep his own close counsel but his sergeant and his men-at-arms do not. The story in the town is that there was an upset at the spring market and a minstrel boy was involved. They say the boy took advantage of the rumpus to steal something from the Duke of Marcy. The duke has told Lord Thierry that it must be found or he will complain of his poor law-keeping to the king.'

'What thing?' I said, aghast. 'What do they say was stolen?'

'A ring or a brooch, some piece of jewellery. Most likely the boy has sold it already to obtain money for drink. Myself, I find it hard to believe that anyone could steal anything from Marcy with that weasel henchman of his, Bertrand, draped around his neck. But the boy will be found. Thierry is both patient and thorough and does not give up easily.'

'He said he sought the minstrel boy for his musical skills,' I said, thinking again how wise Mistress Anne had been to make me hide the mandolin as well as my clothes.

'Now, that I could believe,' said Giorgio. 'Lord Thierry is said to be very musical and literate. There is a vast library in his castle at Valbonnes where he has the collections of the famous troubadours and manuscripts from the time of the Knights Templar.'

'Then he too should be careful,' I said. 'Aren't the works of the Knights Templar banned by Church and king?'

'Not here,' Giorgio answered. 'The south and west of France has always been more . . . *rebellious* than the north. But,' he added, 'he has many of the new printed books too, and they are certainly suspect.' He looked at me more attentively. 'What have *you* heard about him?'

'That he favours the Protestants, that he might even be a Huguenot.'

'A Huguenot! A Huguenot!' This amused Giorgio highly. He cackled with laughter. 'That is a rich joke!' He shook his head. 'The Huguenots think he is an agent of the Pope. The Catholics believe him to be a sympathizer of the Protestant cause. Perhaps the reality is that he's a vigilant law maker and a fair judge, and strives to keep both warring factions subdued. But' – Giorgio shuffled to his workbench – 'even he will not be able to prevent them ripping each other apart.'

Chapter Thirty-three

I t was several days before I was summoned to speak to
the prophet again.

The sky was darkening and Nostradamus stood by
the window of his inner study, staring out at the rising
moon.

'I have thought about what we spoke of last,' he said as
I entered the room. 'And I have told you all that I can recall
of my premonition of the death of your sister, Chantelle,
but clearly there is some other factor, some link from what
happened then to what will come. Some of that past has a
bearing on future events. It may be that your sister was the
instrument to bring you here. Perhaps your destiny is also
connected to the man who directly caused her death, the
Count de Ferignay.'

At the mention of the Count de Ferignay I felt faint.
'You mean that I will meet him again? I have no wish for
that to happen.'

'This is one of the things that we must try to deduce.
And also we have to determine' – Nostradamus began to

walk away from me at this point and the sound of his voice was obscure – 'if you are truly the one.'

The prophet went to the corner of his room and drew aside the curtain covering an alcove. He opened the door that was concealed there. Inside was a narrow staircase.

'I have consulted all my manuscripts and sacred texts and the only thing that is revealed to me concerning you, Mélisande, is the repetition of certain numbers, all multiples of three. And try as I might I cannot deduce a meaning from them. Now I must seek enlightenment another way. We will go and stand under the stars.' He beckoned for me to follow him. 'Tonight the sky is clear and the moon is full, with no cloud to interrupt her light shining upon us.'

The stairs led to a small platform on the roof. Here a telescope was set up and also a metal table on which stood a jug of water and a bowl.

I stood beside Nostradamus and gazed up at the vast span of stars that speckled the night sky. The more common ones I recognized: Gemini, the twins, Betelgeuse and Bellatrix, and the mighty hunter, Orion, with belt and sword. My father had pointed them out to me. The names of the mythical heroes and heroines would be remembered for evermore; the ancient gods' promise of immortality fulfilled to those they had favoured.

'The table is iron,' Nostradamus told me. 'The jug and bowl are made of silver. I sent for fresh river water. It came from a certain stream unpolluted by any waste matter, clear from the core of the mountains.'

He poured water from the jug into the silver bowl. 'I

have used the purest of substances that I am able. Thus we approach this divination with no base metal or material.' He raised his voice. 'And with no base wish but only to seek to do good.'

From inside his coat he took a long thin stick and laid it upon the table.

'Here is a wand made from the root of the rowan tree. The tree that bears the berries signifying the fire brought to man from Heaven.'

Nostradamus removed his cap and his hair and beard shone white.

'Take off your headscarf,' he instructed me.

I did as he bade me and my hair blew about my face.

'Now regard my moonstone ring.'

I looked intently at the translucent gemstone, and as I did so it appeared to expand to encompass and enfold me.

Then Nostradamus flung his hands into the air high above his head. In doing this he seemed to grow in stature and force.

'Raise your eyes to the lady moon and allow her brightness to flood your senses!'

His voice, with such power and authority, brooked no argument. As I lifted my head, somewhere in my mind curled the thought of Giorgio telling me that if one stared at the moon long enough it would speak to you. But the circumstances and the light and the magical presence of the prophet overwhelmed me, and that doubt was gone and only the light remained . . .

Nostradamus stretched his hands over the bowl and uttered words in a language I did not understand. The moonlight reflected on the water. I looked at the night sky and then to the dish, to the surface, glassy and un-ruffled, and back again to the sky.

Nostradamus dropped his fingers into the water and, lacing them together, he scooped up some of the liquid. He continued muttering as he sprinkled water on his left shoulder and his right foot. Then he stretched his hands out to me and allowed the remaining drops to fall upon my head, and I heard him then distinctly say my name:

'Mélisande.'

He took the wand of rowan root in both hands and, grasping it tightly, he stirred the water in the bowl.

Three times to the left.

Three times to the right.

A thousand pinpricks of light burst across my vision.

Now I was unsure what was in front of me and what was in my mind. I heard the prophet's voice sound out again and then the mutter of a repeated phrase. Repeated and repeated and repeated until it became part of me, at one with the rhythm of my breathing, thudding in time with my heartbeat.

The slow pound of blood in my brain.

Darkness came down, and once again I was in the palace of Cherboucy.

High above the great hall I stood. In the pocket of the roof. Below me swung the vast chandelier. Tiered with candles, each individual flame giving out its own red glow, yet creating one vast blaze of light.

The outer edges of the hall were in darkness. The darkling shadows made by the light from the chandelier became the shape of the outstretched wings of an avenging angel.

The court was assembled. Two thrones. One for King Charles, the other slightly behind and to the side, for the queen regent, Catherine de' Medici, placed so that she could whisper advice in the ear of her son. I could hear whispering now, murmuring inside my head. Rustling louder, the black taffeta dress of the royal widow beating ever louder, like monstrous wings.

The courtiers pressed around, eager to see and hear what was happening. In a cleared space before the king stood Nostradamus. A scatter of gold coins at his feet.

There!

I saw it very clearly.

The pillar where Chantelle and I stood. And she was there, peering round. And I beside her, the light falling on our faces.

But no!

She steps back. My dearest, dearest sister, do not do this! I reach out my hand but I cannot prevent her. She moves away into the shade.

And Chantelle is lost to me. A sob escapes my lips. For now I know I will never see her again. She is gone for ever.

Then I see something else.

In the shadow.

A moan escapes my lips.

Nostradamus is gazing intently at my face.

The shadow moves.

It is the prophet. The second that he brushes against Chantelle, I feel the blood leave my head. Giddiness.

Nostradamus reaches out his hand to me.

'You see it?'

I tried to turn my head away.

He moved his own to face me.

'You see it.' And this time it was not a question.

I nodded. 'I saw it.'

The shadow that had encompassed my sister had reached to enfold another.

A gust of wind from an open door in the great hall caused Nostradamus to shiver. It made the chandelier sway. And the shadow moved across the hall and enveloped the prophet in its grasp.

The outspread wings of the Angel of Death had fallen upon Nostradamus.

Chapter Thirty-four

Had Nostradamus not supported me I would have fallen to the ground.

'Come,' he said. 'Sit here.'

He helped me to where a wooden bench stood against the chimney stack of the house. Then he poured some water onto my headscarf and brought it to me. My hands shook as I wiped my face.

'You already knew,' I said.

'Yes,' Nostradamus replied. 'Nine months ago when I was preparing this year's almanac there was a configuration for the month of June that would not resolve itself. To begin with I could not calculate its meaning. It was not connected to a crop failure, a tragic event, or a royal birth. As I could not resolve this conundrum I put it to one side and continued to work on my almanac of predictions for the last six months of this year. The usual happenings presented themselves and in addition a few of prophetic import. However, there was one significant difference.' Nostradamus sat down wearily beside me. 'In the past I have always seen myself in the visions I have of these present times. Yet, for the ones in the second half of this year, 1566, I *am not there.*'

He leaned against the stone of his house and closed his eyes. I studied his face. The long beard, the high brow and aquiline nose. The deep lines etched around his eyes. His eyes that had seen more fiendish sights and catastrophes than any one person should see.

'I believe that I will not be alive much longer on this earth.'

On an impulse I placed my hand on his.

'You've known since last year,' I said to him. 'How could you bear it?'

Nostradamus turned his head. His face, on a level with my own, bore a look of supreme sadness. 'It is not given to everyone to know the date of their death, although every year we pass that date as surely as we pass the date of our birth.'

This thought was a new concept to me and one I did not like.

'It's not something to fear too much,' he comforted me. 'Soon I will either know nothing or I will know all. For me, now, there is relief in contemplating that.'

'If you already knew of your own death then why did you ask me what I had seen in the great hall of Cherboucy Palace?' I asked.

'I suspected that my allotted time in this world was running out, but I wanted verification.' Nostradamus's voice was calm. The tone was tinged with regret but there was no fear in it.

'What made you think that *I* would be able to confirm it?' My thoughts were drawing to a conclusion that I wanted to avoid.

'I am still seeking insight into the pattern of your life course, Mélisande,' he replied. 'If you recall when you first spoke to me you said you too had seen the wings of the Angel of Death spread out over the great hall at Cherboucy.'

'No!' I whispered. I would not accept what he was trying to tell me, that what I had seen was a premonition. I did not want this gift, this curse. I did not want to be like Nostradamus, who had no time of his own to reflect and enjoy life, whose days were living nightmares of confused visions. 'I saw only the shadow cast by the chandelier! I don't have the ability to foresee the future!'

'Perhaps not.' He laid his hand on my shoulder. 'I cannot state whether you do have the ability to prophesy or not. Though if you have, know this, you cannot gainsay it by force of will.' He turned to me on the bench and said very seriously, 'I will tell you what I do know. You were sent here for a reason. And that reason was not only to tell me that which I already suspected, that I am soon to die. There is some other reason that our lines in life have met and merged. You have a purpose to fulfil and I am to guide you to do it.'

'My purpose is to rescue my father.' I broke down and began to sob. 'That is my only wish.'

'It may be that you can accomplish that,' Nostradamus replied. 'Nothing in my divinations indicate that you should not pursue that course, but there is yet another mission that you may undertake.'

'What is it?' I cried. 'Tell me then what I must do!'

'It is not clear to me,' he said wearily. 'I need more time to find out.'

As he got up from the bench we exchanged looks of anxiety. We both knew that time was the one thing he did not have.

Chapter Thirty-five

Despite his wife's protests, Nostradamus insisted on another consultation with me late one morning during the following week.

Giorgio's curiosity was piqued enough for him to enquire as to the reason I would be absent from my duties in assisting him. He stared at me for a moment when I brushed his question away.

'It is a trifling matter,' I said. 'I asked the prophet about the stars. When I did not understand his answer he said he would talk to me further about it.'

'It must be a difficult question indeed that you, Mélisande, require it to be explained twice,' Giorgio said as I hurried from the apothecary shop.

I went upstairs to the top floor and the inner room. There a space had been cleared. In the centre of this Nostradamus had positioned a tripod stool which he invited me to sit upon.

'This stool is similar to the one used by the oracle at Delphi,' he told me. 'As the hour of noon approaches

I will light a bowl of incense and put it at your feet.'

I sat where the prophet instructed me, under the depiction of the sun blazing across the ceiling, with flames of fire radiating from the closed circle. As I tipped my head back to look up, heat struck me, like a physical force upon my upturned face.

But that was impossible.

Hot though the day was, we were inside.

A finger of white light pierced my eyeballs. Crying out in pain, I bent my head and squeezed my eyelids closed tightly. My vision splintered into dazzling, spinning red stars. I held my hands over my face and then slowly opened my eyes again. My gaze came level with a mirror hanging on the opposite wall. I had not noticed it before. Larger than all the rest, its surface was not clear, the reflection muted.

'I see that you have found the mirror, Mélisande, without any guidance from me,' said Nostradamus in approval. 'I unearthed it many years ago in the ancient ruins around Salon. It has special properties which even I have not fully discovered. Usually I keep it covered, but today we will allow the merciless light of midday to fall upon it through you, and see what may be revealed to us.'

The ache in my eyes lessened and I peered at the looking glass.

I was a shadow only.

'We have tried scrying by water and by the light of the moon,' said Nostradamus. 'It is now the turn of the sun to burn out the truth.'

He tugged at a cord hanging by the window. There

must have been a hidden pulley, for the heat over my head increased, and I thought then that some aperture to the roof existed there that he was able to open and close as he wished.

Nostradamus stepped forward and placed a round, flat plate of burnished copper into my left hand. 'Hold it thus.' He showed me how to tilt the disc so that the light from above was caught there and directed towards my reflected image.

I recalled seeing myself in the mirror at Cherboucy and how it had shimmered as I looked into it.

The tenebrous surface of the mirror before me lightened.

'Look!' said Nostradamus. 'The veil is lifting!'

Within the gloom, an image of myself appeared. I stared at this Mélisande, at the contours of her face, her mouth, her eyes, her hair . . .

I reached up and pulled off my headscarf to let my hair fall free.

The very pulse of my life became muted.

The objects in the room where I sat seemed to recede. The passage of time became liquid, a constant flowing around me. I moved my head. My mirror image was slow to follow. Was it because of the profound lethargy I sensed overwhelming me?

Nostradamus was beside me. He held his wand of rowan root in his hand. He gestured with it to my reflection.

'You may speak aloud whatever comes into your mind.'

'She is some years older than I am,' I said, 'that Mélisande.'

'Which Mélisande?'

'The one there, in the mirror.'

I tried to lift my hand to point but felt such languor in my bones that I could not.

The Mélisande in the mirror looked back at me with great staring eyes. She had seen more than I had seen in my younger life. My breathing became faster.

Ah! This Mélisande sees horror, unspeakable horror.

Behind her, two figures in the shadows. One of them steps forward.

'Papa!' I whispered.

I rose from the stool.

'Do not go close.' Nostradamus's voice was sharp with warning.

'Speak!' he commanded my image that was not my image.

But this Mélisande did not speak.

She shook her head slowly and I found that I too was shaking mine.

The disc of burnished copper fell from my grasp.

Nostradamus went to stand at his desk.

'Does it reassure you to see your father there, in the future, when you have become a young woman?'

'It gives me hope,' I said. 'But what year was it and where was I?'

'I cannot tell you the date,' said Nostradamus, 'but I believe that you are in Paris. My dreams of a massacre there when the king himself may perish have haunted me for three years now, since the summer solstice of 1563. You will note that is *three* years ago. In each dream and divination I have had of this dreadful happening, it is the number three that is always constant. Three or a multiple of three.'

'Three is a magical number.' I repeated the words Catherine de' Medici had uttered in the king's bedchamber at Cherboucy.

Nostradamus inclined his head. 'You have walked in these dreams with me, Mélisande, and when we met at Cherboucy I was aware that your life and mine were fated to mingle. Now' – Nostradamus waved his hand at the paper on his desk – 'I begin your horoscope and every entry I make brings you closer to the prophecy. You were born on the fifteenth day of the first month in the year of 1553—'

'I was born in 1554,' I corrected him.

Nostradamus started. 'At Cherboucy I asked you how old you were and you replied that you were in your thirteenth year.'

'Like any young person, I wish to appear older than I am,' I explained. 'I am in my thirteenth year but I have only had twelve birthdays.'

'12,' Nostradamus muttered. 'Again a multiple of 3. You would have been nine then when my dreams began. Yet another multiple of 3.'

He took his pen and altered my year of birth on the horoscope and read it aloud. '*1554*.

'1554,' he repeated.

He bent over the chart and I came to stand beside him. 'Three to make fifteen in the circle of one.'

He raised his head and his eyes had become fixed. 'The planets falter in their courses but the numbers do not. Numbers cannot lie.

'The year you were born, therefore, was 1554. The sum of that year's numbers totals 15. The year my visions of the terrible slaughter began is 1563. The sum of that year's numbers also total 15.'

He made a simple calculation.

'The next configuration of the century to give the number 15 would be 1572.

'Six years from now, again a multiple of 3.

'1572.

'The numbers add up,' he whispered. 'For the first time in the many months that these visions have haunted me, the numbers add up.'

'What numbers?' I asked him.

He wrote out the numerals in his elegant script.

'Six years from now is 1572. 1572,' he said again. 'Not only does it total 15. If we read each numeral from right to left, subtracting as we do . . . See! See the result!'

'Take 2 from 7 leaves 5.

'5 from 5 leaves 0.

'0 from 1 leaves 1.

'Do you realize what this means, Mélisande?' Nostradamus pointed with trembling finger at the single number written on the page.

'One!'

'It is confirmed,' he intoned. 'There will be one who will be The One.'

* * *

I watched as the prophet worked on, calibrating the numbers.

He bent over his desk, pausing from time to time to pull out another manuscript or consult an ancient chart from its place on a shelf. I could see that he was weary. But now that he believed he might deduce an understanding, a strange burning energy throbbed within him, part disturbing, part fascinating.

Could Nostradamus be right? Was I destined to save the king – the person anointed by God over his subjects here on Earth to keep them safe and tend to their well being? Was I to be an instrument in protecting his holy personage?

I spoke my thoughts aloud. 'If what you say is true then I should go as soon as I can and warn the king.'

'You saw what happened when I tried to do this,' Nostradamus replied. 'And I'd already spoken to the queen regent, Catherine de' Medici, when she visited me here in Salon in 1564, the year following my first vision of this kind.'

'The queen regent would want to know that you have discovered more,' I said.

'Yet I hold back.' Nostradamus stared at me. 'A sense of dread compels me to wait, a foretaste of doom that says Catherine de' Medici should not know of this until after you have been given the chance to save the king's life. It will be revealed to me through the numbers when the time is right for you to act.'

'Why then did you go to Cherboucy to deliver your warning?' I asked him.

'Even though I had no specific information, I thought

that Catherine de' Medici and her son might pay heed to me. But although the queen regent listened, the king laughed and would not mind me. I became convinced the reason I was moved to journey from my home to Cherboucy was not, in fact, to speak my prophecy, but so that our life lines, yours and mine, Mélisande, should merge. As I am now convinced that the time to act will be in 1572, six years from now.'

'*Six years!*' I wailed. 'I will not wait so long to save my father. I wish you to write me a letter to take to the queen regent and the king to tell them that my father and I are innocent of any crime.'

'Would you desert the king in his need to go to your father?'

'Yes,' I cried out. 'Yes, I would!'

A shudder went through Nostradamus. He stepped back and raised both hands in the air.

'In 1572 a vile pestilence sweeps through Paris. The Moon falls in the house of Death, in trine with fiery Mars. The great King of France faces certain death. There he stands, defenceless, against the powers that threaten to overcome him. It is for the good of the people and for his subjects that he must be saved.'

'I cannot wait so long to see my father again.' I began to weep.

'Would you not wait so long to see him alive?'

'I don't understand,' I sobbed. 'What are you saying to me?'

'I am saying that I believe that you will both be together again, alive, in 1572.'

'But not before?'

Nostradamus shook his head.

I studied his face more closely. 'You saw more than I did in the mirror. What was it? What did you see?'

'I saw King Charles by a window in the Louvre in Paris. You were there, Mélisande.' Nostradamus paused and he smiled at me. 'I saw you, Mélisande, with your father by your side. Believe me, if you save the life of her son, the queen regent will thank you. She will ensure that you and your father are pardoned for any offence that you may have caused.'

I sniffed and began to wipe away my tears.

'But remember,' said Nostradamus. 'None of this takes place until the next year of fifteen, which is 1572.'

'I need more,' I said. 'There must be more, surely. How do I get to Paris? How do I meet up once again with my father?'

'The planets speak strongly,' Nostradamus declared. 'I will endeavour to discover the way that your fate is entwined with their energies. However, there is something I must tell you.'

He turned and placed his hands upon each of my shoulders.

'I believe that you are the one, Mélisande.' Nostradamus spoke solemnly. 'And I believe that there is a particular path that you might follow to do a great deed. But I must give you warning. The person who does this takes Death by the hand.'

Chapter Thirty-six

As the month of June progressed Nostradamus worked feverishly on his charts and divinations. The weather became oppressively hot. And with the heat came the Plague.

It began in the streets near where the canal from the north entered the city. These were the dwellings of the poorest people, those with barely enough to eat and certainly no spare money to buy medicine of any kind. The first fatalities were five children from the same family, all under the age of eight. As soon as he heard of it, Giorgio sent a box of expensive rose tablets to be distributed to the households in the afflicted area. It was a generous act, for when word got out that the Plague was in Salon we lost a lot of the income from our richer clients. No one who could avoid it would risk travelling into a town where it was known there were Plague victims. From the first weeks of June we had very few visitors of distinction or affluence, and even our ordinary customers came less often. People stayed indoors and the streets became quieter. But Giorgio and I worked day and night making the precious tablets that Nostradamus believed could stave off this most dreaded illness.

Berthe brought the news one day that the Lord Thierry had ordered the gates of the town closed.

'He means us all to die shut up in here while he stays safe at Valbonnes,' she complained as she washed the empty breakfast bowls in the kitchen sink.

'The Lord Thierry has written to Master Nostradamus,' Mistress Anne told her curtly, 'to say that he is taking up residence in the Château Emperi until this crisis is over. He will deal with it directly. You would do well to mind to your work, and not make false accusations against a respected nobleman.'

'It wasn't *me* saying these things, mistress,' Berthe replied. 'The Duke of Marcy was proclaiming it in the town square. He states that Lord Thierry is an agent of the Reformers and an enemy of the true Catholic Church. There is to be a procession today organized by the friars of the Cloise monastery, to seek atonement and beg God to spare the town.' She glanced at Mistress Anne. 'All devout worshippers are to come to their house doors and kneel and pray as the holy men pass by.'

I returned to the shop and relayed this message to Giorgio. 'The bishop means to sprinkle sacred water in the canal,' I told him.

'They should boil the water rather than bless it,' he observed wryly. 'I'd put more faith in the bats'-blood cure that the pedlars are selling in the market place just now.'

'Be quiet, Giorgio!' Mistress Anne had entered the shop

from the house so suddenly that we had no warning of her coming.

I had never heard her speak in this manner to Giorgio. It was clear that she was harassed and anxious. Even though Master Nostradamus had directed me to tell no one of his belief that he was soon to die, his wife must know that her husband's health was failing. As she had been wedded to him for so many years and borne him six children, she would also sense his gloomy mindset.

Giorgio bent his head. 'Madame,' he said.

'We must be extra careful,' Mistress Anne went on in an attempt to justify her brusqueness. 'With the Plague in the town the religious tension has become worse. Both sides say it is God's vengeance for the other side's heresies and misdeeds. Outbreaks of violence are increasing and you know these fanatics seek the slightest excuse to attack someone. The workshop where our almanacs are produced had the windows broken and the roof set on fire. The printer said the Duke of Marcy's henchman, Bertrand, told him that printing warnings of coming disasters caused them to happen.'

'That's always the way,' Giorgio answered her in a neutral tone. He did not appear to have taken offence at her rude manner. But with Giorgio it was never obvious what he was thinking. 'When fearful, people often strike out at those nearest to them. Even at those who would help them if they could.'

Two spots of colour appeared on Mistress Anne's cheeks as she absorbed the full meaning of Giorgio's words.

'You could help me now, Giorgio, if you would,' she

said stiffly. 'My husband, who is scarcely able to stand up by himself, went out yesterday evening to attend to the canal lock keeper at his house beside the Avignon Gate. When he returned he worked late preparing some remedies which he says he has left ready to be delivered.' She pointed to a small bottle and a package sitting on the workbench. 'Would you be good enough to take them there, please?'

Giorgio picked up the bottle quickly and left the shop, limping more than usual. I thought of how precarious were his living conditions here. With his broken body there was little else he could do to earn his keep.

'I will wait in the shop with you until Giorgio returns,' said Mistress Anne. 'As my husband is becoming increasingly infirm I should spend more time here, and acquaint myself with what goes on.' She wandered to the sinks and work tables. Then she tutted. 'In his haste Giorgio has gone without the poultice that is part of the remedy.'

'I'll take it,' I offered. 'I know the way to the Avignon Gate.'

She hesitated. 'I don't want to put you in any danger.'

'I won't be in danger. I trust Master Nostradamus and he says he believes that the Plague is not spread through the air but by uncleanliness and vermin.'

'The lock keeper is a special friend of my husband,' said Mistress Anne. 'He came here last night for help because his child was ill and no doctor would go near his end of the town for fear of Plague. Master Nostradamus says his child does not have Plague, only a lung condition.'

I lifted the parcel. 'If I run I'll catch up with Giorgio before he has walked very far.'

'If you do get near to the canal you must cover your mouth and nose with your apron,' she called after me.

I only got to the next street before my progress was blocked by two men in the livery of the Duke of Marcy.

'This street is closed for the Penitents' Procession,' one of them told me.

'And you should be at home, waiting for it to pass,' the other said menacingly. 'Those are the duke's orders.'

The first soldier looked at me with suspicion. 'Are you a Huguenot?'

'I hardly think so,' I said, pointing at my bright blue headscarf.

I backed away quickly and went along a lane and across an open square. But when I emerged at the other side my way was cut off again. This time I saw the duke's men before they saw me and I dodged down another lane. I began to track back, hoping that I could loop round behind the procession. Now I could hear the rhythmic beating of side drums and the harsh racket of wooden clappers, and a vision of that other procession I'd seen as a child in Spain jumped into my mind. There was sickness in my throat. I turned and hurried along an alleyway, coming out the other end directly into the path of the procession.

Advancing towards me was a terrifying figure dressed all in black. He wore a monk's habit and a high conical hood which concealed most of his face, apart from the cut-out eye sockets. His body was draped in chains which trailed onto the ground and he dragged these along, painfully putting one foot before the other, while moaning and crying out to Heaven for forgiveness. Behind him, in lines of two, were a dozen barefoot men wearing black breeches, stripped naked to the waist. They carried small whips made of knotted cords and beat their bare backs with these.

'Get out of the way!' a woman standing watching at the roadside advised me.

I backed against the wall. The street was packed. Old people on balconies and at windows, men and women kneeling in their doorways, children being held up to witness the spectacle and be blessed by the priests.

As they came level with me I saw the men's backs. They were already scarred and bleeding from their mortification. The knots on their whips were flecked with their own blood. The monks who followed also wore black and had the cowls of their habits drawn close about their faces. Then came another group, less soberly dressed, with blue and white sashes in the colours of the Virgin. They carried her image in a large statue borne up on a wide wooden platform bedecked with ribbons and flowers. They prayed and sang and chanted litanies as they coiled past.

I went into a side street and managed to get further behind the procession where it was quieter. I stood while the remainder of the penitents walked past until I saw a break in the ranks. Then I took my chance and skipped across the street through the gap.

'You, girl!' A hand grabbed my arm. I recognized Bertrand, the Duke of Marcy's henchman. 'Why did you do such a sacrilegious thing?'

'I don't understand,' I stammered.

'You should kneel as the procession passes. Not show disrespect by running across in front of the penitents.'

'I'm carrying medicine for a sick child,' I explained.

'What is it?' He snatched the package from my hands. 'Who made this medicine?'

'It's a poultice from Master Nostradamus—' I began.

'Aha!' he said in triumph. 'A magical preparation from the sorcerer himself!'

'It is not,' I protested. 'The child is sick and needs help. Let me go through.'

'If the child is sick then it needs God's grace. As do you.' He pushed me down roughly. 'You should be kneeling, as everyone was told to do by the Duke of Marcy.'

I tried to pull myself free from him and I was beginning to succeed. His grip was loosening for he was not strong, this Bertrand, and I was equally as tall as him. 'You witch,' he spat at me as we struggled. 'The duke himself is at the other end of the street. He can deal with you himself,' and he bawled out Marcy's name.

'Help me,' I called out in turn to a woman standing in her doorway. She responded by going inside and closing her door.

Now I was truly frightened, for the street had emptied as the tail end of the procession went by. I would be here alone, an unprotected girl, with this man and the Duke of Marcy, who had a reputation for arresting people who were never seen again.

I broke free and ran up the alley with Bertrand screeching curses behind me. But there was no way out at the top,

241

for it led to a street where I could see some more of the duke's men stationed. So I took a left fork down another lane. I could hear the thud of boots behind me. Now I was sweating and desperate, and my breath was coming in terrified gulps. But there was the side door of a church. It was open. I ran inside.

Bertrand was close behind me and almost immediately after him, his master, the Duke of Marcy.

'Sanctuary,' I gasped. I ran to the front and climbed the steps of the altar. 'I claim the sanctuary of a holy place.' I turned to face them. 'You cannot touch me here.'

Bertrand hesitated, but the duke did not. While pretending to be a devout Catholic he did not respect the life that God gave to His creation. He seized my shoulders and, hustling me from the steps, he pressed me against a pillar. With the unyielding stone at my back I felt the force of him against me.

'Let me go,' I pleaded. 'I've done nothing wrong.'

'I'll judge whether that is true or not.' He grinned. 'But first I'll have to question you.' He put his hand on my headscarf and pulled it down from my head. 'That's better. Now we can see what you look like.' He studied my face.

My heart was rattling so loudly inside my chest I thought he might hear it.

'Why hide such beauty away?' he said. 'Most girls would want to display—'

His voiced choked in his throat as an arm came round his neck and pulled him off me.

It was an elderly priest who had thrust Bertrand aside and come to aid me. His outrage had given him strength.

'How dare you desecrate a church with your violence!' he thundered.

'Get off me, you black crow!' the duke yelled in anger at being thwarted. He swivelled round and pushed the priest in the chest with both hands.

'You will respect the house of God and that girl who has come here for sanctuary,' the priest commanded him.

'That girl has connections with those who practise the dark arts,' the duke replied in fury. 'And I will deal with her as I see fit.'

'You are not the law,' the priest told him. 'And if you do not leave this church forthwith I will report you to the man who is the law, Lord Thierry.'

At the mention of the name of his hated enemy the duke went into a rage. He drew his sword and hacked at the priest with a long sloping swing aimed at his shoulder. The priest ducked his head away. With a sucking crunch the sword bit deep into the side of his neck. The priest gave a great groan of agony as a huge spurt of blood gushed out of him.

'You have killed him!' Bertrand shouted in dismay.

I screamed. The priest fell hard onto the tiles of the nave.

The duke stepped backwards. His bloodied sword clattered from his hand.

Bertrand rushed forward and knelt down. The priest was breathing but his face was the face of a dead man. 'Thierry will have you hanged for this!' Bertrand cried out.

The duke looked around wildly. 'We can dump the

243

body and conceal this somehow.'

'There is too much blood,' said Bertrand. He was shaking and trembling at the same time. 'There's blood on the carpet and the altar cloths.'

And on my hands too, I saw. Some drops of blood had spattered onto me. I held them out in front of me as far away from my body as I could.

'What to do?' the duke was shouting at Bertrand. 'What to do? Think of something.' He went forward and kicked his henchman viciously. 'It's what I keep you for, you dog. Think what to do.'

'I don't know!' Bertrand shouted back at him. 'Murder before the altar of God is sacrilege. Even the bishop, who favours you, will not support you on this.'

'Then if we cannot conceal this act we must blame someone else.' Marcy began to recover himself. 'We'll say we saw a Huguenot running from the church.' He strode to the altar and knocked over the candlesticks. 'Let's smash some things. Then when the priest's body is discovered every loyal Catholic will believe it was the work of heretics. Apart from us there's no one to tell what really happened here.'

In the long seconds it took them to remember me, I gathered my skirts and ran. Down the aisle and out of the door. Back through the lanes and alleyways I raced. Terror of being murdered like the priest made me run as I had never run before. Never once did I look behind me, hoping that their armour would slow them, and I being more nimble would reach the shop before they caught me.

Giorgio was already returned ahead of me. 'What's

wrong?' He lifted his head, startled, as I banged the shop door behind me. 'You act as though a demon was chasing you.'

I ran behind the counter without answering him, making for the door that led to the house. With surprising swiftness Giorgio moved to intercept me.

'Who has harmed you?'

I shook my head and tried to push him aside.

'No one,' I said. 'No one.'

'There's blood on your hands.' A note of real fear and concern was in his voice.

Outside a loud clanging noise rent the air. We both stopped to listen.

The alarum bell of the town was ringing.

Chapter Thirty-seven

'What has happened?' Giorgio held my wrists with an unyielding grip. 'If I'm to help you, then you must tell me.'

I gabbled out my story of the Duke of Marcy and the murder of the priest.

'*Jesu.*' Giorgio's eyes stretched wide. 'This is a disaster.'

'I didn't know that crossing in front of the procession would anger them so much,' I sobbed.

'That's not the real reason they picked on you. You're more attractive than you know, child, despite wearing frumpy clothes and keeping your head and half your face covered up.'

Giorgio released my wrists and cocked his ear towards the house. Then he pressed his eye to the spy hole. 'Here comes Mistress Anne.' He gave me a push towards the sinks. 'Fix your kerchief on your head and wash your hands. Say nothing of this until I think what's best to do.'

I was bent over the sink scrubbing my fingers when Mistress Anne whirled into the room.

'Don't you hear the alarum bell, Giorgio? We should put the shutters up.'

'I hear it, mistress.' Giorgio opened a drawer and took out a bunch of keys.

'Lisette' – Mistress Anne caught sight of me – 'assist Giorgio. The sooner the windows are boarded the better. There must be something serious gone wrong if they are ringing the bell.'

'I do not want to go into the street,' I whispered to Giorgio when she had left.

'There's no need for you to help me,' he said. 'But stay in the shop. We need to talk after I have done this.'

I watched from a window as he shuffled outside and began to fold over each shutter, slide its metal rod between the spars, and lock it in place. He had just reached the last one when a group of young men came down the street.

One of them called out loudly, 'Heyo! It's Giorgio!' They began to caper about behind him, imitating his hunched posture and his limping walk.

He ignored them but they came closer and began to nudge and poke at him.

'He's Italian, don't you know,' said another one. 'Like the queen regent, Catherine de' Medici, the one who is supposed to be Catholic but sides with the Huguenots, the sly Italian maggot!' This man grabbed Giorgio by the ears and spun him round so that he staggered and fell to the ground.

'He's like a beetle on its back!' Giorgio's tormentor crowed.

'And like a beetle, should be crushed.' The first man came forward and lifted his heavy-booted foot to bring it down on Giorgio's face.

I was outside in the street before I knew what I was doing. They were so intent on their cruel deed they neither saw nor heard me and so I was able to slip between them. I seized the metal rod of the window shutter where it had fallen onto the ground and I swung it before me in an arc.

'Stand away!' I cried. 'Stand away, and depart from here!'

They scattered, but as soon as they saw that I was a girl they began to laugh.

'A firebrand!' Giorgio's chief tormentor cried. 'Now this is better amusement for us than a crippled old man!'

Giorgio got to his knees. 'Go into the shop,' he implored me.

But it was impossible for me to do that.

The men moved into a half-circle, forcing Giorgio and me to back ourselves against the window. They began to advance towards us, watching for a chance to rush in. One of them jumped near in a feinting move and I jabbed the rod at him. It struck him in the stomach and he doubled up, winded. But immediately one of his companions grasped the end of the rod. And now I was grappling with a man much stronger than myself and the rest of them came round us, laughing at the sport. I knew this man was playing with me, that he could wrest my weapon from me in an instant. I could see the broken teeth in his mouth as he grinned, and said, 'Little lady, I think I prefer to be closer when we tussle like this.'

And he pulled the rod and me to him while his companions caught hold of Giorgio, who had tried to help me.

'Beware the Sixth Extinction! Leave off thy abominable deeds!'

A voice boomed out above our heads.

We all looked up. High above us Nostradamus stood on the roof platform of his house.

'It's the necromancer,' one of the men said in a fearful tone.

'Leave off thy abominable deeds!' Nostradamus repeated. He raised his hands high above his head and the sleeves of his coat slid down and hung like wings on either side of his body. 'Fire will pour down upon your head!' he roared. 'The seas will rise and the earth will flood. The sun will burn with a thousand fires! By man's own hand will this be done!'

The gang of men drew away from us. Even the boldest one let go his hold on the metal shutter rod.

'A thousand suns will scorch the earth! The green land will dry like the barren desert!'

Into the heat of the June noonday spiralled a thin yellow mist. It came from the paving stones at our feet, insinuated itself around our legs, then came creeping higher, causing us to cough and choke.

'Do you see that?' one of the men asked in a quaking voice.

But his friends did not answer. They were already fleeing along the street.

Giorgio too looked shaken. And I don't believe it was

the cruelty of the men that affected his composure. It was what Nostradamus had said that struck his soul, as it had mine. No doubt the ruffian youths thought that the prophet was threatening them. But what we had witnessed was not empty blustering. The words of Nostradamus were a prophecy of happenings to come:

Fire will pour down upon your head.
The seas will rise and the earth will flood.
The sun will burn with a thousand fires!
By man's own hand will this be done!

What was the meaning of his mysterious warning for the world to beware the Sixth Extinction?

I looked up again but Nostradamus had gone.

The trailing mist had already dispersed as if it had never been. But words do not disappear. They sear the mind like a comet coursing across the night sky.

Chapter Thirty-eight

As soon as we re-entered the shop Giorgio locked the door from the inside.

Then he turned and said, 'I thank you for risking your own safety to come and defend me. Giorgio will not forget that.'

'What am I going to do, Giorgio?' I asked him.

'The first thing to be done is to make another poultice to replace the one stolen from you,' Giorgio replied. He went over to his work tables and began to do just that.

I followed him. 'I think I should talk to Master Nostradamus and his wife and tell them what happened to me today.'

'No!' Giorgio turned to face me. 'It will only add to the load they bear.' He hesitated. 'You do know that Master Nostradamus is gravely ill.'

'Yes,' I said. I sat down on a stool, overcome by the hopelessness of my situation. 'But at least I should give them warning to expect trouble. The Duke of Marcy and his henchman, Bertrand, were close behind me and they might have seen me enter this street. They know I carried medicine prepared by Nostradamus. If they find out that I live here they will come and kill me.'

'Listen,' said Giorgio. 'The alarum bell is still sounding. The law of the town states that all citizens are obliged to go indoors while the bell is tolling, and after it stops no one must bear arms in a public place until Lord Thierry has posted written permission. Those ruffians who attacked me outside would not care if they spent a night in prison, but Marcy would not risk being humiliated by Lord Thierry in that way. You are safe here for a little while.'

'But—'

He put his hand on my head.

'Be calm,' he said. 'Now I am going to take this poultice to the lock keeper's sick child.'

'But you will be arrested if you go into the town.'

'Doctors attending to the sick are exempt from the rule,' said Giorgio. 'I want you to wait here until I return. Will you do that for me?'

I bent my head. 'Yes,' I said, for I did not know what else to do.

But after Giorgio left I thought more of my predicament. The Duke of Marcy had to get rid of the only witness to his terrible deed. He, or more likely his henchman, Bertrand, would be lurking somewhere nearby keeping watch to make sure I did not escape.

Escape.

I must escape.

If I left the house it would mean less trouble for Master Nostradamus and Mistress Anne. Nostradamus was ill and becoming more ill as he searched in vain for the key to his premonition that I had some great role to play in the history of France. He'd said I had a purpose but I did not know what it might be, and neither did he. Despite poring over his charts and casting my horoscope several times, nothing was revealed to him. Day by day he became more frail. Seeking my destiny was hastening his end.

If I went away he would be forced to give up. Nostradamus would believe I had deserted my purpose. Once he knew that I had gone there would be no need for him to pursue the knowledge that eluded him.

And I had no choice but to go. I could not seek justice from Lord Thierry. He was such a meticulous man that if he heard my case he would most certainly find out my true identity. Then I would be sent under escort to Paris and Nostradamus would be charged with harbouring a fugitive from the king's justice. By remaining here I would bring disaster on them. A feeling of utter despair swept over me. Due to my impetuous behaviour my father was in prison and a good priest who'd tried to protect me lay dead. It was better that I left now before I upset the lives of yet more people who had helped me.

I opened the door leading into the house. The lower floor was empty. I could creep through the kitchen and out of the back door. I thought of myself on the street, a girl alone. When I'd been dressed as a boy I'd felt much safer, and if I used that disguise again perhaps I could elude Marcy and his men. I remembered where Mistress Anne had put my travelling cloak and the rest of my minstrel's garb. I crept up the stairs to the first landing and listened.

Outside the mournful tolling of the alarum continued. Inside the family room I could hear the children talking. Since the Plague outbreak they had all been kept at home. Now the younger ones were excited by the sound of the alarum bell and the older girl was chiding them to keep away from the windows.

I tapped on Mistress Anne's bedroom door. There was no reply. Either she was resting or she was upstairs with her husband. The door creaked as I opened it. The bedroom was empty.

In the corner was the chest wherein lay the clothes that Melchior had given me. I padded across the room and opened the lid. Despite the serious danger I was in I felt my spirits lift. There was my minstrel's garb and my russet travelling cloak. I stretched out my hand to touch it.

Suddenly there came a battering on the front door.

I dropped the lid in fright. The battering sounded again.

'Open up! Open up!'

I ran to the window and looked out. There were men in the street. Armed men. I heard Mistress Anne calling out, 'I am coming!' Her hurried footsteps went past her bedroom door and down the stairs. I came out of her bedroom and went to the turn in the stairs where I could see Mistress Anne opening the front door.

I cowered on the stairs. There was no way past for me, I was caught by the duke's men! But then I saw that these soldiers did not wear the livery of the Duke of Marcy. The colours on their surcoats were black and red.

'There has been an incident in the town,' I heard one of

the soldiers tell Mistress Anne. 'The Lord Thierry has sent me to ensure that Master Nostradamus, his family and servants are all safe at home.'

'We are,' she replied. 'Please send word to Valbonnes to thank the Lord Thierry for his concern for our welfare.'

'Lord Thierry has arrived in the castle,' the soldier replied. 'He intends to stay there until this crisis is over. We are to remain to guard your doors so that no harm will come to you,' the sergeant went on. 'You are to lock and bolt this door from the inside and also any other entrance to your property. The Lord Thierry's instructions are that no one enters or leaves the house until he can come and speak with Master Nostradamus himself.'

Chapter Thirty-nine

I heard Mistress Anne closing the front door and go towards the kitchen.

I took my chance to run downstairs and into the shop. I squealed in fright as Giorgio appeared from behind the door. 'Where did you go?' he said. 'You didn't think to try to run away, did you?'

'Yes – no. Yes.'

Giorgio gave me a little shake. 'Because the Duke of Marcy is not visible does not mean he isn't out there awaiting his chance to pounce. I told you to remain here and you said you would.'

'I know I did,' I replied miserably, 'but after you left I thought that if I went away it would mean less trouble for all the people here who have helped me so much.'

'Much good it would do us if you were found in the canal with your throat cut.' He gave a dry laugh. 'Even Nostradamus has no cure for that condition.'

I put my hands to my neck in fright as I thought of the

fate of the priest now lying in a pool of his own blood on the floor of the church.

'And anyway,' Giorgio went on, 'there is nowhere for you to go. The town is closed down. The gates are shut and will remain that way until the Lord Thierry decides they may be opened again.'

'He has sent soldiers to be stationed outside this house,' I told him. 'One of them said to Mistress Anne that they have to wait there until such time as Lord Thierry himself arrives to speak with Master Nostradamus.'

Giorgio went and peered through a slit in the shutter. 'Ah,' I heard him murmur, 'that is what he decided to do.' Then he said more loudly, 'Yes, I see them there in the street. He must already be in the château; his banner is flying from the tower.'

I joined Giorgio at the window and looked to where he was pointing. Lord Thierry's black and red standard fluttered on the highest point of the battlements. The bulk of the Château Emperi loomed over the town. The flag of their overlord would be visible to all citizens. This tangible evidence of his presence might alone be enough to quell any thoughts of riot or disorder. His subjects would know that he had them under his watch. A tremor went through my body. I felt that the eye of this vigilant man was upon me.

'Well then' – Giorgio turned from the window – 'we can be assured that you are definitely safe.' He glared at me. 'As long as you remain within the house.'

'I will,' I said meekly.

'And when Lord Thierry comes to the house you will

ask for an audience with him to tell him of the murder of the priest.'

'I cannot!' I gasped.

'Why not?' Giorgio looked at me searchingly. 'Only by placing the matter in his hands will you be rid of the responsibility.'

I did not speak.

Giorgio continued to stare at me. How could he know my dilemma? If I spoke to the Lord Thierry my true identity would almost certainly be discovered. I couldn't take that risk. Better to wait until I could change into my male clothes and leave quietly.

'I do not understand you, Miss . . . Lisette.'

I glanced up as Giorgio hesitated over my name. 'Very well then,' he went on, 'I will say nothing. You must decide yourself if you will speak up about what you saw happen.'

He went to his workbench and began to stack up the crucibles he used for melting metal. 'When I was out delivering the child's medicine I did hear something that might interest you. You recall the mist that appeared in the street and startled both of us?'

I nodded.

'It appears that Lord Thierry ordered a quantity of quicklime and ammonia salts to be poured into the underground sewers. He saw this done in the eastern countries where he travelled. It's used as a means to help curb outbreaks of disease. His soldiers are now occupied in fishing hundreds of dead rats out of the canal. So, you see, once again a strange phenomenon can be explained. There is a sewer running under the street outside the shop and obviously the fumes from the ammonia rose up from below our feet.'

'And appeared at exactly the same time as Master Nostradamus was moved to utter his prophecy?' I said.

'Quite.' Giorgio busied himself with his work. 'For us, a fortunate coincidence. Now, let us continue making such things as we can to combat this affliction on man.'

But neither of us could settle to any real work that afternoon.

In the evening the soldiers outside changed watch and, despite the sultry weather, they brought a number of pitch torches with them. They set these out along the street, down the lane beside the shop, and round the garden walls.

'There are so many of them and they are so heavily armed,' Mistress Anne said nervously as we ate supper that evening. 'It seems more than an ordinary escort.'

'Master Nostradamus is more than an ordinary man,' Giorgio said soothingly. 'Lord Thierry will be ensuring that you are all well protected.'

As night drew on we all got set to retire. Giorgio made himself a pallet bed upon the floor of the shop. The children went to their rooms and Mistress Anne to her own bedroom. I drew aside the curtain of the alcove in the family room where my own bed was laid out, but I did not get undressed to sleep. Instead I took out the almanac Nostradamus had written with his predictions for this year, 1566.

The sun blushed crimson in the western sky. I'd little need of the candle as I held the page close to the window.

Then I raised my head and looked at the glorious sunset, the long slanting rays that brought heat and light and nurtured life. What if Nostradamus's words of this morning came true? Could this enormous ball of fire somehow become malignant? But how could that happen by man's hand? How could we change circumstance to make the sun scorch our green earth? I flicked the pages of the almanac. The month of June, 1566. I had been so occupied these last days I'd hardly realized that the last day of June had just passed. What special notations had Nostradamus made to help us through these difficult times?

None that I could see.

June the thirtieth.

The page fluttered and turned.

July the first.

Today's date.

I read the entry.

A Strange Transmigration.

Transmigration. Of what? A human soul?

Despite the stuffy heat I felt cold. I blinked and read the words again.

A Strange Transmigration.

A shadow fell across the page.

I looked up.

Master Nostradamus stood there. He held out his hand and spoke to me.

'It is time.'

Chapter Forty

As if in an enchantment, I followed Nostradamus up the spiral staircase to the top rooms.

Every candle was lit, every lamp shone forth as though to stave off the inevitable. The mirrors and coloured glass increased the brightness tenfold and more, causing reflection upon reflection to cascade around the room.

'Come to the inner room,' the prophet instructed me.

Once there he walked to the window and looked out. The red sunset poured into the room, but as the light left the sky the weather changed abruptly. The atmosphere became heavy, the air humid and charged with a strange force. Jagged forks of lightning scarred the horizon on the edge of the town, and as we watched, the storm seemed to lull, then gather more force. Thunder rolled in with a great crashing crescendo and the lightning flickered ever nearer.

'You will quit this house tonight, Mélisande, and go to a place of safety. There you will wait until the time comes when you must act.'

Before I could question him on this Nostradamus pointed to his desk and said, 'See what is here.'

On Nostradamus's desk lay three scrolls.

Nostradamus spoke to me slowly and carefully. 'Three papers I now give to you, Mélisande.' He lifted one of the scrolls and held it up. 'This is the first one, though in truth it is the last. My own last prophecy. It concerns the days long after you and I are gone from this earth, when humankind must heed the warning I have written therein or suffer the consequences brought about by their own folly. As my own end approaches, the time of the destruction of man presses in upon me.'

'Man does not completely quit this earth?' I said in anxiety. 'The Lord must come again before that happens.'

'We squander the bounty that was gifted to us.' Nostradamus spoke with the utmost fatigue. 'The blessings that were bestowed, the harvest of the seas and the soil, all freely given for us to use, we have devoured without thought. The mountains and the rivers are there that we may enjoy them, and the beasts of field and forest, the birds of the air. Yet we do not husband them nor share our fortune well amongst ourselves.'

An image of court life came to me. Nobles weighed down with gem-encrusted clothes while peasants stood behind the royal hunt looking for a small amount of food to ward off starvation. As Nostradamus spoke I fancied I could see it all before me. Visions of what had passed, what is, and what was to come, unspooled before my eyes. Bizarre sights I saw, and sounds I'd never heard before. Unimaginable noises, the clamour of many voices filled the room, the heaving of massive machinery, marching men, loud reports as if of mighty cannon. I saw fires rage without ceasing, thick clouds mushroom amid a profusion of winged monsters in the sky; carriages of metal soared higher than eagles and plunged down into the depths of the seas.

I squeezed my eyes shut and put my hands over my ears.

'Ah, Mélisande,' Nostradamus sighed as he watched me, 'I see you have enough foresight that you too are able to share my vision of the Sixth Extinction and the end of days.' He made such an exhausted heave of his shoulders that I thought he would sink down to the floor. 'There is nothing I can do. Nor you either.' He handed me the manuscript. 'But I charge you with finding a safe place to keep my last prophecy until the time comes for it to be revealed. We can only hope that those who come after us are alert and listen to the warning therein.'

As I took the scroll from him I looked into the eyes of the prophet. I realized that death was encroaching and these would be his final words to me, and at once my mind became clear and my thoughts focused.

Nostradamus regarded me seriously. 'That is the simplest of your tasks, Mélisande. The other task is more difficult and to accomplish it you will need this pass I have prepared for you. My status is such that it should assist in your freedom of movement.' He gave me the second scroll, which was stamped with his seal and stated that the bearer was acting on instructions of the famed Doctor Nostradamus, personal friend of Catherine de' Medici. It requested that the person carrying this pass be allowed free passage wherever they chose to go.

'As for this prophecy . . .' He lifted up the last piece of paper. It was blank. 'This is the one that concerns your destiny, Mélisande.'

'There is nothing written there,' I said.

'I had hoped that I would have more to add than the lines I do know. But now there is no time left to me. So I will write what I can.' And saying this, Nostradamus took up his pen and wrote two verses upon the paper.

'In the space of six years my prophecy of the slaughter in Paris will come to pass,' he told me. 'During that time you must tell no one of the existence of these papers.'

'But surely we should let the queen regent know that her son's life is in danger, then she can prevent this awful deed from taking place?'

'Know this, Mélisande: you cannot alter the course of this most vile massacre, but you may help the king who will lift France out of the mire in which she wallows and lead her to greatness and prosperity. And in all of this one thing is clear to me; six years must pass before these events take place, as Leo, the sign of princes, is rising. Therefore you must be patient, and wait until the time is favourable to act, yet not be distracted from that which has to be done.'

'Is there no more that you can tell me?' I asked him.

'In many visions I have seen you grow taller, fuller. You are as a boy again, a minstrel, and have found favour with a royal house.'

'It must be with the French court,' I said, 'if, in some way, I am to save the king.'

'That part is obscured and unclear to me. What I do

know is that now approaches the hour of my passing.'

I looked at the paper he held in his hand and read the words written there. The prophecy I had first heard Nostradamus proclaim in the great hall of Cherboucy Palace.

Thus the first four lines read:

With fire and heartless hangings
The treachery of royal line holds sway
Deeds done by stealth will come to light and all but one
*   consumed*
Safe from the sword, saved only by the word.

And to this, Nostradamus had added another quatrain:

This is your destiny, Mélisande.
You are the one who,
In the way known to you, can save
The king who must be saved.

Nostradamus handed me this last scroll and I placed it with the other two in the pocket of my apron.

'Mélisande' – he spoke gravely – 'I appoint you most solemnly the custodian of these papers.'

Then, as if completely exhausted by his efforts, he staggered to his day bed and fell upon it.

'That is all?' I cried out.

'That is all,' he replied. Then he said his last words to me. 'I have written everything I know.'

Chapter Forty-one

I went down the stairs, my eyes filling with tears.

Mistress Anne was standing by her bedroom door. 'My husband bade me wait here until he spoke with you. Has he told you all that you need to know?'

'Not all of it, but as much as he was able to. The remainder I will have to discover for myself.'

'He is dying?' she asked me, tears beginning to spill from her own eyes.

'Yes,' I replied sadly. 'His end is very near.'

As she made to move past me, I spoke. 'I will say good-bye and thank you, for I may not be here in the morning.'

'I know that there was a purpose in you being here, although I do not understand what it was.' She kissed my cheek. 'I am sorry to bid you farewell and' – she started to sob – 'I am heartbroken to lose so good a husband.'

She went to the door of the family room and called her children to her. Clinging to each other, they mounted the stairs to the top floor. I went into Mistress Anne's bedroom and, more boldly now, opened the lid of the chest and took out my boy's clothes. In some way I must escape this house. I would invent a story for the guards and show them the pass signed by Nostradamus. The strange thunder and lightning flashes in the sky might serve to spook them enough that they would let me through. If they did not then there was nothing I could do. If they did, I would do the same at the city gate. After that I did not know where I might travel – perhaps try to reach my father's house on the Isle of Bressay? Although apprehensive, I was assured of my purpose. I knew now that I had a sacred mission to protect King Charles.

I gathered up my clothes and went into the family room to my bed alcove. I took my travelling cloak and unpicked the stitches from the end of the hem. Keeping aside the pass Nostradamus had given me, I rolled the other two papers very tightly and slipped them inside. I wrapped up my boy's clothes inside my travelling cloak. I would go to the outside privy to change my clothes. I turned towards the door.

Lord Thierry stood across the entrance.

'Are you leaving?' he enquired politely.

'Master Nostradamus has given me a pass to do so.' I said this with as much assurance as I could.

Lord Thierry held out his hand. He read the pass and gave it back to me.

I watched him warily. Had he seen me conceal the other papers in the hem of my cloak? Would he seize me and take them from me? But this was not the way this man worked.

'I feel that I should inform you that my law governs this

town so your pass is of no value here,' said Lord Thierry.

'Nevertheless, I must go.'

He pointed to a stool standing beside the table that occupied the middle of the room. 'Sit down!' he commanded me.

With trembling legs I walked to the stool and sat down.

He came and sat on the other side of the table. The moon was up but the room was gloomy. He made a gesture of irritation and brought the candle closer.

'There has been an incident in the town. This morning a priest was murdered in his church. Do you have any information about that?'

'What makes you think I would know anything?'

'It is impudent of you to answer my question with one of your own,' he said tersely.

I bent my head.

'A girl of your description was seen running from the church, and this' – he placed a small packet on the table in front of him – 'was found beside the body of the priest.'

It was the poultice prepared by Nostradamus for the sick child.

'I know that you can read so you will be able to see the name of the pharmacy attached to this house and the name of the child for whom it was intended is writ plainly upon it.'

I said nothing.

'Do you wish me to question Mistress Anne or the Doctor Giorgio and ask them if you were sent into town this morning to deliver this?'

Still I did not reply.

'Have you nothing to say?' he asked impatiently.

I shook my head.

'Know this then. A young man, a Huguenot, was found in the vicinity. He was arrested by the Duke of Marcy. According to the duke, the Huguenot was carrying the contents of the church poor box and an altar cloth. The duke intends to have this man hanged at dawn.' He paused. 'If you know anything of this matter, now is your time to speak, else this man's death is on your conscience.'

I kept my head down. I could not say anything, else all my history would come out and I would be prevented from undertaking my mission. But was my purpose so important that this young Huguenot had to die for it?

'Place your hands on the table,' Lord Thierry said suddenly.

What was he up to? I brought my hands up and put them on the table.

'Stretch them out where I might see them,' he ordered.

Reluctantly I stretched out my hands towards him.

He moved the candle closer. His mouth twisted in a grim smile. 'You have washed them well. But see, there upon the cuff of your dress, there is a spot of blood!'

I jerked my wrist away.

Our eyes met. He dropped the candle and raised his hands to his face as if scorched by a flame. I reached out and righted the candle as he jumped to his feet and began to pace around the room.

I examined my dress cuffs. There was no spot of blood. He had tricked me. By acting in a guilty fashion I had proved to him that I had been in the church with the murdered priest.

'You must tell me what happened.' He said this strictly, but his voice shook.

'I cannot.'

He continued his pacing of the room, then he said, 'I sense that you are very frightened, of something, or someone, and that prevents you from confiding in me. Let me ask you a series of questions. But before I do I will tell you what I will *not* ask you. I will not ask who you are or where you come from or where you intend to go. I will only ask what relates directly to this dishonourable murder. Agreed?'

I gave my head a quick nod.

Lord Thierry sat down opposite me. 'Were you in the town today?'

'Yes,' I whispered.

'Were you in the church?'

'Yes.'

'Did you see the priest murdered?'

'Yes.'

Understanding seemed to come upon him and he asked me, 'Was the priest trying to protect you when he was killed?'

I nodded and slow tears edged from my eyes.

'Ah,' Lord Thierry breathed. 'Now I begin to see. Did you see the person who murdered the priest?'

'I did.'

'Name the man.'

'The Duke of Marcy.'

Lord Thierry swore and struck his fist upon the table.

'I had the poultice to deliver most urgently for the sick child and I crossed the Penitents' Procession.' Now that my silence was broken I wanted the story out as fast as I could tell it. 'The duke's henchman, Bertrand, saw me and tried to take me away for questioning as a heretic. He called for the duke and I ran into the church for sanctuary. They would not respect the holy place and began to assault me. The priest came to help me. I do not think the duke meant to kill the priest. He meant to strike him to drive him away, but . . .'

'Yes, yes, but it is murder nonetheless and sacrilege in a holy place. This is why the duke wants the Huguenot hung quickly. Then the affair is settled and done with.' Lord Thierry paused. 'Except for one annoying detail. There remains a witness to dispose of.' He regarded me seriously. 'You are in the gravest of danger.'

'I know,' I replied. 'That is why you should allow me to leave.'

He laughed harshly. 'If you left on your own you would not reach the next street before being cut down.' He cocked an eyebrow at my bundle of clothes. 'No matter what disguise you affected. The town is infested with Marcy's spies and informers. You are safer to remain where you are. Although I cannot keep soldiers posted here indefinitely on the pretext of my visiting Master Nostradamus.'

'Master Nostradamus is dying,' I said. 'He will be dead before morning.'

'What!' Lord Thierry stood up. 'That changes every-thing. Where is Mistress Anne?'

'She has taken the children to be with him as his end approaches.'

'You must be removed at once to a place of safety. The

funeral of Master Nostradamus will be an enormous public occasion. Crowds of people will come to the town. In a situation like that you would be vulnerable to the assassin's dagger. And with you dead and the Huguenot hanged the matter of the murdered priest would be closed.'

'But you know the Huguenot did not do this,' I said. 'You cannot hang him.'

'The Duke of Marcy will hang the man. It will be a popular decision as he is the only person under suspicion of the murder. If I try to prevent it without producing another culprit then he will have the populace turn against me.'

'You must stop it!' I cried. 'The man is innocent.'

'How much you have to learn about the ways of the world,' said Lord Thierry. 'I *will* try to stop this execution. Not just to spare the poor fellow's life, but for the fact that if a Huguenot hangs, then the ensuing violence will consume the town. This is what Marcy wants so that he can move in and replace me. He will take power as the man who has a more firm hand over our Protestant brethren.' He stood up. 'That is a problem for the morning. For now' – he moved quickly across the room and lifted me bodily from the stool – 'I am taking you to Valbonnes.'

'No!' I struggled against him.

'You must come with me.' Lord Thierry swung off his cloak and wrapped it round me. 'While it is dark we will go through the town gates and get away. Keep your face concealed until I say otherwise.'

He hustled me downstairs and out of the back door of the house. My state of mind was such that it was not until much later that I remembered and grieved for the loss of my beloved mandolin. One of his men brought his horse round and Lord Thierry hefted me, clutching my bundle of clothes, onto the front of the saddle before him. Surrounded by a tight escort, we cantered off.

I heard him speak to his sergeant at the Pélisanne Gate. 'Inform the Duke of Marcy that I have made an arrest of the person who murdered the priest. I will appear tomorrow at noon in the castle forecourt to hold trial. He is to bring the Huguenot and I will produce my prisoner with the evidence, and all will see who is guilty.'

I heard the sergeant repeat his orders.

'Now I must ride out to Valbonnes secretly,' said Lord Thierry in a low voice. 'My escort are to return and guard the house of Nostradamus. Open the gate and let me through.'

'Sir,' replied his sergeant. 'You cannot go alone.'

'I will. I must. Speed and silence is what we need tonight.'

Chapter Forty-two

As we trotted through the town gate Lord Thierry bent his head and spoke in my ear. 'Hold tight to that saddle pommel as though your life depends upon it, for in truth it does.'

I gripped the leather with both hands as he spurred his horse to a hard gallop. We rode along the highway that led away from the town and turned south-east towards Aix. But he soon left this road and veered west towards a dense forest and I thought that he was leaving a confusing trail for anyone who might try to follow us.

The rain which came after the thunderstorm had made the path less clear; stones and scrub hampered our passage. The horse ploughed on. For an hour or more we rode at the same relentless pace in a westerly direction towards Arles. The terrain changed, from forest to plain, then rocky escarpment, and finally we were on more level land where the animal had to labour less to keep going. Through it all horse and master seemed at one with each other. I sensed Lord Thierry's command of the reins as firm and sure.

Finally he spoke to me, saying, 'You may raise your head and you will see the loveliest castle in all of France.'

The sun was edging up over the horizon and light flooded across the plateau. Gold, pink and grey-white rays lanced down from the clouds onto a bluff. On it perched the castle of Valbonnes, as if drawn from an ancient legend or one of the old folk tales of Europe. It sat foursquare with crenellated walls, a turret at each corner, and a moat all around.

'It is beautiful,' I agreed.

'Why I ever left it to go wandering I do not know.' He smiled. 'Every time I see it after an absence it gives me such happiness.'

There was a sudden ache within me at his words. This was an experience I would never have, for since I was small I had led an itinerant life.

Lord Thierry's castle was made from the same warm mellow stone as the city of Carcassonne, but his home was more compact, more symmetrical. As we approached we heard a shout from the battlements.

'Ah,' said Lord Thierry in satisfaction, 'they are not asleep at their posts.'

He raised his hand in the air and called to his soldiers. 'It is I, your lord, Thierry.'

The clanking chain of the drawbridge unravelled and we rode across and into the courtyard.

He dismounted first and held out his arms to me. I had no choice but to go into his embrace as my legs were numb. He helped steady me as I stumbled against him. Then he set me aside in order to speak to the tall soldier who was hurrying to greet him.

'Robert!' he said, and clasped the hand of this man who was obviously one of his trusted commanders.

'It is good to see you, my lord,' said Robert with enthusiasm. 'We have been concerned for your safety and hungry for news. There are rumours as to the spread of Plague and other more serious trouble in Salon. They say the famous necromancer, Nostradamus, is dying and many strange portents have occurred already. The canals are full of giant frogs which are leaping about and gobbling up babies and small children. And a holy priest tried to intervene but one of the frogs turned into a demon with a sword and cut off his head. Is this true?'

'How plain facts can become distorted!' Lord Thierry laughed. 'It's dead rats that float in the canals in Salon. I caused them to be flushed out by a noxious mixture poured into the sewers, a remedy I saw when travelling in the east. It may have saved the town, for as the rats left, so has the Plague. But it's true that a priest was murdered, and the prophet is dying, so the combination of these events might bring chaos. And therefore' – he gave Robert a firm look to quell further questions – 'I have little time before I must return there to keep matters under control.'

'You will find everything here as you ordered it, sir,' Robert said proudly.

'I thank you for that,' Lord Thierry replied. 'Now rouse my old nurse, Marianne, but with care, mind. Tell her there is no alarm, only that I need her to attend to a lady.'

I was startled to realize that he was referring to me.

'And I want two swift messengers sent out; one to go to the garrison at Febran, and one to Alette. I'll write an order for the commanders there to send thirty men each to Salon. They are to ride at full tilt to the town and once there take orders from me alone.'

'You are expecting trouble?' said Robert. 'Let me guess. It's young Marcy who is using the circumstances to make an attempt to seize power for himself.'

'You're right, as always, dear friend. But I will crush this upstart before he has time to draw breath on another day.'

'Be careful how you play this hand, sir,' said Robert. 'Don't go too far and antagonize the boy's father. He can muster other armies from his friends at court.'

'I think I may outsmart him this time.' Lord Thierry stopped as an elderly woman came running towards him. She was in her nightwear with a blanket thrown over her shift and her white hair bound in two long plaits. 'Marianne.' He reached out to her.

'I heard the fuss,' she said as she hugged him, 'and knew that it must be you. I'm glad to see you safe and well, my lord.'

'Marianne' – he put his arm around her shoulder and led her towards me – 'this lady needs attention. She will require warm food and drink and a bed to rest in. I would ask you that while she is my guest here you spoil her as you did me when I was a child.'

Marianne nodded to me and then said to him, 'Let me also spoil you for a while now. You look in need of a hot meal.'

'There is no time. I will take some bread and cheese and

a glass of wine as I write out some orders. Then I must return to Salon.'

As Marianne went off to see to this and we followed her into the castle, Lord Thierry spoke to Robert. 'Listen to me most attentively. Until I return, no one, unless it is a single soldier known personally to you and carrying a message from me, must be allowed to enter within these walls.' He stopped and gripped the man's arm. 'Pay me heed in this, Robert. When I say no one, that is what I mean. No person is to be admitted to this castle when I am gone. No pedlar, nor vagabond, no mendicant monk, no trades person nor travelling pilgrim. Take charge of no goods, allow no deliveries to come in. You understand?'

'Yes, sir.'

'This is very important. In addition to the castle you are guarding this lady's presence.'

Robert glanced at me. I bent my head.

'Furthermore,' Lord Thierry said, very distinctly, 'no one is to be allowed to leave.'

There was a pause, and then Robert said, 'I understand, sir.'

'Make sure that this rule is kept.'

'I will, my lord.'

We arrived in the great hall, where already Marianne had kitchen staff scurrying with boards of bread and cheese. She herself was pouring out wine from a flagon. I sat down on a bench and she brought me a cup and gave me a sympathetic look. 'Drink this. It will restore the colour to your cheeks.'

Lord Thierry came and stood before me. 'I must go to

my library and write various orders. This matter is complicated and therefore it may take a long time to resolve. You will remain here until I return.'

I saw that this was a command, not a request. And I saw also that he had allowed me to hear his conversation with Robert so that I would not attempt to leave. But now I was so weary with the events of the previous day and my gruelling and uncomfortable ride from Salon that I had no urge to argue. I only wanted to lie down and rest.

'Marianne will take good care of you,' he said. 'Now I must get back to Salon and put a curb into the mouth of the Duke of Marcy.'

PART THREE
THE CASTLE AT
VALBONNES

Chapter Forty-three

Igh summer passed and the reapers in the far fields began to gather in the harvest, yet no news of Lord Thierry's doings came back to Valbonnes. During this time Robert, captain of the guards, kept the castle locked tight. This was a hardship for someone like me who was used to wandering through the countryside, but I knew better than to suggest that I might take a walk or ride a horse outside the walls. I had to be content with gazing out from the battlements or turret windows and imagining what life was unfolding beyond the castle gates.

In front of the castle there stretched a plain with a river and the rim of trees of a forest. Beside and behind the castle was a wide swamp where at night the darkness was pierced by the glow of fireflies and other insects. Occasionally an eerie greenish mist would settle in the evening and lie just above ground level, only dispersing as the sun climbed into the sky next day. When this happened the old nurse, Marianne, would cross herself and say a prayer. Then she would relate to me a tale of the doings of the evil spirits who collected there to plot mischief for the human race.

These things did not disturb me as much as they might once have done. Nostradamus had explained to me how certain elements take the insubstantial form of the air we breathe, and although we cannot see them, they exist as much as if they were solid wood or rock, and have colours and smells of their own. In particular he'd told me of marsh gas. Salon itself had a similar marsh near the town where, like this one, it was dangerous to venture. Unwary travellers who wandered there vanished from sight. Grass tussocks which appeared solid gave way under the weight of a man or woman and the poor unfortunate sank without ever being seen again.

Marianne had many stories to tell, some legend, some factual. She was delighted with my presence in the castle, and glad to have another woman to chat to, or sit with and sew in happy companionship.

Lord Thierry had left written instructions. Marianne showed them to me. I was to be treated as an honoured guest. I was to eat the best food, drink the finest wine, and use any dressmaking materials as I wished. Apart from leaving the castle, no restriction was to be made on my movements. I was allowed free access to all public rooms, including the library.

'Such an honour,' said Marianne. 'Rarely is anyone allowed into his library, especially if Lord Thierry is not present.'

Bit by bit she gave me his life story. Marianne had never married. She had been brought to the castle as a young girl by Lord Thierry's grandfather to look after his son. So she had nursed Lord Thierry's father, and then Lord Thierry himself. Being her only charge, he had had all her affection lavished upon him. It was clear that she adored him, though she admitted he had been a difficult and troublesome child.

'Strong-willed,' she told me. 'He always liked to have his own way and would get it by force or by guile.'

He had little changed in that, I thought.

But according to her, Lord Thierry had altered greatly since his youth. He no longer resembled the wilful boy who had stormed from his father's house at the age of twenty to go away and seek his own fortune. At that time he had not wanted to be schooled in the management of the castle or the lordship of his domain. So he had fallen out with his father and run off to see the Holy Land in the manner of the Holy Crusaders.

'His grandsire was one of the original founders of the order of the knighted men who guarded the Temple of Jerusalem,' she informed me.

'A Knight Templar?' I asked in surprise.

Marianne nodded and chattered on.

'They became so powerful that the ministers who ruled the Church feared their strength and sought to destroy them. Branded as heretics, they were hunted down and killed.'

Most people in the south of France had heard tales of these holy knights who had guarded pilgrims on their way to visit the shrines and places of the Holy Land. But the Pope of that time, growing wary of their power and riches, banned the Templar Order and cast out the members. He claimed they indulged in sacrilegious practices.

'Did they hold strange ceremonies here within this castle?' I asked Marianne.

She told me that she was not old enough to recall this.

'But perhaps there were stories?' I prodded her mind for more information.

'There are always stories,' she replied. 'And at least half of them have a basis in fact.'

'But despite his noble ancestors this Lord Thierry decided to leave his lands and castle?' I asked.

'Just a normal tempestuous youth,' she defended him. 'But now he has learned to control those outbursts and become more considered and thoughtful.'

'Very considered,' I agreed. And as I did, I wondered how he was faring in dealing with the scheming Duke of Marcy and his henchman, Bertrand. The Lord Thierry would need an agile mind to outwit them.

'But then he tired of his wanderings,' Marianne went on. 'The old man, his father, died just before he returned. And although the place had fallen into disrepair Lord Thierry did not move his headquarters to one of his towns. He remained here and worked hard to make the castle of Valbonnes wind- and watertight again.'

When I was not sitting with Marianne sewing new clothes for myself or walking in the gardens or on the walls, I spent time in the library. Mainly I read his books and manuscripts, although Lord Thierry owned a collection of musical instruments, including a zither and also a mandolin. It was not as fine an instrument as mine, but when I first saw it lying there on one of the tables my hands strayed towards it. I lightly touched the strings and heard a sound like tumbling cherry blossom.

Ah! How my soul ached for my precious mandolin left behind in my flight from Salon. I wanted to lift this one and cradle it to me. I craved the solace of music to comfort me as I mourned the loss of my family and every friend I'd known in my short life: Melchior and Paladin, Nostradamus, Giorgio and Mistress Anne. Was it to be my fate to be always torn away from those who cared for me? But I did not dare take up this mandolin to play upon it. The music would be heard and, I did not doubt, would be reported to Lord Thierry. I hoped that if I could but keep my identity secret I might yet go free from here without anyone knowing who I was. If only it was possible to settle the trouble of the priest's murder.

Yet I could not imagine how Lord Thierry might deal with the Duke of Marcy without rousing the whole countryside. He could not execute a duke without permission from the king. The Duke of Marcy's father, according to Marianne, was a very powerful man at court and would raise a petition to prevent this, and might even unseat Lord Thierry in the process. But if an innocent Huguenot were hanged then the strong local forces of Protestantism would rise against him.

Marianne seemed unconcerned. 'Don't fret,' she told me. 'He will find a way out of this maze. He is a clever boy, always was.'

Chapter Forty-four

But I became more anxious as each week passed and we had no news.

And then, as the first frost was riming the windows in the early morning, two messages arrived at Valbonnes.

Marianne examined them and declared them to be written in Lord Thierry's own hand so we were able to believe the contents. They were addressed to Robert but with a separate packet to me so that I also might know what was happening. And for this consideration I was very grateful.

They gave a clear account of events in the outside world.

The young Huguenot arrested for the murder of the priest had been released due to the fact that a prominent Catholic nobleman had stepped forward and declared he had seen the boy in his father's shop at the time of the murder.

'Aha!' Marianne declared when I told her the name of

the nobleman. 'He is one of my Lord Thierry's friends. Perhaps Lord Thierry prevailed upon him to do this to prevent civil strife.'

Lord Thierry had instigated his own investigation and had issued a warrant for the arrest of the man, Bertrand, an aide of the Duke of Marcy, on suspicion of the murder of the priest. There had been a witness to him abducting a girl. This witness was a woman who had been standing at the door of her house.

I knew who this was. The woman who had turned away from me when I had cried out for help. Lord Thierry must have visited her and persuaded her to be a witness. She had made a statement that she had seen a girl struggling against Bertrand.

Soon another witness came forward to say that he had seen Bertrand chasing me into the church. Bertrand was seized and imprisoned in the dungeon of the Château Emperi, closely guarded by Lord Thierry's men. He was to be put to the rack to elicit his confession. However, this questioning would take place at Lord Thierry's pleasure, and he would wait to decide a suitable time to do this.

What devious plan was this? I thought as I read this part of his letter. There must be a reason why he delayed torturing a confession from Bertrand.

Then a gang of ruffians tried to break into the château in Salon to help Bertrand escape. More likely their intention was to assassinate him, for when the rescue attempt failed, arrows had been fired through the bars of the cell where Bertrand was imprisoned.

On at least two occasions after this, poison had been

put in the prisoner's food but those who had done it were unaware that a portion of Bertrand's meals were first fed to stray dogs before he received them. Several of these hapless curs had died yowling in utmost agony within hearing of the prisoner. Now it was rumoured that Bertrand had declared himself ready to tell all he knew of the murder of the priest.

Lord Thierry had written to the Duke of Marcy to sympathize with him at having such a base companion. It was rumoured that on receiving the letter the duke had smiled a glassy smile, knowing that it would not be long before Bertrand told all to save himself from torture and death.

Thus at the beginning of December Salon awoke to discover that the Duke of Marcy had departed abruptly to go to his country estate. He had stated that his mother was unwell and he had gone to attend her.

I saw then how clever Lord Thierry was. Following my conversations with Marianne and the knowledge I had of this man's character, I also sensed that all of these occurrences might not have been happenstance. Had he been so artful as to construct the failed rescue attempt and fake the poisonings? It was those two incidents that had prompted Bertrand's willingness to testify. To begin with he would have been terrified to say anything, knowing that Marcy would kill him if he did. But now, with the delay, and his life in jeopardy, Bertrand would reckon that he would die if he didn't speak out. He probably hoped that if he gave evidence and Marcy was arrested, then he might be able to flee somewhere and save his own life.

And so it would not be Lord Thierry who had accused Marcy but another man, his own henchman, Bertrand, in fact.

Now Lord Thierry could sit and wait and hold the peace of the region in his hands.

The other letter that Lord Thierry sent gave news of the funeral of Master Nostradamus. It had been a massive affair with a huge turnout of people and many dignitaries travelling long distances to attend. The queen regent, Catherine de' Medici, had sent her personal envoy. She was reported to be troubled at the death of the prophet and to have asked anxiously if he had left no final message for her. She lamented his passing, declaring that no longer would she be able to seek his insight and assistance in the troubles that beset her.

For myself I experienced a similar emotion. Having Nostradamus's death confirmed in writing made me brutally aware that I was now on my own. I was left, utterly alone, to determine what might be the best course of action to take regarding the prophecies he'd made just before his death.

That night I took out the papers Nostradamus had given me from the hem of my cloak. I unrolled them and re-read the lines he'd written. His last prophecy made no sense to me at all. I was glad that it was not the one that I was supposed to act upon, for its words had a strange deadly inevitability, as if no one person could avert the course predicted therein.

The prophecy that pertained to me I now knew by rote:

With fire and heartless hangings
The treachery of royal line holds sway
Deeds done by stealth will come to light and all but one
    consumed
Safe from the sword, saved only by the word.

And then I puzzled over the second quatrain:

This is your destiny, Mélisande.
You are the one who,
In the way known to you, can save
The king who must be saved.

The king who must be saved. Saved from what? What
could be the terrible danger facing King Charles? What
grisly fate awaited him if I did not prevent it happening?

In the way known to you. What did that mean? I was no
skilled physician that I could save lives. Like any other
young girl, when growing up, I'd learned some folk
remedies for headache and stomach upset. And in my time
in the apothecary shop I'd learned more advanced recipes
for curing certain sicknesses, but despite that, I had none
of the doctoring knowledge of Master Nostradamus
or Giorgio.

The obscurity of the lines unsettled me deeply. If
Nostradamus, the greatest seer in all the world, could not
divine my part in this, then how was I supposed to
ascertain it?

Another chill thought entered my mind. Catherine de'
Medici had specifically enquired if there was anything

among the effects of the prophet that pertained to the royal house of France. Therefore any last message from Nostradamus would be of enormous interest to her.

The very thing that I held in my hand.

I, Mélisande, had the papers of Nostradamus. Papers that Catherine de' Medici sought. Catherine de' Medici, the Queen Regent of France, who was known to ruthlessly eliminate anyone who stood in her way.

Chapter Forty-five

The month of January brought weather of bitter cold.

Marianne had sewn me a new dress of thick wool with a matching fur hat and I wore these to wander in the garden. If I could not play my music there was nothing to stop me composing, so I sat among the trees and plants as the colours faded through burnished autumn to the monochrome of winter. The restricted palette chimed with my emotions. Yet the stillness of the atmosphere was absolute purity and the fretwork of frost on the plants as crisp as new-starched lace. I inhaled deeply, and as I breathed out I fancied that the notes and the words tinkled and sparkled into the air before me.

> *Clear and light*
> *Snowy night*
> *My delight . . .*

I had taken pen and paper from the castle library and I

began to write. But it was not fluid; the words jarred with the music. I'd crossed it out to write again when there was a shout from the guard room, and almost immediately afterwards a gong sounded.

I dropped pen and paper and ran with all the others to the battlements. A column of men rode towards Valbonnes, too far away to distinguish their colours. But there was no mistaking the bearing of the man at the head of the group and the dignified tread of his charger.

Lord Thierry had come home.

He made me wait two days before he summoned me to his presence.

Marianne told me that he was conducting his business from the library so I avoided going there. As soon as I knew for sure that it was him returning I kept to the rooms that had been allocated to me, taking my meals there and walking for exercise upon my own terrace.

He was seated behind his desk as I came into the library. Documents were piled up to one side, packets of letters and official papers tied with cord and closed with his official seal. On the other side of his desk a black cloth covered a bulky object.

I held my head high to try to indicate that I was not afraid, but my breathing was rapid. He nodded at me abruptly in greeting.

'You have been treated well?' he asked.

'Very well,' I replied quietly. 'I thank you for your kindness.'

'You read the letters I sent?'

'Yes.'

'So the matter that troubled you, the murder of the priest, is settled as well as it can be. As long as I hold Bertrand I can keep the Duke of Marcy in check and he knows this.'

I thought about what he said and replied, 'Yet the duke is headstrong and will constantly seek a way to overcome this setback.'

Lord Thierry regarded me. 'You are observant and accurate in your assessment of character,' he said. 'What else are you?'

'My lord?' I replied.

'I have done my best for you. What will you tell me of yourself?'

'There is nothing to tell,' I said, my heart's pace beginning to quicken. 'I am a plain girl from the countryside.'

'That you are not,' he interrupted me. 'I made enquiries in the area you claim to come from. There is no one of your name, nor ever has been. It's true that Mistress Anne, the wife of Nostradamus, does have cousins living there. But none of them knew of anybody with the name of Lisette. There is no record of your birth in the church's baptismal certificates.'

I shook my head. 'That cannot be, sire,' I said. 'I lived on a farm in that area. Perhaps you looked in the wrong parish?'

He waved his hand impatiently. 'We both know that is nonsense. You've never worked on a farm in your life. That fact alone is obvious. Look at me,' he commanded.

I raised my eyes and looked at a face, weather-beaten by the elements, not unlike the mien of the huntsmen who worked for the king. Tanned and healthy, the countenance of a person who had been outdoors most of his life.

'You have not spent hours in the fields tending crops or watching cattle,' he stated firmly.

'Sir, I came to work at the house of Nostradamus. I am a cousin to his wife. I am Lisette.'

He shook his head. 'No, not a farm girl. Nor an apothecary's assistant.' He glanced at the door then he leaned forward and with a sudden swift movement he flung back the black material on his desk.

My mandolin lay there.

I gasped.

Lord Thierry smiled in triumph,

'There is no doubt in my mind. I know you for what you are.' He paused, and then he added,

'My friend, the minstrel.'

Chapter Forty-six

I could not speak, only stare as he rose from his chair and approached me.

He stood in front of me and my face was almost in line with his. When he spoke his breath smelled of cinnamon.

'You are the mandolin player. The minstrel boy who came to Salon on spring market day and was embroiled in a row outside a tavern with the Duke of Marcy.'

He took my hands in his own and turned them, palms up.

'Look at your fingers; they are calloused at the tip. No maidservant has such marks.'

'I did not serve Mistress Anne as an ordinary servant.' My voice trembled. 'I worked in the apothecary shop.'

He shook his head and smiled. The lines around his eyes creased, with the effect of making his face appear less severe.

'I agree the skin of your hands has some wear on it, no doubt with preparing the potions and handling the medical components of medicines. But your fingers are those of a musician, in particular a mandolin player.'

My eyes strayed to where the mandolin lay on his desk. The instrument seemed to murmur to me. I saw the gleam of the polished wood, the harmonious rise of the fretwork, the gloss of the pearl inlay. My fingers tingled to touch the strings, to feel the instrument thrum as it nestled against my cheek.

'You long to touch it, don't you?'

His voice had sympathy. I felt myself waver. But I must not be seduced by his kind manner. 'I don't understand you, sir,' I replied.

He walked away then to a shelf in one of his bookcases. What was he up to now? He reached up and took down a book.

'Look at this,' he said in a casual way. 'In one of my old music manuscripts, there is an illustration of a lady sitting in a tower. She is playing a mandolin. This folio contains the work of a woman named as Cecily d'Anbriese. She was very gifted and talented. Did you know her fame spread throughout Europe? It is a pity there were not more like her.'

'But there were,' I said. 'France was famed for its women troubadours.'

He turned swiftly and I saw his delight in catching me out so easily.

I put my hands to my face. I felt heat and knew that my cheeks were red.

'I have no wish to humble you,' he said. 'Yet . . . you were the mandolin player, were you not?'

'It was necessary.' I spoke slowly while my mind sifted rapidly through a number of reasons that I could offer him which he might believe, but would not reveal my true identity.

'In what way *necessary?*'

'My father was killed, and I was left on my own,' I improvised. 'I had been promised to a local squire, but . . . but I did not wish to marry him, so I ran away.'

He clicked his tongue against the roof of his mouth. 'You are an impossible liar. Apart from the fact that I have already made enquiries as to who you might be, it is also plainly obvious that you are unskilled in deception.'

I hung my head.

'Oh, don't be upset about that. I'd mark it as a virtue, and a rare one in the world we live in. There are too many women and men who are accomplished liars. Indeed they tell untruths with such ease that they begin to believe their own stories.'

He put down the book and came close to me again. He studied me. 'I would say that you were not one of those. But now is the time you must tell me your true history.'

I hung my head.

He leaned back and sat on the edge of his desk. Near enough for me to be aware of his physical presence but not looming so close as to intimidate me too much. This man calculated his moves very carefully.

His voice had hardened when he next spoke. 'Let me give you some information of which I think you should take account.' He paused. 'Know this, my overlord for this region is the Count de Ferignay.'

A cold quiver ran over my skin.

'Ah, I see that you have heard of him. Now, if I am troubled or perturbed by any event in my own domain I am obliged to report it to the Count de Ferignay. Do you think this case warrants such action?'

I glanced at him in fear.

He tilted his head to one side. 'I wonder if the said Count de Ferignay would be at all interested in a wandering minstrel, with no name. That is, more specifically, a girl, with some skill in singing and mandolin playing. One who will not divulge her past history. What do you think?'

He knew very well that his words had unsettled me. But I would not give in to him.

'Also,' he went on, 'let me tell you that if I did send word to the Count de Ferignay and he wished you brought to him for questioning, I don't think it would be the count himself who came personally to escort a prisoner to his presence. Most likely he would send his own bodyguard for such an important errand. You may know of him. A man called Jauffré.'

I raised my head in alarm.

'If I am to help you then you must be absolutely honest with me.' Lord Thierry went and sat down behind his desk.

'What is your true name?' he asked me briskly.

'Mélisande,' I whispered.

'Mélisande.' He repeated my name in the accents of the south and made it sound like water flowing among river reeds.

'Mélisande. Yes, that is a good name for a minstrel. And how is it that you have chosen to spend part of your life going by a different name, Mélisande, and' – he raised an eyebrow – 'by a different sex?'

I felt myself blush under his scrutiny.

'I do not mean to shame you,' he said. 'It's only that I am intrigued.'

And quite suddenly I was tired. My emotions and my brain were exhausted with everything that had happened to me, and I felt myself rebel against the way this man was manipulating me. I no longer cared if I was captured or not. At least if I was taken and imprisoned I might see my father again. If Lord Thierry chose to report me, then so be it.

'Do your worst, sir,' I said. 'Send for Jauffré. Let him take me from here. I no longer have the strength to cope with all this. And if I survive the journey north with him, then let me be conducted into the presence of your over-lord the Count de Ferignay.'

Chapter Forty-seven

There was a silence in the room.

Then Lord Thierry raised his hands and let them fall upon his desk.

'You have outmanoeuvred me,' he declared. 'And, I must concede, in the most skilful way.' He raised his hand as I opened my mouth to protest. 'I do realize that it was not by guile or deviousness. Your innocence shines through, Mélisande. It is one of your most attractive qualities.' He sat back in his chair. 'But what am I to do with you?' He was speaking half to himself. 'You are safe enough here as long as Marcy does not find out that the only other witness to his foul deed, apart from Bertrand, is still alive.' He glanced at me. 'I have to tell you that I let it be known in Salon that on the night of the prophet's death you fled the house of Nostradamus, taking some of the family silverware with you.'

I gazed at him, aghast.

'It means,' he added, 'that you cannot adopt the persona of the farm girl Lisette ever again.'

'You are an underhand and cunning man,' I said angrily.

He blinked. It was the first time I had ever seen him discomfited. 'I am unsure whether to take that as a compliment, and therefore thank you for it,' he said formally.

I realized that I'd offended him, and although I was not comfortable with his displeasure, some part of me was glad that I had at last scored a point against him.

'It was a difficult matter to deal with and it was all I could think of,' he explained. 'Mistress Anne was in accord with me. It was she who then gave me your mandolin to return to you. She would not reveal any information about you or anything you had told her. But she did agree that for your own safety it was best that your absence was covered in this way. Don't you see? There needed to be a reason for your sudden disappearance from the house. And it's a story that Marcy will believe. He would think you were terrified by the incident in the church so it's a likely thing for you to do. To steal what you could and run as far away from Salon as possible. If he thought anything else, believe me, he would not rest until he had hunted you down.'

I absorbed the sense of his words. Then I gave my head a quick nod.

'Good,' said Lord Thierry dryly. 'We are at least agreed on that.'

He paused. 'I would suggest that you also agree to remain in Valbonnes and accept my hospitality. As I go about my domain trying to keep the peace I can report back to you as to when it may be safe for you to leave.'

The words that Nostradamus spoke to me on the night he died echoed in my head:

'*You will quit this house tonight, Mélisande, and go to a place of safety. There you will wait until the time comes when you must act.*'

Lord Thierry was awaiting my answer. I nodded again, whereupon he reached down and opened a drawer in his desk. He took something out and laid it on the table beside my mandolin. It was the chamois leather bag.

'I looked after this as though it was my own,' he said. 'Please take both these things and, and . . .' – I looked at him in surprise as he fumbled with the words – 'be content here until such time as we can work out the best thing to do for your future.'

I moved forward. With shaking hands I lifted my mandolin. I opened the drawstring of the bag and placed it inside.

I fancied it sighed as it settled there again.

Chapter Forty-eight

So at least I had my mandolin to sustain me in my years of waiting.

And while outside the castle religious wars of attrition ravaged France, inside the walls of Valbonnes I found a kind of peace.

I played old tunes on my mandolin. The ones that required little thought or effort; my fingers mechanically stroking the strings, my mind hardly aware of the notes. But I was experiencing an emptiness of spirit. My thoughts turned to Melchior and the leopard. I knew that by this time they would be far away in the kingdom of Navarre, where I would most likely never see them again. Within me my soul stretched as bleak as the flat land around the castle, hardened with frost and pitted with puddles of ice.

I needed new music. In the past, composing words and tunes would send me soaring, but now when I searched inside myself there was nothing there. One evening, after a day of deepening melancholy, it came to me that I might find inspiration in Lord Thierry's library. I remembered the book he had shown me of the woman troubadour, Cecily d'Anbriese. I would enjoy reading her poems even if I was not stimulated to write any of my own. I knew that Lord Thierry had left the castle that morning. It was likely that he would not return for a few days.

As soon as I told Marianne of my intention she sent a servant to light the lamps and build a fire in the grate. I took my mandolin with me and as I browsed among his books I felt that I was gaining an insight into the man who had collected them. I found the bookcase with the music book and took down the one he had shown me. I opened it up and brought the page close to the lamp to read, when the door of the library opened and Lord Thierry strode in. He had reached the centre of the room and thrown his gloves upon his desk before he noticed me.

'I didn't think you were returning today.' I hurriedly put the book down and edged towards the door.

'No, no,' he said. 'Don't let me disturb you. I will go. I need to change from these riding clothes and eat something.'

He shivered as he spoke. I saw how cold he was, so I said, 'The fire is here. Why don't you go close and take some warmth?'

'Would you play for me?' he asked suddenly. 'Trying to keep peace between these opposing sides is exhausting. Some music would be a balm to my troubled mind.'

How could I refuse? He'd saved my life and kept me well fed and cared for. And besides, I had not played my music to an audience for a long time.

He lifted my mandolin and as he handed it to me his fingers brushed mine. I felt again the current between us that I'd experienced when he'd first touched me in Nostradamus's rooms in Salon. Immediately he looked into my face. Had he felt it too?

I played him a song of the south. It was a traditional song, a song from the time when this land had been free.

'Gather in the grapes, gather up the olive fruit,
Sing as we tramp out the juice,
Sing as we press out the oil.

'Reapers in the early morn, sickles swinging in the fields,
Sing as we stack up the ricks,
Sing as we mill down the grain.'

'That song has another level of meaning,' he observed when I had finished.

'It's a song of freedom,' I agreed. 'Of people being able to exist happily under the protection of a benign overlord.'

'As I strive to be,' he replied.

'You are following the example set by your ancestors?' I asked him.

'My grandfather's grandfather was a Templar Knight,' he replied. 'As a boy I loved to hear tales of their time in the Holy Land. How they guarded the Temple there, and how they protected pilgrims as they journeyed to see the holy places. My mind was fired with stories of the battles fought, the many deeds of honour, acts of bravery, of the respect, even friendship, between Saracen and

Christian. I was desperate to grow up and go and live the life my ancestors had.'

'So you are not a Huguenot?' I asked him.

'I am not.' He paused. 'Although I have sympathy for their beliefs.'

'How is it then that people think you are?'

'Because the concept of tolerance is extremely challenging. It is something that many people never learn.'

'How have you learned it?'

'By having to deal with the aftermath of intolerance. Every day I see the result of man's inhumanity on the lives of my people.'

Chapter Forty-nine

A curiosity about the women troubadours of France, coupled with my own needs for an outlet for my music, prompted me to return to the castle library each day.

And if Lord Thierry was at home he would come there in the evening and stay and talk for a little while.

I found that I looked forward to his visits and was disappointed if duty or politeness kept him away for more than a few days. I welcomed his interest and his knowledge, for it was so long since I'd spoken of music to anyone. Nostradamus had been concerned only with his visions. Mistress Anne, his wife, was kindly, but her appreciation of music was to the extent of how much it helped soothe her fractious child. I was bereft of my sister and my father, with no one to appreciate how the lilting patter of rainfall or the soft sweep of snow upon the hills could be translated into a combination of sympathetic sounds.

I began to transcribe some of the old songs and music.

One night Lord Thierry asked me if I needed help with the language.

'I am not so very familiar with Provençal,' I replied, 'but my father made sure that we were taught to read French, English and Latin.'

'Us?'

'I had a sister.' I stopped. Tears were brimming in my eyes.

He looked at me but did not speak. He neither pressed me to continue nor hastened to make me quiet in the way some men do at the sight of women's tears.

'Her name was Chantelle,' I said at last.

'She is dead?'

'She is dead.'

My tears flowed then, but again he said nothing

After a few minutes had elapsed he went to his desk and poured a glass of wine. The dark red claret was like blood in the glass. He held it out to me and I took it and drank some. He poured another glass for himself and went and sat on one side of the chimney breast. The fire shifted, a log fell and sparks flew up.

So then, halting at parts, and in my own time, I told Lord Thierry of the circumstances of my sister's death and how my father had been arrested. I came to the part where Melchior had helped me escape and his eyes widened as I described how I had hidden in the cage of the leopard.

'The boy has great command of this animal,' he said. 'The leopard must view him as an equal, if not its master.'

Then I related how Melchior had put together the

disguise that had transformed me into a minstrel boy. There was a look of satisfaction on Lord Thierry's face when I related this part of my life story to him. He nodded his head once or twice and murmured something to himself.

Eventually he had heard all of it. It took the space of several weeks, because at certain points I was overcome and could not continue. But it was also because Lord Thierry wanted to know everything. He would ask me to repeat conversations I'd had or explain how such an event had come about and what I had been doing before and afterwards. He was curious about my father's life, of how he had met my mother and been captivated by her. Of how her parents' disapproval had given way under the constancy and intensity of their love for each other.

The Isle of Bressay was about a week's ride from here, Lord Thierry told me, and yes, he said, he knew enough about it to see why any man might covet it for his own property.

'It's a sizeable house with pretty gardens all around. It sits on an island in a lake well stocked with fish. The land is very fertile so the yearly yield for the landowner would be good enough to live a comfortable life.'

He went on to quiz me on any detail I could dredge up from my past. He was very interested in the countries I had travelled through. He had never been to England but he had been in Spain. He too had watched the result of the courts of the Inquisition: condemned men and women walking to their deaths by burning or hanging.

'If only the two Christian faiths could live in harmony,' I said.

'There are more than two now, Mélisande,' he pointed out. 'And soon, where now there are three or four, there will be a dozen or more. It's the nature of things. All will seek their own interpretation, with the accompanying discord. It would fit us better to think of ways of addressing how we might accommodate, rather than destroy, each other.'

'Each thinks the other worships God in a false way and will not yield their own belief.'

'They do not have to. But the fighting that is tearing France into pieces is not about Faith. It's about greed and power and the acquisition of wealth and man's wish to control another and have him work to save himself the labour of doing so. It is what drives this strife. The Duke of Marcy no more cares about his God or Holy Church than does the kitchen cat. That was evidenced in how he slaughtered the priest who tried to prevent him molesting you.'

'So there is no solution?'

'I don't know.' He shrugged. 'Not now, perhaps never. The person who truly rules France, the queen regent, Catherine de' Medici, is convinced that what she does is for the greater good. She is deluded with what she believes to be her divine power.'

'At least she tries,' I protested. 'Here in France to be Catholic or Protestant does not necessarily make your life forfeit.'

'Yes, but what drives her is self-interest. She holds her family's right to rule as paramount. Watch her tolerance dissipate if she thinks her children's sovereignty is threatened. If necessary, our so-called accommodating queen would fight like a she-wolf to defend her young and their right to sit on the throne of France.'

And so it was.

A senior member of the House of Guise was murdered. In retaliation a leading Huguenot lord was attacked and summarily executed. The royal family were threatened with abduction and came close to being captured. The Constable of Paris was killed when the city was besieged by a Huguenot army. Spain sent Catholic troops to the Netherlands to quell rebellion there. Catherine de' Medici was outraged that they tried to pass through French territory without her permission. Elizabeth of England responded by sending soldiers to aid the Protestant cause. Reports came to us of atrocity and counter-atrocity. Violence escalated as the economy deteriorated. France was being driven to the brink of ruin, watched by two predatory neighbouring nations of opposing beliefs.

Lord Thierry reported these things to me and we discussed religion and politics. He was fascinating company, part instructor, part friend. He shared with me his thoughts and experiences, and I told him everything about me.

Except for one thing.

Of the papers that I carried containing the prophecies of Nostradamus, I said nothing at all.

Chapter Fifty

In the year of my fifteenth birthday Lord Thierry informed us that he was undertaking a long journey and might be away for many months.

He instructed Marianne to pack up for him an assortment of formal and elegant clothes. This was very unusual, for normally he wore the plainest of dress. Then he set off with an armed escort of six of his best and most trusted men-at-arms. I knew that he'd not gone to any of the nearby towns, for the messages he sent to Robert in Valbonnes contained instructions for dispersal to other garrison commanders. In this way he was seeking not to make it known that he was absent from his domain.

Over the first six to nine months these messengers came at frequent intervals, but then there was no word from him at all. The weeks passed. Marianne and I fed on each other's anxiety. We imagined him set upon by highway robbers, or the victim of an accident. Perhaps his horse had thrown him and he was lying in a gulley with a broken leg, dying for want of attention? Only Robert remained calm.

He'd been with his master for more than fifteen years and his faith in Lord Thierry's return was unswerving. But as time elapsed he too started to worry at his absence and silence. And then, on a late spring afternoon of the first year of the new decade, Lord Thierry came riding in from the north, both horse and rider covered in dust. He spoke briefly to Robert before going to the library, where he asked me to join him as soon as I was able.

He was standing by his desk when I entered the room.

'I am glad you are returned safely, my lord,' I said. And I was surprised at how very happy I was to see him again. Only as Marianne had rushed to find me to say that the sentry had recognized his horse on the approach road to the castle had I realized how much I'd missed him.

Lord Thierry acknowledged this by inclining his head. Then he said, 'I have some news for you.'

Something in the tone of his voice made me wary. 'News that I will be glad to hear?' I asked him.

'Perhaps not all of it,' he said. 'Some of it is worrisome, but part of it is the best news you might want to know.'

'The best news?'

'Your father is alive.'

I flung out my arms and Lord Thierry caught me and held me. It was he who stepped back first. 'Now,' he said. 'The rest is not so joyous.'

'My father is in prison?' I cried out. 'He is ill? He has been tortured! They have beaten and maimed him. Oh no!' I put my hands to my face. 'Have they broken his fingers so that he cannot ever play again?'

'Hush! Hush, hush.' He took my hands away from my

face and held them lightly. 'I will tell you what I know. But you must not allow your mind these wild imaginings.' He led me to sit by the fire and sat opposite me. 'Firstly I went to Paris, for you'd told me that your father was taken as a royal prisoner and I reckoned that's where he would be sent. I made enquiries there but no one knew much of him. A few people had heard of a talented minstrel who was in the employ of the king. So I thought that I must seek out the place where the court was in residence.'

'Are they in hiding as everyone says they are?'

'Not quite, but the political situation is very bad. Much worse than I thought. We think it is tense here with constant outbreaks of quarrelling; in the north it is far more volatile. These grasping nobles will rend each other like mad dogs and take all of the land and populace of France with them. There are towns under siege. The roads are horrifically dangerous. Where the rule of law is disregarded then every murderer and brigand roves the highways looking for easy prey. I located the court at Finderre, but it proved hard to gain access to the château there. Only by dint of claiming kinship with an old friend of my father's was I able to get close enough to find out what I wanted to know.'

'You went all that way and took such risks to find out this for me?'

'I did,' he replied.

'I thank you,' I said. 'I—'

'No matter,' he interrupted me, and went on quickly. 'The security was strict but finally I was able to stand in the hall while the king held audience for the local clergy on the feast of the birth of Our Lady.' He raised his head and smiled at me. 'Beside the king's chair stood a minstrel.'

'Ahhh.' I clasped my hands to my heart.

'Even though I was some distance away and have never met your father I would have recognized him immediately.'

'How so?' I asked, for I was not said to be very like my father at all.

Lord Thierry smiled. 'The manner in which he played. It was obvious to me that your love and skill in music is inherited from this man. He is an exceptional and gifted musician.'

'He is very talented,' I agreed.

'His daughter doth surpass him if she but knew it,' Lord Thierry murmured in reply.

I felt myself blush. 'How is he?' I asked.

'My impression, and from enquiries I made, is he seems thinner than he was some years ago when tragedy befell him. Apart from that he is well, but troubled in his mind about the disappearance of his daughter, Mélisande.'

'Did you not speak to him?'

'I was unable to do that.'

'But you got word to him to tell him that I was alive and enjoying your protection?'

Lord Thierry shook his head. 'He is watched at all times and sleeps in a locked room. I could not get to see him without arousing suspicion. Already it was noted that I was at court. This caused comment for it's known that I never attend functions unless commanded to do so by royal summons.'

'You could have sent my father a secret message!' I wailed in disappointment.

'Mélisande, I could not. It would have endangered both your lives. Who could I trust to do this for me? The court is full of liars, thieves, charlatans and cheats.'

'You might have written an anonymous note!'

'Think of the number of informers and spies that cluster round King Charles,' said Lord Thierry. 'I would have been arrested within the hour. And supposing I had done so? I believe your father would not have been able to conceal his happiness. His change of manner would have been remarked upon. And in this way he would have betrayed you. You know he would not have wished this.'

Despite my agitation I saw the wisdom of his words.

'Although his freedom is curtailed he is not suffering serious deprivation. He has the favour of the king. It seems his music eases the frequent headaches from which King Charles suffers.'

I slumped in my chair. Lord Thierry sat back in his. I saw the weariness in his face and I recalled that he'd only just ridden into the courtyard on his horse, caked in sweat and dust. I was ashamed of my ungraciousness. 'I am sorry if I sound ungrateful,' I said. 'You have brought me good news. My father is alive and not languishing in a dark prison cell. I am happy about that. And despite your protest,' I went on, 'I *will* thank you for travelling halfway across France to catch up with the court just to find out about my father.'

'Don't thank me yet. You may not welcome the rest of the news I learned.'

I raised my head and looked at him anxiously.

'The Count de Ferignay has laid claim to the Isle of Bressay.'

'What!'

'The count claims this on behalf of his kinsman, Armand Vescault, who is his vassal, and therefore all of Armand's goods are his.'

'He killed Armand!' I cried out.

'No body has been found. Armand is missing, and—'

'Tell me,' I said as he broke off.

'And so are you,' he continued. 'The Count de Ferignay is a perfidious man. He is moving to have all of the Isle of Bressay signed over to him. He has put it about that perhaps you pushed your sister, Chantelle, from the window of the tower on her wedding morning so that you and Armand could run off and marry.'

'Eeeeee!' I screamed.

Lord Thierry started up in fright. 'Mélisande! Control yourself. You will scare the wits from Marianne, who will run to Robert and he will arrive here with a dozen armed soldiers.'

'I'm sorry,' I sobbed, 'but that is the most base accusation I have ever heard.'

'Your father has refuted all of it. Because of his high standing with King Charles it has been decided there has to be a proper hearing of the matter. This will take place when the country is more settled and there has been time to gather evidence to place before the king.'

'Armand was never married to Chantelle,' I pointed out.

'An engagement can be equally binding. Contracts were exchanged and signed.'

In my head now I heard the Count de Ferignay's reply when my father had first told him of Chantelle's inheritance. Interest had resonated in the count's voice when told that she would inherit in her own right.

'That man is wicked. Is there no end to his perfidy?'

'The Count de Ferignay owes money to many important people. As his debts grow he becomes more desperate.'

I got up and went to the window. Better perhaps that I was thought dead. Then my father could at least have my half of the Isle of Bressay. I leaned my forehead against the glass panel. 'What's to be done?' I said in despair. 'There is no way that I can see to solve this.'

'There is one thing that you could do that would grant you safety' – Lord Thierry paused before continuing – 'and would guarantee you enough status that you might approach the king direct to make your case.'

I turned from the window. 'What is that?' I asked him.

Lord Thierry looked up from the chair in which he sat and said,

'You might marry me.'

Chapter Fifty-one

H e took me completely by surprise.

And, realizing that, he rose up from his chair and stood in front of me.

'Forgive me,' he said. 'You are a young girl, you have read the romantic poems and the love ballads and I should have made this suggestion in a more gentle and courteous manner.'

'I'm not a woman whose head is turned by flattery and compliment,' I said unsteadily.

'Nevertheless I would not like you to think that I only wish to marry you to help you fight for justice for your family.' He took my face between his hands. 'You captivated me from the first moment we met.'

I smiled then, despite the turmoil of the emotion within me. 'You mean when I was a minstrel boy, sir?'

'Do not mock me, Mélisande. Yes, there was a stirring in my soul when I first heard you play. The way you bent your head as you cosseted the mandolin made me long to be near to the person who made such music. And in the house of Nostradamus, when I encountered you as the servant girl I felt my spirit move again. I was unsure, confused, as to what was happening to me. I have known women and this was different. Can it be that a soul has a twin, as the people of the east believe? That we are separated at creation and we have to search the world for our other half? And, in rare cases, a person might find the one who makes him or her complete?'

He raised his hands and let them fall by his side. 'I did not know. I thought that I would wait and see if my attraction for you faded, but it has become stronger.'

I asked him to give me time to consider my future. I was just sixteen. He was at least twice my age. But it was not unusual for a girl to marry a man older than herself. He was kind and good, and I realized with some shock that I was deeply attracted to him. And how I longed for some constancy in my life.

He had the good sense to leave me alone for a while. There was a lot of business for him to catch up with. Information had come to him that the Duke of Marcy had been stockpiling ammunition and armaments and that his network of spies was active again. The duke was obviously plotting some uprising but what form it would take and when it would happen was unknown. Lord Thierry rode out to Salon to check personally on the prisoner Bertrand and to be seen about the town again.

When he was gone I had a dream.

Lord Thierry and I were riding in the forest and I dismounted in a clearing as he rode on. He asked me to wait for him there, but as I did the trees grew in around me. All the old tales came whispering into my head. Goblins and sprites, wood faeries and tree demons flitted around me and spied on me from the undergrowth. Then the lines scored on one tree trunk took life before my eyes: the grooves filled out and curled into hissing snakes which twined and intertwined with each other.

I walked towards the tree. It was a mountain ash. The rowan, which carries the red berries to signify the fire stolen from Heaven, and is a sacred tree. The rowan, from whose root Nostradamus had fashioned his divining rod. The snakes became still and then re-formed into the shape of a man. The figure detached itself from the bark and stood apart. So bent over, so stooped and frail was this person that at first I took him to be Giorgio. But then I saw it was the prophet himself.

Nostradamus.

He wore his ring that shone with the milky white of the moonstone and he leaned upon his silver walking stick. He acknowledged me. Then he opened his mouth to speak. And his tongue was a tongue of fire, and flames came from his mouth. In the centre of the flame I saw the sun burn like a ball of white light.

And I was afraid.

His voice was in my head.

Mélisande. Are you mindful of my vision for you?

'I do not know what to do,' I said and began to cry.

To which Nostradamus replied, 'Do not be upset. It is not given to everyone to undertake the task that may be allotted to them. The person has to accept the charge.

They must believe that they are the one.'

I came out of this dream in terror and bewilderment. And I knew that I did not want to live any longer in confusion.

And I would not, I decided.

I would step away from a fate of fear and uncertainty, of a life filled with darkness and danger. I would not go on and try to interpret the half-told prophecy, where I might find only death and never be successful. I would not risk being subjected to torture and any other monstrous inflictions upon my body.

Once, my sole purpose in life had been to find and rescue my father. Now I'd had a chance to rest and I was strong again, that is what I would do. Being wedded to the Lord Thierry would give me access to the court, to the king himself. We could travel to Finderre or Blois, or wherever court was currently held and, as the wife of a lord, I would petition the king.

By the time Lord Thierry returned to Valbonnes I had made my decision. I would accept his offer of marriage.

Chapter Fifty-two

Our wedding was set for midsummer.

Marianne was overjoyed when I told her the news. She said she hoped she might soon have babies to look after again.

I stared at her in shock.

'I never thought I would see this day,' she babbled on. 'My Lord Thierry is a silent man, awkward, and difficult to get to know.' She stopped, and mistaking the expression on my face, she asked in an anxious voice, 'You would let me stay on? Please,' she begged. 'I am not so old that I cannot manage to nurse your children.'

Children! I had not thought of the physical side of this union. What might be expected of me.

Marianne understood at last. 'He will be kind,' she whispered to me. 'Do not be anxious or afraid.'

Now I appreciated Chantelle's predicament when she was waiting to be married to Armand. In the absence of a mother how was one supposed to know what to do? My father, in protecting us from the salacious comments of the worldly wise women of the court, had given us little information on the duties of a wife.

But the Lord Thierry wooed me in a proper manner. He brought gifts of jewellery and soft leather gloves. I hardly rewarded him with a smile or a kiss. I only enquired how soon after we were married we might travel to the royal court and see my father. His thoughts were for my wellbeing. He questioned me on how I was. I replied by asking how our marriage would be proclaimed, did he need permission, and when would be the most suitable time to declare who I really was.

My selfish concerns meant that I neglected to notice how busy the castle had become, with messengers riding in almost daily. I assumed that a lot of the hurrying to and fro was to do with preparations for our marriage.

Even Marianne's comment one day did not make me realize that unrest in the domain was increasing and the situation outside the castle was becoming dangerous.

It was the middle of May and I stood in my room while Marianne fitted me for my wedding dress. As she knelt, adjusting the hem of the gown of gold, we heard a noise in the courtyard below. She stood up to look out of the window.

'More men arriving. He must think he needs all of them here, else he would not leave the other garrisons so undermanned.'

I joined her and watched a troop of soldiers file in under the archway.

'They must be early wedding guests,' I said,

unconcerned. 'I did tell my Lord Thierry that I would be happy with only a few people present.'

Marianne opened her mouth as if she would say more but instead said brightly, 'Let us finish sewing this hem and you will be as a queen on her wedding day.'

I looked in the mirror and saw myself. I did appear very grand. My dress was not the plain white that Chantelle had worn but a gown that befitted the wife of a noble lord. A stab of sadness welled up inside me but I thrust it aside. I had decided that I would not think of anything from the past. I would set my mind to the future and the clearing of my father's name.

'You are beautiful,' Marianne told me.

But I knew that she loved me for making her Lord Thierry happy and she would say that. I regarded myself and saw a young girl. Slim and tall with no pleasing plumpness either in figure or in face, yet even under my critical assessment I did look passably attractive.

That night at dinner Lord Thierry gave me the head-dress that had been worn by brides of his family for many generations. He placed it on my head as I sat at table with him. A circlet of thin gold, no more than a twisted wire with a veil of golden gauze attached to it.

He brought something from behind his back. 'I plucked this for you from the garden. It's one of the prettiest wild flowers that bloom here.'

He laid it beside my plate.

I looked down. Pale pink petals.

Artema.

And suddenly I remembered the crushed flower inside

my mandolin and my dream of Chantelle, and it was as if she was in the room with me and the bittersweet memories flooded through me.

'You're trembling, Mélisande.' Lord Thierry leaned towards me. 'What is wrong?'

I rose with such violence that I knocked over my chair.

'What ails you?' he cried out in fright.

I looked around wildly. 'I should not be here.'

I pulled the veil from my head. Soft and fragile as moth wings, it tore as I cast it onto the table.

I ran into the garden and he followed me.

I sat down on a bench and he, this wisest of men, did not approach me until my storm of weeping had passed away. When I was calmer he gave me a kerchief and wiped my face. He went away and fetched some wine mixed with water and insisted that I drink some. Then he sat down beside me.

'Come to me,' he said, and he pulled me to lean against his shoulder. 'This is not merely an attack of nerves before your wedding day, is it?'

I shook my head.

He gave a long, deep sigh. 'Then tell me now what I need to know.'

'I have betrayed a sacred trust,' I whispered.

'I long suspected that you carried some secret,' he replied, 'for I saw how sometimes it would weigh upon your mind. You would be playing music, when without warning you would revert into a dream state and hardly be aware that you had done so. I supposed it to be you thinking of past times with your father and sister.'

'Not only that,' I said.

'There is more?'

'Yes. I cannot tell you. It would endanger your own life and I would not have that happen.'

'Why not?'

It was such an unexpected question that I did not know how to answer it. 'Why not?' I repeated his question.

'Yes, why not?' He spoke quite sharply. 'I saved your life, it is true, but I would be obliged to seek justice for any person in my domain. You owe me no debt of gratitude.'

'It is more than gratitude that I feel for you, sir,' I replied tremulously.

'What is it then?' His tone was almost cold.

'A deep affection,' I said.

'But not love?'

'I do love you,' I protested, 'in a way . . .'

'Mélisande.' He held me very tightly. 'Although you are young, you must know the kind of love that I want from you. Wholehearted and passionate and complete.'

'I will be obedient to you,' I said. 'I will do all that you ask of me. I will do my best to give you children. I will—'

'Oh, Mélisande, Mélisande,' he interrupted me. His mouth was in my hair. 'For some couples that might be sufficient, and it may be that it would do for me, for I'd take whatever crumb you might give me. But' – he tilted my face to his and looked into my eyes – 'I love you too much to allow you to lead an arid life. I lived such a life once, and I know how it shrivels the soul.'

'I have a destiny to fulfil,' I whispered. 'Master Nostradamus himself told me this.'

'Ah,' he said.

'It's not some foolish whimsy,' I assured him. 'It is a matter of great importance. He spoke to me about it on the evening of his death.'

'I believe you,' he replied. 'I will help you undertake whatever it is. I will accompany you.'

'That's not possible.'

I knew that with Lord Thierry by my side I would have a good protector and my road would be easier, but I held back from agreeing that he might come with me.

In doing so I truly thought that I might save his life.

For the words of Nostradamus were in my head.

The person who does this takes Death by the hand.

Chapter Fifty-three

A week later Lord Thierry came to my room and woke me in the night.

'Get up and put on these clothes,' he ordered me. 'Be as silent as you can and when you have dressed meet me in the library.'

His manner was such that I did not argue. I rose and lit my bedside lamp and looked at what he had brought me. Men's hose and a long tunic. A hat, dark jerkin and stout boots.

I dressed and went downstairs. He stood by the fireplace and in his hand he had a pair of cutting shears.

'I am informed that an army marches towards my castle and by morning we will be under siege,' he told me. 'Therefore you must leave tonight and I deem it safer that you go in male attire.'

When I tried to protest he told me very brusquely that the Duke of Marcy was in command of the approaching forces. I stood with head bent as he hacked my hair into a semblance of a male style.

'Not quite the wedding day I'd planned for us,' he said grimly.

When he had finished I said that I wanted my own travelling cloak to go with me and I ran upstairs to collect it and the precious papers it contained.

On my return he handed me my mandolin and I slung it over my shoulder. Then he took a torch of burning pitch from a bracket on the wall.

Down into the cellars we went. He opened door after door, and finally we walked into a long tunnel whose walls were slimy and green.

'Where are we?'

'Under the moat.'

'Leading to . . . ?'

'You will see.'

We came to a hollowed-out cave. It was of a circular shape. A stone table stood in the centre and radiating from it were six stone sarcophagi. On top of each one lay the effigy of a knight in armour. The walls were drier than those of the tunnel and were covered with designs not unfamiliar to me. I stood in the centre of the cave and with a steady drumming in my head I turned round and round and round, whirling, until the floor slipped from me.

He caught me or I would have fallen.

'Are you ill?' he asked me.

There was a thought, an elusive memory that I could not quite catch. As though I'd entered a room where an echo still sounded.

'What is this place?' I replied.

'When the Knights Templar were banned and

persecuted they needed a place to meet. My grandsire offered this hidden chamber in his castle at Valbonnes and in time the last knights were buried here.'

I reached out to the wall and traced the intertwining loops, the carvings, the knot that unknotted and retied itself. The end I could not find. And there was something there too in my head like the aftermath of a note in the air.

He took my arm. 'We must go on.'

'Where?'

'Outside the castle ramparts.'

'What army is coming here?' I asked him as we walked on.

'The Duke of Marcy has ties on his mother's side to the Duke of Guise. You know that he in turn is allied to the Count de Ferignay. Marcy's spies found out that the girl who witnessed his murder of the priest was in the castle here and he sent to both these men for soldiers to help him raise a force against me.'

'You have your own network of spies who tell you this?'

'It is prudent for me to have eyes and ears in the community. And I have one expert in Salon.' He laughed. 'How else do you think I was able to have knowledge of your movements there?'

'Berthe,' I said with confidence. 'The kitchen maid who listened at doors.'

'Who is Berthe?'

'She was a servant in the house of Nostradamus.'

'I know no one of that name. Soon you will meet the person that has kept me up to date with all the happenings in Salon.'

The tunnel curved upwards, bringing fresher air to relieve the dank smell. We arrived at a set of stone stairs. Thick tendrils of cobwebs faced us and on the floor insects, pale with living in dark places, scuttled away at our approach.

'There is only one road to Valbonnes,' I said as we passed outside through a small wooden door set in a mound on the other side of the castle moat. 'Will I not meet the army as it approaches?'

'I have arranged a guide for you. This person knows the way across the marshes where others will not tread. Mind well the path for there are sucking bogholes that would pull you under. Most travellers who venture there are never seen again.'

Lord Thierry pointed to an old bent tree. The figure that stood there was also stooped and walked towards me with a familiar shuffling gait.

'Giorgio!' I exclaimed.

Dr Giorgio, once apothecary to Master Nostradamus, pulled his cap from his head and made a little bow.

So it was not Berthe who had reported the things that went on in the house of Nostradamus.

'You are the one person in all of that household that I would have trusted,' I said to Giorgio as he greeted me.

'Which shows just how good a spy he is,' remarked Lord Thierry.

'I take that as a compliment,' said Giorgio. He replaced his cap and spoke to Lord Thierry. 'The situation is graver than you or I imagined. Both Guise and Ferignay see this as more than helping the Duke of Marcy on a personal matter. They mean to control the whole of the south of France with him as their puppet. To that end they have sent many soldiers and artillery too. You have very little time to get away.'

'I am not going with you,' said Lord Thierry.

'The walls of Valbonnes are not thick enough to survive cannon balls and siege machines.'

'It is my duty to defend my castle. And the longer we withhold, the more time you have to take her to safety. Marcy seeks the girl here and as long as they think she is within the castle they will remain in siege.'

'Sooner or later they will ask you to bring her to the battlements and when you cannot do that then they will burn the castle with you inside it,' warned Giorgio.

'That is the point when I will sue for peace,' replied Lord Thierry.

'They will enter and find her gone. Then they will kill you.'

'Perhaps not. And even so, by that time you will have had at least three clear days' grace and the girl will no longer exist.'

Giorgio gave him a puzzled look. 'How so?'

In answer Lord Thierry lowered the hood from my head and drew open my cloak.

Giorgio looked with interest at my man's clothes. 'Now is explained your mysterious appearance in the house of Nostradamus.'

'On your journey together this minstrel boy can tell you whatever he wishes you to know. But for now' – Lord Thierry paused – 'I must say goodbye.'

It wasn't until that moment that I realized that most likely I would never see him again.

'Why can't you escape with us?' I asked.

'If I did, it would decrease your chance of reaching freedom.'

'But by staying you put your own life at risk.'

Lord Thierry shrugged.

'Why are you doing this?' But even before he answered me I knew the answer.

'Because I love you, Mélisande,' he said. And he took my face between his hands and he kissed me full on my mouth. And his mouth was warm and he was gentle and he stirred something inside me. And I almost turned back then. For I knew that I could save this man's life. I had something that might ensure our safety. If I told the Duke of Marcy about the Nostradamus papers he would see the huge power that ownership of these would give him. I could bargain with him for free passage out of the country, perhaps to the New World. I would buy security for Lord Thierry and myself, and we would find a place to live out our lives. And I knew that life with such a man would be full of joyous music. We could banish sadness, he would adore me, and I should be granted any wish that he could provide.

He broke away and he searched my eyes with his own. He'd sensed my wavering, my inclination to stay. I fell against his chest and began to weep.

'It is not to be,' he whispered into my hair. 'I think I knew from the beginning it was not to be.'

'I too have a duty to perform,' I said.

He set me away from him and stood me at arm's length. 'Let me look at you. Do not cry, Mélisande. Allow me to see you smile one last time. This is the vision I will bring to mind when my darkest hour approaches.'

Giorgio touched his sleeve. 'There are torches among the trees.'

We both looked to where he pointed. The forest twinkled with the movement of hundreds of lights.

'They have yet to cross the river,' Lord Thierry said calmly. 'But I must go back to the castle now and sound the alarm. I'll return the way I came and will engineer a rock fall in the underground tunnel so that none may enter that way.'

Without saying anything more he walked away from us. At the entrance to the tunnel he turned and raised his hand. 'Goodbye and fare thee well, Mélisande.'

PART FOUR
THE NOSTRADAMUS
PROPHECY

Chapter Fifty-four

The night that I left Valbonnes I did not ask Giorgio where we were going. I only took his hand as he held it out to me and followed him with complete trust into the foul-smelling swamp.

The swamp was not vast but we took several hours to cross it. Inch by inch Giorgio prodded with his stick ahead of us to find a firm path. The moon was up in a fairly clear sky, which helped, for we couldn't risk striking a flint. It proved a circuitous snaking route that sometimes left us with no option but to jump over boggy patches to reach a safe tussock of grass. I watched and marvelled at his dexterity in doing this.

'You are not so disabled as you make out to be,' I commented on one occasion when we stopped to rest.

An impish look came onto his face. 'My arms and legs have not the co-ordination that they once had, but yes,' he agreed, 'I have more ability than I pretend to others.'

'Why do you wish to appear more infirm than you actually are?'

'It's useful if you are a spy. I've found that most people viewing my injuries assume that it must follow that my mind is equally compromised.'

'How very patronizing,' I said.

'How very convenient,' replied Giorgio. 'When you have an infirmity like mine people do not see you as a threat. The common perception is that body and brain are as one. The conversations I have heard in taverns, the secrets that patients have told me, they would never have divulged if they thought my wits were not as disjointed as my limbs.'

'Did Master Nostradamus know?' I asked him.

'I'm sure he did, else he would not have trusted me to measure and mix his recipes. He never commented, but he put me through a strict apprenticeship where he watched and checked everything I did. We were both aware that if I did not have a degree of accuracy in my work I might terminate the lives of half the noble houses of Europe! Now let us go on.' Giorgio stood up and lifted the knapsack that Lord Thierry had given him. 'The Duke of Marcy's troops will not come near the swamp because it is thought to be impassable and also for fear of evil spirits. But if daylight comes and they see two figures moving across it they might send soldiers to try to cut us off on the far side. I want to be out of this and under the cover of the edge of the forest before daylight.'

'What do you think will happen to Lord Thierry and the castle of Valbonnes?' I asked.

Giorgio shrugged and did not answer. But when the sun rose early the next day there was no need for me to ask again. It was plain to see the fate that awaited the beautiful castle and all within it.

We'd come to the end of the swampland and had climbed quite high on a thickly wooded slope. As the sun cleared the tops of the trees we stopped to look back.

On the plain in front of the castle an army was mustering, with cannon and siege engines.

'Lord Thierry's castle cannot withstand an assault by cannon for very long,' I said.

'Long enough that we might be far away before it falls,' said Giorgio. 'Let us use the time as he wanted us to, and get you to the Isle of Bressay as quickly as we can.'

So I was going to the Isle of Bressay. I should have realized that. Where else would I go? Where else *could* I go? My heart lifted at this thought. In some way I would be nearer Chantelle and my father. The tenants on the land would welcome me. I wondered if they'd had any news of what had happened recently to threaten their livelihood.

It was well that the weather was warm, for in the time that it took us to reach my true home we never once spent a night inside. We had a haversack of food and blankets that Lord Thierry had given us. Giorgio avoided towns, farms and any type of habitation. Once when it rained heavily he would not even shelter in a remote barn.

'These are the type of places that Huguenots use to come together for their worship,' he told me when I begged to be allowed to rest inside until the downpour stopped. 'It would only take one nosy traveller or farm worker to notice us and make comment at the next inn for a spy to pick up a piece of information.'

'I'm travelling as a man now,' I pointed out, 'and would not be so easily identified.'

'But I would,' he said. 'Spies know other spies and it would be simple to link a limping Italian from Salon to two people hiding as they travelled on the road away from Valbonnes.'

After that I did not protest. We walked and rested and walked, and on the way I told Giorgio the bones of my life history, my connection to the Isle of Bressay and why Lord Thierry had instructed him to take me there.

'Before this day is done I think you might see your father's land.'

Giorgio said this to me just after noon one day while walking through a meadow. We came over a gentle hill and there before us was a lake. Around the edge were small wooden houses where the fishermen lived and near to these was a causeway leading to an island. On the island among meadows and gardens stood a large house with its tall chimneys reflected in the peaceful waters. My tiredness sloughed from me. I began to run.

Giorgio flung himself after me. 'Hold back!' he cried. 'Hold back!'

He gripped my arms and hurried me into some bushes. 'Don't you see that the house gate is locked? That there are armed men guarding the entrance to the causeway?'

We knelt down, and then, keeping low, went closer that we might better see what was happening.

'Was it your father's custom to have soldiers patrolling his boundaries?' Giorgio asked me.

I shook my head. 'I don't believe so.'

We waited and watched for a while. Then a messenger rode out from the house. He was challenged by the soldiers but allowed to pass. His route was near to where we were hidden and he galloped close enough for us to see the colours on his tunic.

They were royal blue, quartered with the lily of France. The coat of arms of the Count de Ferignay.

Chapter Fifty-five

Giorgio and I ran to the foot of the hill and in among a small group of trees.

Giorgio was clearly agitated. 'That could have been disastrous.' His face was white and he was trembling. He gave my arm a shake. 'You must never rush away like that again.'

'I'm sorry,' I sobbed. 'I'm sorry.'

My tears were genuine. I'd had a bad fright, but I was also crying because I knew that I would not be able to go onto the Isle of Bressay, or sit at the window of our music room, or play in the gardens. I wept for the fate of my home with the Count de Ferignay's soldiers trampling everywhere.

'I am become careless that I didn't think he would have already sent soldiers to strengthen his claim to the property. Or else,' Giorgio mused, 'he might have thought that if you were alive, this is where you would go and he has placed men there to watch for you.'

'What can we do now?'

Giorgio sat down upon the ground. 'I must give this matter some thought,' he said.

As Giorgio pondered our situation I stood under the trees, staring at the Isle of Bressay. Memories began to stir in my mind. The house was always full of glorious sound and brightness. Its setting on the island, surrounded by the sparkling lake, meant that light poured in through the windows from dawn until sunset . . .

I swivelled round and stared at the hill behind us.

From my bedroom window I had been able to see this hilltop.

The Hill of the Standing Stones.

Rising in the morning and going to bed at night, I would gaze in fascination at the circle and the huge cairn that stood within it. Every day I saw the sun rise and set upon the stones. And the middle of the summer after my ninth birthday I had gone to the hill one evening . . .

'What day is this?' I asked Giorgio.

'It is late June,' he replied. 'The exact date I could not tell you. But listen to me, Mélisande,' he went on, 'there is a place where I have some contacts and you might be safe, but it will have its own dangers and—'

I was not listening to him. I had begun to walk away and up the incline of the hill.

He got up and came after me. 'Where are you going?'

'I must go and look at the stone circle,' I told him.

'There is not enough time,' said Giorgio. 'We should put some distance between ourselves and this place before another day passes.'

I shook my head and kept walking. 'First I must see the stones.'

I had no idea why I said this. When he saw that I would not be dissuaded, Giorgio urged me to ascend from the other side so that we might not be seen by any watcher in the house. He glanced around but he went with me up the hill until we both stood beside the cairn inside the circle of giant monoliths.

Giorgio was uneasy and kept urging me to leave. I hardly heard him. There was another sound ringing in my head. The air moved around me as if I were inside a huge cathedral with every bell pealing.

I had been nine years old when I'd last stood here . . . on Midsummer's Eve.

I had gone to bed that night but had got up again. The sky was still light, it being the longest day of the year. The sun, sitting on the rim of the horizon, spread long fingers of light over the earth. I had risen and walked from my house and climbed the hill of the ancient stones as if in a dream. When I got there, one red ray of sunlight was touching the huge stone slab around which the central cairn was built. I went towards the beam of light and placed my hand on the spot where it rested on the ancient stone.

The stone had rotated and I had stepped into a secret chamber . . .

The door had closed behind me.

But I had not been frightened.

It was not totally dark. Along the sides of the door was enough of a gap to allow slices of light to come through to illuminate the walls that surrounded me.

A wedge of gold sunlight slid across the far wall, and as it moved, the surface was revealed to me. I stretched up and with my fingers I touched the lines inscribed there; the grooves imprinted by stone on stone.

Then I'd heard Chantelle calling my name, and also the voice of my father, fraught with anxiety. So I'd turned and pushed the keystone, and the cantilever was so well balanced that, even after the space of a thousand years or more, it swung open. I appeared behind my father and sister. They thought that I had been sleepwalking. And in the morning I believed it to be a strange dream which I then forgot about.

Now, here with Giorgio standing beside me, I raised my hand to the collar of my cloak. I had not known myself how deeply this pattern was imprinted on my mind. It was this same design that I'd drawn and pinned as a template to stitch and embroider my cloak.

And also . . .

Nostradamus!

His visions of the massacre in Paris had begun in the year of my ninth birthday.

'At the time of the summer solstice.'

The year of my ninth birthday, 1563, added up to 15. The year of my birth, 1554, added up to 15. The year of his prediction of catastrophe for France, 1572, added up to 15.

I thought of the papers concealed in the hem of my travelling cloak and I drew it closer around my shoulders.

Giorgio took my movement as coming out of some reverie. 'Now that you have seen the stone circle,' he said, 'can we go?'

349

'Giorgio,' I said. 'There is something here for me and I must wait until I find it.'

'Listen,' he said. 'Do you recall on the second day we left Valbonnes we looked from a mountain slope and saw huge columns of smoke in the sky? I believe it meant the castle had fallen. With my broken body I can only travel slowly, and you merely have the stamina of a young girl. Those who are probably following our trail are armed and experienced horsemen with fresh horses, good food and supplies. No matter how careful I am they will pursue us. While you live, the Duke of Marcy's life and position are threatened. He will keep at least one of the inhabitants of the castle alive until they confirm that a girl of your description arrived in Valbonnes at the time that Master Nostradamus died. He will find out that the same girl disappeared just before the castle fell. Then he will deploy men in an ever-widening circle to seek you out and kill you.'

'None of Lord Thierry's staff would betray him, not for all the money in the world.'

'Not for money, no,' Giorgio conceded. 'But there are persuaders more powerful than money. I suffered the *strappado*, which is reckoned to be the most civilized method of torture. After a few sessions of it I would have told my questioners everything without them quizzing me further. Believe me, when they heat up the pincers in the furnace fire and lay out the torture implements where you can see them, and you smell the burning flesh and hear the screams of the others being questioned, you speak out what you know.'

I shuddered. Lord Thierry would die bravely, but I thought of the old nurse Marianne and hoped that her death had been merciful.

'I would rather my name was absent from that particular guest list,' said Giorgio. 'So you see why we must press on.'

'It troubles my mind that I have brought misfortune to people who have tried to help me,' I told him. 'But for that very reason I must wait a little longer in this place. Otherwise they have died in vain.'

He gave in to me for he could do nothing else. Although not as disabled as he had pretended in the past, he was not fit enough to force me to go somewhere against my will. As he sat down upon the ground I said, 'Today is Midsummer's Day.'

'If you say so,' he answered me. 'I have no reason to doubt you.'

'So now this is the summer solstice?'

'Ah, yes. A significant date.' He looked around at the stones.

I sat down beside him. He studied my face with interest.

'I do not understand what you meant when you said that these people will have died in vain.'

I almost told him then of the papers that Nostradamus had entrusted me with. I was tempted to share with him the secret of my mission. Only the promise I'd made to the prophet prevented me.

'We will wait,' I said. Although I did not know what I waited for.

We ate some food as the sun began to go down. Then

suddenly Giorgio lifted his head and said, 'Can you hear anything?'

I too listened and then shook my head. The lowering sun's long rays slanted across the sky from the west. They inched along the ground before us.

'There is no birdsong,' said Giorgio.

He was right. The chirruping had ceased as the shadows crept over the grass. A cloud passed across the sun and we both shivered.

Giorgio got up and paced to the edge of the hill. He knelt down and stretched out on his stomach on the grass to look at the Isle of Bressay. 'Nothing seems amiss,' he called back over his shoulder.

His voice came to me from far away. In idle fancy I had counted the number of stones.

15.

The number Nostradamus had puzzled over.

3 times 5.

15.

The clouds parted. A red line of light blazed out. It struck the central stone of the cairn.

I stood up. Giorgio was keeping watch and had his back to me.

I walked forward. I touched the stone. It swung open and I went through.

Chapter Fifty-six

The chamber was filled with rosy light that made it vibrate with energy.

Now sixteen years old, I was much taller than I'd been at nine, and I could both see and reach into the farthest corners. The complex pattern inscribed upon the walls throbbed with life. It was the design that had been in the cave of the Knights Templar. The intertwining circles. The writhing, roiling lines flowing into each other, the slanting ellipses, the snake-like coils crossing and recrossing. I stretched out both arms trying to grasp it all, to encompass and memorize and draw it to me and within me.

I felt my head swim and I sank to the ground.

The pattern was a force of life.

It pressed down on my head. And on the knights assembled in a circle there.

Each knight was dressed in a pure white surcoat with a large red cross emblazoned across his chest.

One by one they stepped forward and as they did, each

one drew his sword from its scabbard and kissed the blade. And then they spoke, their voices rolling like summer thunder in the mountains.

'Let me not be judged on the ill that I have done, but on the good that I intend to do.'

The Lord Thierry was the youngest among them. His face illuminated from within, his shining spirit so dazzling that when he stepped forward I did not at first recognize him. With firm hands he too swore the oath of fealty and justice.

'There is a pestilence upon the land.'

'The prophet has shown the way.'

'He has passed on. His time on earth spent out.'

'Another has been given the prophecy to safeguard.'

Then their voices began to overlap and clamour. And the noise was the sound of a thousand wooden clappers and I could make no sense of any of it. And I clutched my ears with hands and pressed hard on each side of my head to keep my mind from splintering into madness.

It was the smell of the *artema* flower that brought me to my senses. I opened my eyes in the utter darkness and the soft fragrance of Chantelle's wedding posy drifted into the enclosed space. I rose to my feet. I groped my way towards the door and outside.

The sun was lying just below the western horizon.

Where was Giorgio?

Above me the canopy of the heavens was a cloth of midnight velvet sprinkled with vibrant pulsating light.

Giorgio still lay on his front on the grass. He was so deeply asleep I had to shake him awake.

'I will go now,' I said to him.

He put his finger to his lips. 'Speak quietly,' he whispered, 'for sound carries over water.'

As we gathered our things together we could hear the voices of the sentries, then a wailing child from one of the fishermen's dwellings.

Using the stars as our guide, we turned south.

'We have only a few hours of near darkness before the sun rises again,' Giorgio whispered. 'Then I think we should hide during the day.'

So that was how we travelled for the next week or so. Giorgio would not move at all in daylight. As the weather was fine it was no hardship to walk by night and hide during the day.

It was on the afternoon of the fifteenth day that Giorgio pointed out a rocky mountain range in the distance and said, 'Hopefully on the other side of that lies safety.'

I ventured to ask, 'Where is it? Where have you taken me?'

'The only place I can think of where we might find refuge,' he answered. 'The kingdom of Navarre.'

Chapter Fifty-seven

It was clear that we were in a Huguenot town. Most of the inhabitants were dressed in cloth of dark hues relieved by white ruffs or headscarves.

'We are so travel-stained and covered with dust,' observed Giorgio, 'that even the prim Protestants will not find our dress too gaudy.' He looked at me critically. 'I think it's better to be clean if we are to present ourselves for employment anywhere.'

He left me sitting by a fountain for an hour and returned with an almost-new pair of dark breeches and a tunic in my size. He had also bought a jacket in blue cloth with a very plain white collar and cuffs and a blue cap with dark red corded trim which matched the russet of my travelling cloak. From his own knapsack he unfolded his black physician's coat with matching square hat and put it on.

'It will be difficult for me to make money in a Protestant town if they do not approve of music or other forms of entertainment,' I said when I had changed my clothes.

'That is a falsehood put about by their enemies,' said Giorgio. 'The Queen of Navarre, Jeanne d'Albret, is herself an accomplished musician and loves concerts and musical celebrations. What she objected to at the French court was its frivolous ways and scandalous actions.'

'Do you know someone at the court of Navarre who might give us employment?' I asked him.

'There was a magistrate in this town who came to Salon four years ago and asked me to prepare a potion to help his wife conceive a child. He was desperate, as they had been married a dozen years and she had failed to give him an heir.'

'And was your medicine successful?'

Giorgio grinned. 'So much so that when his third set of twins was born last year he returned and requested me to make him an antidote. I'm hoping that he remembers the skilled physician who helped him have four strong sons and two beautiful daughters.'

We found the house of the magistrate who had sought Giorgio's help. When Giorgio declared who he was to the servant at the door the man's wife herself came to greet him.

'My husband is away on business at La Rochelle, but I know he will be pleased to see you when he gets back. Meanwhile I'm happy to be able to thank you in person, my good Doctor Giorgio. Before I took your remedy I was becoming afraid that my husband might have our marriage annulled as I was barren.'

'I am pleased that all is well with you and your family,' Giorgio said. 'I will come straight to the point. You may have already heard that Master Nostradamus has died. His wife has taken to running his business so I decided to move on. I hoped that your husband might make a suitable recommendation for me. And' – he indicated me – 'my young nephew here, who is my assistant, and has also some talent as a musician.'

'You have come at the right time,' said the magistrate's wife. 'If you are prepared to travel then there are many appointments being made by the master of the royal household for the excursion to Paris.'

'The court of Navarre is going to Paris?' Giorgio said in astonishment. He glanced at me. The last news we'd heard in Salon was that Queen Jeanne of Navarre had declared that she and her son would not enter French soil again. 'I thought that the wars of religion would have meant it was safer for the Huguenots of Navarre to remain within the boundaries of their country.'

'It probably still is,' said the magistrate's wife, folding her arms and settling herself against the doorway as she realized that we were not aware of the latest doings and she could be the one to tell us. 'But there's been a Pact declared by the King of France, most probably engineered,' she added, 'by that Italian maggot who is his mother.'

In saying this, it didn't seem to occur to her that Giorgio, being Italian, might be offended by this remark.

'The queen regent, Catherine, is a true Medici,' Giorgio replied silkily.

As the magistrate's wife took this as an affirmation of her own opinion and gossiped on, I saw now how Giorgio was very effective at garnering information.

'This Pact, the Treaty of Saint Germain, is to bring peace to both sides. And to seal it properly . . .' The magistrate's wife held her breath to savour the moment of imparting her most exciting piece of news, then she burst out, 'We are to have a royal wedding!'

'A wedding?' Giorgio made his eyes huge in anticipation. 'Who is to be married?'

'Our Prince Henri of Navarre will marry the Princess Margot, sister of King Charles of France!'

This did seem to nonplus Giorgio. 'What!' he exclaimed.

The magistrate's wife was well satisfied with his reaction.

'You cannot tell me that Prince Henri and his mother, the Queen of Navarre, have agreed to travel to Paris for the ceremony?' said Giorgio.

'Not yet. But the most eminent Huguenot in France, Admiral Gaspard Coligny who sits on the French State Council, is to negotiate terms. My husband says he is a resourceful man and will succeed in his aims. Both sides know that without some kind of resolution England and Spain will begin to encroach on the lands of Navarre and France as we destroy ourselves from within. He says it is the one truth that both Protestant and Catholic accept.'

'It must also be to strengthen Navarre's own claim to the throne of France.' Giorgio mulled over this momentous development as we returned to the rooms we had rented.

'Prince Henri can never be the king of France,' I said. 'King Charles will marry and have children and in any case he has two other brothers.'

'When royal marriages are made, the game is a long one and is for life,' Giorgio said enigmatically.

The proposed wedding was the main conversation in the inn where we ate our dinner that evening.

'Coligny must be mad to stay among that nest of vipers,' said Giorgio.

My own impression of Gaspard Coligny was of a man with courteous manners and skilled diplomacy which he'd used to good effect. 'Perhaps he seeks a way to stop the wars of religion?'

'He should know that being a Medici, Catherine, the Queen Regent of France, will concede little. It must already be a thorn in her flesh that the Huguenots effectively rule La Rochelle and other towns inside French territory.'

Like the magistrate's wife, the innkeeper was keen to share his information with anyone who would listen. He told us that the recent agreement meant that the Huguenots were to be allowed the same access as Catholics to hospitals and schools and universities. 'They give us this as if it were a privilege, when it is our right,' he complained.

'And there you have it,' observed Giorgio as the innkeeper went away after setting down our dinner plates. 'Catherine de' Medici tries to placate each side and annoys both. Another man has told me that the family of Guise are once again fomenting rebellion, being bitterly opposed to paying recompense as ordered by the king for lands and goods seized during the last war.' He picked up his spoon to begin to eat. 'Surely the Prince of Navarre would not be so foolhardy as to accept this proposal.'

I remembered my impression of young Prince Henri. His prowess in the hunt, his rough but engaging ways, and how the Princess Margot had run to hug him when they were parting. She had been a child then. Now she was a woman. Did she retain an affection for him? Or was she being bartered against her will to bring reconciliation between opposing sides?

Chapter Fifty-eight

B y Christmas Giorgio and I were attached to the royal court of Navarre.

The gratitude of the magistrate at achieving a healthy family so quickly prompted him to use all his connections to secure us both a place. Giorgio was appointed an apothecary physician, with myself to assist him and play occasionally in the minstrels' gallery. We were given separate but adjoining small rooms, two of many boxed-off units in a long dormitory-type accommodation, which was rapidly filling up as the court of Navarre began preparations for the impending journey to France.

And in the midst of this, news came from Provence that the castle of Valbonnes had fallen, that the Lord Thierry had died defending his domain. And I knew then that it had indeed been his spirit that I had seen in the cairn of the standing stones on the hill overlooking the Isle of Bressay. But I grieved when Giorgio brought me the news and so did the Huguenots, for they had judged Lord

Thierry to be a fair ruler of his domain. Now there would be unrest in that region until the king appointed a new overlord, for the Duke of Marcy had also been killed in the battle.

Giorgio urged me to take comfort that I need no longer fear being pursued by Marcy. And I did have a sense of relief, but it was tempered by the sadness I felt for the death of a man who had loved me faithfully and given his life that I might live – and had made it possible that I might reach Paris to see my father and fulfil the prophecy of Nostradamus.

Since my vision at midsummer among the standing stones I was now even more convinced of the truth of Nostradamus's portents and my place in them. I had no understanding of what it was I had to do, but my life's path had led me to Navarre and I was now part of the court that would accompany Prince Henri to Paris for his marriage to Princess Margot.

For although during the whole of the following year Gaspard Coligny sent missives from France telling of the constant stalling of the matrimonial contracts, the wrangling over the type of religious service acceptable to all parties, the disagreement of the contents of the bride's dowry, the lack of concessions granted on both sides, no one really doubted that the marriage would take place.

Princess Margot was said to be unhappy as she had hoped for a more refined bridegroom. There were rumours that she had fallen in love with the young Duke of Guise and begun a liaison with him and that her mother, on hearing of this, had gone into a paroxysm of fury.

Catherine de' Medici had run to Margot's bedchamber and, stripping her nightdress from her, had struck and pummelled her daughter repeatedly, pulling handfuls of hair from her head. I recalled Princess Margot's miserable little face as she sat that evening in the king's apartments in Cherboucy Palace as the queen regent, Catherine, berated her children. The Princess Margot might protest, but what choice did she have?

Another memory came to me of that night: of the mirror above the sideboard, the pattern on the frame, the fluidity of the surface and how it had rippled and become still. And then a vivid reflection was before my eyes – the boy and the leopard.

Melchior and Paladin.

Had they ever been returned by King Charles to the Prince of Navarre?

In our first six months at court we did not see the young Prince Henri of Navarre. He spent time with his mother as she taught him statecraft and tried to instil some finesse into her somewhat uncouth boy. Queen Jeanne was attempting to do this before they went to France so that Henri's manners would not disgrace him among the French courtiers.

But this man's passion was hunting and at any opportunity he was off to one of his many hunting lodges. His quest of the moment was to capture a huge bear that had killed several hill shepherds and was becoming a scourge to the mountain villages. Henri used this as an excuse to his mother, saying that he needed to hunt the beast down as it was his princely duty to safeguard his people. When the bear was at last sighted he ordered his chief huntsman to call the royal hunt to muster. So once again I looked down from a palace window and watched the men and horses and dogs assemble.

And a boy bring a leopard into a courtyard.

But Melchior was no longer a boy. He was a man. He stood below me and my heart beat faster as I saw his dark tousled hair, his chest filled out broadly under his leather jerkin, his legs sturdy in black breeches and long boots. His arms hung down by his sides. One held the looped chain attached to the collar of his leopard.

Paladin was fuller, muscular, more dangerous.

I looked to the distant mountains where they planned to hunt. These were where Melchior had been born, and where he'd vowed that one day he would return so that he and Paladin might run free.

The hunt was assembled, the weapons sharpened and ready, the animals exercised and stabled in the surrounding buildings. It only required the presence of Prince Henri himself to lead it. He was delayed: he had gone to Eaux-Chaudes to bid farewell to his mother, who was setting out early for Paris as she would travel more slowly.

While we waited for the prince I mostly helped Giorgio with his work. He was in competition for custom, for there were other doctors and apothecaries at court. Giorgio had brought with him from Salon a bag of instruments and dishes and now used some of Lord Thierry's dwindling money to buy herbs and powders. I helped him mix and prepare his most popular remedies. Soon word spread, helped by the gossiping magistrate's wife, and we began to make enough for us to live on.

I had also presented myself and my mandolin to the master of the queen's music. To begin with he was disinclined to let an unknown lad be any part of his band of players. But I proved myself by dutifully strumming chords in accompaniment to their daily psalm singing. By the time Prince Henri arrived to lead the hunt I'd been allowed a place in the minstrels' gallery, which was positioned halfway up the wall on one side of the main hall.

Prince Henri's dinner was not the sedate formal meal that usually took place when his mother was present. The young prince was less strict with his religious duties and more lax in every way.

His favourite dogs were allowed into the room as he ate, whereas his mother would have had them tied up at the door. As dinner progressed Prince Henri sprawled in his chair, chewing at a haunch of meat. One of his hounds nuzzled its head into his lap and tried to seize it from him. He grunted and cuffed it. The dog reared up and put its paws on his chest and slobbered its tongue on his face. Henri allowed the dog to gnaw the bone and pull off a piece of meat. He ate another mouthful himself before he threw it on the floor where the rest of the dogs leaped upon it, barking. I thought of the fastidiousness of the French, and in particular Princess Margot's love of baths, and decided that this kind of behaviour by Prince Henri would repel her.

I was not the only person thinking of the upcoming meeting with the French.

The prince was a popular fellow with his men, his attendants and his friends. He had a broad sense of humour and a liking for practical jokes. This night he was in high humour and his laughter was constant because of the anticipation of a good day's hunting tomorrow. It became obvious, however, that his companions were concerned for his welfare.

When one commented that hunting a bear was more risky than stag or boar, Prince Henri's close friend, Denis Durac, quipped, 'Far safer for our prince to be in the Pyrenees than in Paris.'

'Hush, Denis,' Prince Henri scolded him. 'The queen regent, Catherine de' Medici, has given assurance to my mother that we will be under no threat. Gaspard Coligny wrote to me to say that King Charles now treats him as a revered father.'

'The promise of a Medici does not fill me with confidence,' replied Denis Durac. 'I think you need more safeguards than the word of that duplicitous woman.'

'I will be well protected.' Prince Henri laughed. 'I will take my leopard with me.' He raised his hand in summons. 'Bring him here to me.'

From my station in the gallery overlooking the hall I could see both Melchior and Paladin enter the room and stand beside Prince Henri's chair. I watched them from under the brim of my cap. The animal raised its head as if to sniff the wind. Did it recognize my scent even from so far away? Melchior bent and scratched Paladin behind the ear. Then he straightened up and looked around to see what had aroused the animal's interest.

The dogs slunk away to the far end of the hall. There were some birds of prey on perches there, two falcons and a hawk. On the appearance of the leopard they squawked and flurried their feathers, and would have flown off if they had not been tethered.

I kept my face averted.

We played on during dinner until we had almost exhausted our repertoire. The other musicians went in and out to relieve themselves or to find food or drink, or dally with the women. All at court took advantage of Queen Jeanne's absence. The master of the queen's music had drunk a lot of wine and was tired, but we had not been given permission to retire.

'You then, my lad,' he yawned as he rummaged in his box to find another piece of music. 'If you can make a decent sound with that instrument, play a tune to take up some time.'

I bent my head to my mandolin.

I began to play.

> *Proud prince of royal blood art thou,*
> *Paladin, so nobly named.*
> *Prisoner of others, yet*
> *Thy spirit, like the wind, untamed.*

I played but five notes. Melchior raised his head.

The leopard stood up. A low growl came from its throat.

Melchior placed his hand on Paladin's collar. With slow, almost imperceptible movements Melchior's eyes began to quarter the room. The leopard's tail swished and it too looked around.

> *Swift son of a mighty hunting race,*
> *Conquest falls to thee.*

I saw Melchior say something and the leopard sat back on its haunches. But its head remained high, its body tensed for action. As was Melchior's.

I had almost finished the song before he found me.

> *Silent shadow, fleet among the chase,*
> *Chained now, yet thou shall be free.*

Melchior stared hard but without expression deep into the corner of the minstrels' gallery where I stood. When I had finished playing he dipped his head in the faintest of nods.

A warm glow enclosed my heart.

Chapter Fifty-nine

Within a week a hunting party set out to track down the bear.

The animal had wreaked destruction through a group of villages on the outskirts of the forest of Navarre, therefore Prince Henri's chief huntsman organized the hunt to be assembled in that area. As the royal party progressed to the assembly point the villagers declared that they were being terrorized by the biggest and wildest bear they had ever seen. It was said to be enormous, possessing huge jaws with fangs dripping blood.

'It would seem that this bear's strength and prowess grows with every telling,' Prince Henri remarked in amusement on the first night we arrived at the hunting lodge in the foothills of the mountains.

His friend, Denis Durac, said seriously, 'It does sound as if it is of monstrous size.'

'I know that within exaggeration there usually exists a kernel of truth,' Prince Henri observed wisely. 'But in the space of one day I have heard men who claim to have seen this bear with their own eyes describe it as black, brown, or black and brown, or even, in one instance, pure white.' He laughed. 'Perhaps it is all of these colours.'

'There is no denying the damage it has caused,' said Denis Durac.

'Yes,' replied the prince, 'the mother I spoke to earlier moved me deeply.'

As we had ridden through the last village Prince Henri had stopped upon hearing the keening of a woman lamenting the loss of her child. He was told that the bear had seized the little boy as he'd played outside his family hut. Upon hearing the mother's screams everyone in the village had run to help. They had managed to drive the bear off with stones and fire but too late to save the life of the boy. The child's badly mauled and half-eaten body was brought for the prince to examine. Prince Henri ordered money to be given to the grieving woman and she had run after him as he rode off and grasped his stirrup and kissed his feet.

The prince was obviously embarrassed by this display of emotion. But he reined in his horse and, looking down on her kneeling there on the earth, he promised to bring her the head of the bear who had robbed her of her son.

'Now that is the mark of a true prince,' Giorgio had murmured to me.

I was surprised at his comment for it was not Giorgio's custom to give praise, and also he was very out of sorts at having to accompany the hunt at all. He was in pain being jolted around on horseback and would have much preferred to remain in the safety of the cosy royal palace than be out trekking over wild countryside. I felt some guilt at his discomfort for it was me who had encouraged him to come along. I'd learned that a physician was required to be in attendance at the hunt and I'd gone to Giorgio and asked him to volunteer for the post.

'Why would I do that?' Giorgio said. 'I'd much rather be at court and attend to the ladies here who pay well for my remedies.'

'Prescribing water tinctures for women's fainting spells when they would be better advised to lace their bodices less tightly is not true doctoring,' I told him.

'Mélisande!' He affected to be shocked. 'I have told you before that physicians have to heal the mind and spirit as well as the body. In any case, you have not explained why you think I should offer my services on this occasion.'

'It would be very prestigious, and bring you to the notice of Prince Henri,' I said.

Giorgio narrowed his eyes. 'Is that all?' he asked me.

'Of course,' I replied. 'I only wish for your advancement.'

'Now I am even more suspicious,' said Giorgio. 'Is it your intention that you accompany me on this expedition?'

'I think you would most certainly need an assistant with some apothecary skills. Someone who could also play the mandolin in case Prince Henri needed any musical diversion.'

Giorgio considered this idea. 'Going about the court discreetly as you do, dressed as a young man, is relatively easy. But on a hunt, when men are in close physical contact, and are wont to relieve themselves whenever and wherever they choose, is somewhat different. All manner of things might be very awkward for you.'

'I appreciate that,' I told him. I was already becoming used to the careless, open way men did this. I'd learned to turn my head away, and also to drink sparingly and control my own functions until I was sure of privacy.

'I will manage,' I assured him.

'I hope so,' he said seriously. 'For if you were found out you might become sport for men of crude tastes, and I might not be able to protect you.'

But I might have the protection of another, I thought.

When we stopped at the hunting lodge Giorgio and I established our sleeping arrangements and pharmacy in a tent under the trees. He had been asked to attend to one of the prince's men so I unfolded the portable stools and table we had brought and set out herbs, tinctures and some surgical instruments and bandages in case of any serious injury to the hunters. I finished and sat down on a stool, took up my mandolin and began to play. How good it was to be outdoors again! The trees rustled and whispered to each other. The moon rose in the sky and the night owls hooted.

Giorgio returned and informed me that he was now more unhappy than ever at being away from his more gentle duties of the court.

'Lancing a boil on the backside of Prince Henri's valet is not what I envisaged as the rise in status you promised me,' he said.

I noticed that there was some satisfaction in his voice and I enquired sweetly if inflicting pain on another eased his own discomfort.

He was about to reply in kind when a shadow of a man appeared at the door of the tent.

'I am looking for a salve.'

My pulse began to race.

Giorgio waved his hands towards his medicines in an agreeable manner. 'I have many salves. Is there a particular one that you seek?'

'A most particular one,' Melchior answered him. 'It is of arnica with the addition of borage flowers.'

Giorgio shook his head. 'That is not one of my remedies.'

'Perhaps your assistant has heard of it?'

'I do not think—' Giorgio started to reply.

I stood up and came forward nearer to the door of the tent.

Melchior held out the little dish I had given him all those years ago at Cherboucy.

'I know that recipe,' I said to Giorgio.

Giorgio tilted his head to one side. He looked at my face, at Melchior's, and back to me. Then he said, 'I think I may go now to where the evening meal is being served.' Melchior and I watched him as he slowly unrolled his sleeves, fastened up his shirt cuffs and put on his coat and hat. He stared hard at Melchior before he left. 'I will expect my assistant to join me within ten minutes,' he told him distinctly.

Melchior returned Giorgio's stare.

They both knew that if Melchior chose to disobey him there was nothing he could do.

When Giorgio had gone I found that I was suddenly shy.

I bent my head and sat down again on the stool.

Melchior came and knelt before me. His face was on a level with my own. I looked into his eyes and felt myself drown in their depths.

Melchior reached out his hands and took mine in his own.

'Mélisande,' he said. 'Tell me how you have fared since last I saw thee.'

Chapter Sixty

Before we began the hunt proper the next day Prince Henri sought advice from his huntsmen.

He called Melchior to him and spoke to him most cordially. I saw how the prince listened and discussed how they might deploy the hunting animals, the horses and his men. His ambition was to rid his people of the threat that terrified them, but he showed concern for the safety and wellbeing of the hunters.

We made our way into the Pyrenees following the path shown to us by a local shepherd. This man knelt down before the prince as the bereaved woman had done the day before. He thanked Prince Henri for coming to his aid. He explained that his livelihood was at stake. Three of his sheep had been killed, the rest of his flock scattered in terror.

We went deeper into the mountains. Now the terrain was rocky, with woods dotted on the hillsides. It was in one of these that Melchior and the leopard, Paladin, had been born. Some trader or noble had brought a leopard to this land and it had escaped to the wild. The animal must have been pregnant before leaving the country of Africa where it had been captured.

At midday we paused to eat. The men took their meals in rough order. Prince Henri sat among them. For all his uncouth ways his conversation was not coarse as is sometimes the case in men without the presence of women. They talked politics and the fate of human kind and the influence of God and Church. The prince refused to condemn any man for his beliefs. We had earlier passed a wayside shrine dedicated to the Virgin Mary and our shepherd guide had gone forward, blessing himself, to place some flowers there. Then, remembering the company he was with, he had turned in sudden fear. But Prince Henri had already nudged his horse to move on, keeping his eyes firmly on the road ahead.

We mounted again and continued our tracking. The wind was blowing from behind us, carrying our scent forward and preventing us from picking up that of our prey. Giorgio and I were in the rear, as our horses carried the boxes of medicines and instruments, but the party was small and we could see ahead very clearly.

The shepherd showed us the place where his sheep had been killed a few days previously.

'Let the leopard smell fresh blood,' Prince Henri ordered.

Melchior brought Paladin forward and took the muzzle from the leopard's mouth. The animal was restless, ears flattened against the relentless mountain breeze. Melchior slipped free the chain. Then, despite the coolness of the air, he removed his shirt.

Once again was revealed the twisting pattern of ochre and violet colours on his painted back.

Within me every sense heightened. As if my mind and body were in accord.

I was aware of Giorgio watching me. He turned away but not before I had seen the look of concern on his face.

Suddenly, without warning, the bear attacked.

It leaped from the mountain rocks above and landed on the mount of Denis Durac. Under the weight of the bear and the tremendous force of the assault, horse and rider crashed to the ground. The bear's attack ripped the shoulder of the horse to the bone.

Without waiting for a command the leopard launched itself in retaliation. The bear raised itself up. With a wide sweep of its huge paw it cuffed the leopard away. Paladin was sent hurtling through the air and thudded to the earth, rolling over and over down the mountain slope.

I bit my hand to stop myself screaming.

The huntsmen released the dogs. They yipped frantically, barking and circling, but too cautious to try to run in. The bear was immense. Twice the height of any man. And broad as a house. The horses neighed in terror. Eyes rolling, they reared and thrashed and tried to bolt. Some managed to do so, galloping off down the path with their riders clinging on desperately. Prince Henri kept control of his own, urging it forward to the place where Denis Durac lay on the ground, trapped under the body of his own horse.

The bear stood over the stricken man, snarling and growling, small red eyes blazing hatred, drool and blood hanging from its jaws.

Prince Henri snatched off his cloak. He stood up in his stirrups and flung it over the head of the bear. The cloth spun out and caught the bear about the ears. Half blinded, with its head covered, the beast twisted this way and that, forelegs flailing like one demented.

It gave the respite needed. In an instant Prince Henri had his lance in his hand. There was a blur of almond fur and Paladin had the bear by the neck. The leopard clung on as the bear clawed at his body and tried to shake free. The hunters closed in, and with spear and arrows finished the kill as quickly as possible.

The shepherd was weeping with both fright and delight. The rest of the men hauled the horse off Denis Durac. He lay there, white-faced, while one of the huntsmen mercifully slit the throat of the stricken animal.

Prince Henri came and knelt by his friend. Denis Durac grasped the prince by the hand. 'Sire, you saved my life.'

Prince Henri cuffed his head in comradeship. 'As you no doubt would have saved mine, dear friend, had our positions been reversed.'

I saw now why these men loved their prince and would go with him to the mouth of death.

Prince Henri raised his hand in summons to Giorgio. 'Doctor! Your presence is required here.'

We gathered ourselves and made our way back to the hunting lodge. Giorgio insisted on a litter being made to transport Denis Durac. He declared Durac's ribs to be broken, and if they were to heal without further internal injury then they must do as he recommended. He spoke with such conviction that the prince paid attention and insisted that Giorgio's orders were followed.

After we had eaten, Prince Henri spoke of his promise to the village woman. He had the bear's head sawn off before setting out with an escort to take it as a gift to the mother of the dead child. The prince had placed Denis Durac in his own bed. I left Giorgio in attendance on him there and went to pack up our boxes and prepare for our return to court the next day.

Melchior was waiting for me.

'How is Paladin?' I asked him.

'Sore, but satisfied with his kill.'

'Do you need ointment for his cuts?'

Melchior shook his head. 'He will lick his wounds clean. His saliva has healing properties.'

I looked to the mountains behind us. 'This is where you were born?'

'Yes, not so far from here.'

'You told me once, that the day would come when you would seize your chance and escape.' I gestured with my hand to indicate the hunting lodge, empty save for a few servants. 'This is an opportunity.'

Melchior nodded. 'I know of a secret pass through the mountains.' He waited. 'What would you do?' he asked me.

'I must go to Paris.'

'To find your father?'

'Yes . . .'

'There is something else?'

'Yes.'

He looked at me but I shook my head. I'd already decided that I would not tell him of the strange prophecy of Nostradamus. As the day approached when I must take the papers I carried nearer to the presence of Catherine de' Medici, my terror of her vengeance grew. If she tore the hair from her own daughter's head for falling in love with the wrong man, what would she do to me, a mere minstrel, who had concealed from her a prophecy concerning her son, the king? I had too much regard for Melchior to involve him in anything that might bring him harm.

'If you go to Paris you will be in great danger,' he said.

'I know that.'

'Then I will go too that I may help thee.'

His fingers brushed mine.

And my heart trembled.

Chapter Sixty-one

We made a triumphant return from the hunting lodge, dragging the remainder of the bear's carcass through the villages on the way. The villagers ran out to strew flowers at Prince Henri's feet and to try to kiss his hand as he passed. They surrounded the litter carrying Denis Durac, including us all in this outpouring of gratitude and affection. It was plain to see the high regard in which the people of Navarre held their royal leader.

Arriving back at court, we discovered that finally an agreement had been reached as to the terms and format of the marriage of Prince Henri of Navarre and the French princess, Margot. The wedding would take place in August of next year, 1572.

1572.

The year Nostradamus had predicted when the streets of Paris would echo with the screams of the dying.

The organization began for the long cavalcade of court members, nobles, dignitaries and royal staff to set out from

Navarre to Paris for the wedding ceremony. Queen Jeanne d'Albret went to Paris a few months ahead of her son. She wished to get settled there to prepare for the various royal receptions. Prince Henri intended to follow later. King Charles had specifically asked his cousin to bring the leopard, Paladin, with him.

Over the months as the court got ready to move, Denis Durac made a full recovery. This caused a lot of comment for it was quite usual for a person suffering internal injuries to take an infection and die in agonizing pain. Thus Giorgio's fame at healing spread enough for him to be one of the doctors chosen to go in the vanguard of staff travelling to the French capital. Prince Henri requested that he attend to his mother, Queen Jeanne, who did not keep good health.

Now the hour of my destiny was near. The night before we were due to depart I lay unsleeping and trembling with apprehension in my cot, staring out the uncurtained window at the moon in the sky. The night noises of the castle came to me and I recalled how Chantelle and I had whispered together each evening in the palace of Cherboucy in happy sisterhood. I must set my fear aside. I owed my sister justice. If I saved the life of the king then surely he would grant my father liberty and avenge the death of my sister and her lover?

Although we'd been provided with a coach in which to travel, the journey was harrowing. Long hours with wheels jarring over rough roads did not help Giorgio's condition, but it was the sights we saw on the way that disturbed both of us much more than any physical discomfort.

The countryside was ravaged with the constant religious wars of attrition. Crops rotted in the field while starving orphaned children stood by the roadsides holding out their hands for bread or alms. We passed burned-out villages, and manor houses and châteaux with the walls torn down. Nearly every crossroads had a gibbet with a dangling skeleton. Despite this my spirits lifted as we approached Paris. I was hopeful that, after all this time, I would see my father again and my memory of the city in my extreme youth was of a happy, vibrant place.

How this city had changed! The wars of religion had battered the buildings and the mood of the citizens in equal measure. The jubilant, noisy sounds I'd heard in my youth had been replaced by angry voices and arguments.

The markings on our coach declared us Huguenot. Once through the gate horsemen in the street would not move aside to let us through. In front of us carts slowed to delay our progress and stallholders and passers-by shouted names and crude words after us.

Suddenly a rough hand pulled aside the window flap and a face was thrust through,

'Heretics!' the intruder screeched at us. 'Here, take this as a wedding present for your Protestant prince!' And the man spat into Giorgio's face.

I gave a shriek. I heard our coach driver curse and one of our escort rode up and beat the man off with his whip.

Giorgio calmly wiped the sputum from his face. 'Can you blame them?' he said. 'It's not so long since they were starving when the Huguenot army besieged Paris and killed the constable of the city.'

Giorgio and I had been given accommodation in the house of the Viscount Lebrand where Queen Jeanne was residing. We were allocated space on a basement level with a sink and a bench for the preparation of remedies, and prior to our arrival, Giorgio had sent orders to various Parisian suppliers for special ingredients. Our rooms had an outside door from which stairs led up to the street, which meant we could come and go from the house as we pleased.

Almost immediately Giorgio was summoned to the apartments upstairs to examine an ulcer on the leg of Viscount Lebrand. He left me with the job of unpacking our boxes while he went off to attend to this. I had just hung up my travelling cloak and mandolin on a hook on the wall when the door from the street opened and a man of ill features walked in.

'Where is Doctor Giorgio?'

'Not here,' I answered him in alarm, annoyed at my own foolishness in leaving the door unlocked. 'Who are you?'

'Tell him Rodrigo sent this.' He handed me a small package. 'It must be used immediately.'

'Does it contain fresh ingredients?' I asked him. 'Will it spoil?'

'Oh yes,' he laughed, 'a lot will be spoiled if it is not used right away.' He gave me a toothless smile and left.

I knew that Giorgio had been searching through his books for a remedy for the ulcerated leg of the viscount. But I did not know what this ingredient that he'd sent for might be, that it would spoil if not used at once. I decided I had better unwrap it.

I opened the package. It contained a vial with white powder. When I removed the stopper a familiar fruity smell lingered in the air. The powder did not seem to have the density to be useful for a salve and I was curious as to what it contained. I wet my finger, dipped it in and was about to place it into my mouth when Giorgio entered the room via the inside door which led from the house.

'What have you there?' he asked me sharply.

'A man delivered this package for you, for immediate use or it would spoil,' I told him. 'I supposed it to be the powder for the salve but I was about to taste it to be sure.'

Giorgio rushed forward and jerked my hand away from my mouth so violently that I fell against the table. I stared at him in amazement. 'What's the matter?'

'That is – that is,' he stuttered, 'for a special mixture. I had – I had it prepared – for the purposes of disinfection.' He lifted a cloth and wiped my finger clean. Then he gave me a little push. 'Go and find a pumice stone and scrub your fingertip until it's raw,' he instructed me.

As I went to the sink to do as he'd ordered I saw him meticulously fold over the packet and tuck it into the inside of his tunic.

'How is Queen Jeanne?'

'What?' he said. 'Why do you ask that?'

'Because Prince Henri hoped you would make his mother well enough to enjoy his wedding,' I reminded him.

'Of course,' said Giorgio, 'yes, I am aware of that. I'll

consult with Queen Jeanne tomorrow, then I will know what to do.' He looked around in a distracted manner. 'Now I must go out. There are things I have to deal with.'

I didn't bother myself much about Giorgio's errand that evening. In Salon and in Navarre he was always able to source the scarcest ingredients for his recipes. I assumed that already he had established a similar network in Paris. But I was concerned as to his safety. As the date of the royal wedding drew near the city was becoming crowded and dangerous.

As well as the highborn travelling here to view the ceremonies and processions, a vast number of every low type of person was pouring through the gates every day. The wars that had scoured the land had caused famine, and Paris was full of peasants seeking free handouts from the wedding feasts promised for the public to enjoy. All the inns and taverns and monasteries were overflowing with travellers. By day they thronged the streets, at night those without lodging houses lay huddled in the doorways and alleys.

It was past midnight before Giorgio came back. I'd returned to the small room where I'd made a bed for myself, but I awoke when I heard his key turn in the lock of the outside door. He was not alone. There was a murmur of voices and then, to my complete shock, someone very quietly opened the door of my room. I remained still. Giorgio had never before intruded on my privacy in any way. I kept my breathing even, but my body tensed to run or strike out if attacked. I heard Giorgio speak reassuringly.

'I told you, the boy sleeps deeply. He will hear nothing and suspect nothing, for although useful, he is slow-witted.'

I realized instinctively that Giorgio was saying this to protect me, but even so I felt offended. My impulse was to rise up and declare, 'I have wit enough to know that there is something wrong with a person who chooses darkness to consult a doctor.' But the years had passed and I was no longer the reckless young girl I'd once been. So I lay without moving and did not speak.

My room door closed and I heard nothing more. And I was too frightened to rise from my bed to try to eavesdrop on the conversation in the other room.

Chapter Sixty-two

In the weeks leading up to the wedding the heat in the
city grew oppressive.

And as the heat increased, so did the discord
between the citizens of Paris and the peasantry from the
countryside, between the native French and the visitors
from Navarre, between Catholic and Protestant.

Thieves and street girls stole openly from the visitors,
innkeepers charged inflated prices, shopkeepers cheated
and fleeced anyone and everyone. Beggars formed themselves into gangs and became belligerent if refused alms.
The rule of law crumbled under the onslaught.

The main target of discontent became the Huguenots.
They were easily identified by their dress and
manner. They found themselves ostracized, denied food
and lodging, jostled and insulted whenever the opportunity arose.

Clergy from either side preached openly against the
marriage. The words of the preachers inflamed the senses
of the congregations. As the days went on the mood of the

people rose through irritation to annoyance and boiled over into outright anger.

The situation in the city was mirrored within the house of Queen Jeanne d'Albret. While we awaited the arrival of Prince Henri, his mother was subjected to an endless stream of messages from the French court, containing instructions, suggestions and in some cases demands. When she was informed as to the format of the ceremony Queen Jeanne stated that her son's Protestant faith meant that he could not enter the cathedral of Notre Dame to be married. A compromise was suggested by Gaspard Coligny. It was arranged that a platform would be erected in the square in front of the cathedral where Prince Henri and Princess Margot could be married. The queen regent, Catherine de' Medici, insisted that a ceremony must be held within a Catholic church. So it was agreed that a proxy would take Prince Henri's place for this.

In return Queen Jeanne sent messages to King Charles, who had taken up residence in the Louvre, asking to speak to him directly and not through his mother. But the young king had been completely captivated by another adviser, Gaspard Coligny. King Charles now called the Huguenot leader 'Father' and allowed him greater and greater influence over decisions of state and defence.

Giorgio and I were in constant attendance on Queen Jeanne of Navarre as her health varied with the stresses upon her. Recently Giorgio had become waspish and short-tempered. He'd had at least two more visits in the middle of the night from people unknown to me. When I'd awoken again to hear voices in the outer rooms I'd kept my eyes and my door firmly closed. But on one of these occasions I'd heard Giorgio raise his voice and say, 'It is *not* necessary to do this. Time will bring the same conclusion.'

The conversation continued at a level I could not hear.

His manner with Queen Jeanne was sympathetic and caring but he did not discuss her treatment with me as he would normally have done with any other patient.

She meanwhile complained less about her health and more and more about the French royal family and their imperious ways.

'I am of royal birth and an heir in my own right,' she protested on one occasion, 'a grandchild of a king of France. My son, Henri, is of the blood royal, from my ancestry and from his father's Bourbon family.'

To which Catherine de' Medici was said to have replied, 'It is by my permission that the Bourbons hold any title and I am minded to withdraw that licence.'

One day as Giorgio was removing leeches from Queen Jeanne's arm, Gaspard Coligny arrived for an audience.

'You are better today, madame?' He kissed her fingers.

'I have the attention of a good doctor here,' said Queen Jeanne, 'sent to me by my son.'

Gaspard Coligny's hair had become more grey and sparse since I last saw him. He nodded briefly to Giorgio.

'And how do you fare, my friend, Admiral Coligny?' Queen Jeanne enquired in turn. 'Do you manage to keep your patience with that foolish and self-indulged boy they revere as king?'

Giorgio handed me the basin of blood and began to

remove the tourniquet from the queen's arm. Suddenly there was a flurry of movement at the door. Giorgio looked round and dropped the cloth he was holding.

The queen regent, Catherine de' Medici, accompanied by her son, had arrived unexpectedly to visit Queen Jeanne.

'Father!' King Charles cried out in joy, and hurried forward to embrace Gaspard Coligny.

Both older women in the room looked on in disapproval at Charles's precipitate behaviour.

'I do hope that you will recover sufficiently to attend the wedding of my daughter and your son,' Catherine de' Medici said smoothly.

'It is my hope also that the wedding will take place, madame,' replied Queen Jeanne.

There was a pause as Catherine de' Medici digested the veiled threat that had just been made by Queen Jeanne d'Albret.

'I came to thank you for the many gifts you have bestowed upon my daughter and myself.' Catherine de' Medici chose to ignore the implication that the wedding might be cancelled by the Navarre side. Her eyes roved around the room as she spoke. Her gaze alighted on me for a second then passed on.

'As I thank you for yours,' replied Queen Jeanne.

'Yes . . .' Catherine de' Medici paused. 'There was a most particular present sent to you earlier today.' She smiled, and somehow this was more sinister than any of her severe looks. 'I had a pair of white leather gloves of the softest kid-skin made especially for you.'

'I received them with pleasure,' said Queen Jeanne.

'I am happy about that,' said Catherine de' Medici. And she smiled warmly at Queen Jeanne as if this small courtesy had pleased her enormously. 'And I would be most grateful if you would at least try them for size very soon so that if there is any alteration needed then I can have it attended to immediately.'

As Queen Jeanne tried to rise from her day bed, Catherine leaned forward solicitously. 'I hope your health will improve that you may see your son joined to the noble house of France.'

Queen Jeanne ignored the insinuation that her son Henri was not already part of the French nobility and said, 'I have been unwell, but the attentions of the doctor my son sent to care for me means that I will be fit enough for whatever ceremonies I may have to attend over the next few weeks.'

Despite having his presence pointed out to her, Catherine de' Medici did not glance in Giorgio's direction.

And that did make me wonder, for my memory of this woman was very clear in that respect. When she entered a room her eyes searched out every corner. She noted who was there and what position they occupied. She weighed up an individual's importance, their threat, their influence. Assessing each person as to how much use they might be, or what amount of harm they could do.

There was shouting from the street and the noise of horsemen passing. 'No doubt another contingent of your countrymen entering Paris,' Catherine de' Medici commented haughtily.

Queen Jeanne returned Catherine de' Medici's look

with an equally proud stare. 'My son has many friends who wish to rejoice with him on his wedding day.'

Catherine glanced from the window. 'But that body of soldiers are French!' she exclaimed. 'And they are marching away from the centre towards the gates. I gave no order for troop movement.'

Gaspard Coligny smiled towards King Charles as he replied smoothly, 'You know of this, sire. The Protestants of the Netherlands need help from their brethren in France and Navarre. It's a noble act to send arms to assist them else their Spanish overlords would execute them all for their beliefs.'

'You have allowed a contingent of French troops to go to the Netherlands to fight against Spain?' Catherine's voice was incredulous.

Charles looked in confusion from his mother to the man whom he now called Father. 'When Gaspard explained the foreign situation I deemed it the right thing to do.'

Catherine strove to keep her voice calm. 'Spain could deem this an act of war and invade us.'

'It seems a reasonable thing to me,' King Charles pleaded with his mother.

Catherine controlled her anger and managed a grimace of a smile before saying, 'What is reasonable is that I should always be kept informed before such a thing should happen.'

'Your pardon, madame,' said Gaspard Coligny. 'But I did not think it necessary to explain the orders of the king himself to anyone.'

I heard an intake of breath from Giorgio.

'Perhaps then you might explain this to me,' said Catherine de' Medici. 'I note that many of the Huguenots walking about the streets of Paris carry weapons. When does it happen that guests at a wedding are armed?'

'When it is that the hosts are also armed,' Coligny replied without hesitation.

Catherine de' Medici looked to her son, waiting for him to reprimand Coligny for speaking to her in this impudent manner. But Charles only nodded and said, 'That is a fair comment.'

Queen Catherine bit her lip. With her skirts swirling she swept from the room.

Giorgio nudged my arm. 'Take away this basin of blood,' he ordered.

I hurried off with the basin to our rooms to empty it into the sink. A jumble of pots and trays were lying there, awaiting cleaning. I hesitated. Giorgio's rule of good hygiene took precedence over everything else. Bad blood could contaminate, and must be kept apart from all other things. I recalled seeing a drain just outside our door. I went outside and knelt down to empty the contents of the bowl into the opening. Thus I was positioned out of sight directly under the stair arch of the main doorway of the house as the queen regent, Catherine de' Medici, hurriedly left the villa.

As she ascended into her carriage I heard her speak. In a voice shaking with fury she gave an instruction to her equerry.

'Send this message privately to the Duke of Guise. Tell him that the time has come.'

Chapter Sixty-three

That night I was once more roused from my sleep in darkness.

But this time it was not by the sound of lowered voices and someone creeping quietly near my room. The noise was loud and the person was crying in a high voice, 'Doctor! Doctor Giorgio!'

I sat up in bed. The door to the inside corridor of the house shook under the pounding of fists. I scrambled for my clothes and cap and was opening the door before Giorgio was fully awake.

A dishevelled servant stood there. 'The doctor must come at once! Queen Jeanne is sick unto death!'

Giorgio grabbed his doctor's bag and hurried upstairs in his nightgown with me running after him. It was clear immediately on entering the queen's bedroom that there was nothing he could do. There was nothing anyone could do. The corpse of Queen Jeanne sat propped up on pillows with eyes fixed and staring straight ahead. Her face was as white as her hands lying on the bed coverlet.

'I need everyone to go away.' Giorgio spoke out firmly.

The servants of the bedchamber did as he asked. Giorgio opened up the bag he'd snatched up on his way out of our rooms. 'You too,' he said to me in a low voice. 'I will verify that the queen is dead and make the announcement. You must attend to any of her ladies who may become hysterical.'

I did as he requested. Giorgio loosened the bed drape so that it fell across his back as he leaned over the body of the dead Queen. A small collection of people began to gather at the door. The Viscount Lebrand appeared and pushed his way through.

'What is amiss?' he demanded. He strode towards the bed and pulled the drapes aside. 'Has the queen suffered another attack of her illness?'

Giorgio straightened up. He closed his medicine bag, turned to the viscount and said, 'I am sorry to have to tell you that Queen Jeanne has passed on from this earth. She has been dead at least an hour.'

At Giorgio's words wailing broke out among those round the door. Just as he'd predicted, one of the ladies began to shriek and moan and rend her garments.

Giorgio glanced in her direction. 'Let me go now and bring some smelling salts and soothing medicines to calm these ladies' nerves.'

The viscount nodded at him gratefully while the queen's attendants clutched each other, weeping.

As Giorgio lifted his bag and hurried off, one of the ladies ran to the bed and, grasping the queen's hand, began to sob plaintively. I put my arms around her shoulders and tried to draw her away. But she resisted, and held on more tightly, kissing the back of the queen's hand with its yellowed and age-mottled skin. The Viscount Lebrand intervened, and coaxed this lady out of the room to be with the others. Soon the whole house was filled with lamenting. Like her son the Queen of Navarre was loved by her subjects.

Despite the death of Queen Jeanne it was agreed that the wedding of her son, Henri, was still to take place. It was not to be delayed, though Henri did grieve for his mother. She had been serious-minded while he was light-hearted. She was refined while he was more casual in his manners and speech. But they had cared for each other. Out of respect for what he believed were her wishes Prince Henri declared himself content to go ahead with his marriage on the eighteenth day of August.

After the funeral there was a short period of mourning and then the final preparations went on for the wedding. The city became more tense and this mood was reflected within the walls of the house. The queen's servants missed her presence deeply and even Giorgio, normally so stoic about such things, seemed to be upset at her passing. He was short-tempered and distracted. I too was now on edge for I'd discovered from the kitchen servants that Melchior and the leopard had arrived in Paris. They'd gone, as arranged, to specially prepared quarters within the palace of the Louvre. Melchior was now positioned closer to my father and he'd told me he would try to find out any information he could. I wondered if I might be able to catch sight of the one other person that I longed desperately to see.

When I asked Giorgio if, now that Queen Jeanne was dead, we would attend any court functions, he snapped some non-committal reply. I was startled at his rudeness and bent my head to my work, puzzled as to why he was so touchy about my question. I glanced up. Giorgio was staring at me and I could not read the expression on his face. It was as if a stranger had entered the room, and yet his eyes had a look I recognized. A coldness came about me as I realized that the last time I'd seen a man regard me in such a manner was when I'd struggled to free myself from the Count de Ferignay.

It was a look of calculation, the way a predator might survey a potential victim.

And suddenly it was as if some other sense within me was alive.

I sensed a trap encircling me.

I lifted my head up. The way the leopard raised its head seconds before the bear attacked.

Giorgio drew his hand over his brow.

'It is too warm, yes?' he said. Drops of sweat ran on either side of his temple. 'I am overcome by this heat.' He paused and smiled. 'As you must be too, Mélisande. You must rest more, my dear. I will make you another soothing preparation to help you sleep at night.'

So it was nothing. My prickling uncertainty was only the stifling heat of the city. Giorgio's close regard was merely his concern for my welfare.

All through the days of that sultry, suffocating August Giorgio continued to watch over me. I began to drink his sleep remedy every evening for each batch he made was sweeter than the previous one. And it meant that I did not lie awake at night bathed in perspiration, listening to the increasingly frightening noises of the rabble that occupied the city streets in the hours of darkness. His potion drove away my nightmares, where I saw myself kneeling at the feet of Catherine de' Medici, begging for mercy as she summoned the executioner from Carcassonne to lead me to the stake.

Chapter Sixty-four

When the wedding day arrived, we, as medical advisers to the Navarre royal house, were allocated places near enough to view the proceedings. While everyone's attention was fixed on the wedding ceremony I was hoping that this was the day I might see my father once more.

Prince Henri arrived first, accompanied by his good friend Denis Durac and Gaspard Coligny. They mounted the special platform erected for the ceremony outside the cathedral of Notre Dame in order that the Protestant bridegroom would not have to enter a Catholic church. Here they were made to wait for nearly an hour before any dignitary of the French court deigned to join them. For once the Huguenot men were not clad in drab clothes. Although not gaudily attired, they were richly adorned as befitted their station and the circumstances. They wore suits of silk, with Prince Henri's doublet thickly encrusted with silver embroidery. Their hats bore white plumes fastened with pear-shaped pearls.

To pass the time the two young men strolled about exchanging words with the onlookers. They kept mainly to the sides where the Huguenot supporters had gathered, although once or twice Henri did come near to the stalls where French courtiers stood and made conversation with some of them. He did not approach the furthest end, the back of the platform, where the common people and the citizens of Paris were crushed together waiting to view the spectacle and hoping for generous distributions of largesse to come their way. But it wasn't necessary to be near this group to sense their mood. They had booed and shouted remarks at Henri, Denis Durac and Coligny on sight, and their surging restlessness signified a crowd that could very easily become a mob.

'Hey, Monsieur Coligny, you don't really believe what the Medici woman has told you! That this wedding will unite Catholic and Protestant!'

'If the Princess Margot wears a white dress today then you'll know that, like her mother, she too is a liar!'

In contrast the Parisians greeted the arrival of the Guise family with roars of approval. The Duke of Guise, whom I remembered as an impetuous fifteen-year-old, was now a handsome man of twenty-two. He had a short manicured beard and a bold expression on his face. He was the nobleman with whom Princess Margot was said to have fallen hopelessly in love. The duke acknowledged the loud cheers and swaggered to his place.

And now the quips became more personal and bawdy.

'Hey, Henri! You should ask your bride where she slept last night! Her answer might surprise you!'

'And that might not be your first surprise, Huguenot!' a wit in the crowd added quickly. 'Look for a wedding gift in nine months' time. It will be your surprise from the Duke of Guise!'

The Duke of Guise laughed loudly at this play upon his name. Henri ignored it all and began a conversation with Denis Durac.

Then Catherine de' Medici arrived. She had left off her customary widow's clothes of black and wore a gown of deep purple brocade. A high ornate neck ruff emphasized her haughty air. The crowd became quiet as she swept onto the platform and took her seat.

On seeing the queen regent I shrank back against Giorgio. He had provided me with a high-collared coat and a large floppy hat to wear in the style of a doctor's assistant. It covered my features very well, but on seeing Catherine de' Medici apprehension overwhelmed me. This year, 1572, was the year that Nostradamus had predicted I would come to Paris. The year when the planets would move into aspect and my destiny should be fulfilled. But what was I supposed to do? Should I try to get closer to where the king would be? Was I supposed to step between him and an assassin's dagger? Perhaps I should have brought the prophecy with me. It was still concealed inside the hem of my travelling cloak, hanging on the coat hook with my mandolin.

A fanfare of trumpets announced the bridal party. The clothes of King Charles made it look as if he were trying to outdo his sister in splendour. His tunic and breeches were crimson, his hose mauve. The tunic was ornately decorated, stitched, corded and pin-tucked with dozens of beads, his breeches and sleeves slashed with yellow silk. Clusters of ribbon decorated his garments and diamonds blazed from his fingers, neck and ears. On his arm he escorted the bride.

Like the others beside me in the crowd I gasped at the appearance of the Princess Margot. The healthy and vibrant young girl I had seen all those years ago in Cherboucy had become a darkly beautiful woman. Her bridal gown was cloth of gold studded with all possible jewels. Emeralds, rubies, diamonds and sapphires shone in the sunlight as she moved up the stairs to the platform. On top she wore a sleeveless overdress of shimmering blue which trailed for many feet behind. Picked out on this train, in a repeated design of exquisite golden embroidery, was the fleur-de-lis of France. On her head was a crown trimmed with ermine and beneath this her face was composed, but her colour was high and her eyes flashed rebellion.

King Charles led her to Henri's side and he extended his hand to her. Margot ignored him and, helped by her attendants, she sank to her knees on one of the prie-dieus before the altar. Henri shrugged and knelt beside her.

We saw King Charles beckon to Gaspard Coligny to bring his chair closer to him. Catherine de' Medici raised her head higher and became immobile.

The choir started to sing. Clouds of pungent incense drifted into the air. The Huguenots coughed and tutted their disapproval. The choir ceased chanting. The archbishop began the wedding ceremony.

Henri of Navarre made his marriage vows in a flat unemotional voice. The archbishop then turned to the bride and asked her if she would accept Henri of Navarre as her husband.

Princess Margot did not reply.

The archbishop repeated his words.

Margot stared straight ahead and refused to say 'yes'.

A murmur began amongst the onlookers.

Still Margot did not answer.

Then the crowd began to make comment.

'Speak out, Margot!'

'Tell him to go back to Navarre!'

Catherine de' Medici whispered to the king. Charles rose to his feet and laid his hand upon Margot's neck. When the archbishop, for the third time, requested her to make her vow, the king pushed his sister's head forward in assent.

Henri of Navarre affected not to notice. There were whistles and catcalls from the crowd and a number of rough-looking individuals surged forward. I saw Denis Durac put his hand to his sword hilt but his master swiftly checked him.

The incident went by word of mouth like a forest fire, and as we followed the long procession to the reception in the Episcopal Palace we heard opinions being loudly voiced:

'The Princess Margot has been coerced to marry the heretic!'

'Paris should rise up to protect her!'

Being in the Huguenot party, we began to be jostled and Giorgio put his arm around my shoulder to protect me. As official guests Giorgio and I were permitted entry to eat from long tables set up in the courtyards while the wedding party ate inside.

We stood in ranks as the dignitaries filed past us. Upon entering the gates, Gaspard Coligny glanced up and saw above him the Huguenot banners captured at the time of one of their defeats in the recent religious wars.

In a voice deliberately loud enough to be heard by the Duke of Guise he said, 'Be assured these will be taken down and returned to their rightful owners soon enough.'

Immediately the Duke of Guise snarled a reply and leaped in front of Coligny to bar his way.

Chapter Sixty-five

Giorgio pushed me behind him.

Supporters of both Coligny and Guise collected round them, but before anything could happen the king's voice was heard above the noise.

'Cease at once!' he called out. 'It is my sister's wedding day and I will have no trouble!'

A space opened and King Charles walked towards the two men. 'Understand me now, what I say to you.'

There was a silence. Catherine de' Medici appeared behind the king. She gave an almost imperceptible tilt of her head.

The Duke of Guise stepped away. 'I perceived an insult to your majesty,' he said by way of explaining his action.

'It was a jest,' said King Charles. 'No more than that. Come' – he reached out to embrace Coligny – 'the man I call "Father" will sit with me as we eat.'

They went on without further incident into the great hall of the palace while the rest of us stood at tables set up outside. I ate and drank very little. My anxiety made my hands shake and fits of trembling seized my body. Giorgio, seeing this, enquired kindly as to my wellbeing.

'I am fretting to see my father, nothing more,' I assured him. All the time my eyes darted among the faces around us and I strained to listen to anything that might help me find Papa.

It was afternoon before the banquet was over. Our tables were cleared and we were herded to upper balconies overlooking the courtyard as the royals and their guests assembled below us. There were to be special tableaux for them to view. Chairs were brought for the wedding party and, to the obvious irritation of Catherine de' Medici, her son, King Charles, seated Gaspard Coligny at his side. I stood with Giorgio and looked down upon the ambassadors, nobles and high churchmen. The clusters of Huguenots in their darker clothes were a stark counterpoint to the splendid robes of the others, their badges of honour, sashes and decorations of high office.

A gong sounded and a procession of peasants from the various regions of France came to pay homage to King Charles and to present him with gifts for the bride and groom. These men and women were dressed in their traditional costumes; from the Auvergne, Picardy, Brittany, Normandy, Gascony . . .

'Look how uncouth the Gascons are!' someone on our balcony said in a mocking voice. 'So like their brethren of Navarre.'

There was a shifting in the crowd about us. Giorgio looked nervously over his shoulder and he drew me away.

'There will a fracas before this evening is over,' he murmured in my ear. 'We should leave soon.'

I knew that he was right. There was nothing for me here. Nostradamus had told me that he had seen me with my father by a window in the Louvre, not on a balcony overlooking the courtyard of the Episcopal Palace at Notre Dame. There was no reason for me to wait any longer. It was not the time for me to act to save the king. And now I had little hope of seeing my father today.

Then I saw a figure that filled me with terror and I knew that I must leave at once.

The Count de Ferignay!

I ducked my head and, pretending to yawn, I covered most of my face with my hands.

Giorgio glanced at me and then into the courtyard. I spread my fingers wide and risked another look.

The count was more portly than he had been six years ago. His face had widened, the skin around his jaw was looser, his face showing the ravages of years of self-indulgent living. He was standing to one side, part of a group surrounding the Duke of Guise.

With Giorgio following me I edged along the wall towards the furthest staircase to lead us down to the exit gate.

In the courtyard the peasants had begun to perform. Their voices chimed in harmony and their clogs clattered merrily on the cobbles as they swung round and round in a song and dance celebrating the gathering of the harvest.

Suddenly the Princess Margot stood up. She marched forward, clapping in time with the music, and made an attempt to join in the dance.

The Huguenots appeared scandalized by her behaviour. Small knots of them gathered, whispering together.

Margot cast off her overdress. She ran into the courtyard, flung out her arms and danced wildly. Her golden gown was dishevelled, one shoulder was bare, the crown upon her head becoming unsecured as her hair tumbled down. Catherine de' Medici half rose to her feet. Her face showed suppressed fury at the sight of her child behaving wantonly in public. King Charles flung out his arm to forestall his mother interfering.

'It is my sister's wedding day,' he said. 'Allow Margot some liberty. For the rest of her life she will live in Navarre wearing drab clothes, with neither dance nor music.'

The Princess Margot skipped down the cloister among the pillars and then out again into the centre of the courtyard. She swirled round and round, took a few steps, tripped and stumbled.

Shouldering his companions aside, the Duke of Guise leaped forward. As she fell, he gathered Margot into his arms and her head dropped onto his shoulder.

'*Dieu!*'

Giorgio was not the only spectator who took the Lord's name in vain.

In the courtyard there was an instant of silence. Then Denis Durac stood before the Duke of Guise and addressed the princess. 'Majesty, your bridegroom seeks your presence.'

Margot straightened up. She thrust aside both the Duke of Guise and Denis Durac, and calling to her attendants, quite soberly and steadily walked away inside the palace.

Taking advantage of the ensuing outbreak of chatter, Giorgio grasped me firmly by the arm and escorted me down the stairway to the outer door.

The sun was descending in the western sky. Its heat filled my mind and the fierce rays from this burning ball of fire stabbed across my vision. I put a hand to my temples as a migraine came on me.

Then I heard King Charles speak as clearly as if he were standing beside me:

'This commotion has caused my head to hurt. I need something to soothe the ache within my mind.'

And through a gap in the crowds I saw him wave his hand in summons.

And then . . . and then I heard a sound I had dreamed about for the last six years. A sound I feared I might never hear again.

A lute played by a master musician.

I stopped. I craned my neck and strained against Giorgio that I might see.

The king was still seated in the chair placed for him in the courtyard. Behind him stood a tall man.

A man much stooped since last I saw him, but un-mistakable to me. Before falling in a faint I cried out one word:

'Papa!'

Chapter Sixty-six

I opened my eyes.

I was lying on my mattress in my room in the house of Viscount Lebrand, with Giorgio kneeling by my side.

'You fainted. I had to carry you home.' Giorgio said in a worried voice. 'I am very concerned for your health, Mélisande.'

I struggled to sit up. A wave of sickness rose within me but I managed to say, 'Did you see him, my father?'

'If you mean the minstrel who came to stand behind the king's chair then, yes, I saw him. But to cry out like that was a very dangerous thing to do, Mélisande. You were lucky that in the mêlée after Princess Margot's shocking behaviour no one paid you any heed.'

'There are more wedding festivities planned,' I said urgently. 'Do you have invitations for these?'

'It may be possible for me to attend some functions in an official capacity,' Giorgio replied. 'Why do you ask?'

At his question, made in such a solicitous and caring tone, the dam broke, and the whole burden of the tragedy of my life came sweeping through me. 'My father,' I sobbed. 'I saw my father today. I've not seen him for many years, not since the death of my sister.'

So then I related to Giorgio the full details of my family history, exactly how Chantelle died, and how I was parted from my father and had to flee to Salon.

'Ah, yes,' he said when I had finished. 'It's all much clearer now.' He leaned forward and stroked my forehead. 'Yet I sense there is more, Mélisande. You have not told me all.'

But after having seen my father in person I was now so focused on reuniting with my beloved papa that I did not care about the prophecy or want any attention given to the papers of Nostradamus. 'No.' I shook my head. 'There is no more. That is the tale I have to tell and I only want to speak to my father again.'

Giorgio stood up. 'There must be something that can be done about this situation.'

'But now Queen Jeanne has died we might be sent back to Navarre,' I said. 'There is so little time.'

'I agree.' Giorgio spoke slowly. 'There is not much time. But it would make you happy to see your father again?'

'It would!' I clasped my hands together.

'And if it proves impossible for you to actually speak to him, is there any message you might want to give your father, or anyone at court?' Giorgio asked casually.

'I would like to let Papa know that I am safe and well,' I replied.

'Nothing else?' He hesitated. 'No written word of any kind?'

'I could write out something if you think that might be appropriate,' I offered.

'No, no,' said Giorgio. 'I thought perhaps you already had some piece of paper, a letter perhaps . . ?' His voice tailed off.

'I will make one now.' I began to rise from my bed.

'No, better not to.' Giorgio seemed disconcerted. He went towards the door. 'I will try to ensure that you meet once again with your father, Mélisande. You deserve that at least.'

Following the royal wedding there were four days of celebrations: all kinds of parties, ornate spectacles, masked balls, concerts and lavish feasts, both public and private. But despite the bountiful distribution of food the mood of the city was charged with resentment. The house servants gossiped about this but I barely noticed. Mainly I kept to our rooms for I was sick with nervous tremors at the thought that I might soon see my father.

Would he recognize me? I found a mirror and stared at my reflection. I was shocked at my appearance. My face was thin, my complexion white, my eyes circled with fatigue. With my short hair and cap pulled down I could pass for a boy, but surely my own father would not be fooled by this disguise?

Over the next few days Giorgio went out in the evenings, not returning until late. Each night when he did return he seemed more careworn and disinclined to talk.

He explained that this was because he was frustrated that he could not secure a pass for me to go with him inside the palace of the Louvre. And all the while, as I fretted, he was very solicitous of my health and sat with me as I drank my nightly medicine.

But then towards noon on Friday, which was the twenty-second of August, a messenger came with summons for him to attend the Louvre immediately. The new bridegroom, Henri of Navarre, when about to play tennis with King Charles, had fallen and injured his ankle.

Giorgio glanced to where I sat on a stool, listlessly stirring a pot of alum.

'This small emergency means that both of us will be permitted to enter the Louvre,' he said. He looked at me with compassion. 'It could be your one chance to see your father, Mélisande.'

I stood up, swaying.

'I am ready,' I said.

In the few days since I had been out, the streets of the city had deteriorated. I was taken aback at how unsafe and filthy they had become. Raw sewage was heaped in stinking mounds and passers-by gave us suspicious looks as we passed. Giorgio kept tight hold of my arm as we hurried along. Arriving at the main gate with the messenger sent to escort us meant that we were both allowed inside.

Henri of Navarre sat by the side of the tennis court in an inner courtyard with his ankle resting on a cushion. Gaspard Coligny stood beside him and the queen regent, Catherine de' Medici, was also there. She stepped to one side as we approached without acknowledging our presence. Henri's ankle was swollen but he was joking with King Charles.

'Had I known this was how you treated your opponents, I never would have agreed to play a game with you,' he joked.

'You should be glad that it's only a torn ankle muscle you suffer,' came a distinct murmur from the ranks of the courtiers present. 'Much worse could be done to a heretic.'

It was a voice I recognized. The Count de Ferignay! I felt a sickening cramp of fear in my stomach but I kept my head down and face averted.

If Henri heard this jibe he ignored it, but his friend Denis Durac bent close and whispered in his ear, 'Mark well, sire, you were tripped up by one of the men of the house of Guise as you entered the courtyard. The blow was deliberate, so now they have you hobbled.'

'You must take my new brother-in-law's place.' King Charles addressed Gaspard Coligny petulantly. 'It is my royal wish to play tennis at this moment and you can be my partner.'

'I beg pardon, sire,' Coligny excused himself, 'but after the State Council meeting this morning I must go and prepare orders to allow more of our troops to muster in the face of Spanish aggression in the Netherlands near our borders.' Coligny smiled openly at the queen regent in an insulting manner. It was well known that Catherine felt that any confrontation with Spain should be avoided.

'You may go.' King Charles glanced defiantly at his mother and waved his hand in dismissal to Coligny.

Catherine de' Medici looked away as Coligny quitted the room.

'I will play tennis with you, sire, if you would do me the honour.'

The Duke of Guise had stepped forward from among his supporters grouped around him. The king nodded impatiently and returned to the tennis court as the Duke of Guise took up a racket. My eyes searched the rows of spectators and courtiers ranked in the gallery and milling about the doors. There was no sign of my father. The duke walked lazily to the court. The king was becoming more irked at the delay to his game.

'Let us commence then,' he snapped. 'I've had to put off my morning's sport long enough while my so-called advisers, Coligny and the rest, argue over whether we should be at war with Spain.'

Catherine de' Medici drew in her breath. 'May I remind you, sire, that to provoke war with Spain would be disaster for France.'

'I do not care!' King Charles's voice was shrill. 'I will not discuss that matter any more. I want to play my game of tennis *now*!' And he flung the ball and hit it wildly with his racket.

The Duke of Guise, despite obviously trying to allow the king to score, took the first point.

Charles flushed with anger, struck the ball viciously in return. The duke gave it a soft pat. The king ran forward in glee. He drew back his arm to make the stroke that would certainly have resulted in his gaining a point, when suddenly a furious commotion was heard in the corridor. Several men-at-arms rushed into the court-yard.

'Assassination! Assassination!'

Charles screamed in alarm and fled to hide behind his mother. She remained completely still, smoothed her dress, and demanded, 'What is the meaning of this outrage?'

The first soldier went down on one knee before her. 'The Admiral Gaspard Coligny has been shot.'

'What!' King Charles threw his tennis racket on the ground. 'Am I to have no peace?' he shouted in fury. 'Can I not play one game without constant interruption?'

At the news Henri of Navarre had tried to rise to his feet.

A babble of voices broke out and men began to rush towards the doors.

'Stop!' commanded Catherine de' Medici. The courtiers shuffled to a standstill. 'Secure all entrances and exits to this place,' she ordered her personal guard. 'We are sad to hear of the death of Gaspard Coligny but we must safe-guard the presence of the king.'

During the upset, another man, by his dress a Huguenot, ran in and conferred with Henri of Navarre. Helped by Denis Durac, Henri now stood up. He then spoke, commanding those present to listen without raising his voice. 'I have just been informed that Admiral Gaspard Coligny is not dead, but has suffered injury after being shot.' There were audible sighs of regret from the house of Guise. 'We should be grateful that the Lord has seen fit to spare his life.'

Charles turned a look of irritation on his brother-in-law.

'Grateful? *Grateful?*' he screeched. 'My tennis game is disrupted. It is now completely spoiled. And I was about to make a point,' he added sulkily.

The comparison between these two men could not have been more obvious. The kingly attributes of Henri contrasted with the temper tantrum of Charles when contemplating losing a tennis match.

On hearing that Coligny was only wounded Catherine de' Medici's disappointment was palpable but she recovered quickly. She made the slightest movement of her head.

'Is there a doctor who might attend to Admiral Coligny?'

Giorgio stepped forward.

At once Henri of Navarre said to him, 'Giorgio, be good enough to take your assistant and go now to the house of Admiral Gaspard Coligny and give him your best attention.'

Both Henri of Navarre and Catherine de' Medici ordered an armed guard to protect us on our way. The streets were seething with men, shouting the news to each other and jostling the soldiers as they pushed their way through with us in the centre of their formation. The calls between the various groups let us know that the shot had been fired from a house owned by the Duke of Guise.

'Was this planned, do you think?' I asked Giorgio.

He gripped my shoulder so hard that I cried out in pain. 'Say nothing,' he hissed at me. 'Do you understand? Say nothing.'

We were ushered upstairs in Gaspard Coligny's house.

His friends, who were clustered around his bedside, stepped aside upon hearing that we had been sent by Henri of Navarre. Giorgio looked at the wound on Coligny's left arm.

'If I may, I could apply a poultice,' he suggested.

'I do not recommend that course of action,' a voice interrupted him.

Ambroise Paré, the king's surgeon, had arrived, sent by the king, who now regretted his lack of concern at Coligny's injuries. Paré's integrity was above reproach and Giorgio immediately deferred to the more experienced doctor's opinion. He glanced at me as he passed but his face showed no recognition. We had only met once briefly when he had gone to attend my sister Chantelle and declared her dead.

'First we must remove the musket ball, else the wound will fester,' Paré stated after conducting his own careful examination of Coligny's broken arm.

'And afterwards we should take Admiral Coligny to the Louvre for safety,' added Giorgio.

'No!' There was a grumbling from the Huguenot men at the door. 'If we let him be taken to the Louvre it would give them the chance to finish off their botched attempt to murder him!'

Paré gave Giorgio a curious look, saying, 'It is my belief that moving Admiral Coligny would kill him most effectively. His wound would have a better chance to heal if he remained in bed.'

Giorgio drew me towards the window as Ambroise Paré began to probe for the bullet.

'We must get away from here,' he said in a strained voice. 'For soon no one will be able to gain access to or exit from this house.'

I looked down. The alleyway below us was crowded with Huguenots who had hastened there from all parts of the city. They made a dark heaving mass as they crushed closer to find out what was happening.

We found our escort stationed at the front door and Giorgio persuaded them to conduct us safely to the house of Viscount Lebrand. In order to gain passage the soldiers had to walk with halberds extended out before them.

'There will be a riot before the night is out,' I commented.

'Or worse,' said Giorgio tersely.

The house of Viscount Lebrand was also in turmoil. He had heard the news but could not go to aid his Huguenot brethren as his abscessed leg was suppurating. He asked Giorgio to change the dressing.

'To lose Gaspard Coligny so soon after the death of our queen would badly damage the Huguenot cause,' he told Giorgio.

Viscount Lebrand had taken the death of Queen Jeanne hard, feeling that it reflected badly on him as she had succumbed while in his house.

'Queen Jeanne was exhausted by the visit of King Charles and Catherine de' Medici during that day,' the viscount went on. 'Perhaps if I'd sat with her that night I would have seen her weaken and sought aid and she might not have died.'

'You should not berate yourself,' Giorgio told the

421

viscount as he began to drain the wound into the bowl that I held close to the infected leg. 'Time would have brought the same conclusion.'

I felt the floor of the room slide away as the pus oozed out.

'Take the bowl away now and rinse it out,' Giorgio ordered me kindly, 'then go and rest. And be sure to take your medicine before lying down.'

'Your assistant is unwell?' I heard the viscount enquire politely as I went towards the door.

'I believe it may be the first stages of querain,' Giorgio said in a very low voice.

The viscount tutted in sympathy. 'Such a pity. Good assistants are hard to find.'

Querain? In Salon we had treated patients who had contracted that fatal illness and I knew that I did not have it. As Giorgio must also know. Why would he say such a thing? I did have a headache though. A tearing fierce burning behind my eyes.

The bowl shattered as it slipped from my grasp and fell into the sink. I stared at it stupidly. I had no energy to clear up the mess. A throbbing sensation pressed from behind my eyelids.

I needed to take something to ease this. There was a remedy Giorgio used for migraines that was very effective. I groped my way to the shelf but the bottle was empty. The pain was now an iron band around my temples. I must have relief. I knew that Giorgio had some of his most popular remedies in his doctor's bag. It was always kept beside his sleeping mattress, but I reckoned he would not mind if I took something from it.

I opened Giorgio's doctor's bag to find the tincture and rummaged all the way to the bottom. A small soft parcel was lodged in one corner, roughly wrapped in paper. Might the remedy lie beneath it? I pulled the parcel out, and as I did so the paper wrapping tore and the contents dropped onto the floor at my feet.

A pair of gloves.

White gloves.

Why would Giorgio keep gloves in here? He never wore gloves of any sort. These were ladies' gloves. I had seen them before somewhere . . .

I bent to pick them up. Then I stopped. A fruity scent wafted from the open parcel. And this time I recognized the smell for what it was.

Cherries.

And with stunning clarity all else crashed into my mind.

I sat down upon the floor. The door from the house opened and Giorgio walked in. He looked at me and the open bag. He saw what lay on the floor beside me.

'Ah, Queen Jeanne's gloves,' he said. 'I should have burned those accurséd gloves.'

Chapter Sixty-seven

Giorgio closed the door and locked it behind him.
I stared at him. My friend. My protector.
Giorgio.

He had killed Queen Jeanne.

Using the Medici poison he'd once told me about in Salon, he had murdered the Queen of Navarre. I recalled now the symptoms Giorgio had described: the smell of cherry, the yellowing of the skin on the backs of the hands. My mind jerked back to the night of Queen Jeanne's death. When we had entered the bedroom her hands on the bed-spread had been white. She must have been trying on the gloves, as urged by Catherine de' Medici who had sent them as a gift that day. Giorgio had gone to the bedside, ordering all others to go away. He had taken the oppor-tunity to remove the gloves and hide them in his doctor's bag. I remembered that later, when her lady-in-waiting had rushed forward, the queen's hand had been ungloved, the skin brown-spotted with age but also yellowed with poison.

I raised a stricken face to him.

'You killed Queen Jeanne of Navarre.'

'The Medici poison was delivered here and I made it up into a cream that was rubbed into the inside of the gloves,' Giorgio said quietly. 'And I ensured then that after Queen Jeanne died the gloves disappeared so that there should be no evidence. But Queen Jeanne was very ill. She would have died in any case. Time would have done the job had they had the patience to wait.'

'That is what you just told the Viscount Lebrand,' I said. '*Time would have brought the same conclusion.* The same words you said to someone who visited here late one night some weeks ago.'

'Ah, so you *were* awake that night.' Giorgio tilted his head and regarded me. 'So I was right then to start to use the sleeping draught on you.' He came towards me and demanded abruptly, 'What is the message that you carry, Mélisande?'

'I do not know what you mean.'

'We both know what I mean.'

He was standing over me. Suddenly I was very frightened. I got to my feet and pushed him in the chest. He allowed me a little space and then said in a friendly manner, 'We can trade secrets if you will.'

'What secret do you know that I might want from you?' I asked him.

'Information that would help your father. Proof of how Armand Vescault died.'

'How could you possibly have that information?'

'The Lord Thierry truly loved you.' Giorgio shook his

425

head in wonder. 'You inspired such devotion in him that he gave his life that you might live and did this thing for you.'

'What thing?'

'Lord Thierry paid for a private investigation into the disappearance of Armand Vescault. As you would be travelling in disguise he arranged for the results to be sent to me to give to you. Before we left Navarre I received a letter from the magistrate of Carcassonne. His officials thoroughly searched the palace of Cherboucy. In a deep well they found the body of Armand Vescault stabbed to death with a dagger bearing the coat of arms of the Count de Ferignay. This shows that the Count de Ferignay lied when he said that he had spoken to Armand and had seen him riding away. It is enough to clear you and your father of any wrongdoing. So that letter would be very useful to you, I think.'

As he was speaking I noticed that Giorgio had moved between me and the outside door.

'You should give me that letter!' I cried out. 'Out of loyalty to Lord Thierry.'

'I am not employed by Lord Thierry,' said Giorgio. 'It suited me for a while to let him believe that I was.'

'Who then employs you?'

He hesitated before replying, 'The highest in the land.'

'King Charles?'

Giorgio laughed in amusement. 'How innocent you are, Mélisande, that you believe the king to be the most powerful person in France.'

'Catherine de' Medici!'

'Hush!' He glanced up at the ceiling.

'But why would you work for her? I thought the Medici subjected you to torture as they suspected you of trying to kill one of their noblemen.'

'No,' said Giorgio. 'It was not because I tried to poison one of their noblemen that the Medici had me tortured. It was because I *failed* to poison one. The Medici asked me to effect this man's death. I was a newly qualified doctor with high ideals and dedicated to saving lives. When I saw this man in so much suffering I could not continue. What the Medici did to me as a result of that made me vow never to disobey their orders again.'

'If you work for Catherine de' Medici why were you in Salon at the house of Nostradamus?'

'For years now the prophet Nostradamus has been tormented with premonitions regarding the blood royal of France. You know that Catherine de' Medici believed in him. I was instructed to ingratiate myself with Nostradamus and collect all information that I could. Catherine de' Medici felt that he had a specific prophecy to foretell about the succession to the throne. And she was right.' Giorgio looked at me intensely. 'Was she not?'

Within my chest my heart began to clamour. The Nostradamus papers! What did Giorgio know of these?

He was studying my expression. 'I know that you carry some kind of message, Mélisande. It's why I risked my own life to help you escape from Valbonnes. I had not much access to the top floors of the Nostradamus house, but I used the maid Berthe to do some of my spying for me. I'd give out some flattery about her hair or dress and she would readily divulge what she knew. From yourself, too, I was aware that you had consultations with Nostradamus. Therefore I know that there is something of great importance that you have to divulge. Catherine de' Medici has told me of the fate that awaits me if I do not find the prophecy and bring it to her secretly tonight.'

'If Catherine de' Medici thought I carried something of value to her then she would have had me arrested and tortured long ago,' I protested.

'I did not inform the queen regent that I believed it was you who carried the message from Nostradamus,' Giorgio replied. 'I told her only that there was a person I was following who might lead me to the knowledge that she sought. If I had mentioned your name to the Medici woman you would have been taken immediately to their most vile torture chamber and unspeakable things done to your body until you screamed for mercy. No, I did not want you to suffer as I had done. Long ago, Mélisande, you were kind to Giorgio, and ran to help me when I was attacked outside the apothecary shop in Salon. So I thought to use another way to inveigle you to tell me about the secret you know.'

'There is nothing,' I said but my voice shook in fear. I realized now why the queen regent had not acknowledged Giorgio's presence in Queen Jeanne's bedroom or at the tennis court earlier today. She did not want to be associated with him in any way. Yet she had skilfully engineered that he should be the first doctor to attend to Gaspard Coligny, and if Ambroise Paré had not arrived in time, perhaps Giorgio would have managed to kill Coligny by not treating his wound properly. He would have bound the wound with the musket ball inside, causing it to fester.

'No wonder Ambroise Paré looked at you so strangely when you suggested moving Gaspard Coligny,' I said. 'He would know that any skilled doctor would see that was the worst thing for the patient. And that was why you wanted to leave so hastily,' I went on, 'in case any of the Huguenots realized that too, and saw that you did not have Coligny's best interests at heart.'

'No matter,' said Giorgio. 'Gaspard Coligny will die tonight none the less.'

'How can you be sure of that?' I asked in surprise.

'Mélisande, you are not so stupid and naive not to see that Paris is a bundle of dry kindling into which a spark has been thrown. The militia are locking the city gates even as we speak. I will make a bargain with you.' From inside his coat Giorgio took a letter and handed it to me. 'Here is the letter from the magistrate in Carcassonne that proves you and your father are innocent. Take it from me as a sign of my good faith. Now tell me where you have hidden the Nostradamus papers.'

I quickly read the letter in my hand. The contents were exactly as Giorgio said and it bore the official seal of Carcassonne.

Now I had what I needed to free my father! I tucked the letter from Carcassonne inside my tunic. But I could not betray the trust of Nostradamus and give Giorgio the papers containing his prophecies. Instinctively I glanced towards the hook where hung my mandolin and travelling cloak. Giorgio intercepted my look and at once he reached out and snatched down my mandolin.

'I should have guessed that was where you would have concealed any precious papers!' he cried, and he smashed my mandolin against the wall.

For a dreadful moment I thought my heart had stopped beating.

In frustration Giorgio hurled the broken pieces from him as he realized there was nothing inside. A fury came over him. He drew a stiletto from the sleeve of his coat, stepped forward and put the blade to my throat.

'I have had enough of coaxing you. Tonight my own life is forfeit. You will tell me where you have hidden the prophecy or I will kill you.'

Sick at heart at losing my beautiful mandolin and having no wish to die, I told him what he wanted to know. 'The Nostradamus papers are sewn into the end of my travelling cloak.'

He flung me away from him, ran to the cloak and ripped the hem open with his dagger.

'Very neatly concealed,' he said as the rolls of papers were revealed. He turned. 'And now,' he said, advancing towards me, 'I am truly sorry to do this, Mélisande.' He spoke with what seemed like genuine remorse. 'As in the past you saved me from harm I would have preferred that you did not suffer. For choice I would have made your end painless with a more potent sleeping draught.'

'You have been poisoning me?' Now I knew the reason for my sickness and headaches.

'Yes,' Giorgio replied. 'I was giving you enough of the

drug each night that your senses were addled. It made you more easy to manipulate. I thought, once I had coaxed you to give me the prophecy of Nostradamus, I would finish your life in a merciful way. But the matter has to be dealt with now.' He raised the stiletto.

'You will be arrested,' I squealed in panic. 'You cannot conceal a stabbing. In the morning when my body is found Viscount Lebrand will have you arrested.'

'When the massacre begins,' said Giorgio, 'believe me, no one will care about you. In the morning one more body will mean nothing at all.'

'What are you saying?' I looked at him in stupefaction.

'The queen regent, Catherine de' Medici, removes enemies from her path,' Giorgio said. 'It is her way. She believed Queen Jeanne was about to change her mind about the wedding. Therefore she told me to eliminate her. Now Catherine de' Medici cannot allow Coligny to go forward and take us to war with Spain. It would ruin France completely, and if we were conquered her sons might lose their inheritance. Thus the Huguenots must be sacrificed.'

'You mean the Huguenot nobles?'

'The Duke of Guise and his supporters will deal personally with Gaspard Coligny and his lords. As for the rest, lists have been compiled of those lodged in the inns and boarding houses. Once it starts, the city will rise and none will survive. Tonight every Huguenot in Paris will die.'

'Tomorrow is a holy day,' I protested. 'The feast of Saint Bartholomew. And anyway, King Charles will not allow it. He has an affection for Gaspard Coligny.'

'In the end the king will do as his mother advises him,

even though tomorrow is a feast day. I tell you, the slaughter will begin inside the king's own palace of the Louvre,' said Giorgio. 'There will be a signal to start the attack. And anyone not wearing one of these' – he pointed to a white ribbon pinned to his coat – 'will die.'

But I would not credit what Giorgio was telling me. 'It is impossible. There are thousands of Huguenots. They will not be so easily overcome.'

'That is why it must be now,' said Giorgio. 'It is whoever strikes first that will win this fight.'

And, saying this, he moved towards me very quickly, thrusting the stiletto at me.

I jumped away and ended with my back against the sink. He had me trapped. There was no way out. My throat closed in terror and I could not scream. And if I did, no one would hear me, for we were at the bottom of the house. He came at me again, lunging, and I ducked, but the stiletto sliced my upper arm. The sight of my own blood galvanized me into action. I put my hands behind me, and holding the sink edge for support, I kicked at him with both feet. Because his limbs were loose from his torture sessions he did not manage to avoid my blows. But I was weakened by the sleeping potions he had given me each night and I barely checked his progress.

He grabbed hold of my hair, trying to pull my head back that he could cut my throat. I clawed at him and we struggled together. He was overwhelming me. I put my hands behind me again, but instead of finding the sink edge I had hold of something else.

I felt pain.

I'd grasped a piece of the broken bowl that had smashed in the sink earlier. My fingers closed around the long shard of pottery. I gripped it in one hand as tightly as I could. Then I brought it up, and with all my force I rammed it under Giorgio's chin.

He screamed only once. Then he began to gurgle. He threw the stiletto down and clutched both hands to his neck. But there was no stopping the blood as it bubbled out from beneath his fingers.

Giorgio collapsed onto his knees. As his life left him his hands fell away from his face and his body sprawled twitching at my feet. For a long time I stood, unable to move. I had killed a living person. A man I thought was my friend but who had betrayed me. And yet I could not hate him for it. He had done what he had in order to preserve his own life. As I must do now, to preserve myself and those I loved.

Averting my eyes from his face, I took a pair of scissors and cut the white ribbon from Giorgio's coat. I snipped the remaining stitches at the end of the hem of my travelling cloak and eased out the rolls of papers contained there. I placed these inside my tunic beside the letter from Carcassonne.

Then I staggered to the outside door, wrenched it open and ran out into the night.

Chapter Sixty-eight

The old bridge of the city was before me.

The waters of the Seine slid smooth and glassy below the arches. Despite the hour there were some people about, shadowy figures moving in the darkness. From a nearby alley came the grunting sounds of a struggle. Whether made by assassins or lovers, I did not know nor care. I had wisdom enough now not to stop to investigate any strange noises. The very stones of Paris crackled with tension. Giorgio had made a correct assessment. Fuelled by the heat of the fetid summer and the recent wedding of the king's sister to the hated Huguenot prince, the citizens' hostility towards the thousands of Protestants billeted in their midst simmered, ready to explode.

I touched the Nostradamus papers inside my tunic and wondered if this was the night when the first words I'd ever heard the prophet utter would come to pass.

'The king's life is forfeit! I see blood running red in the streets of Paris!'

It had been so many years ago since King Charles had

laughed at this prophecy. But now would be the fulfilment of the astrological predictions of the Seer of Salon.

I saw again Nostradamus with his hands raised above his head.

'*A hundred dead!*

'*No! More! Two hundred!*

'*Yet more! And more still!*

'*Three! Four! Five hundred! Five times five!*

'*The bell is pealing. Paris screams in agony. Children are torn from their mothers' arms. They try to escape, running through the streets. Their bodies clog the river so that the water cannot flow. Murder most foul!*'

Nausea rose from my stomach. For now I believed, without doubt, that an enormous atrocity was to take place. And it would be tonight. Beginning within the royal household, with some signal to summon the whole city to rise up against the Huguenots.

What signal?

This was what I did not know. Only that it would happen and the two persons I loved most in all the world were in danger. My beloved father, who had allowed himself to be taken captive in order to save me, and Melchior, both somewhere in the palace of the Louvre. If they were not to die I would have to find them and warn them. And I would not trouble myself over the fate of the king, or try any more to decipher the words of the second quatrain Master Nostradamus had written out for me.

This is your destiny, Mélisande.
You are the one who,

435

In the way known to you, can save
The king who must be saved.

King Charles was in grave danger tonight. But I did not have any great desire to save this crazed and murderous man who would agree to the ghastly butchery of his invited wedding guests.

A brazier burned at the entrance to the bridge. There were usually three watchmen on duty here. I could only see one, standing there alone. His two companions were at the side, busy with a couple of street girls.

'Who are you?' the single soldier demanded as I approached. 'State your business.'

The man grabbed at me and I twisted away from him. My cap and grimy face proved an effective disguise. I showed him the white ribbon I'd pinned on my sleeve.

He sighed in disappointment. 'A boy. No use for any kind of sport.' He prodded me with his lance but not too unkindly. 'Go away home to your mother, little fellow. And tell her to lock and barricade her door. It's almost daylight and when it comes there will be trouble. No one will be safe.'

I thought quickly. To reach the Louvre I had to cross the river. From inside my tunic I took out the parchment which bore the seal of the prophet. 'I am to be allowed through,' I declared.

The soldier peered at the paper I'd thrust under his nose. 'What nobleman gave you this pass?'

'This bears the mark of someone who, although dead, has far more power than any earthly prince or lord.'

'And who would that be?'

'Nostradamus.' I hissed the name at him.

The man started back, and I slipped past him.

On across the bridge I ran, and now the dark bulk of the Louvre was before me. At the far side of the river I paused to lean against the wall of the embankment. It was only for a minute or so, to ease the pain in my side and to tuck the parchment securely into my tunic. But then the moon shone out from behind a cloud. I glanced up and shivered, and I heard Nostradamus's words again:

'The Moon falls in the house of Death.'

These few minutes hesitation I was to regret.

As I left the shelter of the wall a church bell began to toll. I turned my head to listen.

The bell is pealing. Paris screams in agony.

I cried out.

I was too late!

It was the signal for the start of the massacre.

Chapter Sixty-nine

As the bell began to sound, the main gates of the Louvre opened and a large body of men on horses galloped out, led by the Duke of Guise. They rode off in the direction of the house of Gaspard Coligny. Swords held aloft in hands, they called out to each other in high excitement. Thus I knew that the admiral's fate was sealed.

As the gates began to close I ran forward. I was risking all, but had a desperate hope that my boldness would see me through.

I held out the pass that Nostradamus had given me, displayed the white ribbon on my sleeve and declared importantly, 'I come from Doctor Giorgio and have a paper that the queen regent, Catherine de' Medici, must read. It is very urgent.'

At the name of Catherine de' Medici the soldier fetched an officer of some rank.

'It is vital that the queen regent sees this message,' I told him. 'It concerns a prophecy of Nostradamus. She awaits this information with impatience and I must give it into her own hand.' Catherine de' Medici's obsession with the occult was well enough known for me to be allowed inside the gate. And if it happened that I was taken before the queen regent then I would show her the prophecy concerning me and my destiny to save the life of the king. I decided to do this despite remembering that Nostradamus had said Catherine de' Medici should not know of it until after I had saved the king, for now my only thought was to reach my father in any way I could. I must try to convince the queen regent that I had been told by Nostradamus to come to her especially at this time to save her son. Then she might look on me with favour, and I could plead my case for my father and myself. 'If you say that it comes from Doctor Giorgio,' I added to the officer, 'you will find that I will be allowed into the presence of her majesty.'

This officer took the pass from me and led me to the guard room. He bade me wait there while he went off to investigate whether I was to be allowed to speak to Catherine de' Medici. When he'd gone there was a sudden shout and then a prolonged scream from inside the palace. One of the guards grinned at me.

'It has begun,' he said.

'Now these Huguenots will see what Paris thinks of them,' said another.

He had hardly finished speaking when a group of dark-clothed men ran from the palace towards the walled gardens. Close behind and firing arrows upon them came a number of soldiers.

'Aha!' the first guard shouted. 'The rats are running. Let's have some fun with them.' He collected his lance from where he'd propped it against the wall and, followed by his companions, chased after the fleeing men.

I took my chance and slid out of the door, making for the stable block. Pitch torches burned in brackets all over the yards, where grooms and stable lads were leading out mount after mount to waiting cavalry officers and militiamen. I went past the line of open doors. I had no knowledge of where my father might be. But I knew this was where Paladin and Melchior were quartered, and Melchior had promised me that he would discover all he could about my father. I went round to the side of the building to where I thought I saw the outline of the leopard's cage. A figure I recognized was standing in the shadows.

'Melchior,' I whispered.

He pulled me towards him and before I could say anything he said, 'I was coming to find you. There is a massacre planned. We must leave this place of corruption as soon as we are able.'

'My father?' I said.

'I have found out where he sleeps in the palace.' Melchior unfastened the cage door and brought out Paladin as he was speaking. He bent his head close to the animal's ear and spoke to it before removing the muzzle from its head. I remembered what Melchior had told me in the palace of Cherboucy and I stood unmoving. The leopard came and sniffed me, then nudged its nose into my hand.

'This way,' said Melchior, and we crept out into the night.

With the leopard padding softly beside us, we swung away from the main wing of the palace, where lights were beginning to shine from windows as people looked out anxiously, wondering what the disturbance might be.

We went to the oldest part of the building and then via an outside staircase to a high level. Here an iron door led into a long low-ceilinged corridor with a row of skylight windows letting in milky moonlight. A series of small cramped rooms were situated under the eaves. It was obviously rarely used as most of the room doors were lying open and the rooms were dusty and empty. But we came finally to one which was shut and locked.

'This is where your father is kept. He is watched closely but tonight his guards will be elsewhere.'

'You are wrong,' said a voice behind us.

We turned.

The Count de Ferignay stood in the doorway of the room opposite, sword in hand.

'It came to me tonight, as I prepared for the sport of killing Huguenots, that the diversion it offered would be a perfect opportunity for someone to rescue the minstrel. So, after my lord, the Duke of Guise, had left to deal with Admiral Coligny I thought I'd come here and see if I was right.' Ferignay stepped forward and snatched the cap from my head. 'It *is* the wayward younger daughter,' he said triumphantly. 'The rumours that you were here in Paris and attempting to reach your father are indeed true.'

My spirits, so high and hopeful a moment before, now

sank to the lowest level. I should not have paused to rest —
to watch the moon — after crossing the bridge. Had we
been here a little earlier we might have eluded Ferignay.

Melchior turned his head a fraction. Paladin growled
deep in his chest.

'Do not think to resist me,' the count warned him, 'for
I have Jauffré to hand and we are both well-armed.'

At this Jauffré emerged from the next room, also with
sword drawn.

And we have no weapons, I thought. When I had taken
Giorgio's ribbon and the papers, why had I not thought to
also pick up his knife? We had nothing to protect us.

Except for the one that I had forgotten: Paladin that
would give its life for its master.

As the Count de Ferignay stepped towards him,
Melchior spoke one word.

Paladin leaped forward.

In a furious uncoiling burst of energy Paladin sprang,
jaws wide open, at the throat of the Count de Ferignay.
Ferignay slashed out. Man and beast crashed to the floor.
The count screamed and tried once more to use his sword,
but the creature now had its prey gripped at the collar. The
leopard's teeth fastened on, grinding through blood and
bone. Ferignay howled in his death agony, rolling on the
floor in a contortion of legs and arms as the leopard sav-
aged his neck and face.

But Jauffré had his sword ready and before we could
prevent him he had plunged it twice into Paladin's
writhing body. The leopard whirled, snarling, mortally
wounded. Melchior jumped at Jauffré and wrested the

sword from him, then he thrust it in turn through Jauffré's chest. Jauffré toppled to the ground and both Melchior and I rushed to Paladin.

The leopard had been pierced in vital organs and was clearly dying. With tears on his cheeks Melchior knelt down and cradled Paladin's head in his lap. Within minutes the leopard's breathing stopped and Paladin's tawny eyes closed in death.

More noble than any knight upon the field of battle. More loyal than any comrade. Bringer of justice for my sister. Swift and courageous avenger. My own heart bruised with pain as I beheld the death of Paladin.

Proud prince of royal blood art thou,
Paladin, so nobly named.
Prisoner of others, yet
Thy spirit, like the wind, untamed.

Swift son of a mighty hunting race,
Conquest falls to thee.
Silent shadow, fleet among the chase,
Chained now, yet thou shall be free.

Melchior sat, stunned.

Relief flooded my senses at the sight of the dead bodies of the two men who had committed murder and robbed me of my youth and happiness. But grief also swamped my senses at the fate of Paladin. I felt shock beginning to numb my body. I knew that we had to act now or we would die.

I knelt beside Melchior and put my hands over his.

'Paladin is free now, though it be in death. Thy princely leopard has avenged my sister, and given its life to save yours. You must not squander this sacrifice.'

Below us I could hear running feet and hysterical yelling. I took the dagger from Jauffré's belt and cut the bloodied white ribbons from his sleeve and from that of the Count de Ferignay.

'It's a special ribbon to be worn as a sign to the soldiers and the militia that those wearing it are to be spared,' I explained to Melchior as I tied one around his arm.

Melchior stroked Paladin's head one last time. Then he stood up and broke open the door of the room where my father was held prisoner.

The figure slumped on the floor got to his feet. He was as thin as a barley stalk with eyes that glittered bright with fever.

My heart buckled.

'Mélisande?' my father said in amazement. He swayed, about to fall.

I rushed to hug and support him. 'We will talk later, Papa,' I said, and I tied the other ribbon onto his sleeve.

Melchior took my father under his arms and easily hoisted him across his shoulders.

'Now let us leave this accursed place.'

On the lower levels we could hear shrieks and the sound of furniture being hauled about.

'They are trying to barricade themselves inside their apartments,' I said.

'It will serve only to delay their deaths,' Melchior replied.

We hurried back along the corridor and opened the outside door at the end. Coming towards us on the staircase was a Huguenot woman. Behind her in close pursuit were five men. Her dress was ripped from bodice to skirt and her hair hung free. When she saw us she stretched out her arms and begged, 'Help me! For the love of God! Help me!'

As we watched, two of the men caught her by her hair and began to drag her cruelly back down the stairs. The other three looked up at us and started to mount the stairs in menacing manner. I held up my arm to show the white ribbon. They hesitated and then turned and went down the way they had come. In the area at the foot of the staircase a number of women had been penned by soldiers, who were pushing and slapping them. Melchior pulled my sleeve.

'Come inside,' he said. 'There is nothing we can do for them.'

The women cry for succour, and you, Mélisande, can do nothing to help them.

We went to the other end of the corridor, found an inner stairway and began to descend by feeling our way in the darkness. It was an unused servants' staircase but still we were able to hear the screams of the dying in the main passages as Huguenots were pulled from their beds and murdered. All around us in the dark labyrinth of the Louvre, men and women were being hunted down.

And among all of it I thought only of getting my father to safety. We reached the bottom of the stairs. One side led to a dimly lit passageway. At the other side, the exit door, of crumbling stone decorated with ancient symbols, was locked and bolted across with iron bars.

'This door has been closed off for many years,' said Melchior as he examined it. 'That's why we encountered no one on our way down this staircase.' He eased my father from his shoulders and set him on the ground. 'I will venture into the corridor and see if I can find out where we are in this maze.'

'Have this,' I said, and I gave him Jauffré's dagger which I'd taken from his body.

When Melchior had gone my father reached out to touch me.

'My headstrong daughter,' he said.

I leaned my head against his chest. 'Forgive me, Father, I have caused you so much grief.'

'No, no,' he shushed me. 'It was the thought of you free that gave me strength over these long months. I'd sing your songs. Imagine you roaming on the Isle of Bressay. Did you ever reach our home?'

'I did.'

'Was it as beautiful as you remembered?' he asked me.

'Yes, it was,' I replied truthfully.

'I could hear your voice in the wind that blew outside the castle walls,' my father said dreamily. 'King Charles was not cruel to me. He loves music and he would send for me when his head ached and I would play for him. So my life was not so bad.'

Melchior returned.

'Where are we?' I asked him.

He sat down beside us on the steps and regarded me

very seriously. 'Mélisande,' he said, 'I do not know. But raving madness is unleashed in this place tonight. To go out into any of these corridors is to meet certain death.'

The person who does this takes Death by the hand.

Before we could speak further we heard the clash of swords and shouts of men duelling. We carried my father up some stairs as fighting men came into view below us. Henri of Navarre and Denis Durac had been set upon by four men of the house of Guise.

Henri was stocky but powerful, Denis less strong, but skilful with his rapier. They stood side by side within the arch of the stair entrance and fought like men possessed. Two men fell to their swords but it was clear that both Huguenots were weakened. Due to his bandaged ankle Henri was less agile. Denis Durac had a cut to his face and several slashes to his sword arm, and as he parried a further blow, he dropped his guard. Directly beneath us one of the Guise noblemen dashed forward to take advantage.

Melchior sprang down and landed on this man's shoulders. He had Jauffré's dagger in his hand and he stabbed it into the man's neck.

'Melchior!' shouted Prince Henri in glad surprise.

Denis Durac recovered himself. The other Guise nobleman lunged at Henri of Navarre and would have delivered a fatal blow had not Denis Durac leaped between him. Henri's opponent's sword stuck Denis through his stomach. Denis sank dying to the ground. In rage Henri killed the soldier who had inflicted death upon his friend.

Then he cast his sword aside and ran and knelt by Denis Durac.

'I am no longer in debt to you, your majesty,' said Denis Durac, groaning in his pain. 'I have paid back the favour you did me when the bear caught me in the Pyrenees.'

'It was not a favour I wished returned,' said Henri. 'I am not ready to lose such a good friend.'

To which Denis Durac replied, 'I can think of no better way to die than to give my life to save the king, who must be saved.'

Chapter Seventy

*T*he king who must be saved.

I sat upright on the staircase.

Denis Durac had just uttered the last line of the quatrain that Nostradamus had written to show me my destiny.

This is your destiny, Mélisande.
You are the one who,
In the way known to you, can save
The king who must be saved.

But why had Denis Durac called Prince Henri of Navarre 'king'?

And then I knew why. The death of the Queen of Navarre, Queen Jeanne d'Albret, meant that her son was no longer Prince Henri. He became a king, the King of Navarre.

And Henri was king in more than name. In conduct and in kind he was indeed a king. A king to be kept safe.

My destiny.

As prophesied by Nostradamus.

Henri was the king who must be saved. The great King of France was not to be the son of a Medici. It was Henri of Navarre.

This is your destiny, Mélisande.
You are the one who,
In the way known to you, can save
The king who must be saved.

The prophecy and the presence of Nostradamus spoke to me.

"Know that you cannot alter the course of the awful deed but you may help the person who can lift France out of the mire in which she wallows and lead her to greatness and prosperity. For France to prosper Henri must live. He will bring end to chaos and many lives will be saved if you save his. Mélisande, in the way known to you, save the king who must be saved."

In the way known to you.

Often, during my years of waiting, I had puzzled over the way it could be known to me that I might save a king. I had considered my inadequate medical skills and knew that I was lacking in that field.

In the way known to you . . .

I raised my eyes to the stonework above the bricked-up door, the arch inscribed with the ancient symbols.

The way *was* known to me.

The pattern fluctuated before my eyes, as had the one

on the frame around the mirror in the palace of
Cherboucy. The tomb of the Templar Knights. The walls
inside the central cairn of the Standing Stones.

My destiny. I knew what I must say and do.

'Mélisande, look there.' Melchior pointed along the
corridor to the far end, where some soldiers were
marching towards us. 'We have just helped kill noblemen
of the house of Guise. Our white ribbons will not save us
now. We must prepare ourselves to die. Know this' – he
cupped my face in his hands and looked into my eyes –
'I do love thee.'

'And I thee,' I said. I took his hands from my face and
held them for a moment. I addressed Henri of Navarre,
who had picked up his sword and was preparing to fight.
'Sire,' I said. 'Destiny has brought me to you this night, for
I give you my word that I am the one who can lead you
from this place.'

Henri indicated the men coming towards us. 'We are
grievously outnumbered. If you know a way to escape then
show it to me quickly.'

I walked out into the corridor and turned immediately
to the left.

Supporting my father, Melchior and Henri followed
behind me.

'I have explored this passage,' Melchior called to me as
I hurried on, 'and it only turns in a circle to where we have
come from.'

'Which is why the soldiers have stopped pursuing us,'
said Henri of Navarre. 'They know if they wait where they
are that we will fall into their clutches.'

'In here,' I said with confidence. I opened the door of a small closet, went to the tiny window and pushed aside the panelling underneath.

'This looks only like a hole in the ground,' said Henri doubtfully.

'It is not,' I replied with confidence, for I knew every turn of this maze. I had known its pattern since I was a child. The design imprinted in my mind, and re-imprinted again and again, until it was part of me. Each loop and curl, the tracks and lines, the coiling, snaking passages embedded on my soul.

We helped my father inside. Then we all crawled along between the wainscot and wall of that room and of the next and the next. I struck out a piece of the panelling in the third room and from there I led them to the doorway. Musket fire rattled close by.

'It is necessary to cross to the rooms on the other side,' I said.

'You are certain of this?' King Henri glanced from me to Melchior.

Melchior nodded. 'I would follow this girl wherever she leads.'

'Girl?' Henri looked at me more closely. 'Girl you are. But how are you here, and where is Paladin, the leopard, Melchior? I have never once seen you without him by your side.'

'Paladin is dead, my lord.' There was a catch in Melchior's voice as he said this. 'Defending my life.'

'I am sorry to hear it though glad the leopard died well. Such is the nobility of animals,' commented the king.

452

'Would that they could teach men to have that quality then we would not be witnessing this slaughter tonight.'

I opened the door and beckoned to them.

We slid into the room opposite. I stood there a moment with my eyes closed until the lines of my destiny once more unravelled before me.

'Here.' I pointed.

Melchior knocked on the wood and found it hollow and once more we squeezed inside. We burrowed down under the floorboards and along our secret way.

And on every step of that hazardous journey we were accompanied by sounds that no human should hear. Sometimes we were in darkness, sometimes light shone through. At one stage Melchior stopped and applied his eye to a crack. He reeled back and then urged us to hurry. On and on we went under the corridors. Ignoring the howls of terror and clash of battle, we crawled in single file. I led and the king followed, until we came out via a loose floorboard into a small salon. Melchior went to the door and looked into the corridor.

'There are soldiers not three feet away,' he whispered. 'They wear the livery of the personal guard of Catherine de' Medici.'

Henri put his hand on his sword.

'You have brought me to a trap!' he exclaimed.

I shook my head.

'My word is true.' I crossed the room and touched a tapestry. 'Behind this is a hidden door.'

I ran my fingers over the wood carvings, until I found what I sought. A soft click and a small door opened. We clambered inside, down some stairs and into a low-roofed alcove. In front of us was another door. I opened it and encountered a heavy curtain which I drew aside.

We stepped into the private study of the King of France.

Chapter Seventy-one

Charles sat weeping in a chair by the window.

'Your majesty!' Henri of Navarre announced his presence.

So distraught was King Charles that he did not remark on it being strange that his cousin with several other people should appear from behind a curtain in his room in the middle of the night.

'Are you aware of what is happening in your palace,' Henri asked him, 'and in your city?'

'I did not wish it!' cried Charles, rocking backwards and forwards. 'They bullied and harangued me until I could no longer think sensibly. They have murdered Gaspard Coligny, whom I loved as a father. I did not want anyone to die.'

'Then, sire,' said Henri of Navarre, 'you must give the order to stop the slaughter.'

'I cannot,' the king sobbed. 'Look down there and you will see that nothing can stop it now!'

We crowded to the window and looked down.

Unspeakable horror met our eyes. Terrified fleeing Huguenots, the survivors of the first wave of the massacre, had been rounded up and herded into the main courtyard. There, archers fired on them as the guards pressed forward, stabbing and impaling them on their pikes. Piles of dead bodies were mounting up as the soldiers, in uncontrolled mania, stripped and mutilated the corpses.

Henri of Navarre recoiled. I leaned for support against the window frame. Melchior put his arm around me and pulled me away. I held my father close.

'What to do now?' said Henri, addressing Melchior. 'Who is this girl and why did you trust her enough to allow her to lead us here where we may be worse off than before?'

Melchior explained to Henri of Navarre about my presence there, and how we came to be in a position to save his life.

'And I would ask for my freedom, sire,' Melchior said when he'd finished his story, 'and that we all may leave this place tonight.'

'Your freedom I grant you.' Henri nodded. 'But as to how you or I might safely quit Paris, I do not know.'

As he was speaking, the door of the room opened and Catherine de' Medici entered. Despite it being after three in the morning she was fully dressed in her customary robes of black. Her hair was carefully coifed with all her jewellery in place. It was clear that she had not just arisen from her bed but had been awake and dressed for some time, if not planning the massacre then certainly not unaware of it happening.

456

Although she must have been astounded to see Henri of Navarre in a completely different part of the palace from where she believed him to be, she held her ground. 'It is most improper for anyone to be with the king without the knowledge of his chamberlain,' she said. She took a step back towards the door she had just entered, no doubt to summon help.

Henri brought forward the sword he still held. 'Madame,' he said, gesturing at the king.

Catherine de' Medici stayed calm. Without haste she inspected us all in turn. When she looked at me I saw recognition in her face.

In an abrupt movement Henri cast down his sword. 'Now I am unarmed,' he told the queen regent. 'I wish neither you nor your son any harm. In fact, I came to warn him that the men of the house of Guise have begun an armed rebellion and are killing Huguenots indiscriminately.'

Catherine de' Medici stared at the man whom she considered an upstart yet who had just outmanoeuvred her in diplomatic skill.

'I concur,' she replied after a small hesitation. 'We must rein in these soldiers,' she addressed her son. Then she turned quickly to me and said, 'I know you for who you are. The captain of my guard brought me the pass given to you by Nostradamus. Where is the man known as Giorgio who swore he would bring me something of interest that he had obtained from the seer before he died?'

'Giorgio remained at the house of Viscount Lebrand,' I answered her very carefully. 'For it was in me that the seer confided. I have the paper with the prophecy written in his own handwriting.'

Catherine de' Medici held out her hand. 'You will now give to me this prophecy of Master Nostradamus and tell me what you know of its meaning.'

Very slowly and carefully I took from my tunic only the paper on which was written the two quatrains relating to my destiny and tonight's events. I presented them to Catherine de' Medici and said, 'This is the paper Nostradamus wrote out for me and all I know is that it pertains to the King of France.'

Catherine de' Medici unfurled the parchment and read out the first one of the two quatrains.

'With fire and heartless hangings
The treachery of royal line holds sway
Deeds done by stealth will come to light and all but one
 consumed
Safe from the sword, saved only by the word.'

She paused. 'Are these first four lines not the words Nostradamus spoke in Cherboucy when he came to warn us that the king's life might be in danger?'

'Yes,' I said. 'Nostradamus foresaw this night of bloodshed in Paris.'

'These clearly refer to the actions of the house of Guise,' said Catherine de' Medici firmly. 'They are of the royal line and have treacherously betrayed us all tonight.' She turned to her son, the king. 'We must stop the slaughter.'

'We must stop the slaughter. We must stop the slaughter.' In distress and repeating his mother's words over and over, King Charles rose and opened up the window and began to call out to his archers to leave off their firing.

'Close the window!' Catherine de' Medici snapped out.

King Charles jumped back at the sound of his mother's angry voice, and I, who was nearest the window, obeyed her order. As I closed over the casement a quantity of arrows struck the glass, for in the darkness the marksmen below saw what they thought was a Huguenot attempting to escape.

Catherine de' Medici shouted in alarm and rushed to her son. King Charles fell upon his mother's neck, sobbing. She cuddled him and soothed him as if he were a four-year-old child. Then she guided him to a chair and settled him. She straightened up and looked at me intently and said, 'You are Mélisande, the minstrel's daughter. The one who ran away on the day her sister fell from the tower at Cherboucy.'

'I am, your majesty,' I replied, 'and if I may be so bold, I would like to present to you this testament.' I brought out the letter written by the magistrate of Carcassonne stating that they had found the murdered body of Armand Vescault with evidence of the involvement of the Count de Ferignay.

'I know all of that.' Catherine de' Medici waved her hand in irritation as I tried to explain. 'My own spies eventually discovered the truth of the matter. The Count de Ferignay is a known liar and philanderer. I did not believe one word of the tale he told me.'

I could not quite comprehend what the queen regent had just said. Had she really kept my father for years without trial although she knew of his innocence?

Noticing my look of incredulity, the queen regent said, 'It was necessary. My son, the king, suffers frequent headaches. He finds your father's music soothing, therefore I decided the minstrel should not leave the court. It was the simplest way to ensure that he remained here. Had the truth come out then he would have gone off to look for you.'

How little the happiness of ordinary lives matters to those who rule, I thought.

'And I did it for the good of France,' she added enigmatically.

Nothing was ever straightforward with this woman. A memory came to me of Cherboucy. In the great hall as the queen regent listened to my plea for justice, I'd seen her eyes searching the room, counting the number of soldiers belonging to the house of Guise and those of her own. Perhaps she did not dare to arrest the Count de Ferignay, connected as he was to the powerful house of Guise, without endangering the stability of the crown. It was always said of her that she was so devious that she did not even tell herself the truth.

'And it has been so decreed by mystical signs that I was guided to do this,' the queen regent continued. 'For as you have come to save your father and bring me this letter you also saved the life of my son, your king. This is the other verse that Nostradamus has written here in which he foretells the deed that has just come to pass.'

Catherine de' Medici held up the paper I had given her and read out the second quatrain of the prophecy:

'This is your destiny, Mélisande.
You are the one who,
In the way known to you, can save
The king who must be saved.'

Henri of Navarre caught his breath. I did not need to meet his gaze to know that he understood the full meaning of the quatrain. Avoiding his eyes, I looked to the queen regent.

Catherine de' Medici nodded her head a few times. 'Even from beyond the grave Master Nostradamus has not failed me. My contrivance has brought you to this room. Thus you, Mélisande, were at the window and able to close it over as the archers fired. And so my beloved son, Charles, King of France, was saved from death.'

I glanced at Melchior, who made the slightest movement of his head. And I understood him to indicate to me to say nothing.

The queen regent had a satisfied look upon her face. As the Lord Thierry had once told me, Catherine de' Medici thought that her children were destined by divine decree to rule France. Thus she believed totally that fate had conspired to save Charles from dying this night.

But I knew my true destiny and I had to ensure the safety of the king who would be great. I found courage and

I spoke out. 'Your majesty, if I may be so bold, the wise seer, Nostradamus, still strives to assist you—'

'Yes.' Catherine de' Medici spoke impatiently. 'What else do you have to say, girl?'

I looked beyond the queen regent to where a mirror hung on the wall. And fixing my gaze upon it, I intoned,

> '*Two persons joined in holy bond*
> *Two realms . . .*'

Catherine de' Medici half closed her eyes. 'I recall those words. They were indeed also spoken at Cherboucy by the seer Nostradamus. I interpreted it to be a union between my son, King Charles, and Elizabeth of England. But that did not transpire.'

I pointed to Henri of Navarre. 'Majesty, perhaps you did interpret the prophet's words correctly.'

The eyes of the queen regent opened very wide. 'Now I see that I did!' she exclaimed. 'It was hidden, yet I was given the gift to determine the right path to take.'

'You arranged the marriage of Prince Henri and Princess Margot,' I prompted her.

'And this union must be preserved,' she agreed. She clasped her hands to her bosom. 'Nostradamus speaks to me from beyond the grave.'

The queen regent turned a more benign look upon Henri of Navarre, and I knew then that I had completely fulfilled my destiny as charged by Nostradamus.

'My son.' Catherine de' Medici spoke to King Charles.

'We will make a royal warrant to declare that Henri of Navarre should live.'

'And Mélisande and her father and Melchior must be allowed to go free,' said Henri of Navarre.

Such were King Henri's skills of diplomacy and authority that Catherine de' Medici went to sit down at the king's writing desk. And she wrote out an order for a safe passage that my father, Melchior and I might go unharmed from Paris that night.

Chapter Seventy-two

E ven when that heinous night was over the killings did not stop.

For, although the king issued instructions for all men to lay down their arms, he was ignored. The mob ruled the stricken city of Paris and inevitably the people began to turn on each other.

As word seeped out to the provinces, the violence began to spread throughout France. In many cities known criminals roamed the streets plundering premises and committing murder. In the countryside, downtrodden peasants formed large gangs wreaking havoc wherever they went. Houses were set on fire with the doors barricaded and the occupants still inside. Hangings took place without trial or mercy. Neither Protestant nor Catholic was safe. Amid scenes of wild carnage old scores were settled and personal vendettas carried out by those mad with blood lust.

My father was very weak and not fit to travel far. Once clear of the city Melchior led us to an abandoned woodsman's hut in one of the forests where he had hunted with King Charles. We burned fallen branches to keep warm and Melchior trapped animals to feed us. At night, as we sat by our fire, he grieved for the loss of his companion and fellow hunter, Paladin, the noble leopard who had died to save his master's life. Papa and I joined him in his lamentations, and we recounted many stories of the goodness of Chantelle and used the time to properly mourn my sister. And I told them of the things Nostradamus had seen in his visions, and of his last prophecy, and what he had asked me to do.

We spent the autumn and winter there in safety while the terror took hold of France. In an orgy of hatred thousands upon thousands of people, innocent men, women and children, died, and the words of Nostradamus came true. Rivers ran red with blood.

The royal family became virtual prisoners in the Louvre and, in a horrible irony, the Duke of Guise, seeing that all control of the country might be lost, used his own soldiers to try to restore order on behalf of the king.

Wildly varying stories of congratulations and censure were reported from the other courts in Europe. It was said that, upon hearing the news of the murder of so many leading Protestants, the King of Spain had joyfully thrown his hat in the air, but the Queen of England had at once put on a black veil.

Catherine de' Medici denied that there was a Catholic conspiracy to exterminate all Protestants. She made a declaration that a Huguenot plot to kill the king had been uncovered and swift action, as undertaken by the

Duke of Guise in killing Gaspard Coligny, had been necessary. Thus she blamed the Guise family, while they in turn insisted the order had come from the king.

The old year spent itself and the new year had begun before gradually peace was restored to all parts of the country. As the nobles bickered over responsibility the people were left to carry the burden of recrimination and bitterness.

Isolated as we were, away from all other habitation, we heard none of these happenings until we arrived eventually at the Isle of Bressay.

We had waited until the spring following the massacre before we left our forest shelter. We travelled very cautiously and in easy stages, therefore it was May of that new year before we saw our own land again. The soldiers of the Count de Ferignay had gone, disappearing, our tenants told us, when news came of their master's death and of the events in Paris.

My father's health was not robust, but when summer arrived in glorious beauty his mind and body began to heal enough for us to go walking out together.

So it was that one evening in late June I went with him and Melchior to the hill of the Standing Stones overlooking the Isle of Bressay. I had wrapped the last prophecy of Nostradamus in a package of oiled leather and brought it with me on this day of the summer solstice.

'There is something I must do,' I told Melchior, and, leaving my father, we went together into the circle of the standing stones.

I thought of the prophecy contained in the package. I

remembered what Nostradamus had said when giving it to me:

'I charge you with finding a safe place to keep my last prophecy until the time comes for it to be revealed. We can only hope that those who come after us are alert and listen to the warning therein.'

'This circle has been here a thousand years,' said Melchior.

'And will survive a thousand more,' I said. 'There is a place here where the last prophecy may be hidden.'

'It is a good choice,' said Melchior, 'for men will not move these stones.'

'Yes,' I said, 'though metal beasts roam the fields and metal fish swim in the sky, mankind will always respect the standing stones.'

Melchior touched my forehead. 'Sometimes,' he said, 'I do not know if you are quoting the prophet or if it is your own prophecies you utter.'

'I know not myself,' I replied.

The sun was going down, sitting low along the western sky, its rays spreading upon the New World on the other side of this planet, and out to others that spin among the mighty oceans of darkness in the skies. For the terrifying truth, obscured for so long, was that we were not, and never could be, the centre of this universe. We are one among many, but there are some things so enormous in their construct that our frail minds cannot encompass them. Nostradamus was himself, in the end, overwhelmed by his own visions.

He wrote what he knew to warn those who will come

after us. So I will hide his quatrain of doom in the hope that the people of a future time will discover it and avert the apocalyptic catastrophe as predicted by the Seer of Salon:

The Sixth Extinction

Cometh after the Five that have been

    when Land, Sea & Sky will burn without end.

The waters flood, yet there is none to drink.

Creatures and crops wither and perish.

The earth groans with the burden of mankind

    & all living things cry out for succour.

A shaft of sunlight reaches out and blazes onto the central cairn.

As if in a trance I walk there, and I touch the keystone. The great slab pivots. Inside the secret chamber is where I put the last prophecy of Nostradamus.

And there it lies, waiting.

* * *

I tell my story now for those who come after me so that they may find the last prophecy and pay heed to the warning.

It was only given to me to do one thing. It is up to others to avert the disasters to come.

I walk with Melchior back down the hill. Above our heads the stars throb in the firmament. And as we walk, for the first time since my mandolin was destroyed, music, clear as starlight, stirs within me. I think of the ballad I will compose that will tell our story, Melchior and I. Of how we met and were parted, how we came together again, and the manner in which the leopard, Paladin, saved our lives.

I will name this ballad, *The Song of Mélisande and Melchior.*

We return to the quietness of the house and to our own rooms therein. And I light the lamp and pick up the new mandolin my father has gifted to me and I say to Melchior,

'Tonight I will make music.'

Melchior takes the mandolin from my hands. He leans over and blows out the lamp and says,

'Let us first make love.'

And as I lie down with him that night I know that I have truly come home.

Epilogue

Despite being kept under close supervision for several years Henri of Navarre managed to escape. In time he succeeded to the French throne and became one of the greatest kings ever to rule France.

AUTHOR'S NOTE

Although based on real historical events this book is a work of fiction.

To tell the story of Mélisande and Melchior I have added characters, happenings and prophecies – specifically the ones referring to the massacre of St Bartholomew's Eve and the Sixth Extinction – to those that we know definitely existed at that time.

The massacre of St Bartholomew's Eve did take place in Paris in 1572.

One can visit the house of the famous seer, Michel de Nostradame, known as Nostradamus, in Salon de Provence.

The prophecies of Nostradamus can be read seriously or with scepticism. It is the choice of each individual to believe or disbelieve as they choose.

There have been five previous 'Extinctions' in the history of the world when cataclysmic events wiped out a huge number of species. It does not take any gift of foresight to see that our current disrespect for the resources of the Earth will lead to disaster. The human race may be the species who are annihilated in this 'Sixth Extinction'.

The warning is there, hidden among the standing Stones, as written in *The Nostradamus Prophecy*.

The author would like to thank:

Margot Aked
Lauren Buckland
Laura Cecil
David Clayton
Sue Cook
Marzena Currie
Annie Eaton
Julie Gormley
Diane Hendry
Sophie Nelson
Chris Newton
Hugh Rae
Hamish White
Museum staff in Salon de Provence
Random House staff
& the usual suspects . . .

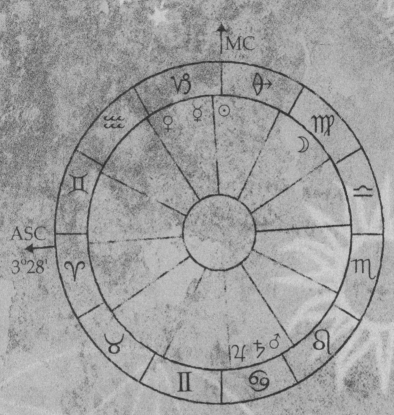

MC

☊ ⇗

♑

♒

♍

☿ ☉

♀

☽

♎

Ⅱ

♈

ASC
3°28'

♏

♉

♌

♃ ♄ ♂

Ⅱ

♋

Nostradamus
14th December 1503
Noon chart
St Remy, France
46°N46' 04°E50'

☉ ♂ ♀

♃ ♂ ♄ ♂ ♂